ALL OR NOTHING

Taking the Odds Book Three

JAMES BUCHANAN

mlrpress

MLR Press Authors

Featuring a roll call of some of the best writers of gay erotica and mysteries today!

M. Jules Aedin	Drewey Wayne Gunn
Maura Anderson	Samantha Kane
Victor J. Banis	Kiernan Kelly
Jeanne Barrack	J.L. Langley
Laura Baumbach	Josh Lanyon
Alex Beecroft	Clare London
Sarah Black	William Maltese
Ally Blue	Gary Martine
J.P. Bowie	Z.A. Maxfield
Michael Breyette	Patric Michael
P..A. Brown	Jet Mykles
Brenda Bryce	Willa Okati
Jade Buchanan	L. Picaro
James Buchanan	Neil Plakcy
Charlie Cochrane	Jordan Castillo Price
Gary Cramer	Luisa Prieto
Kirby Crow	Rick R. Reed
Dick D.	A.M. Riley
Ethan Day	George Seaton
Jason Edding	Jardonn Smith
Angela Fiddler	Caro Soles
Dakota Flint	JoAnne Soper-Cook
S.J. Frost	Richard Stevenson
Kimberly Gardner	Clare Thompson
Storm Grant	Lex Valentine
Amber Green	Stevie Woods
LB Gregg	

Check out titles, both available and forthcoming, at
www.mlrpress.com

ALL OR NOTHING

Taking the Odds Book Three

JAMES BUCHANAN

mlrpress

Published by
MLR Press, LLC
3052 Gaines Waterport Rd.
Albion, NY 14411

Visit ManLoveRomance Press, LLC on the Internet:
www.mlrpress.com

Editing by Kris Jacen
Cover art by Deana Jamroz
Printed in the United States of America.

ISBN# 978-1-60820-147-1

First Edition 2010

All alone with the new pictures. Maybe he didn't see them taken. Dark hair cut short so you could see his face and know who it is. Smiling, looking to the side, a little toward the camera, but not seeing it.

Play with the mouse, click, click, clicks in outline. Cut around careful, taking everyone but him out. Remove all the other people who didn't belong, focused only on who mattered to the plan. Nobody but him mattered. Put the picture next to the other pictures and then, like magic, all of it came together…the whole plan. What had happened and what needed to happen so everything would be just right. Only a little bit longer. Be patient. Stay focused and everything would come together like it was supposed to.

CHAPTER 1

Nick eyed the baby-blue, slope-hooded, four-wheeled box taking up the end of his driveway with unbridled suspicion. Drawling out, "What the fuck is that?" as he glared at Brandon, Nick looped one arm across his chest and cocked his hip.

He'd told Brandon just to come over and let himself in with his key when he hit town—the key Nick had made for Brandon back in October. Still, Nick expected to hit home and find the Harley parked out front, not a blue minivan.

Between the vehicle and a pile of luggage, Nick's driveway bordered on impassible. Nick parked his Kawasaki on the lip of the cement, by the back bumper. Just as soon as Brandon's luggage got stowed, the bike went into the garage. No way was he leaving his bike out all night. Especially not in Vegas. Especially not in Vegas in December; not with the cold wind carrying the hint of rain in its touch. A winter thundershower and the bike would be toast. If no one stole it. Nick didn't live in the best part of town.

Brandon snagged a duffle from the rear seat, stepped back and slid the door shut. "What?" he mumbled as he turned.

Pointing, like it wasn't the huge, hulking and completely obvious monstrosity that it was, Nick hissed. "The thing in my driveway." Although, scarily enough, the van fit the neighborhood quite well: one time suburbia sliding into inner city disrepair.

Brandon looked at the minivan then looked back at Nick. "It's a car, Nicky." He tossed the bag on a pile of suitcases that looked like it might do for a month instead of the week they'd had planned. And since most of the cases were pink leopard print, Nick figured those must belong to Brandon's daughter, Shayna.

While he might be gay, Brandon certainly wasn't swish.

Brandon's daughter and her luggage were part of the plan. Not the best plan, but the only feasible one under the circumstances.

Nick'd been the one prodding Brandon, since August, to step up to the responsibility plate and spend more time with his daughter. He couldn't very well bitch when Brandon's ex asked him to take Shayna for the week between Christmas and New Year's. Well, he could bitch, but not to Brandon's face. And it was either have Brandon and his daughter come to Vegas or not see Brandon for yet another month.

There were a lot of reasons why not seeing Brandon wouldn't work.

"It's a minivan," Nick drawled out the correction. "Four doors of soccer-mom hell." Shifting his weight to the other hip, Nick asked what seemed to be the obvious question. "Why?" He had suspicions about the reason, but he wanted to hear it out of Brandon's mouth.

"I bought the thing off my stepbrother, Jacob, for fifteen hundred." Brandon shrugged. "It belonged to his wife, Carol."

Nick shook his head. Trust Brandon to sidestep the question. "I didn't ask how...but why? What compelled you to go out and buy a Yuppie mobile?" Nick stepped back and considered the whole picture. Brandon stood in his typical attire: jeans, biker boots, T-shirt and black leather jacket. The tips from the pattern of his full back tribal tattoo were visible at the collar of his shirt. A series of rings strung through the edge of his left ear matched the bar in his left eyebrow. Behind Brandon hulked the ten-year-old minivan. It was probably the most discordant set of images Nick could imagine.

"You," he drew out the word as he pointed first at Brandon then the vehicle, "are as far from Yuppie as a Goth cop can be. Your tattoos alone should bar you from ever owning a car like this." Rolling his eyes for emphasis, he added, "Didn't it like blow a fuse when you tossed *Everything Dies*, *Black Number One* or, hell, just about anything you've downloaded from Type-O Negative on the CD."

"Why did I buy a piece of crap that I can't stand?" As Brandon crossed his arms over his chest he snorted and shook his head. "Dian's exact words, 'You put my daughter on the back of that damn bike of yours and ride to Vegas, I will hunt you down, cut your balls off and feed 'em to the dog.' So Carol just got a new station wagon and I offered to buy this off Jacob."

"You baby your bike." Not quite understanding the thought process of Brandon's ex, Nick shook his head. "You could eat off the goddamn engine it's so clean. This thing's, what, ten, twelve years old?" He kicked a tire and was surprised when the van didn't collapse into a pile of rust and spare parts. "Gotta have at least sixty thousand miles on it..."

Brandon interjected, "Close to one hundred."

"A hundred thousand miles on it." Holy crap that was a lot of mileage for an American built tank. "It's beat up as all hell. How many accidents has it been in?" Dings and nicks dotted the paint and the front driver's side bumper was crumpled up. "Your ex would rather have you take some junker you don't care about across the desert than your bike?"

With a snort, Brandon leaned against the side of the van. "Look, one thing you never do is get between a Jewish mom and what she believes is right by her kids." He laughed. "Don't ever doubt that if I defied her, Dian would castrate me and when she did it, the blade would be dull."

Looking around, Nick asked the obvious question. "Ah, so where's the little demon spawn?" Evidence of Shayna's existence littered his driveway, but so far he hadn't seen her.

"Inside," Brandon waved at the house, "somewhere."

"You know," Nick stepped up close, almost nose to nose, and teased, "I don't see you as Jewish."

Brandon bumped Nick's knee with his own. "I don't see you as Catholic."

"Point taken." God, Brandon smelled good: cloves, leather, and a faded hint of cologne. Nick leaned into his body just a hair more, not quite touching but close. "We're both lapsed former whatevers." Maybe he should just pin Brandon to the van and give him a real Vegas welcome. Make sure Brandon's ex hadn't already cut off his balls...at least literally. She seemed to have done a fine job on the mental end. Unfortunately, a hard-core make out session would probably have to wait. The whole kid-lurking-about-somewhere put a damper on his hormones.

Nick stepped back and ran one hand through his hair, trying to put his thoughts into words. "Which brings up another point. I haven't, like, bought anything special. I mean, you mentioned, *you know, last night*," he groused, "thank you so much for the advance warning —that Dian is a lot more, ah, into the whole cultural/religious life. Are we going to get in trouble with, like, food and stuff?"

"Naw," Brandon shrugged like it didn't matter. "Dian's observant, but not completely *Frum*." Apparently that meant something, but Nick was clueless as to what. "She ain't gonna freak if the milk's in the same fridge as the meat."

There were rules about refrigerators? "Huh?"

"She don't expect me to keep kosher." Another shrug, then Brandon stuffed his hands in his back pockets. "I got some rules," his tone sounded like he'd gotten an earful beyond some rules, "written out: beef franks, no cheeseburgers, and the dishwasher's good enough for sanitizing. Dian says Shayna's practically a vegetarian anyway, doesn't like meat much. Don't worry, we're good."

"Okay," Nick grumbled. "I'll take your word on it, but I'm going to be so completely freaked out on this." He wished he could be mad at Brandon for putting him in this position, but it was his own damn fault. Step up to the plate; be more responsible, he kept prodding. And Brandon'd been making little baby steps toward that. Then Dian got hit with training at the same time as her new husband had to go back to New York for business…and for the first time she'd actually thought of Brandon to help out.

Nick's own damn fault and he'd have to live with it. Still, it was hard enough knowing he had to play their relationship down because of his pint-sized houseguest. The whole kosher thing added another layer of stress to the whole visit. "I mean, maybe we should just stick to paper plates or something?"

"Look, Nicky." Brandon reached out and gripped his shoulder. After a squeeze, he used the touch to pull Nick in closer. Almost whispering, he reassured, "I'm the complete and utter fuck-up of the ex-husband." One of his come-hither smiles flashed and Nick's annoyance faded under the onslaught. "I get Shayna back to Grover Beach with brushed hair, bathed more than twice and in one piece…we could feed Princess ham and cheese sandwiches the entire week and Dian would consider it a roaring success."

Any effort was better than no effort. Dian probably gave Brandon more leeway than she might if he'd been around more. Most likely she didn't want to scare him off of his tentative steps to reconnect with his daughter. Nick had never met the woman, but since Brandon never trashed talked her and she seemed enthusiastic about the attempt, she possibly was a reasonable person.

Even with the van thing.

"You know," Nick grinned, "the van kinda suits you."

Brandon choked, "What?"

"Yeah," with two fingers, Nick goosed Brandon in the ribs, "matches your baby blue eyes there."

Brandon jumped. "Get over here, Nicky." With his hand already on Nick's shoulder, he managed to twist around and wrap his arm around Nick's neck. "I'm going to kill you ," he taunted as they wrestled a bit.

Brandon's body was warm in the cold afternoon. "Getting rough with me?" Nick taunted. He didn't, however, resist much. "You know I like that." Stepping back a little, Nick managed to push his ass against Brandon's hip. He ground into the touch. "I sure as hell know you like that."

Brandon pushed him away. "Quit it, Nicky."

"You started it." Nick pointed out the obvious as he straightened his winter-weight street-style motorcycle jacket. As a concession to high desert cold, matching overpants covered his business slacks. Wasn't quite the slick, crotch rocket biker look he'd prefer, but Brandon had seen him in far worse shape. At least he'd been able to score a set in black and red to match the jacket with the red demon face on the back. Wouldn't want to trash the look completely.

"Fuckhead." Brandon thumped the back of Nick's head as he backed away.

"Okay, I can fuck you with my head." Nick tugged off his riding gloves before shoving them in his pocket. "And the rest of my cock, too." He grinned.

"Stop." It was Brandon's turn to growl. His came off more threatening than gruff. "Last thing I want is for Shayna to overhear something like that and go spouting off to her mom."

"Sooner or later," Nick grabbed one of the bags and slung it over his shoulder. His helmet, resting on top of the baggage, got tucked under his arm. Then he reached for the handle on a wheeled suitcase. "You're probably going to have to say something to Dian, you know about you and me? Didn't she ask about why you were spending a week in Vegas with another guy?"

"I don't think she even thought to ask about that. I mean, I told her we'd planned this trip a while back and you're one of my best law enforcement buds." He shrugged. "And, you know, Shayna apparently started bitching about getting left with her two baby brothers and her aunt Marion. Marion treats her like she's still four. I think Dian was just relieved to give Shayna an option and stop the whining." Somehow Brandon managed to tuck a duffle and a rolled up matching sleeping bag under his arms while toting his own leather backpack and another one of Shayna's bags toward the back door. "And on the whole coming out to Dian? Maybe, someday," Brandon hedged. "But when she finds out, I want it coming out of my mouth not Princess-Phone-Stuck-In-Her-Ear in there." Nick just shook his head and followed.

Once inside, Nick asked about the new nickname, "Phone in her ear?" He hooked the small bag he carried on the handle of the suitcase before plunking his helmet on the counter. Shucking his jacket, he tossed that over one of his high backed kitchen chairs. "What do you mean?"

"Shit," Brandon dumped the luggage in the center of the kitchen and leaned against the table. "Dian brought her down yesterday, on her way to San Diego." With his other hand he made a swooshing motion down and out. "Shayna breezes past me, flops on the couch, flips on cartoons, grabs the cordless and says, 'I got to call my friend Beth.' An hour later, I'm like, 'get the fuck off the phone.' I mean, I didn't use that word, but what the hell can two nine-year-olds talk about for an hour? They're like watching the same cartoon and telling each other about it. I didn't think that started until they were sixteen or something."

"Don't look at me on that." Nick laughed and dropped into one of the chairs. As he stripped off the overpants, he pointed out, "You, at least, are a dad. I don't even got the title."

"Well, expect your phone bill to be like triple." Brandon hooked another chair with his boot and pulled it out. As he sat down, backwards, he hooked his arms over the back and rested his chin on the spine. "I'll try and keep her off, but you know, she's nine and she's addicted."

"Where is she now?"

"I think, in the living room." Brandon jerked his head, indicating the room through the door at his back. "Playing your video games and, probably, on the phone."

As long as she wasn't digging through his closet and finding the fun toys, Nick would deal with a long distance bill. "I guess your road trip went all right?" He added as he jerked off his tie. Man, time to ditch the monkey suit and put on some proper clothes.

Brandon grinned. "Yep, except I had to listen to pre-teen pop for four hours."

"Hey." Nick pooled the tie on the table. "Can I say one thing?"

Rocking the chair onto the back legs, Brandon teased, "You can say more than one thing."

"Asshat." Nick picked up the tie and tossed it at him. Not much of a threat. It kinda drifted down to the floor into a pile of

Escher print jumbles. "No, I mean thanks."

"For what?"

"For putting it on the line like this."

Brandon honestly looked confused. "I don't get you." Trust him to be obtuse in the relationship arena.

Nick shrugged. "Bringing Shayna out here." He wanted to tell Brandon how he felt, but didn't want to scare him off. "I mean, this a big step for you, and for you and me."

Brandon dropped his gaze to the floor and chewed on his bottom lip for a bit. Finally, he looked back up and smiled. "Yeah, it is." For agreeing with him, Nick thought that smile was awfully forced.

"Thanks for trusting me." He tried to ease it a bit.

"Hey, you know, it's," Brandon fell silent for a moment, then the rest of his thought came pouring out in a rush, "well it's not easy and I thought a lot about it. But, if you're going to be around, it should happen."

That was as close as a declaration of, well something, as Brandon had ever got. Shit, the only times he'd ever said *I love you* was after he shot his wad. "I intend to be around." Even with all the other crap, Nick did intend to be around. That is, if things went well in the next few days and if Brandon didn't freak with what Nick needed to talk to him about. The reason that the whole trip couldn't wait. Now wasn't the right time to broach it, though. He needed things to settle down a bit, get Brandon relaxed and then they could talk.

Brandon shot him one of his thousand watt smiles, then twisted in the chair and yelled through the doorway into the living room, "Princess, get off the phone and come here, I want you to meet someone."

"I'm busy," floated back to them.

As darkness dropped into Brandon's expression, he yelled again, "Get off the phone before I shove it down your throat."

"Fine," she snapped back. They heard the rattle of a remote

or controller hitting the floor and small feet stomping toward them. "Beth, Brandon says I have to go," came from the other side of the bar style doors leading out of Nick's kitchen.

"She calls you Brandon?" Nick hissed the question. "What does she call her stepfather?"

Brandon looked at him funny, like he wasn't sure what Nick asked. "Daddy."

The hem of a floral skirt, pink leggings and a set of glittery sneakers became visible under the bottom half of the door. "Yeah, it's so lame. Bye." She added as she pushed through the door. "What?"

Shayna…Nick had only ever seen pictures of her and most were not terribly recent. A sharp face with bright blue eyes was framed by masses of curly brown hair. Gangly knees and elbows seemed at odds with the more feminine clothes. Well, fem for a little girl, Nick supposed. He'd never call himself an expert on kids' duds or women's for that matter. A long sleeve T-shirt stuck out under a baby-doll short skirt, but with leggings. It all looked *almost* hip, like Shayna fought for stylish against a heavy hand of a mom. He remembered similar battles with his folks over things like: "boys don't wear eye-liner."

"Shayna," Brandon stood and held his hand out indicating Nick, "this is my best friend, Nick O'Malley."

"Hi, Mr. O'Malley," Shayna drawled it out as though she were supremely pissed that Brandon interrupted a scintillating discussion so that she could meet an adult.

Well, okay, new situation for everyone, Nick let the tone pass. "Why don't you call me Nick?" In three days, if she kept up that snot attitude, then he'd have a discussion with Brandon. Right now he could live with it. It had to be difficult for her, too; stuck for a week with a dad she didn't know well and dragged off to visit one of his friends. "Less of a mouthful."

"Mommy says," those two words dropped Shayna's speech into the smug, *look at me, I'm listening to my mom* mode, "I shouldn't call adults by their first name."

"It's okay." Nick smiled, reminding himself that baby steps were needed to win Brandon over, why should it be any different with his daughter? "Otherwise it's going to be weird all week hearing Mr. O'Malley." Then he pointed out, "Besides, you call your dad, Brandon."

"I guess," Shayna huffed and rolled her eyes. Okay, maybe Nick wouldn't wait three days for that discussion.

"Okay, hey." Like he was trying to break the tension before someone cracked, Brandon dove into his duffle. After a little bit of searching, he stood up and shoved a bundle wrapped in holiday paper at Nick. "Look I got you something."

A for the thought, *B-* for the wrapping effort, and *D+* for timing; Nick took the package. "I was thinking we could open Christmas presents over at Miri's. She wants us to come for breakfast day after tomorrow."

Again the superior tone out of a yard-ape's mouth, "We don't celebrate Christmas."

Fuck the discussion with her dad. "Great then," Nick snapped, "I'll just take the stuff I bought for you back. Maybe take the things to the alliance center, someone there will appreciate it."

"Play nice," Brandon glared down at his daughter, "it ain't going to corrupt you to open a couple gifts." Taking a deep breath, Brandon turned to Nick and smiled. His voice sounded strained, "Open it, *now please.*"

"Why?" Oh shit, he sounded as snotty as the kid. Nick figured a deep, relaxing breath wouldn't hurt him either. A little calmer, he asked a more reasonable question, "Sure you don't want to wait?"

"Now. Please." Brandon's smile grew so tight it threatened to rip his face apart.

Try and be nice and what do you get? With a huff, Nick ripped open the paper. "Hey, skull camouflage lounge pants." Why would Brandon buy him something like that? Commando all the way, Nick couldn't stand to sleep with something between him and the sheets. To be polite, he smiled and tried to sound appreciative, "Just what I needed." Wadding them back up into the paper, he added, "I don't usually wear stuff like this to bed."

"I know." The way Brandon said it, both words getting separate, slow emphasis, spoke volumes. Not so subtly, Brandon rolled his eyes toward where his daughter stood bouncing the phone handset against her knee. "But you have a nine-year-old house guest...so wear 'em."

"What does *Nick* normally wear to bed?" Out of everything else going on, how did she pick that one comment out?

"Really ratty stuff." Brandon shot Nick a glare like he was daring Nick to contradict him. "Why don't you get a soda, snack or something? Take it in to the TV." Apparently, that was all she needed. Shayna hit the refrigerator like she'd been starved. Maybe her mom kept the sweets on a leash, too.

Nick looked at the present in his hands and then over at the pint sized Diva raiding his refrigerator. "Only for you," he hissed, low enough so only Brandon would hear, "you know that, right?"

They both watched as Shayna dashed out of the room cradling a Coke.

"Thanks man." When he turned his attention back to Nick, Brandon managed a rueful smile. "I owe you."

Nick tossed the bundle on the table and then pinched the bridge of his nose. "If this is how the week is going to go...yeah, you do, 'cause I don't, like, sleep well with anything between me and the sheets."

"Okay, well," Brandon grabbed the luggage off the floor, "you said you had one of those cots you could put up?"

"Yeah." Still trying to rub the tension out of his forehead, Nick stood. "Borrowed it off Miri, it's in the front room."

"Let's go get it set up." Backing out of the room, Brandon added, "It'll be okay, really. I promise."

Nick would withhold judgment on that.

CHAPTER 2

Nick sat at his computer and logged into one of his many web-based email accounts. Behind him, Brandon messed with the borrowed fold-out cot. There wasn't much room in Nick's home office, but at least Shayna would have a little privacy. He'd tried to help Brandon at first. Setting the thing up turned out to be more of a one-man operation. Especially after he'd caught Brandon's fingers in the locking strut for the leg.

Talking to Brandon without looking at him, Nick clicked through into the inbox. "We should head to dinner." Twenty-five messages, ninety percent likely spam, Nick began the daily weeding of the mail. "I thought it might be fun to go over to the strip. Find someplace there. The casinos are all decorated up, Caesar's has the big tree out front, Bellagio has their whole display." About the tenth message down, he hit it. "Damn it."

"What?"

Did he really want to explain? Might as well, there wasn't much point keeping his cyber life private. "Another e-mail from this idiot, *cynicforlife*." Nick spun his chair around, reached back and tapped his monitor. A ten-times forwarded email about some not quite new virus alert filled the screen. "Met 'em on a forum." Not only was the warning fairly out of date, but Snopes had debunked it weeks ago.

"What?" Brandon tossed Shayna's sleeping bag on the mattress and then sat down on top of it. "You posting dirty pics of you in leather again?"

Nick kicked Brandon's shin. "Not that kind of forum, jackhole." For emphasis, he added a glare. "Get your mind out of the gutter. Not everything I do online is porn."

"Well, that's what the song says the Internet's made for." Grabbing Shayna's pillow off the floor Brandon smacked Nick's thigh with it as he brought it up. "And, hell, you showed me a couple of those places." He tossed it at the head of the tiny bed.

"Some of those chat rooms are raunchy."

"No." Nick wrinkled his upper lip in disgust, not at what went on in the chats, but that he would interact with this cynic character in that way. "This forum is for reviewing techno stuff." Brandon had to know him better than that. "Sometimes I'll print out threads from there and give them to people at work. You know," he shrugged, "some new product or something that kind of deals with what we do." Leaning over, Nick rested his elbows on his thighs and let his hands dangle between his legs. "Then cynic turned up on like three or four other forums I'm on."

Brandon raised his eyebrows and smirked, "Tracking *Disdain99*?" He sneered. Disdain was the user ID Nick used on the Goth forums and dating sites, back when he needed those types of places. Brandon knew about most all of them. Nick believed in being open, at least when you were fairly serious about someone.

"Naw, that's my alt for fun stuff, this was under *2TechNick*. Never seems to have hit anything but the *2TechNick* stuff. Always has these stupid fucking responses. Not mean or anything, just like they didn't quite get the point of the post, you know?" Actually explaining it to Brandon made the whole scenario seem almost creepy. "Sends me links to articles on crap I already know about, music I don't listen to…trying to connect I guess, but like the tip of the iceberg in alternative music, but not Goth."

"Why don't you block 'em?" Brandon stood.

Nick turned back to the computer. "I just delete it or ignore the posts." As he said it, Nick chucked the email into the trash folder. Pushing back from the desk, he added. "Said, 'thanks,' a couple times and then got more." Nick got up as well. "So I just ignore the e-mails."

Brandon repeated, "I'd block the sender." He patted Nick on the arm and, as Nick turned, cocked his thumb over his own shoulder indicating that they should head out. "Let's do the strip." He grinned. "Sounds fun, I don't think Shayna's ever seen it." Walking out of the office, Brandon yelled into the living room, "Bundle up, Princess, we're going out."

Getting Shayna out of the house ended up being a major undertaking. She'd only been at Nick's place half a day and already misplaced her coat and one of her sneakers. Nick let Brandon sort that out while he changed into black jeans, red T-shirt and combat boots. Then he pulled his black leather duster out of the closet. He headed into the living room expecting to be off and then the plans derailed again. Another search ensued for a necklace Shayna insisted—like wailing, yelling and slamming doors insisted—she needed.

Thank God Shayna didn't live with him. He couldn't take this 24/7.

Brandon rifled Shayna's jacket pockets in the living room while she searched her luggage back in the office. How many places could a kid lose stuff in that short of time? Nick was about to head into the kitchen to see if she'd maybe left it on the counter when Brandon found it. He pulled out an egg shaped pendant on a lanyard from between the cushions of the couch. "Found it, Princess!" he yelled. Seemed to be the communication option of choice for the time being.

Shayna had described it, vaguely, but the description didn't prepare Nick for just how ugly the thing was. "What the fuck is that?" Nick plucked the odd little bit from Brandon's fingers. The gray plastic oval only weighed a few ounces and had a red button in the center. It wasn't even techno-cool like some of the kids' pocket games out there.

"This child-finder thing Dian bought." Dragging his own jacket off the arm of the couch, Brandon pulled out what looked like a small remote from the inside pocket. "Princess goes missing, you flip it open, hold down green button. You can also set it for, like, a minder mode. If the kid wanders out of a certain radius the alarm goes off." He flipped open the cover and stared at the tiny LCD screen. "What the hell does she have the distance set at...fucking thirty feet? Nooooo, no. I'll reset for max distance."

"Sure you want to set it for max?" The system reeked of Big Brother, but changing the settings didn't seem real wise.

Brandon shrugged and kept fiddling. "Okay, half max that's

two-hundred-fifty feet. That's half a block." He flipped the cover closed. "Means one of us can go to the can and not have the piece of shit go off."

"Why'd your ex buy it?" Nick bounced the fob in his hand. Speaking of missing kids, where the fuck was Shayna? Wasn't like his house was big enough to get lost in...her stuff apparently, but not her.

"Dian's paranoid." Brandon tucked the remote back into his pocket and then put on his jacket. "I mean, I'm a cop, I'm not half as paranoid as she is about this."

"Does Dian have one for each of her kids?"

"I guess, the individual sensors I think." He patted his chest where the locator rested. "She said this was the babysitter's remote." At that point Shayna wandered back into the room, wearing different clothes than she'd been in five minutes ago. Both he and Brandon stared and then neither decided to say anything. Nick figured an explanation would just drag things out longer.

They bundled into the minivan. The inside had been kept up better than the outside and Nick hoped that meant, maybe, Brandon's stepbrother maintained the mechanics as well. Nick directed Brandon up Tropicana; short hop since Nick didn't live all that far off the strip. First they dumped forty bucks in change at the arcade at Excalibur and ended up hauling out half a dozen stuffed animals in neon colors. They probably could have bought the lot for less, but it wouldn't have been as much fun as whacking bean bag catapults and racing Viking boats with water guns. He and Brandon let Shayna decide what they'd play. Nick snapped pictures with his cell phone until Shayna complained that he was being embarrassing.

Then, on a tip from one of the attendants, they wandered over to New York, New York and an allegedly kosher deli. Brandon may have been nonchalant about the whole issue, but eventually Dian was going to make decisions about Brandon— and ultimately Nick—based on this trip. They needed to at least try to do things right. At least if Brandon really wanted to be more involved with his daughter. Besides, heading across the street gave them an excuse to wander through another casino, or at least the non-gambling portions, and see the decorations.

They grabbed sandwiches and parked themselves at a table on the fake street corner that made up the food court. A little corned beef and a beer fed the gnawing in Nick's stomach. Brandon chowed down on one of the specialty sandwiches made of half a dozen types of meat while Shayna stuck to Matzo ball soup. Brandon had just taken a massive bite when the phone at his hip began to scream in a demented cartoon character's voice.

"What the —" Nick self edited before the word *fuck* slipped out "—is that?" Shayna glowered over the rim of her bowl. She might have actually been old enough to understand what word he'd dropped.

Brandon grimaced as he swallowed. "Dian." He dropped the sandwich and wiped his hands on a napkin before grabbing the phone. "Text." Flipping the phone open, Brandon snorted. "She wants to know what's for dinner." Nick thanked God that at least one of them had the sense to care about their choice. "Shall I tell her chili-cheese dogs?"

Identical glares from Nicky and Shayna didn't seem to faze Brandon. He punched a short string of keys and hit send. "What'd you tell her?" Nick tried to probe without sounding too nosy. The message seemed way too short.

Brandon stared at his phone and grinned when it started to scream again. "Food."

"Brandon," Shayna's huff rebuked him better than Nick ever could manage.

"Fine." Brandon rolled his eyes like they were imposing on the most important moment of his life. Pointing the lens of the camera phone at the deli sign, he snapped off a picture and with a couple more keystrokes hit send. "Hopefully she can read the part that says kosher." He dropped the cell on the table and reached for his sandwich. The phone started to scream again. Grabbing it and checking the screen, he muttered, "What's with the fu—texting?" Nick stifled a snort for not being the only one not used to watching what he said. Brandon pointed the camera at Shayna and clicked off another picture. Then he punched a longer message out and sent that off. This time he didn't set the phone down. When it screamed again, he read off, "She's in a meeting. Figures. She says she'll call you at eight-thirty, Princess, when you're in bed."

"Subtle hint there?" Nick took a bite out of his pickle.

"Yeah, and a Howitzer is a little gun." Brandon holstered the phone and dove back into his food.

Apparently, Shayna inherited her mother's sense of timing. She waited until Brandon's mouth was full before asking, "Why does your phone scream when Mommy calls you?"

Nick tried not to choke. Brandon didn't fare so well. Nick had to stand up and slap his back a few times. Finally, after a swig of beer, Brandon muttered, "I don't know. I just picked that ring tone." Then he pointed at her food and ordered, "Just eat, okay?"

Shayna scowled, "But..."

"No," Brandon glared back, "just eat."

After finishing their food, Nick suggested they wander down the strip. Something needed to lighten the mood a little after the not quite father-daughter fight. They had to keep steering Shayna away from the folks passing out leaflets as they walked. Fuck, Nick never really processed how much porn was passed out on the strip via postcards and flyers. And all of it consisted of too thin girls with surgically enhanced cleavage.

To try and distract Shayna, Nick pointed out the tree under the arches at Paris. Then perched on the railing, they watched the Bellagio fountains dance to the tune of *Greensleeves* for a bit. Brandon yanked out his cell and caught some video—narrating in the particularly lame fashion of most people taking video. Shayna groaned, pushed off the rail and started walking. The front of Caesars, to their right, was bathed in golds and greens. They got a great view of the tree at the front of the casino when they walked up onto the pedestrian bridge over Las Vegas Boulevard.

Since the temperature kept dropping and the wind picked up, they turned around to head back. Nick suggested they duck through the shops and interiors. It would take a bit longer, but keep Shayna from bitching every five minutes about how cold it was. Unfortunately, it didn't stop the tide of complaints of how her feet hurt and she was tired. Brandon managed to stifle those, at least temporarily, with hot chocolate and cookies. As they wandered through the displays, Brandon shot a bit more video: from in front of them, behind them and to the side of them. Daddy Paparazzi at its best, Nick just grinned and let him do it. Shayna mostly tolerated the attention, although she kept rolling her eyes like they were the two biggest dorks in existence.

Taking advantage of a pause, Nick whipped out his own phone. "Come on, let's get a picture of you guys in front of this." A rotunda of blue 'ice' staggered up from one of the floral beds. Close to a dozen larger-than-life penguins posed as though caught in mid motion. Above them floated several large crystal stars.

Shayna slurped the chocolate as she looked from the display, to Nick, and back to the sculpture. Finally, she pronounced, "That's Christmas stuff," with a glare for effect, "my Mommy says we don't *do* Christmas."

Nicely, Nick corrected her, "Penguins are not Christmas." He tried to maintain cheerful as he pointed out, "It's a winter theme." Waving toward a vacant spot in front of the display, he coaxed, "Come on, you and your dad. Let's take a picture."

"Really, Princess." Brandon wrapped his big hand around the back of Shayna's neck and used it to gently steer her toward the display. Leaning down as they walked, he added, "What does your mom think of Bubbie's Chanukah bush?"

Nick was about to ask what a Chanukah bush was when he noticed that an older couple, also looking at the penguins, kind of studied them. Then the woman smiled and moved her fingers in the air indicating Brandon and Nick. "Want me to get all three of you?"

"Yeah," Brandon answered for him, "could you?"

Nick shrugged. It'd be kinda nice to have all of them in a picture. "It's already set on camera mode." He turned the phone in his hand and pointed at the various icons before handing it over. "Just point and hit 'okay.'"

As Nick scrambled over to stand next to Brandon, she asked, "Do I need to focus?"

"No." Nick sidled up to Brandon's right side. As Brandon moved her in front of them, Shayna looked up at Nick with one of her tense, not quite sure if she accepted the situation, expressions. Resisting the urge to put his arm around Brandon's shoulder, he added, "It's auto focus."

"All right," the woman bubbled. "Say 'gingerbread.'" Nick was pretty sure she caught Shayna rolling her eyes. At least Princess kept her mouth shut. Hopefully she smiled. After a couple more the woman insisted she take, to make sure at least one came out, they moved on.

As they walked back out onto the strip, Brandon's phone screamed again. He grabbed it off his hip and glanced at the display, then pushed a button and held it to his ear. "Hey." He scowled as he listened to Dian. Nick assumed Dian called, although Brandon could have assigned that ringtone to someone else as well. "No," he grimaced, "I forgot to charge it last night. Of course she ran it out of battery, yakking to everyone on the ride up." Brandon kept his hand on Shayna's shoulder as they walked. With the crowd, it seemed the best way not to lose her. Heck, Nick had a hard time keeping next to Brandon. "We're on the strip, looking at lights and stuff. Yeah, I know what time it is. The three of us are heading back to the car right now." After a pause, probably in response to some question he added, "Nicky's with us." Brandon smiled at Nick. Then his expression fell into something resembling panic, "No! No!" He thrust the phone in Nick's face. "Nicky, say hi to Dian."

Not knowing quite what Brandon was doing, Nick leaned toward the phone and said, "Hi, Dian."

"See," Brandon returned the phone to his ear, "Nicky, it's a dude's name." Then Brandon tapped the back of Shayna's head and handed her the cell. "Here. Your mom wants to say goodnight."

CHAPTER 3

Not bothering to turn on the light, Brandon staggered into Nicky's office. He tried to be quiet, but it was hard laboring under fifty pounds of deadweight. Shayna was completely and utterly out, to the point of drooling on his shoulder out. What happened to *sugar and spice*? And when the hell did Shayna get so big? Ahead of him, at about shin level, was his goal: her cot. No way in hell could he bend down and get her in bed without throwing out his back. Long gone were the days when Shayna could snuggle in the crook of his arm. Not that he'd had many of those.

A little twinge of regret tugged at the bottom of his heart.

Instead of bending over, Brandon squatted enough so that Shayna's feet could touch the floor. It wasn't that far down. When the hell did she get so tall, too? "Come on Princess, you got to stand up." Coaxing, he tried to hold her up and unzip her jacket at the same time. "Help me here, Shayna." With the light bleeding in from the hallway, he could almost see what he was doing.

She swayed and her eyes fluttered, "Daddy?" At least her feet were under her.

That little tug turned into a big wrenching twist. How had it gotten so bad that she called some other man *daddy* and Brandon was just...Brandon? He knew: his own damn fault for not being there.

"Okay, Princess." Brandon managed to slide the jacket off her shoulders and ease her to sitting on the bed. "Let's get your sneakers off." She could sleep in her clothes; they were clean enough. As she blinked and yawned, Brandon pulled the locator up and over her head. Then he tugged her shoes off.

She yawned again. "Brandon?" It must have penetrated her drowsy brain that Brandon wasn't Frank.

Brandon settled her back on the little bed. "Yeah, Shayna." Thankfully, Nicky'd put some extra blankets under the cot. There was no way for him to get Shayna into the sleeping bag.

As he shook out one and spread it over her, Shayna mumbled, "I miss Daddy and Mommy."

Taking in a deep breath, Brandon tried to come up with something profound and fatherly; and not jealous that she missed her stepfather when Brandon was right there. The most coherent thing he could manage was, "That's okay." God, he sucked at this father gig. "Look, Princess, I'm here." He folded the jacket under the bed, put her sneakers on top of that and dropped the locator fob into one of the shoes. "Just yell if you need me."

"Mmm, hmm," Shayna breathed, drifting back under again. Yeah, long day for all of them. Brandon shook out another blanket and laid that over the first. Hopefully, it'd be warm enough. Elbows cocked on the edge of the bed, butt resting on his heels, Brandon stared at *his* little girl while she slept.

Brushing a little bit of stray hair off her face, it hit Brandon. Shayna relied on him to keep her safe. He kind of felt that way about Nicky, but Nicky was a big boy, an adult. Honestly, for the most part, he could take care of himself. Shayna couldn't. It all rested on Brandon's shoulders and the weight was damn near crushing. So strange: a person who was part of him. Depended on him. His responsibility.

As a cop, Brandon knew responsibility—in that big, amorphous global sense. This felt nine kinds of different: personal, concrete and fucking scary.

He stayed there for a while, indulging in a daddy's prerogative, watching his child sleep. At least until his knees started to protest. Then Brandon stood and ran his hands over his face. Man, he was bushed, too. How could just kicking around with his kid wear him out so much? Brandon wandered back out to Nicky's living room. A beer and a shower sounded like heaven.

Pretty much the only lights on were in the hall and a flicker of something on the flat-screen TV. The sound wasn't up so Brandon ignored the idiot box…probably wrestling highlights or extreme fighting: Nicky's mind candy of choice. Nicky sat on his old Victorian couch, his feet kicked up on the coffee table. Black slim-line jeans hugged his legs and rode up over the tops of his combat boots. A red T-shirt, with an upside down cross stenciled in gray and black on the front, stretched tight over a nice layer of muscle and warm-brown skin. Goddamn, he looked like a modern day Dracula. Sans the long hair—Nicky had grown it out some, but it'd only been about six months since they'd had to cut off the mid-back black fall to stitch his head back together. Right now in the growing out process it hovered between grunge-rock mess and heroin chic. Still looked incredible on him. Lean, brown and sexy, with strong features and dark eyes, nobody else ever managed to rock Brandon like Nicky.

And Brandon really didn't need to be thinking about that right then.

Nicky smiled across the dim room. Two beers sat on the table, like Nicky'd read his mind. Who'd have thought that Brandon would ever find someone so right? Second thing that night which scared the shit out of Brandon. Despite all the differences—out and not quite out, biker Goth vs. vampire-Victorian Goth, cop and gaming control—he and Nicky just meshed.

Ignoring the twinge of panic, Brandon walked over, grabbed one of the beers and dropped onto the sofa next to Nicky. "Princess is down for the count." First he took a deep swig then twisted his body so that his head was in Nicky's lap and his legs rested on the arm of the couch. Just that little bit of closeness felt wonderful after a long drive and a long tour of the strip. "I think I may follow her lead." Brandon managed to get it out through his yawn. "You got work tomorrow, right?"

Nicky shifted, dropping one arm over Brandon's chest. "Unfortunately." Nicky snorted. "What, you thinking it's time for bed or something?" His fingers absently danced along Brandon's ribs.

Realization struck Brandon that if he stayed in this position much longer, he'd pass out. He couldn't believe he was that exhausted. "Yeah." Brandon struggled to sit up. "I'll get the couch ready."

Nicky used the arm across Brandon's chest to pull him back down. "What?"

Brandon rolled his head to look up at Nicky. "I'll sleep on the couch."

"No." The stare Brandon got in response was a mixture of frustrated and murderous. Looked damn sexy on Nicky, of course everything looked damn sexy on Nicky. "Ze couch, she is not made for sleeping." He intoned in a fake French accent. Dropping the tease, Nicky added. "Seriously, I own the most uncomfortable couch in the world for that." Nicky shoved Brandon's shoulder, pushing him off his lap. As Nicky struggled to stand, he ordered, "Get your butt in bed. I haven't seen you in three—four weeks. You've been covering everyone else's shifts since Thanksgiving."

Normally Nicky's order would rev Brandon to hot and horny in a matter of seconds. With his daughter in the house—no he couldn't go there. "Nicky, come on." Brandon rolled as he sat up so his legs came off the arm of the couch and hit the floor. Palming his face again, he stifled another yawn. "I'm not sure I'm ready for Shayna to know we sleep in the same bed."

"Sooner or later," Nicky huffed, "she's going to figure that out." He reached out for his beer. Brandon sensed that's what Nicky wanted, grabbed it off the table and passed it over. After a muttered, "Thanks," Nicky seemed to mull things over. Finally, he asked, "Do you really want to start your relationship with Shayna off on false pretenses? Think about it. Are we hiding or not? I'd rather not." After another swig, Nicky sighed. "I'm no child psychologist, but, babe, she's just getting to know you now…if you start with lies, can't be good."

"Damn it, Nicky," Brandon groused. "Going all philosophical on me." They'd winged the Shayna part of this trip without much thought. Fuck, there hadn't been time to actually plan, much less discuss issues like sleeping arrangements. He'd just assumed that Nicky would go along with him. He didn't want a fight, but Brandon wasn't ready to give in either.

Nicky flashed a tight smile. "Look, I don't mean to be a

downer." With another huff, he uncrossed his arms and stuck one hand in his back pocket. He used the beer in the other to point from the couch to the corner of the house where his bedroom was. "But, come on, sleep where you always do when you're here." Downing another swig, he added, "If you treat it like it's no big thing…then it isn't. Get my drift?"

"No." He just couldn't do the sleeping arrangements. If he went to bed with Nicky, one thing would lead to another and they'd end up naked, sweaty and…no that couldn't happen.

Exasperated, Nicky threw up both his hands. "Why not?" Beer sloshed out of the bottle and onto the floor. Nicky glared at the damp spot, then at Brandon like he should have warned him or something.

"Feels weird."

"Well, I'm getting something tonight." Nicky pulled himself straight up and crossed his arms over his chest. The glare his face fell into almost intimidated Brandon. "So, I can fuck you on the living room couch, open to the rest of the house, or in my bedroom which has a door." When he smiled the little points on his canines became very visible. Nicky had Goth-vampire nailed…naturally. It was lecherous, dangerous and fucking hot. "Your choice," he growled.

Still, Brandon couldn't see it. The whole idea just hit him as too creepy. "Not a good idea, Nicky." God, his protest sounded wussy even to his own ears.

"Look. Okay." Nicky dropped the hype. "Let's fool around some. Make out?" He grinned again. "Please, come on, I hate begging, but dude I miss you." Although less menacing, it still came off as lecherous, dangerous and fucking hot. Brandon stuffed the thought down. "You can come back out to the couch afterward." Like he couldn't fathom Brandon's reluctance, he added, "If that's what you really want."

"It's just weird." Glancing back toward the office, Brandon stood. He chewed his bottom lip for a bit. "The thought of screwing around with Shayna in the house."

"You know." Nicky stepped in close and butted Brandon's shoulder with his own. Almost conspiratorially, he whispered, "I have an older sister. That means my parents were screwing around while one of their kids was in the house."

"Why is that so disturbing?" Brandon snorted. He pushed back. "I mean, not your parents having sex...the thought that there's more than one of you out there?"

"Asshole." Nick removed his hand from his own back pocket, grabbed Brandon's beer and set both bottles on the table. Then he slid his arms around Brandon's middle and his hands into Brandon's back pockets. "Come on." He breathed against Brandon's neck. The contact was so tenuous, and so sensual for it, that the hairs on the back of Brandon's neck stood up as every other inch of his body focused attention on Nicky. "It's not like this is a first date." Nicky kissed Brandon's chin before he started walking them backward toward his bedroom. "We have something here. And I'm not going to tie you up or anything."

Despite his words and his misgivings, Brandon didn't resist being drawn to bedroom. He couldn't resist Nicky...ever. "You're too reasonable."

"Horny men are desperate men," he teased, "we'll even resort to logic to get laid."

Well, he could resist that. Brandon jerked back. Pulling Nicky's hands out of his pockets, Brandon growled, "I said no." Still, he had to go into the bedroom, that's where his clothes were. Not unless he wanted to sleep in his jeans. He pushed past Nicky into the short hall.

Nicky's rebuke, "You are such a buzz kill," followed Brandon into the bedroom with its red curtains and purple walls. Like everything in Nicky's house, the room gave off the ambiance of a horror show whorehouse: lots of thick drapes, tons of rich colors and heavy antique furniture—most of it inherited from Nicky's grandparents along with the house. Brandon knew chicks that didn't put half as much effort into their digs as Nicky.

Brandon knelt next to his duffle and yanked out a pair of

pajama pants. Normally at Nicky's, he'd have crashed in his briefs. Without looking at Nicky, but aware of his approach through boots on wood floors, Brandon chastised, "No, you're a horn dog." Shit, he wondered if the damn things fit him. Brandon couldn't remember the last time he wore the bottoms. Probably the last time he'd been up at his dad's place.

Springs groaned as Nicky sat on the edge of his bed. "Guilty as charged," he grumbled.

Brandon looked over to see Nicky fussing with the laces of his combat boots. Nicky sat on the bed, the lounge pants rested on top of the old dresser, right next to the resin demon doing a hand-stand, and the door stood wide open. God, Brandon couldn't decide if winning Shayna over to Nicky was harder than getting Nicky to remember that a nine-year-old girl slept down the hall. With an over-emphasized grunt, Brandon stood. He stalked to the door and closed it forcefully—just short of slamming since he didn't want to wake Shayna. Then he grabbed the lounge pants off the dresser, balled them up and pitched them at Nicky's head.

Pulling one of the legs off his face, Nicky sneered, "Pissy, pissy, pissy." He wadded the pants next to his hip. Kicking his boots off, Nicky asked, "What the fuck is your deal tonight?"

"You're just going to get naked while the door's wide open?" he snapped. Brandon felt his face and shoulders go tight. "Can you not remember that Shayna's here?"

Nicky rolled his eyes. "One, I'm just taking off my goddamn boots and two," speaking slow, like he thought Brandon was too dense to get it, "how could I possibly forget when you remind me every other second?"

Brandon leaned back against the dresser, his hands against the wood, and stared. Nicky sat on the bed and stared back. Seconds ticked by on the clock. Finally, Brandon dropped his eyes. "I'm sorry, babe." He didn't want to be mad at Nicky, ever. "I'm just so nervous." He wandered over to the bed and dropped down next to Nicky. Hands hanging loose between his knees, he sighed and gave a slight shrug. "I don't want to fuck this up."

"I know." Nicky reached out, grabbed his shoulder. With a strong squeeze of his hand, he reassured Brandon. "But you need to relax, okay?" The pressure turned into rubbing, a firm grip working the knots in Brandon's muscles. "Things will be fine."

"Did tonight go okay?" Flopping back on the mattress, Brandon tried to rub the tension out of his temples with his fingers. "You think I did all right?"

Nicky leaned over. His elbow slid into the pit of Brandon's arm and Nicky's hip rolled against Brandon's thigh. "You're asking me?" Running his other palm absently over Brandon's abs, he thought for a moment before adding, "I think so. I think the big thing is you're trying and that counts."

He so didn't deserve anyone like Nicky. "You're too good for me, Nicky."

"No shit," Nicky moved in closer, almost nose to nose, "Sherlock." Then Nicky dropped that last inch or so and kissed him.

Brandon shuddered. Yeah, it'd been two months. Still, he managed to pull back enough to mumble, "Nicky, what are you doing?"

"Come on." His touch worked heat into Brandon's middle. The sensation wicked through his frame making every inch of his body stand up and pay attention to how near Nicky was. Like he didn't even notice Brandon's reaction, Nicky purred, "At least give me a good night kiss."

Bullshit. "A good night kiss?" Brandon wrapped his grip around Nicky's arm, intending to pull him back from the strokes. Instead, Brandon found himself running his hand up and down the warm skin of Nicky's arm. And what he really wanted was for Nicky to kiss him again.

"With tongue preferably." Nicky brushed his lips against Brandon's and whispered, "But I'll take what I can get."

"Fuck you, Nicky." His protest came out half-hearted at best.

"That's what I'm trying for! Sheesh." He laughed and the sound tickled down Brandon's spine.

Brandon breathed deep. The scent of Nicky: sweat, a faint ghost of cologne, and oil from the bike blended into an intoxicating mix. "God, you smell good, you know that?" Brandon had missed that.

"Yeah." Grabbing Brandon's wrists, Nicky wrestled them up and over Brandon's head. "Think so?" Brandon struggled enough to make a show at resistance, but not enough to actually break away. He knew he shouldn't give in. He wanted to give in. Finally, Nicky pinned Brandon's hands against the rails of the wrought-iron headboard and nipped along Brandon's chin. The tiny pricks of pain and a little restraint...Nicky knew just how to make him want more. His prick swelled in response. That reaction caused all sorts of other twinges and pinches. With his hands trapped, Brandon couldn't even adjust his dick to a more comfortable position. All he could do was squirm and twist hoping to relieve the pain. And that—that got him even harder.

Brandon wasn't in control, Nicky was. If Nicky took charge that meant Brandon didn't have to think. He didn't want to think. Brandon wanted to give in, give up, to Nicky. Let him take responsibility out of Brandon's hands.

Nicky straddled his thigh. His leg pressed hard into Brandon's crotch. Brandon writhed beneath him and his prick throbbed. It felt as if it would split his jeans. He groaned and humped, trying for more contact. Nicky thrust against him. That thick, long, demanding cock trapped in its own denim prison, pressed like iron into Brandon's hip. Brandon could feel where it ran along Nicky's leg. If he moved right he could feel the head of Nicky's prick dig into his groin. Close enough to almost feel it against his own aching dick.

Their mouths devoured each other. Hot, desperate kisses wound between them. Brandon sucked on Nicky's lip and his tongue and whatever else he could manage. He broke free of Nicky's hold and buried his hands in Nicky's thick hair. Tangling his grip into that dark mass, Brandon pulled Nicky into another frantic kiss. Nicky's hands wandered over his body, up under his shirt, making Brandon shiver wherever their skin met. He didn't even have control over his lower body. Delicious pressure from the tight confines of denim and Nicky's leg smoked like dry ice through his veins.

With a growl, Nicky bit his neck at the collar. Sucked hard enough that Brandon felt the blood rising to the skin. Insane amounts of friction, need and two months of denial threw Brandon over the edge. He arched his back and gasped out, "Fuck!" as he blew in his jeans.

Nicky kept sucking, raising a welt, and thrusting against Brandon. Somehow, Brandon managed to stay focused enough to wrap his hands over Nicky's butt and grind back. Nicky grunted. He jerked. Brandon held on tight as Nicky shuddered through his own release. Then, panting, Nicky collapsed onto Brandon. They lay that way for a while.

Then it sank into Brandon's brain that he'd cum in his jeans.

He snorted at the indignity of losing it like some horny teenager. Slowly, Nicky kissed up his neck until he reached Brandon's ear. Then he whispered, "You're at least taking me to homecoming right?"

Brandon's snorts turned into laughter. "Well, with the hickey you gave me, all the other girls are going to think I'm easy."

"You are easy." As he rolled off the bed, Nicky chuckled. "Crap." He laughed and cupped the wet spot on his jeans. "Asshole, take me all the way back to freaking high school." The smile took any sting out of his words. "I'll be right back. Bring you a towel?"

Brandon sat up and started to unbutton his soaked jeans. "Yeah." He grunted as Nicky eased out of the door, closing it behind him.

Nicky hit it on the head, flashbacks to high school…although he'd never done it with a guy until he'd graduated. Brandon stood and toed out of his boots. Well, there was that whole nebulous period when he was a kid and experimenting…but that didn't really count. Brandon yanked his T-shirt up to his nose and took a sniff. It would do to sleep in. Nicky sidled back into the room. After tossing Brandon a damp towel and closing the door, Nicky shucked his clothes. Brandon shoved his own jeans and shorts off then cleaned himself off as well as he could manage. Fuck it, he'd do a shower in the morning. He kicked his dirty clothes into a pile near his bag before retrieving his pajamas from the floor and flopping back onto the bed. Brandon took a moment to watch Nicky hop into his lounge pants.

Feral and sexy, Nicky crawled up next to Brandon. "Now that we're comfortable." Nicky stretched along Brandon's side. "What was that about, 'he's a dude?'"

They couldn't stay comfortable too long. He still had to make up the couch. Raising his butt off the bed, Brandon yanked his pajama pants up over his ass and grunted, "Huh?" Brandon rolled over so he could look at Nicky. "What?" Where had that question come from?

"Dian?" Nicky glared and snapped his index finger against Brandon's temple. "The phone? You trying to shove it up my nose out on the strip?"

Oh that. Brandon closed his eyes and tried to explain. "She started going off on me, accusing me of bringing my daughter with me while I was hanging out at a girlfriend's house. I wanted to make sure she knew that wasn't what was going on."

"Bitch," Nicky thumped Brandon's chest with his hand, "that's exactly what's going on. Except you're hanging out at your boyfriend's house." Brandon felt Nicky shift. He opened his eyes to find Nicky leaning over and staring at him. "Which do you think would freak her out more?"

"Don't go there, Nicky." Brandon didn't even want to consider that issue.

"Just saying." Nicky slumped back and Brandon had to adjust his position or be pushed off the bed. "You're playing that whole *I'm straight* game." Now, Nicky's touch moved along his ribcage and made Brandon twitch. "It's going to bite you in the ass. You shouldn't pretend you're not having sex with me to keep your ex-wife from thinking you're up here having sex with some woman. So not right, dude."

"I didn't think." Brandon sat up and swung his legs over the side of the bed. "I just didn't want Dian to worry. She's already like," Brandon held his fingers up in front of his eyes, measuring off a tiny distance, "this close to losing it anyway."

Nicky wrapped his arm around Brandon's middle. With a gentle tug, he coaxed, "Come here."

"Why?" Brandon sighed. "I need to get the couch ready."

Another tug. "It's been almost two months." His hand ran up Brandon's back. "Just be with me for a while, okay?"

A little bit wouldn't hurt. They'd already both gotten off, so nothing would get up and running again for a while. He sank back down on the pillows and smiled at Nicky. "For a little bit."

clickjacked.blogroads.net- Private Post, Dec. 27, 10:55pm

No, no, no. There wasn't supposed to be other people there. Not now. So close and but, no. It was all about being alone. If there was no alone then there was nothing. It wouldn't work right, the plans wouldn't be right. Check the house and there's a car. Not the car that's supposed to be there. And then watch and see, but it's not going to work because the other people are there. The whole night of being there and never alone.

Pictures would help though. Somewhere in them would be cracks. Focus on the cracks, drive the wedges in to get him alone, vulnerable. See what they said. Maybe just a one-time thing with all the people. They'd go and he's alone again. It only worked with him alone.

CHAPTER 4

A little whisper in his ear, "Brandon," registered.

Brandon yawned and cracked his vision on a fuzzy focused world. A twin set of crystal blue eyes, inches from his own, stared intently. "Eh, Shayna?" What was Shayna doing next to his bed? He shifted and felt the weight of an arm across his chest. A sense of the present rammed through Brandon's sleep fogged brain. Fuck, he was in Nicky's bed! His heart suddenly couldn't decide if it wanted to go at a thousand beats a second or stop dead. Fighting back the panic, he managed to keep the dread inside from showing outside. Brandon eased Nicky's arm off and back, trying not to wake him.

As if sensing his thoughts, Shayna whispered, "Why are you in Mr. O'Malley's bed?"

Dredging up Nicky's arguments from last night, Brandon hissed back, "The couch is too uncomfortable, too small." What the fuck time was it? He blinked at the clock: five-thirty. Didn't Shayna know she was on break?

"Oh." She frowned. Poking at his shoulder, right near Brandon's collar, she asked, louder, "What happened to your neck?"

Dear God, the hickey. "I ran into something." A terrible lie, but hopefully a nine-year-old would buy it. Brandon pushed Shayna back a bit and eased out of bed. At least he and Nicky were both dressed. Otherwise this would equal a major disaster instead of just nine kinds of uncomfortable. "Come on." He bent down near her ear. "Let's not wake up Nicky." Then, with his palm cupping the back of her head, Brandon steered Shayna out of the room. "I'll get you some breakfast."

Easier said than done. Shayna examined every box of cereal, every pre-packaged food in Nicky's kitchen, with a dedication Brandon rarely saw in cops processing evidence. She finally stood up holding a box of instant pancake mix. "This."

"Pancakes?" Although Brandon's cooking skills tended toward rusty, he could probably manage the instant variety. "You sure you want that?"

"It has the OU." She slid the box onto the counter and tapped the bottom left corner. "Mommy says if it has that or the circle or star with the K, I can eat it."

"Okay." Brandon shrugged. "Whatever." Dian had their kid *trained* that was for sure. He grabbed a pan from the cabinet and tossed it on a burner. Took a few tries with the lighter to get the stove going. Water and a bowl, even Brandon's meager skills managed that. Of course it looked like he'd have enough to feed half the force. He dropped the batter into the pan, managing a semi-round shape then started on prepping the coffee maker. Only so long before the need for caffeine reared its head.

After he flipped the first one over, he snagged a plate for the pancakes and a mug for his coffee from the dishwasher. "Here." He slid the plate onto the counter. Then he grabbed the mug and poured the two fingers worth of already brewed coffee into it.

As Brandon took that initial, soul-warming swig, Shayna looked at the plate suspiciously. "Is it washed okay?"

"Yeah." What the hell was she talking about? He used the mug to point toward the one sort of modern appliance in Nicky's kitchen. "Came out of the dishwasher just now." He grabbed the plate and held it out to her. "Your mom said that's good enough."

Wrinkling her nose, Shayna didn't take it. "Can I have a paper plate?"

Brandon just stared. This went way past training and into full-blown indoctrination. He took a deep breath. Shayna was well taken care of. She was polite. She had good grades. Lots of things about how Dian raised their daughter rated in the positive end of the scale. And the whole food thing didn't rate as a negative... more as a pain in the ass to deal with. "Sure." Brandon even managed a smile. "Whatever makes you happy, Princess." Digging through Nick's cabinets netted Brandon a slim stack of paper plates with red, blue and white stars on them. No telling how long the things had been stored. Brandon pulled one out of the middle and dumped two not quite burned flapjacks on the paper. Luckily, the syrup and fake butter passed the test as well: circled U's on both the packages.

Shayna balanced the plate with both hands as she stepped back. "Can I," she chewed her bottom lip for a moment. Holy crap, he had the same habit. "Can I watch TV while I eat my breakfast?"

"What does your mom do?" Brandon didn't want to be a downer, but he also didn't want to end up defying any rules that Dian laid down. Especially since he hadn't actually read the ones she wrote out for him.

"Mommy, sometimes she lets me." The way Shayna said it, sometimes equated to pretty much never. "But," Shayna brightened, "Bubbie lets me when I stay at her house."

Well, if Edith indulged Shayna, then it equaled two against one. He'd ride on his stepmother's coattails. "Go ahead." He pushed one of the bar style doors open and let Shayna pass out of the kitchen. For a moment he actually felt like a dad and not a fuck up. Brandon even gave himself a mental pat on the back as he whipped up a few more pancakes.

Nicky wandered into the kitchen as Brandon tossed number six onto the stack. He messed with tying the knot on a white necktie dotted with what looked like blood spray. Casting a suspicious glance at the counter he asked, "You made pancakes?" Nicky looped the tie up and under for the final knot. At least the red matched his shirt. "You've never made me pancakes."

"I thought you were an intravenous coffee kinda guy." Brandon considered the half full bowl of batter. Hell, he had enough pancakes made for the rest of the month. Brandon dumped most of the remaining batter down drain before tossing the bowl in the sink.

"It might be nice," Nick shrugged grabbing a mug from the cabinet, "you know, sometime."

Brandon slid up behind him, "You're jealous."

Pouring a cup of coffee, Nicky tried to ignore Brandon. Brandon could tell by how Nicky held himself: aloof but totally aware of how close they were. "You're whacked," Nick growled over his shoulder.

"You are." Brandon ran the spatula handle up Nicky's stomach. He jumped. Coffee sloshed over the tile. Laughing, Brandon pushed him up against the counter and whispered in his ear, "You're jealous of a nine-year-old…girl." Then his fingers followed the path of the spatula and his other hand slid down Nicky's leg.

Nick shivered. "Fuck you." Halfheartedly he tried to push Brandon away. All it did was grind his ass into Brandon's hips.

"Aw, babe, it's too funny." Brandon could feel Nicky getting hard. Hell, he could feel himself getting hard. Brandon began a line of kisses starting behind Nicky's ear and moving down toward his back. Whispering against Nicky's skin, "Want me to read you bedtime stories and blow the bad dreams out of your head?"

"I can think of someplace I'd much rather have you blow." Nicky turned so that his butt was against the counter and Brandon's hands rested on either side of his body. "Wanted you too last night. I see we've broken through one barrier." He grinned, then taking a deep swig of coffee Nicky purred over the lip of the mug, "So why are you up so early?"

Reminding them both why they couldn't have fun like normal, Brandon backed his pelvis up giving them a few fractions of an inch of space. "Princess." He huffed. Hopefully it came out good-natured instead of mildly pissed off.

"Ahh," Nicky took another gulp, "The way of the Princess, Brandon-san, it is designed to rob you of sleep and sex."

Brandon snorted. He opened his mouth to spit out a snappy comeback when Nicky's phone began to ring. Since it sounded like an old style rotary ring that meant it was Nicky's cell. Stepping around him, Nicky grabbed the phone off the charger on the counter by the back door. He looked at the screen and frowned.

Stepping in and pushing the top of the phone down so that he could view the display, Brandon tried to fathom why Nicky would be bothered by a call. "What?" Well, other than it was damn early in the morning.

"Unknown number." Nicky shrugged. "Been getting a shitload of those lately. Like at least three a day." He dropped the phone on the counter. "Never leave a message. Maybe a telemarketer, but I'm on the do-not-call list."

Irritating e-mails, number blocked calls, both hooked up as freaky in Brandon's cop brain. "You didn't, like, put your number out there…online?"

"Are you fuc—" Nicky stopped mid sentence, his gaze jumping to the doorway.

Shayna pushed back through the doors and Brandon stood up straight using the position to distance himself from any hint of intimacy.

"I'm done." Shayna announced as she pushed the plate onto the counter. Looked like she'd eaten maybe five bites.

"You didn't eat half of what I made you."

Shayna rolled her eyes. "I'm full." She glared at Brandon as if challenging him to contradict her. When he didn't she turned to Nicky and screwed up her face in disgust. "What's on your tie?"

Nicky didn't even pause before responding, "Blood splatter."

Shayna's eyes went wide. "Real?" Brandon stopped himself from laughing. With as smart as she was, there still echoed this deep well of innocence.

"Yeah," Nicky grinned, "I had to murder six people to get it just right." When Shayna's mouth fell open, he laughed, "No, it's printed. A joke."

Shayna retreated into a know-it-all shell. Her little lips thinned into a tight line. "That's gross." She even managed a drawl. "Your house is creepy."

Nonchalant, Nicky took another swallow of his coffee. "Creepy?" His eyes, however, rolled enough that Brandon could sense the irritation under that calm surface.

"Yeah." More confident, Shayna added, "It looks like Halloween."

Nicky didn't seem put out by that statement. "Halloween is one of my favorite holidays."

Shayna scuffed her toes on the floor and looked up at the ceiling. "Scary stuff gives me bad dreams." Then she shrugged and turned to Brandon. "Brandon, your friend is strange." That pronouncement seemed to encompass the world of her thoughts. Shayna nodded and then dashed through the swinging doors toward the sound of cartoon mayhem. Brandon glanced at Nicky. A dark, tight expression blew across his strong features. When he saw Brandon looking, Nicky just shook his head and dropped his mug on the counter. He didn't even say *goodbye* as he grabbed his bike gear and headed out the back door. The only way Brandon knew Nicky was actually gone was when he heard the high velocity whine of the Kawasaki's engine whipping down the driveway.

CHAPTER 5

Nick poured himself a cup of coffee from the break room decanter and teased, "Come on, say it."

Ada, racked-stacked-prim-and-proper, ran one manicured, but unpolished hand, through her heavy, wavy black hair. "No, I won't." From the urinal gossip, all the straight guys at the Board had fantasies about Ada. Heck, even as a gay man, Nick acknowledged that Ada deserved a look. She possessed a natural, serene beauty that every commercial product in the world promised the masses it would bring. As far as Nick could tell, Ada never wore more makeup than a little lip gloss—and being Goth, he did have a reasonable understanding of liner, lipstick and eye shadows, even if he didn't wear them to work; and she tended toward similar outfits as today's: flats, calf length skirts and tops that flattered while not exposing.

Their co-worker relationship rated fairly familiar and rather relaxed, since Ada didn't have to worry about Nick trying to get in her pants. Of course it also blew way beyond tense. Nick knew, that Ada *knew*, he was going to hell because he *had relations* with other men. She'd never said anything openly, but with the church she belonged to and how she weighed in on various issues other than that…Nick figured it had to be that way. Still, he believed in the one person at a time method of winning over the world. If Ada saw him as a person, she'd be less likely to follow the herd when it counted. It wouldn't be *those people*, but *this is Nick*.

"Oh, come on," he propped his butt against the counter and looped one hand across his middle. He took a swig of coffee and coaxed, "I won't tell anyone it came out of your mouth. Admit, you think she's a pain in the rear." He'd gotten so used to self-editing his language around Ada that he didn't even think about it anymore.

Ada sighed. "Jen can be…" she looked like he'd pulled her teeth to make her speak, "difficult." Both he and Ada had been assigned to portions of an internal project. That meant interacting with the administrative end of computer programming…and Jen Saville.

"No, making the left from Flamingo onto the Strip at rush hour, that's difficult." Nick grimaced. "She's impossible." Computer people generally tended toward introverted and socially lacking—Nick figured he had his moments at various times. Jen, however, managed new levels of both. Nick had to wonder how she negotiated the interview process with her stunted personality.

Ada forced a smile. "Everyone has good points." Shit, Nick could have been back on the painkillers from when he'd gotten tossed out of the back of his hearse on the Grapevine and still recognize the expression as forced.

"List them." He snorted and held up three fingers on the hand that didn't hold the coffee cup. "Give me three and I'll shut up."

Eyes rolling to the side, tongue exploring her cheek, Ada looked like she was thinking. Finally she frowned and said, in a tone normally reserved for attempts at funerals to say something nice about complete assholes, "She keeps them well hidden."

"Wow!" Nick sounded stunned…because he was. In all the years he'd worked in Electronic Services and Ada had worked Investigations she'd never trashed anyone. "Outta you, that's amazing." It was one of the reason's Nick tolerated the whole *I have issues with your lifestyle* vibe. At least with Ada, she tried to live the ideal. That included the whole love the person not the act dilemma.

Nick was about to say more when the focus of their discussion burst into the room. Her hair wasn't brown, but it didn't quite rate as blond. While she dressed for the office, Nick couldn't quite categorize it as proper civil service attire either. Both her clothes and hair seemed disheveled and not intentionally so. Pretty average in height, weight and build, Jen was one of those people who faded into the background as completely unremarkable. Pulling through his memories, Nick had difficulty remembering the times he'd spoken with her. He knew it had to be a few times at least, but he couldn't dredge specifics up. And he was pretty sure he was the one who selected Jen for the assignment, although he couldn't really remember why.

For Nick, who could still remember the phone number of his first college crush that meant Jen rated as pretty forgettable; except when he was forced to deal with her. Like now.

She shoved a clipboard with a form under Nick's nose, "Agent O'Malley," she mumbled, "I need your signature on this requisition."

Pushing the form down enough that he could look at her, Nick tried for an instructive tone. "Usually conversations start with *hello* or *sorry I'm interrupting*." He'd been designated as the lead for the team. Some of that meant, like, actually supervising other people.

Without bothering to apologize, Jen blurted, "What were you talking about?" Having done a stint, a short stint, at JPL and gotten his Electrical Engineering degree out of USC, Nick'd run into people who lived on the cutting edge of high functioning autism: bright, nice, but antisocial in spades. A qualitative difference, one Nick couldn't quite put his finger on, existed between them and Jen. Her whole personality just rang as odd. Plus, even though she seemed clean enough, Jen harbored the faint taint of unwashed dogs and clothes that hadn't dried properly. A musty, funky edge.

Ada jumped in with her charitable outlook, "Nick was just telling me what a good work ethic you have. How you can really focus on a task and not get distracted."

"Yeah, okay," Nick grabbed the clipboard, gave the form a quick once over and muttered, "you're very focused, that's one." He added the last part for Ada's benefit. Nothing seemed amiss. A standard requisition for computer data-entry time…diverting minor resources normally reserved for audit to their little slice of administrative busy work. He pulled a pen from his pocket and scribbled his signature. "There you go, Jen." Flipping the clipboard around, he handed it back to her. Nick flashed one of his more subdued smiles. "Knock yourself out."

Then he pretty much ignored Jen. He'd tried to be nice to her when she first came on board a year or so ago, but that just seemed to make her stick around and pester him more. So instead he, like most everyone else, pretended she wasn't really there. He wasn't mean to her. He just didn't go out of his way to foster interaction.

Ada had wandered over past the break tables and toward the door. Since the choices were stay and talk with Jen or walk with Ada, Nick chose moving across the room. As he opened the door for them, Ada smiled up at him. "So," Ada took a deep breath, "how are things going with the visit?"

Ah yes, changing the subject to avoid having to diss Jen. Well, Nick could still tease, "Are we gossiping?"

"No," she took a sip of her tea and corrected, "we're having a co-worker conversation."

Nick was about to say fine and dandy, something about everything being wonderful, instead, "It's been a little rocky," slipped out. Shit. Ada was not one of the people he confided in, not normally, not ever. He guessed he needed to vent.

"Really?" Ada reached out and touched the back of his hand with the tips of her fingers. "Why?"

He'd started, might as well finish. "Apparently, I'm spooky, my house is creepy and is going to give her nightmares and she can't eat anything in my kitchen." Although he'd stop himself if it started to devolve into a Nicky pity-party.

"Picky eater, is she?" Ada smiled and waved her hand in the air between them, dismissing the issue as minor. "All kids that age are." Ada had a house full of yard-apes, she should know.

"No," Nick studied the surface of his coffee, like the subtle licking of fluid toward the rim held ultimate truth, "she's Jewish."

That stopped her in her tracks. "What?"

"Yeah," pausing in the hall, Nick shrugged. "See Brandon never told me, but his ex-wife had this whole religious awakening after they broke up. Went back to her orthodox roots and now keeps kosher. So I've got a nine-year-old telling me I'm forcing her to commit dietary Seppuku because I keep the cheddar in the same drawer as the salami."

"Oh dear." Ada's hand fluttered up to her mouth reminding Nick of a seventies soap opera expression. If Ada hadn't been so damn sincere in her chagrin, the movement, the expression, all of it might have rated as funny. "And what about Brandon?"

"He's so busy playing daddy catch-up that he won't say boo. It's just frustrating, I mean I try and lay down a few rules, like, you know her not playing the Rated NC-17 games on my game console and he jumps down my throat. Tells me it's not my place." Nick snorted. "Dian calls and he pretends nothing's going on, but you know there is. His attitude irritates the heck out of me. It's like, if you're going to be that way, why did you bother coming…just go home."

She smiled knowingly and nodded as she walked. "A little hard, is it?"

"Yeah." Nick shrugged. "And I'm just all keyed up."

"Why?"

"Well, ah." He dropped his voice a little. Ada was the closest he'd ever come to an actual friend at work. Nick need to confide in someone. "Look you can't tell anyone." Especially someone who wouldn't get their own feelings all mixed up in it. "I've got a job offer. Don't know that I'll take it, but it would mean I could move to Southern California. Be with Brandon." Nick's own feelings were mixed up enough as it was. He loved Vegas. He loved his life and his friends. He loved the power and excitement of the GCB. But Brandon, for all his faults, just might be worth a sacrifice. "I haven't talked to him about it. I need to and it's stressing me out."

Ada didn't say anything for a few moments. Then she smiled again. "Well, you can't change what his answer will be." She sipped her tea. "Don't stress over trying to guess the future. It'll work out fine for you. I know it will."

"Thanks." Not that Ada'd said anything profound, but having a live body to articulate it to helped. "You're right. Things'll work out. I just wish it wasn't so stressful right now. I kinda didn't plan for the whole kid thrown into the mix when I asked Brandon to come out this week." A few more steps down the hall and it registered with Nick that Jen dogged their footsteps. He spun and snapped, "Do you need anything else, Jen?"

"No." She shuffled her feet on the linoleum. "I'll go now."

Softer, he said, "Okay." He wasn't mad at Jen, he was irritated with Brandon and nervous about his life. "After you run those figures we'll get together and go over it." They needed to do a team meeting anyway.

Jen bobbed her head, "Sure," and then faded off around a corner.

Nick turned back to Ada. "Sorry." Both flashed embarrassed smiles. Usually, Nick wasn't that much of a jerk with anyone. Jen just seemed to try his patience.

"Look, it's hard for all three of you." Ada started walking again, headed vaguely in the direction of Investigations where she worked. Nick probably should have headed back toward Electronic Services, but he kinda liked the new groove he and Ada were hitting. So, instead, he walked with her. "Your friend, Brandon, is trying to be a father after not being there for a long time. I imagine he's just terrified that he's going to make a mistake and he desperately wants his daughter to like him. He hasn't realized she will no matter what. And she is in an unfamiliar house, with a father she barely knows and his friend...has he told her *about* you?"

"No." A little harder than necessary, he pitched his coffee in a trash bin along the wall. "She has no clue."

Ada shook her head. "Actually, she probably does. Kids are very smart and pick up on that. She couldn't tell that you two are a couple, but I think she probably knows that you and she are both competing for her dad's time, attention and affection."

"We're not competing." They weren't. No way. He just wished

he could have a little more of Brandon's time. "She's his kid, that's the most important relationship there is. I'm not going to get in the middle of that."

"Two things." Ada held up a matching number of fingers and ticked them off as she spoke. "You already are in the middle of it, and she doesn't know that her daddy can do both, that the... love is different." They'd reached the door to Investigations. Ada halted in the doorway. "Any blended family is going to have that happen. It's very hard for kids to adjust to their parents being with someone else. On top of that whole thing, she's trying to adjust to being with her dad. And you're probably sending off signals that you're nervous...about what you need to talk to Brandon about and what his response will be." She added a final smile. "You're all walking on eggshells trying to figure out how it all fits. But it'll be fine, you'll see."

As she stepped inside, Nick added a quick, "Thanks by the way."

"For what?"

"For listening and not saying anything." Nick held up both hands. "Whoa, stop, look I know you don't approve of my lifestyle, but you don't make a big deal over it either. And you're letting me bend your ear about dealing with all this."

"Nick, you're a good hearted person. I think you're trying very hard to do the right things. I would be lying if said I didn't have some conflict about it. But when I think about it, one of the few truly honest and nice people I know...is you. I don't know, but I think that anything that brings a father and child together can't be all bad."

"Okay, well," with an exaggerated false swoon, Nick grabbed his chest. "Now I've had two utterly stunning revelations out of you today and I'm not sure I could handle a third." He laughed. "So, I'm going to head back to the pit and rip the face plate off a slot machine before I get too overwhelmed."

"Get out of here, Dracula, I have numbers to crunch." She flicked her hand at him as though waving him off. "Have a blessed day, okay?"

Heading back toward lab, Nick called over his shoulder. "You too." After he sat down at his station, it took Nick a moment to orient himself. Things didn't seem like they were where they ought to be. Hell, he hadn't been at his station in two weeks. Normally he did a lot more field work; random testing of slot and video poker machines at casinos. But, with Brandon coming and the side project, he'd asked for more scheduled time at the Gaming Control Board's Headquarters.

The rest of the day Nick spent buried in algorithms and reports. He pretty much ignored all distractions, including his cell phone. With all the unlisted calls he'd been getting, Nick tended to let it ring unless he expected a call. And hopefully, if he completely lost himself in his work, he could wind down enough to start the weekend on a positive note. There really was a lot to be positive about. If things went well. Things had to go well.

The whole bringing Shayna had freaked him out. Still it rated as a massive forward step for Brandon. Every other concession in their relationship came as a consequence of some nearly averted tragedy. Actually, if he thought about it, Nick figured getting he and Shayna to meet resulted from a crisis—of the sitter variety. Much smaller in scale than Nick being slated for a hit by the Mexican Mafia and thrown out of the back of his hearse or Brandon thinking he'd been shot during a drug/prostitution raid.

Brandon rated far more reactive than proactive in the relationship game.

That personality flaw, hopefully, would help. Nick hated the ultimatum gambit, but sometimes you just had to play the cards you'd been dealt. This equaled one of those times. If he let Brandon think, mull things over, they'd never move past where they were now. Of course, Nick wasn't really sure he was ready for the next step right now, either. Life, however, didn't always hand you opportunity when you asked for it.

A page broke into his thoughts. He was needed up front. Odd, but maybe they wanted him to sign for some slot parts or something. Wasn't required that ESD personnel be the agents that did it, but sometimes new staff or jittery manufactures needed the extra bit of hand-holding. He stood up and stretched. His shoulder felt tight. His back popped. When Nick glanced at the clock he realized why: four-thirty in the afternoon. Shit, he'd worked through lunch and his afternoon break. Trying to figure out how not to catch hell for that slip, Nick sauntered toward the reception area.

As he stepped around the corner he caught sight of a black leather jacket and the edge of an ear studded with piercings. Brandon knelt on one knee in front of Shayna. She huffed and rolled her eyes. Pink faux-fur jacket, masses of brown curls and a swirly purple skirt...she looked like a perturbed princess being attended by her knight. The incongruity of the situation, the place and the person took a moment to resolve in Nick's brain. "Hey," he finally stuttered out. "You're here."

Brandon stood and held out his hand. "Surprised?" As Nick stepped in, Brandon pulled him into a quick buddy-hug. Just as quickly he stepped back.

"In spades." Nick smiled down at Shayna. "Why'd you come by?"

Shayna's face seemed pained. "Brandon," she whined, "I really have to go."

Brandon coughed. "There's one reason, also—"

"Brandon!" Shayna's tone cracked with frustration and irritation.

"Hey, Nick," Ada's voice bubbled behind him.

Nick turned slightly, opening himself up to her. "Ada, I think you've met Brandon." She'd been one of the few co-workers who'd made a point to stop by, several times, while Nick recovered from the nearly becoming road-pizza incident. He vaguely recalled Brandon being there at least one of those times. Of course, he'd been fairly doped up on pain meds for about a month and a half. "This is his daughter, Shayna." Nick loosely knew where the women's room was, but Ada had the key to it.

"Who really needs the can right now."

With a sympathetic grimace, Ada gazed down at Shayna. "Want me to show you where the restroom is?"

Relieved, Shayna blurted out, "Yes!"

"Come on, sweetheart." Ada held out her hand. As she led Shayna away, she hissed in a stage whisper, "Boys just have no clue what it means to really have to go."

Shayna didn't even bother with the pretense of a whisper. "None at all."

After they rounded the corner, Nick turned back to Brandon. "We've just been dissed by a nine-year-old."

"Get used to it." Brandon snorted.

"So you came here so she could take a leak?"

"That started as we turned into the lot. We, ah, spent the day kicking around. Just got out of the movies and I told Shayna I'd take her over to the mall to spend this gift certificate she got. Figured you could meet us for dinner there." He shrugged. "I tried to call, but you weren't picking up. Since we were in the area, I thought I'd try and catch you before you took off."

"Dinner?"

"Yeah, come on." He playfully punched Nick's shoulder. "Fancy dining at the food court? Kid's meal toys to throw at each other, double burger with chili."

Nick shoved his hands into his pockets and glared. "You're making it sound so romantic."

Brandon threw up his hands in mock surrender. "This is what normal people do with their kids, right?" The forced happy in his tone told Nick that Brandon was trying…too hard. Probably a result of last night combined with this morning.

"She's not my kid, Brandon," Nick reminded him. If he didn't think Brandon played some weird mental game, Nick might have been less suspicious.

Brandon stepped up close. Not touching close, but still

nearer than just a couple of friends might stand. "I want, fuck," he huffed, "Nicky, I want to share that part of things with you, understand?" Holy crap, he was so earnest, Nick almost believed him. "I wouldn't have brought Shayna out with me if I didn't. You know that, right?" That was true…on levels Brandon didn't even get. "I want you to know her and be a part of who she sees me with. If it weren't for you, I wouldn't have gotten back involved with her. You did this. Part of that is, I've been really thinking today, I want to be normal around her…like you and I normal. I know I've fucked shit up a lot, but I don't want there to be any doubt in her mind that I'm okay with being with you."

Okay, Brandon earned points for trying. Nick still had to play devil's advocate though. "No, you're not okay with it." He didn't want Brandon thinking he could get away with telling Nick what he thought Nick wanted to hear.

"All right," Brandon shrugged. "Yeah, I'm still working on it. But I ain't going to hide what you are to me. I can't do that to the two people who mean the world to me."

Nick goaded. "So you're going to sleep in my bed with me tonight then?" He wanted to see how far Brandon was willing to commit to the whole open and honest policy.

Embarrassed, Brandon coughed. "Okay, you know, baby steps here." Then he smiled as if to take the sting out of his reluctance. "Don't push. But, you know it's Shayna, me and you."

"In that order?" When Brandon's face fell, Nick smiled to ease his barb. "I know, she means more to you than I do." Of course he couldn't let Brandon think he'd settled the matter. Nick heaved an overly dramatic sigh. "I just have to play second fiddle all the time." Rolling his eyes, he sighed again. "Nobody loves me like I deserve."

"Bite me, Nicky." Brandon laughed through his growl. About that time, they both caught sight of Ada herding Shayna back to the lobby. Surprisingly, Brandon didn't step away. He called out, "Better, Princess?"

"Much!"

"So." Brandon bumped Nick's shoulder with his own. "Want to meet us for dinner?"

Still a little dumbstruck by Brandon's shift in freak-out level, Nick mumbled, "You know, I skipped lunch." Regaining his ground, he added, "Let me clear it with my supervisor and I'll clock out early." He jerked his thumb over his shoulder and walked backward into the Board offices.

"Yeah." Brandon tapped his jacket pocket, the one he always carried his smokes in. "Meet you in the parking lot."

Nick knew that sign, time for a cigarette. He nodded and then ducked back through the offices in search of the lab manager. When he caught his supervisor, it took a little finessing on the time issue. Finally, though, his manager okayed him busting out early, but told Nick to pay more attention to his time. Nick jotted a quick set of instructions on a large post-it to Jen and added a *thnx 4 the help, appreciate it* at the bottom. That was something he always did. People never got enough recognition for just doing their jobs. After gathering up his gear, he slapped the note on the second batch of reports to go with the set she'd taken earlier and jammed it in Jen's box on the way out the door. He made his way past the other state offices and downstairs. Saluting the security guards on his way out, Nick searched for Brandon's form in the dusk. Night fell early in the desert during winter.

"All clear?" Brandon called from off to the right of the building lobby. Shayna jumped off one of the planters as Brandon flicked his dead butt into an ash can.

"Yeah." Nick waited as Brandon cupped the back of Shayna's head with his big hand and steered her over his way. Using the time, Nick zipped up his jacket. He'd slipped the overpants on upstairs. "I'll grab the bike." Starting toward the parking lot, Nick tugged on one glove. Wasn't really easy with his helmet under his other arm, but years of practice helped. "Follow me, I'll drop it at home and we can head out from there. Where'd you park?"

"I saw your bike." Brandon pointed in the general direction of where Nick left the Kawasaki. "Parked near it."

As they approached the general area, Nick spotted a blue minivan. Brandon must have spied it at the same time. Keys jangled as he yanked them out of his pocket. Pointing the mass at the van, Brandon punched a button. From their last trip, Nick knew when the doors unlocked by remote the lights flashed. Nothing happened. Brandon shook the remote and tried again. Still nothing. "Why isn't the freaking fob working?"

"Well, because, babe, that's not your hunk of junk." By that time, they'd come up close to the van. "Unless you went and registered your mommy-mobile to my address, because this one has Nevada plates." Ignoring them, Shayna, arms out to either side, walked along the painted line between the cars.

Brandon glanced over at his daughter then snorted. "Looks just like mine."

Nick cupped his hands over his eyes and tried to peer through the tinted window. "Actually, I think it's Jen's. I seem to remember helping her get something out of a blue piece of shi—minivan." Wasn't easy in a lot lit by twilight and yellow halogens, but he could sort of make out the interior. Yeah, it was what he remembered of Jen's car. Cages, three of them, two sideways and one stretched across the back, took up the space where the seats would have been. They came up to just below the level of the back windows. "She breeds large dogs. I think that's what she said." It was sad that he could remember Jen's van better than he could recall anything about Jen. Nick stepped back and kicked the bumper. "Pretty much a dead ringer for your junker."

"The hell with this." Brandon muttered and jabbed the red panic button on the fob with his thumb. Two rows away an alarm wailed. Stopping the wail with another jab, Brandon grinned. "Meet you at your place."

CHAPTER 6

"I don't know," Brandon grumbled as he pushed through the crowd, "it's called *Libbi Girl.*" Although the outdoor mall wasn't nearly as packed as in the weeks before Christmas, post-holiday bargain shoppers clogged the walkways. "They got girly crappage."

Unlike most of the mall crowd, they were on a hunt for a specific store, the one where Shayna had her gift certificate. "Girly…crappage?" Nick drawled out as he dodged a woman toting six large bags. Both of them were having a tough time keeping up with Shayna. She darted between people or stopped and reversed direction on a whim. It was like trying to track a lab rat on crack. Brandon suddenly understood the point of that obnoxious child locator device. Let your attention wander for a moment and, damn, you'd lose a kid in a crowd like this.

"You know," Brandon lunged forward and caught the back of Shayna's jacket, slowing her pace. Holding the pink, furry hood like a leash, he grimaced back at Nick. "Lip gloss, necklaces and shit." He managed to slow Shayna's progress. When she turned to glare, Brandon shot the look right back and pointed at the ground near him. Shayna huffed, pouted, but proceeded at a far less frantic pace than before. At least she seemed to get the message to stay near. "Edith says it's all the rage." Brandon shrugged. "Dian says Shayna can do anything there, except get her ears pierced."

"So," Nick grinned, "you going to let her get her ears pierced?"

"Hah, funny, I'll let you explain that one to Dian." With two fingers, Brandon goosed Nick in the side. "She's got a fifty dollar gift certificate from all her aunts. So I have instructions to let her blow it on junk." Brandon grinned at Nick as they walked. It was kind of nice, just being out with Nick like this. "I mean what could she—" Brandon damn near skidded to a stop. "Holy

Fuck!" He hissed.

"Holy Fuck is right," Nicky hissed back.

Brandon swallowed. What the hell had he gotten himself into? A screaming pink and smoked glass storefront confronted them. Stuffed animals and their accessorized carrying cases shared shelf space with cell phone glitter bling. Boy bands throbbed over the sound system. No display was taller than Brandon's chest. Along one wall, miniature, but cartoonishly out of proportion white vanities seethed with tween girls. Hip teenage staff, dressed in hot pink aprons sporting "glamour goddess" slogans, fussed over pint size divas.

The girls giggled while their nails received coats of sparkly gloss or multi-colored ribbons were twisted into braids. A tug on Brandon's belt jerked his attention down.

"Brandon!" Shayna almost squealed. "Look!" She waived the brochure clutched in her hand so fast that Brandon only saw a multi-colored blur. "I have enough I can get the *Libbi Girl* Max Package."

Afraid, but unable to stop, Brandon sputtered, "Great, what's that?"

Shayna's little finger jabbed the paper at various places. "Nail polish, and two hair colors and beads or braids and makeup!"

"Makeup?" Somewhere in the last thirty seconds Brandon's ability to speak without his voice cracking had vanished.

"Yeah! And I'll still have enough left over to buy some things....'cause it's only thirty dollars!"

Brandon choked as Nicky shrugged and deadpanned, "It's only thirty dollars, Brandon, what a steal."

Okay, nine, nine was way too young for half that shit. Brandon growled out, "No makeup!"

"But pleassseeee," Shayna's wheedle clawed up his spine.

Poised and sweet, a teen girl sporting four different stripes of color in her otherwise brown hair slid up from behind, positioning herself between Brandon and Nicky. "Really," she purred, "it's completely washable. Our goal at *Libby Girl* is to make the little girl feel like a big girl." She smiled brightly at Shayna and then whispered so only Nicky and Brandon could hear, "But not really look like it." Her gentle pressure on his shoulder and Shayna's death grip tug on his arm pulled Brandon into the store. He looked back at Nicky for help. All he got was laughter from those dark eyes. "I'm Prayer, by the way, I'll be your *Libby Girl* hostess. The Max Package is our most popular. The girls love it." Her smile wrinkled her nose. "Huh, Princess?" She laughed and held out her other hand to Shayna.

"Princess?" Brandon growled. This girl didn't know Shayna well enough to call her by her nickname.

Another saccharine smile flashed. "All *Libby Girls* are princesses." The line was delivered in the rote patter of a professional sales pitch.

"They're," Nicky's hiss at his ear startled Brandon, "starting the indoctrination earlier and earlier."

Counterpoint was Shayna's wheedle, "Please Brandon. Mommy said it's my gift certificate. I can do anything but get my ears pierced." A dip, hands folded in supplication, scrunched up face, and full-tooth smile preceded the next plea. "This one is nicer than the one at home." Twisting one ankle out, Shayna looked like anything but a little girl ready for temporary hair dye and make up. "Bubbie only ever lets me get my nails done there. But I have fifty dollars!"

Brandon's hand shot out pointing at the various displays. "Do you know how many toys, lip gloss, and nail polish you could buy for thirty bucks?"

Off to his right, Nicky chuckled and fingered a bright colored bauble. "Give up. No use fighting it. The lure of the gal spa runs deep."

Brandon shot Nicky a glare that would peel paint. "How would you know?"

"Flame dame, babe." Nicky stepped close and tapped Brandon's forehead with his middle finger, the one with the

Gargoyle ring. Brandon had given Nicky the bat eared hunk of sterling in Mexico. "Remember, Miri, hairdresser? In the biz."

That Nicky wore the ring, all the time, sent a warm rush through Brandon's chest.

A glance over at Shayna confirmed it. Wide-eyed and hopeful she stared at him. He was so not prepared for this daddy gig. Brandon sighed and swallowed. "It's your money, Princess."

Shayna's squeal echoed the impromptu wiggle pop dance she executed in mid store. Brandon squeezed his eyes shut and shook his head to dispel that image. Nicky laughed and stepped close. "Hey, could be worse, babe."

"Really," Brandon realized Prayer and two moms stared at them. One eyebrow went up and the *don't fuck with me* cop stare slid down. "Worse?" The first person that said a damn thing was toast.

Reaching across Brandon's shoulder, Nick tugged at the piercings running down Brandon's left ear. "She could be trying to talk you into overriding your ex-wife on the whole ear piercing thing." Brandon swallowed again, this time because Nicky was so damn close. And touching him. In public. Of course, if he jumped away or said something, then it would call attention to them.

Prayer's mouth tightened into a thin line, the kind that teens sported when trying to make algebra turn out right. She paused for only a moment then the smile returned. "Hey, Princess," Prayer turned, dropped down with her hands on her knees and shrugged, "why don't you tell your daddies it'll be about half an hour. Okay?"

"That," Shayna pointed at Brandon as she rolled her eyes, "is Brandon, he's my dad. That," her hand and her hip cocked out toward Nicky, "is Brandon's friend, Mr. O'Malley." Shayna leaned in and added, in a conspiratorial whisper, "They're really good friends."

"I can tell," Prayer acknowledged with a smirk at Brandon. Then she clapped her hands and belted out in a cheerleader cadence, "Come on, Princess, let's pick out your polish!"

As they skipped, literally, toward the back of the store, a growl rolled in Brandon's throat. Nicky, still pressed against Brandon's back, slid his free hand into Brandon's front pocket. Brandon froze. "Come on, really good friend." Nicky teased up close near his right ear. "You can't kill a sales clerk for being too perky."

"No." Brandon hissed back. "But I can kill you, if you don't get your fucking hand out of my pocket."

Somehow, Brandon managed to survive both Nicky and the whole *Libby Girl* experience, although he did feel a wave of nausea come on when they started slathering shit on Shayna's lips and eyes. Only Nicky's gentle jibes kept him from total daddy freak out. Still, it felt like everyone in the world was watching them. Several times Brandon turned because the sense hit him so hard. Finally, he chalked it up to nerves: being uncomfortable being a dad, being uncomfortable letting loose with Nicky, and being uncomfortable with a daughter he barely knew as a child playing like a big girl. Nicky was right though, the store was all about *playing dress-up*. Of course, Brandon almost laughed up a lung when Nicky distracted him with a story about almost getting caught with a member of his high school basketball team, rope and a cheerleading outfit stolen off the jock's girlfriend. Put a whole new spin on dress-up, especially as it hadn't been Nicky in the chick's hot pants.

Finally, Prayer released Shayna back into his care: blue nails, glitter cheeks, bubble-gum highlights and all. They managed to get out of the store with only slightly more hassle than trying to get a tweaker in a patrol car. Shayna toted a tiny bag filled with a rhinestone studded cell-phone case for the cell phone Brandon kept forgetting to charge, a few bottles of polish and a cheap charm bracelet for her friend Beth. For twenty bucks she could have snagged twice that shit at the discount store.

Of course, then there was Nicky. They'd paused in front of yet another kiosk, this one hawking stuff you could custom imprint with names. Shayna's begging started when she saw a little dog tag in rainbow hues. He'd been ready to shoot Shayna down when Nicky whipped out his credit card and grabbed the bauble.

"Would you quit buying her crap?" Brandon snapped.

Ignoring him, Nicky handed over the tag. "It's my money." He smirked. "Princess, tell him what you want on it."

"Put it away, Nicky," Brandon ordered in the same voice he used as a cop ordering people out of cars.

Nicky stepped in front of the register. "Nope, buying it." Brandon reached around, trying, not so successfully to grab Nicky's wrist. Nicky shifted. His hip bumped Brandon's groin. He leaned in, slightly, pressing into the touch.

Brandon hissed, "Nicky, quit it." The feeling of being watched, studied, slid over him again. He did not need to get turned on at the freaking mall. Especially when he glanced over to find Shayna looking at them funny. Maybe that's where the foreboding came from. "Hey, Princess," Brandon managed to swallow, "sure you really want that piece of junk?"

"Sometimes you're weird, Brandon." Shayna shook her head and started writing on the little pad the clerk had indicated.

Nicky signed off on his receipt. As the clerk typed up the message, Nicky asked, "Why do you call your dad Brandon?"

Shayna glanced up from watching the machine grind out her inscription. "I don't know." She shrugged.

"'Cause Daddy is Frank," Brandon broke in, "Dian's second husband."

"Dad, pop, papa, pa," sticking his card back in his wallet, Nicky rattled off the options, "or you could be DaddyB and Frank would be Daddy."

"Okay, we're not on the *Beverly Hillbillies* so I refuse to be called pa." Brandon felt strange with all of the alternatives. He'd never really thought about what his little girl should call him. Brandon happened by default since that's what everyone around Shayna had called him. Somehow he'd passed beyond the link-up of him being her dad in Shayna's growing up. He merely rated as 'this guy in her life.' Trying to lighten his own mood a bit, Brandon went for a half hearted joke, "And the DaddyB thing, that just sounds bad. Like I'm some bizarre Rapper cruising and looking for eighteen year olds."

"Mr. O'Malley," Shayna looked over from where the clerk wiped off the finished tag.

"Yeah, Princess?"

Shayna dropped the dog tag over her neck where it rattled against the locator pendant. "Can I ride the merry-go-round?" She pointed off into a park area with slides, several tree houses and a full sized Carousel. Yeah, she'd pegged Nicky as the cash machine. Right for his wallet.

"Sure," Nicky fished in his pocket, "if you promise me one thing."

"What?"

"Call me Nick."

Shayna jerked her chin at Brandon. "Brandon calls you Nicky."

"Nicky would be fine." Nicky's smile drove little shards of ice into Brandon's gut. He wanted them to like each other, but really, Brandon wasn't prepared for the reality of Nicky and Shayna together. "Or Uncle Nicky…I'm your dad's best friend after all."

Shayna blinked. "You know my daddy?" Then it seemed to register. "Oh, yeah, Brandon."

Nicky held out a couple of crumpled dollar bills. "Here's two bucks for the ticket, we'll be right there by the fence watching you." Shayna darted off toward the Carousel in the center of a brightly lit play park. "Okay, we have so got to fix that."

"I love how you just insinuated yourself into my family." Brandon stalked off after Shayna.

Nicky jogged to catch up to him. "What?"

"Uncle Nicky?" Brandon growled. How dare he? It was taking

all sorts of things for granted that Brandon wasn't sure he was ready for Nicky to take for granted.

Oblivious, Nicky teased. "It has a nice ring to it though, doesn't it?"

Brandon hooked his hands over the waist high metal fence enclosing the merry-go-round. Nick sidled up next to him. Brandon counted to ten, backing down his agitation. When he had enough control, he said, "Nicky, don't move that fast."

"Why?" Nicky actually sounded confused.

They'd been over this ground half a dozen times in the last few months. "I'm not ready for that."

"If I wait until you're ready—" Nicky snorted as he hooked his heel over the bottom rung on the fence. "We'll be eighty and you'll still be driving four hours across the desert to come see me."

"Well." Massaging the rail with tight fists, Brandon managed to keep his voice even. "You're just going to figure out how to deal with it 'cause I'm not quitting the force." Why did Nicky have to bring it up here, now?

"I did." Nicky fell silent for a bit. A strange, heavy silence that Brandon wasn't sure how to interpret. They both watched as Shayna scrambled around the interior and chose a white horse on the second ring. Finally, as the music kicked up and the horses began to move, Nicky spoke, "I might be quitting the GCB."

Brandon couldn't have heard right, "What?"

Nicky waved at Shayna as she made the first pass. "Ride 'em cowgirl, Princess." Then, expression anything but playful, he turned toward Brandon. "I got a job offer and I'm seriously thinking about taking it."

"Offer?" Suddenly, the chill Nevada night seemed overly warm. "What do you mean offer?"

Shrugging, Nicky banged the rail with his heel. "I've been offered the regional slot manager position in Southern California for one of the big conglomerates. I have the chance to go corporate. These guys manage a good half of the Indian casinos in the west through partnership agreements. And, well, they figured somebody with my credentials and my *background*, would be good PR." His smile was tight and a little embarrassed. It took Brandon a few moments to process that Nicky felt uncomfortable because it wasn't just his Gaming Control background, but the quarter Indian heritage they'd wanted. "I used that to yank up what they'd be willing to pay me to be their token Indian. Any port in a storm." In the time they'd know each other, Brandon never sensed Nicky as the type to play a race card. "We're still just talking. But, you know, you can only have so many dinners before you have to stop calling it a casual thing and move into dating."

"Why would you do something like that?" To say Brandon was floored would have been a massive understatement. "You love your job."

"Because," Nicky blew out a long breath. "Because, I can be based out of any one of their major casinos and they have two biggies in San Bernardino and Riverside. Then it doesn't have to be a sometimes on the weekend relationship. I want more than that."

"But what if things don't work out?" Nicky was thinking of leaving his job, to be with him? Brandon had to think. It was too fast. Too much. "I don't know, Nicky." Brandon wanted to run and hide and not have to think about anything resembling a future. "I just don't know."

"Look." Nicky grabbed his shoulder and squeezed a little. "I haven't said yes yet. I told them I'd get back to them after the first of the year."

Brandon managed to stammer out, "Like in a week?" It felt like some big beast was ripping the ground out from under his feet.

"Like you got four days to decide whether you can get the fuck over your issues." Nicky's eyes were so serious. "I want to be with you enough that I'm willing to put my whole life into chaos to take a chance on you. So you can buck up and take a little chance on me." He drew in another ragged breath and an awful sense of dread hit Brandon in the balls. "Probably not the best way to spring it on you, but I don't want it to stay like it is," Nicky rushed it out. "Since we're here...if you say you can't deal with it. Then, this is it."

"Huh?" Nicky couldn't have meant what those words said.

"I mean, if you say you can't deal with it, then I can't deal with being with you anymore. I can't handle what we have now lasting years."

"That's not fair, Nicky."

"Neither is expecting me to accept so little when I could have someone to come home to, wake up to...I want that." Nicky moved right up against Brandon's side. One hand covering Brandon's on the fence, the other hadn't left his shoulder. Both of their bodies shook. "I want it to be with you. You got four days, so start thinking now."

"Nicky..."

"Look, Brandon." Brandon's gaze followed Nicky's...tracking Shayna as she spun around the Carousel's circuit. "There's a little girl riding a plastic pony that says, even if you don't want to admit it, you're damn serious. Since you've been broken up with Dian how many of your...ah...friends have you introduced her to? None, right?" All Brandon could manage was to shake his head. "So, I guess that means you think there's something here. So do I. But I want that something to be more than a long distance relationship."

Brandon opened his mouth. He had to say something. Nicky cut him off before he'd even formed a thought. "Stop. I wouldn't push, okay, not so hard, if the opportunity wasn't there. But it is and I'm willing to take the risk. If I don't move on this chance, it'll go." Nicky's voice echoed the uncertainty clawing at Brandon. "So I'm asking you if you're willing to jump, too."

"I'm not sure I'm ready for that, Nicky."

"Sometimes luck is just hearing opportunity knocking. It's at the door and banging hard, babe." Stepping back, Nicky added, "You got four days before I have to answer." Then he turned around, shoved his hands in his pockets and walked off to greet Shayna at the exit gate. She laughed at something Nicky said to her. Then he grabbed her under her arms and spun her around. As Nicky set Shayna down, he looked back at Brandon. What Brandon saw in his eyes, well he knew Nicky wasn't joking. He'd laid every card on the table and it was all or nothing at this point.

Still there. There was only supposed to be him. But then he was there with that guy and that little one, him and the other one. The little one was irrelevant. Couldn't do anything, couldn't mess up anything. Something to be swept off into the trash.

The other one was a problem. No problems. Problems had to go away. There had to be a way to make the problem go away. Not fair to come this far and have problems. Something had to get them away and separate. It couldn't work with this other problem.

And it had to work.

CHAPTER 7

Electronic chaos, punctuated by screams of *die!,* rolled across the small apartment from the boys' room. Mixed in were Shayna's commands to *kill 'em.* She'd have made Brandon's range instructor at the academy proud. And Nicky, apparently, excelled at electronic mayhem selections for the eight-to-twelve crowd. Non-gory shoot 'em ups, virtual pets and various gadgets made for a battery-intensive second Christmas.

So far the morning had proceeded well enough. Shayna and Miri's boys seemed to get along okay...or they were still all in that honeymoon phase holidays instilled in children. A small battle had been waged over breakfast and whether Shayna would or could eat it. Prepackaged, overly sugared cereal seemed to resolve her issues. Brandon had no clue whether *Fruity Pebbles* actually fit guidelines, but hell, if Princess ate it, he was fine. And gifts...well, Brandon figured that the lure of wrapped packages and bows outweighed maternal indoctrination. Only one snide comment about Christmas made it past Shayna's lips before she succumbed to the mad present scramble.

Grabbing torn wrapping paper off the floor and shoving it into bags, Miri looked up and flashed him a sly smile. "Why don't you guys head back to Nick's place and grab some alone time." She ran one hand through her blunt-cut, black bangs before reaching for another wad of paper under the silver metallic tree. With the vintage oriental PJs she wore, Brandon almost swore he was back in the fifties.

"Naw." Brandon cradled a box filled with purple, red and silver ribbons—the colors of a Goth Christmas. "We're good." A palpable tension still oozed between he and Nicky. They kept trying to pretend everything was all normal. Shayna forced that charade, although even she seemed to pick-up on it. Brandon didn't want to spoil the week for her by he and Nicky sniping at each other. Still, the post ultimatum throw-down chipped away at any hint of actual togetherness.

"Okay, take it from a mom of three boys," Miri wrinkled her nose and scowled at Brandon, "when someone offers to watch your kid for a while you say 'thank you' and go fuck like bunnies." Like she was shooing them out the door, she waved her hands in the air. "Out. Go." Then she rolled her eyes in a trademark Betty Page pout. "Take it now before I change my mind and put you to cleaning the breakfast dishes or something."

"Oh God, chores." Nicky snorted over the breakfast bar as he racked dishes in the dishwasher. Hard to threaten someone with something they were doing voluntarily. Given that about ten minutes earlier, Miri's apartment looked like ground zero for a confetti explosion, they'd pretty much contained and controlled the disaster. "Run Brandon," Nicky drawled. "I'll cover your back."

Chucking a wad of crumpled paper at Nicky's head, Miri sneered. "You got a couple of hours before asshole's home. Make the most of it." She reached up and patted Brandon's arm.

Brandon looked over toward the boys' room. All he could see of his daughter was her sock covered feet. "I don't know." Dian wouldn't be thrilled if he left her with someone to babysit. "Shayna—"

"Is having a blast." Coming up behind him, Nicky tossed Brandon's jacket over his head. "Hey, Princess!" He called.

Shayna's "Yeah?" barely carried over the video game racket.

"We're going to head back to my place and do laundry and stuff." As Brandon pulled the jacket off his face, he saw Nicky leaning in the doorway where the kids were. "You can come help or you can stay and play video games." Nicky looked back at Brandon and smirked. "Which would you rather?"

Brandon shouldered into his leather jacket and moved up next to Nicky. All the kids answered, "Video games!"

"You just have to know how to phrase the question." Nicky smirked and elbowed Brandon in the ribs.

Shayna and Cole, Miri's oldest, lay on the floor with game controllers in their mitts and attention focused on the TV screen. Justin lounged on the bottom bunk with a hand held as his little brother, A.J., shouted instructions to the others from the top bunk. They looked like they were having fun. "Are you sure, Princess?" Brandon felt weird leaving her there with kids she barely knew.

Shayna rolled over onto her side and glared at him. The locator fob slid and thumped the floor. He'd almost told Shayna to leave the damn thing at home, they were only going over to Miri's, but she had just slipped it on with her coat and he'd let it slide. "Brandon." Hitting three different pitches with the one word, her voice mocked him as supremely dense.

"Okay." Brandon had enough sense to know when he'd lost. "We'll be at Nicky's. Call if you need anything."

"I can't," she hissed as her character ducked a blow. "You forgot to charge my cell phone again."

Nicky snorted as Brandon growled out, "They have these things called home phones. You know, hooked into the wall. Call if you want me to come get you."

Shayna's dismissive, "Whatever," as she rolled back on her stomach, stung him.

Miri grabbed his shoulder and Brandon jumped a little. He hadn't heard her come up. "Don't let it bug you." Brandon caught the small, sympathetic smile Miri offered. "It's a kid's job to break your heart every other day." Sliding her hand down to his elbow, Miri pulled Brandon toward the front door. "Means you're actually being a parent." Nicky waited there, pulling on his own coat. As Miri shoved them out the door she whispered, "Have fun, babe." Then she stuck her tongue out at him. "Don't say I never gave you nothing."

They walked the few blocks to Nicky's place in silence, except for the two phone calls Nicky got from the unlisted number. Both times Nicky'd grabbed the phone off his hip, scowled at the display, but didn't answer.

The whole ultimatum thing from yesterday put them on a weird footing. Brandon tried to play like nothing had changed. Every minute past last evening's conversation made it harder and harder. Brandon'd spent most of the night just lying in bed, tossing, turning and thinking. Nothing had sorted itself out. He knew exactly the same two things he'd known before going to bed. He didn't want to lose Nicky and he sure as hell wasn't ready for that level of commitment.

Neither of them seemed to want to bring the issue up. And if one of them opened their mouth, the issue would come up. It made the walk strained.

That and Brandon still couldn't shake the feeling of being watched. He figured being with Nicky and Shayna together dredged up all the closeted fear he hadn't quite gotten rid of. On a cold, drizzly and gray Saturday morning in the down-on-its-heels residential section of Vegas, there really wasn't anyone around to create the sense of paranoia. Assorted parked cars, a guy taking out the trash, and a few kids who'd braved the weather raced by on bikes and skateboards. Still, Brandon wasn't used to being *out*. Everywhere he went with Nicky…well, he felt like someone was going to turn around and shout, *"You're gay!"*

It was so strange having people know, even if it wasn't a ton of people. A few department members witnessed him freak over Nicky when Brandon thought he'd been shot. Word seeped around to other officers. Brandon felt it in the cold shoulders of some, but most either hadn't got the memo or didn't seem to care. Although, he'd damn near stroked out when a gal from the Sheriff's Academy called and asked if he wanted to go on a volunteer speakers list for their diversity panel. How the hell she'd found out was anyone's guess. Brandon hadn't even had a chance to get used to that type of attention, and then Nicky had to try and push their relationship to another level.

"Tying up?" Nicky's voice edged into Brandon's thoughts. He looked up to find they'd already made it to Nicky's place. As he stepped onto the porch and slid the key in the door, Nicky added. "Tying down?" The door swung open and Nicky waited for Brandon to move inside before following. "What's your pleasure?"

Well, if they fucked, then they didn't necessarily need to have a conversation. "I get to choose, huh?" Brandon snorted and then realized his tone echoed rather snide. Walking into the bedroom, he used the next statement to take the sting out of his words. "As long as we've got condoms and lube, I'm a happy camper."

The first time Brandon saw Nicky's bedroom, he'd wondered why the bed had been positioned with the headboard cutting across the corner and pulled away from the wall. That one corner of the room seemed useless. The room felt kinda cramped. Plus, the whole wrought-iron bed thing had thrown him: queen-sized but with big square posts and upper rails that looked able to support a steel canopy. Heck, even the heavy red drapes at the back were strung on a rod across the ceiling and not the bed. The only thing that made sense, at the time, to Brandon was the mirror bolted to the ceiling.

Now, of course, he knew that all of it, even the mirror, served a wicked purpose. Behind the bed, hidden by the curtain, lurked enough floor space for stand up play—large eyebolts were screwed into the studs and floor at strategic locations. The bed was specifically designed for bondage. Nicky'd flipped his around, which didn't matter as the metal posted head and footboards were identical, so that when the Murphy mattress flipped up and the curtains were pulled back, he had a whole miniature dungeon to play in.

Nicky followed him into the room, stepped up to the dresser and pulled two short lengths of rope from the drawer: one blue, the other white. The quick and dirty short lengths, he kept there. "Shall I give you your other present now?" Longer ropes, handcuffs and the like Nicky stored in a duffle under the bed.

Teasing, "That's really for you and not me." Brandon sat on the bed. Of course since Nicky was going for the little stuff, they probably wouldn't be flipping the mattress up on the custom-made bondage bed today. Damn. Not like they had a hell of a lot of time anyway.

"In a way, yes." Nicky turned and smiled back. That wicked, feral look, oh yeah, Nicky had something in mind. "But I think you'll get a kick out of the feel."

Brandon started to tug up his T-shirt, but stopped. "Why are we doing things like this if you, you know, intend—"

"I don't intend anything." Nicky came up close, ran his hand across Brandon's hair. "If you have an answer then maybe it might be weird." Drawing the cotton cords between his fingers, Nicky stepped back. "You know, depending on what it is." He stared at the ropes in his hands, folding them in half, slapping his palm with the loops. Finally, Nicky looked up at Brandon again. "Do you?"

Brandon shrugged. "I don't, no, I don't know." Then he yanked off the shirt and tossed it at the foot of the bed.

"Then we just go with the flow, Brandon." Nicky swatted Brandon's bared chest with the ends of the ropes. Hard enough to sting and leave four little welts. "And shut the fuck up, or I'm going to have to gag you." He reached out with his other hand, and smacked Brandon's cheek with a more playful than serious blow. "Or is that what you want, hmm?"

"Right now?" Brandon flopped back on the bed with his arms spread. "I want you."

"Good." Nicky smirked. "Get out of your pants then."

"What about yo—"

As Nicky's smirk dropped in to a glare, he held up his hand. "Ah, gagging in four, three…"

Brandon shut up. Managing to kick off his boots at the same time as he unbuttoned his fly, Brandon shoved his jeans and shorts down. Brandon's legs hung off the side of the mattress. He wasn't hard yet, but things were starting to perk up. Knowing better than to actually touch his prick when Nicky hit one of his moods, Brandon ran his hands over his own chest and waited.

Nicky stepped between Brandon's knees. He let the white rope slide through his fingers to pool on Brandon's belly. Then he took the blue rope, adjusted the way it folded so that the midpoint hung over his thumb. "Put your feet up on the bed. Keep your butt where it is," Nicky ordered.

While Brandon complied, Nicky looped the rope over and around Brandon's cock. He pushed Brandon's legs a little wider, which rocked Brandon's ass off the bed a little. That done, Nicky pulled the rope behind Brandon's balls. With a tug that made Brandon groan, Nicky tied the rope off with a knot back, behind his sac. Brandon felt it press into the sensitive skin there. Then he pulled ends of the rope between Brandon's balls, separating the nuts and then threaded across the lines, between his nuts and prick. Another knot, between his nuts and prick, snugged it down—secure but not too tight— and made Brandon hiss.

Nicky wrapped the rope around the base of Brandon's still soft prick. He tied that off at the top. Quickly, he strung a set of bowline knots, circle under and lace through along top, so that it looked like zippered teeth in thin, blue rope running over the top of Brandon's prick. Swelling into the rope, Brandon's prick began to rise. Not before Nicky tied it off just below the head of Brandon's dick. What rope was left, Nicky wound just below the crown. More blood pumped into his prick and Brandon groaned. There was nowhere for him to grow. The pressure ate his senses, almost too painful, as his cock pressed against the restraint, skin bulging between the rope lines, but delicious.

Grabbing the white cotton rope in one hand, Nicky took hold of Brandon's sac with the other. After fondling Brandon's balls for a moment, he folded the rope in half and slid the loop up under the wrap at the base of Brandon's balls, pushed the ends through the loop and tied it off. Nicky knelt. Brandon could feel, but not really see, what was happening.

Nicky took one ball in his hand, caressed it, kissed it. As he sucked it into his mouth, he began to wrap the rope around it, the skin forcing Brandon's left testicle downward. Then he did the same with the right. Nicky grabbed both nuts and tugged them down. A sharp stab of pain wicked up through into Brandon's belly. He hissed and jerked. The rope slid against his skin as

Nicky began wrapping above where he'd separated the balls. The binding forced his sack further down, acting like a rope ball collar. Brandon groaned. So tight, pain and pleasure shot through his frame. Nicky chuckled as he tied it all off. The sound vibrated through every nerve.

Standing, Nicky held out his hand. "Come on, bitch. Off the bed." He leered. "I think it's time to have a little fun."

Brandon slid off the bed. As he stood, gravity took hold, the weight of the rope settled in, distending his sack farther. Brandon shuddered.

Nicky, who'd knelt again and was pulling the duffle bag with more rope out from under the bed, chuckled. "Yeah, that's pretty nice." He blew across Brandon's prick, the warm breath causing another shudder. "All purple. My favorite color." Bag freed from under the bed, Nicky got to his feet again. "Go to your corner," he ordered. "We're going to play."

Brandon eased between the corner of the bed and the wall. His cock throbbed and each time he took a step the weight on his balls strained the skin, making him tremble. Nicky walked around behind him and jerked the curtains open. Brandon heard the bag land on the bed and then the zipper grind down as Nicky ordered, "Turn around, face the bed." Brandon did. Nicky pulled ropes from the bag. Not really bothering to look at Brandon, he motioned to a spot on the floor. "Stand there." Brandon moved to comply as Nicky stood and swung to face him.

Nicky held one section, almost ten feet of rope, looped in the middle. Brandon snorted to himself, almost every tie Nicky did started as a looped piece of rope. "Give me your arm." When they got in this type of scene, Nicky always barked out his orders. If Brandon didn't comply fast enough, he might earn a slap or a spanking or just sexual tormenting for hours without release. Neither of them was into major pain play. This was about domination and control and pain sometimes went along with that.

Brandon extended his arm out toward Nicky, who draped the rope over it at about Brandon's wrist. Maybe about two feet of the looped end hung down. Nicky grabbed the looped end and, starting near Brandon's hand, used that to wrap Brandon's wrist three times. For some reason Nicky tended to work in threes. Then he crossed back over the bind, tucked it under the wrap a couple of times and pulled the whole thing snug. Finally, Nicky tied the remaining looped bit around the loose ends with a good solid square knot. He strung the leftover rope through an eyebolt, pulling Brandon's arm up and out. With a couple of hitches and a square knot, Nicky tied a trucker's hitch just beyond Brandon's fingertips. It didn't quite qualify as a quick release, but the knot could be undone without Nicky reaching or without too much hassle.

When Nicky ordered, "Other arm," the whole process was repeated with a second section of rope.

Nicky bent down. He banged Brandon's ankles with his fist. "Spread 'em." As Brandon shuffled his feet apart, Nicky paused and peered at something. "What the?" He grabbed at something just behind Brandon and then rocked back holding the barrel of a ballpoint pen. "How the fuck did this get back here?" For a moment, Brandon thought he was going to chuck it, but then a wicked grin spread across Nicky's face. He set the pen back by the leg of the bed. With a little more quick and dirty knot work, Nicky tied off Brandon's ankles to eyebolts set in the wall just above the floor.

Nicky'd done this so many times, even if Brandon only counted his own participation that the process took five minutes at most. Nicky'd strung the rope through the eyebolts high up on the wall and down by the floor, pulling Brandon's limbs spread eagle out in an X. A Saint Andrews Cross—without the beams. At least in this position. As Nicky tied the last rope off, Brandon grunted. Delicious pressure ate into his shoulder and elbow joints.

Still on his knees, Nicky blew across Brandon's bound prick. Brandon shivered. Nicky fished a thin cord from his back pocket. Brandon hadn't even seen him put it there. "We have to get that out of the way." Nicky looped the rope under the cord already wrapped around the head of Brandon's dick. He snugged that into a quick square knot. Then he wrapped the long ends around Brandon's middle, slid them under themselves so that the rope formed a T over the front of his body and pulled Brandon's cock flat up against his groin and belly before Nicky tied it off.

Smirking, Nicky reached back and grabbed the pen. Brandon was mystified…completely. Then Nicky grabbed his balls. "Hmm, good thing you shave." Using the back of the pen, Nicky tapped Brandon's balls, "What should I write?" Given the binding and the frustration, a sharp sting shot up from Brandon's nuts into his stomach with each little beat. "I know." Nicky flipped the pen around and Brandon tensed, waiting for the pain. "Property of Nick." Instead, as Nicky wrote, a sensual tickle wound its way through his sac. "If found, why the fuck are you reading his nuts? This dick belongs to ME!" Brandon had no idea whether all that fit on his skin, but his dick throbbed and he groaned.

Nicky tossed the pen off somewhere. Lost in the sensations playing through his groin, Brandon couldn't care less. Starting softly, Nicky began to slap Brandon's balls between his hands. Brandon's testicles, bound tight into his own skin, smacked into each other. The gooey, amorphous pain coursed out of his groin. It melded into the erotic pull from the combined weight of the rope tying off his sac and the gentle swing. He tensed, anticipating the next blow before it landed. Each tap, no matter how light or how strong, gave Brandon shudders. A little fear worked into his brain. What if the next strike was too hard? Would his nuts just explode?

And his dick…God, the rope practically burned into his skin. A throbbing grinding pain ate through Brandon's senses. Almost too intense, Brandon didn't think he could stand much more. Somewhere along the line, he'd started babbling. Nicky just laughed and let him. Brandon never knew whether the moaning, pleading and begging would end with him gagged or Nicky turned on or both.

Brandon felt helpless, out of control, and it was wonderful. Twitching, shuddering, he sagged into the ropes. Somehow the juxtaposition of struggling against the bindings, feeling them pin him, gave Brandon a release. It meant his mind could wander into the head space of utter, absolute calm. Mentally, Brandon relaxed. The very moment he physically was unable to resist, he could let go of every worry and enjoy the ride Nicky sent him on.

Brandon spent so much of his life locked down into the self-assured cop mode, hiding in the closet for so many years, guarding against anyone finding out, that he just needed someone to take away the options. Nicky was that person. Nicky could do anything to him like this. And, most important, Brandon trusted him not to. Nicky wouldn't ever hurt him. Well, he'd *hurt* Brandon plenty…delicious, private torture…but not more than Brandon could stand. If Brandon ever muttered *peanut butter*, their safe word, he knew Nicky would stop and get him undone.

The immediate pain stopped, although a slow, steady ache remained. Sweat pouring down his skin, nerves frayed almost to breaking, all Brandon could do was pant. He felt and sensed, more than really saw that Nicky stood. Pain bloomed in his left nipple. Nicky must have twisted it. Brandon barely managed to crack open his eyes—he hardly remembered closing them— to see Nicky smiling. Nicky moved in close. He put his right shoulder against Brandon's chest and then loosed the knot holding Brandon's arm up and out.

"It's time, bitch." Nicky whispered and pulled the knot holding Brandon's other arm. Brandon's legs wouldn't quite support him. He sagged against Nicky. Stinging little shocks traveled along his muscles as the blood flowed back into Brandon's arms. Nicky walked a step or two back, took Brandon's hands in his. "Bend over," he ordered as he positioned Brandon's fingers on the top rail of the bed. "Hold on tight, bitch. The ride's going to get bumpy."

Brandon sucked in his breath. Bent over, his legs spread out and just his hands on the bar of the bed—he could barely support himself like that. When Nicky got to Brandon's hip, he reached under Brandon's body and untied the rope around Brandon's middle. With a few jerks and twists, Nicky pulled Brandon's prick back between his legs. Then he unwound the wraps from just below the crown. Brandon hissed as blood flowed in and pain shot up his dick.

Nicky, somewhere behind him, laughed. Brandon felt that thick, hard cock against his ass and the cool touch of gel drizzling over his hole. He pushed and Brandon felt his body give way, allow Nicky to fill him. While gently thrusting, Nicky's nimble fingers worried the knots on the cords tying up Brandon's dick and balls. They gave as Nicky's porn star dick rammed in all the way to his balls. With the knots undone, the bowline truss on Brandon's dick unraveled. Nicky tugged on the cord binding Brandon's balls. It caught, tugged and then spun loose. For a few seconds, blissful release of pressure flooded Brandon's senses. He had no feeling other than he wasn't trapped.

Pain hit.

Every nerve awoke at once. A thousand invisible, infinitesimal wasps stung his cock and balls. Brandon's eyes burned. One long stream of profanity spewed from his mouth as he thrashed against Nicky and that dick invading his ass. It felt like his skin was being stripped off his nuts as blood flowed back into the flesh between his legs. Somewhere in all that writhing and bucking he sensed that Nicky came.

Then Nicky's strong arms held him, helped him. Brandon's breath came in short, barking gasps as he sank to his knees. Like he had no control over his body, Brandon shook. He had to find something to focus on. That something was Nicky: his hands petting, touching and his voice soothing with nonsense phrases like, "I'm here," and "Trust me." Letting Brandon slump onto his body, Nicky reached back and untied Brando's ankles. "Come on." He coaxed and pulled Brandon to standing.

Somehow he managed to get Brandon onto the bed and lying down. Then he brought a warm wet cloth to wash Brandon's skin and cold water to soothe his throat. When Brandon could be touched without hissing, Nicky wrapped his sensual lips over Brandon's prick and sucked. Brandon bucked into his hot, tight mouth. As frayed as Brandon's nerves were, it only took a few minutes of that bliss before Brandon lost it and spunk spewed out of his dick into Nicky's kiss.

They lay wrapped up in each other for awhile, murmuring bullshit and promises. There was a moment where Brandon thought, maybe, it just might work if Nicky moved to So. Cal., but he was too exhausted to put it into words. Finally, Nicky shifted and whispered that he needed to hit the shower. Brandon dozed while Nicky hosed off. Then Brandon hauled himself off the bed and into the bath. Thoroughly fucked and cleaned, Brandon stumbled back into Nicky's bedroom. He toweled off his hair and watched Nicky reach for the phone.

"Calling the flame dame?" Brandon shrugged and tossed the towel on the bed.

Nicky grinned. "Yeah, 'bout time."

Kneeling by his duffle, Brandon dug out new shorts and a shirt. The jeans from earlier, Brandon grabbed off the floor. As he jumped into his briefs and pants Brandon felt a little stab of guilt. He'd almost completely forgotten about Shayna while taking care of his dick. Parenting sucked. "You think she's ready?"

"Probably." Nick punched the buttons for Miri's number as Brandon tugged his shirt over his head. "It's about lunch time. You want to eat in or go out?"

"Let's see what Shayna wants." Brandon sat down heavily on the mattress next to Nicky and began to pull on his socks and boots. "Princess gets everything she wants, remember?" He was a little more relaxed now. Maybe it meant he could focus on he and Nicky and what he really wanted. Thank God he hadn't said anything earlier when his senses and defenses were down.

"Spoil her rotten now and what are you going to do when she's fifteen?" Miri must have picked up the line because Nick held up one finger, forestalling a retort. "Hey girlfriend, wanna send Shayna home? Sick of her yet?" The smile fell from his face. "When? What time?"

Brandon stood, everything going cold inside. "Nicky?"

"Okay, okay, we'll head that way. You head toward us." Nicky tossed the phone on the dresser as he jumped to his feet and headed toward the door. "Come on." Brandon didn't need the prompt; he'd run over Nicky if he stopped. "Miri says she sent the boys home with Shayna about half an hour ago. They've got two or three friends' houses along the way." Grabbing both their jackets off the chair, he dredged up a smile. "They've probably just stopped in someone's yard to play and just forgot the time."

"I'm going to kill them."

Nicky thrust Brandon's jacket at him as they headed out the front door. A nervous tinge cracked his voice as he chided. "They're kids Brandon." Shoving his hands into the sleeves of his own coat, he added, "You're not going to kill them. Don't you remember playing around the neighborhood when you were a kid?"

"This isn't her neighborhood. She knows better." It hurt to breathe. It hurt to think. "Straight home!" Brandon yelled at no one in particular.

"Yeah, okay, whatever." Nicky hit the sidewalk at a jog. "Come on, babe."

Brandon didn't need the prompt. Boots pounding the concrete, he passed Nicky at a dead run.

CHAPTER 8

They rounded the corner from Nicky's street and Brandon almost skidded on his ass he was moving so fast. Cop training finally overrode daddy panic. "Slow down!" he yelled at Nicky. They needed to slow down and actually look. He took two deep breaths and forced himself to walk.

A few feet ahead, Nicky dropped from a jog to a walk as well. Twisting back toward Brandon, he pointed down the street. A bunch of kids on skateboards, razor-scooters and bikes clustered a ways down the block. "See, I told you." Nicky's relief reverberated through his words. In amongst them, Brandon caught sight of the oldest of Miri's kids. "They just stopped somewhere to play." He cupped his hands over his mouth and yelled at the assembly, "Cole! Justin! Shayna!" Two boys, Brandon recognized Justin, the middle, and Cole, the oldest, stepped out of the assembled kids. He didn't see A.J. or Shayna among the group.

His little girl was not there. Fighting down a swell of panic, Brandon bellowed, "Where's Shayna?"

Cole stepped back, almost like he was afraid of what Brandon might do. Justin just jammed his hands in his pockets and waited. Once Brandon got near enough that he didn't have to shout, Justin answered, "She said we were being mean to her and went home." As he spoke, Miri jogged up, her youngest, in tow. The kids all milled around and a black man with a blonde dye job came out the door of the house and ambled over.

Nick knelt in front of Justin. "Home?"

The man with the dye job wore a mechanic's shirt with a name tag that said *Dennet.* "What's the matter?" He put his arm around one of the other boys in the crowd.

"Nick? Brandon?" Miri moved behind Justin and Cole slunk up to press against her side.

"They said Shayna went to walk home," Nicky answered Miri

first. "My friend's daughter hasn't made it home, yet," he added for Dennet's benefit.

"Yeah." Apparently more comfortable with Nicky than Brandon, Cole nodded. "You're only another couple blocks, Nick." Cole whined out the answer as if he thought he was about to be in trouble. "Just around the corner. She said she could find it."

They'd come from those two blocks. No sign of her. Brandon shook. A cold sweat swept across him. Suffocating, he was suffocating he had to remind himself to breathe. Pull in air. Push it out. All the blood left his body. Shayna was in danger. All the training, all the searches, all the words for calming frantic parents vanished. Panic clawed through his stomach. This wasn't some missing kid. This was Shayna.

"You're talking about," Dennet leaned in toward Brandon, "the little girl who was here?"

"Yeah, was she here?" Brandon swallowed, took a deep breath and pushed the panic down. "She didn't come home." He had to stay calm, focused and deal with the right now, not the what if.

"She probably saw you guys pass and was playing hide 'n seek or something. Or there's two little girls who live that way." Dennet pointed off back where Nicky and Brandon had come from. "Nothing to worry about. You all new to the neighborhood?"

"No. I've lived here for years." Nicky shook his head. "Brandon and his daughter are out visiting from California."

Dennet looked like he mulled something over. Finally, he shrugged. "She probably got turned around. What's her name?"

Panic had him so hard that it took a moment before Brandon could remember and stutter out, "Shayna."

"Okay." Dennet cupped his hand on the head of boy with red hair and buck teeth. "Mark, you live by those girls, right?" When the boy nodded, Dennet pushed Mark off. "You run over there. See if there's a little girl, Shayna, there. If that little girl is there, you bring her back here. Got it?" Mark nodded and took off. "If she's not there, come back here and let your aunty know!"

Dennet shouted at the boy's heels. Then he turned to another boy. "Blaze, take your brother inside, okay?" He patted Blaze's back. Then Dennet spoke to Miri's boys. "Cole, Justin why don't you boys take A.J. and go inside, too." They must have played there fairly often. He called after Blaze, who was already leading another boy of around seven into the house. "Tell your mom to get you guys some chips or something." When they were at the porch, Dennet turned his attention back to the adults. "Look, I remember seeing a little girl with Miri's boys a little bit ago. She can't have gotten too far."

"You'll help?" Brandon asked Dennet. "If we spread out we can cover more area."

"Sure." Dennet nodded. "By the way, I'm Dennet Michaels."

"Brandon, Nick, I guess you know Miri." After the quick introduction, Brandon fell into cop mode to save himself from going nuts. "Nicky and I will spread out this way," he waved back in the general direction of Nicky's place, "hit the side streets." Then he pointed left and right. "Miri, you head that way since you didn't see her coming this way." Brandon knew how to handle searches and it gave him something to focus on. "And Dennet if you can check down there. Meet back here in like fifteen minutes."

They fanned across the neighborhood. Looking over fences, peering under cars. Every second was more terrifying than the last. "Shayna!" Their voices echoed through the neighborhood. Each time they called the strident edge cut a little deeper. Every yell carried more panic. About a block into the search, the obvious solution hit Brandon. Shit, if he hadn't been so jangled, it would have come to him sooner. A quick search of his pockets, as he jogged back toward Nicky's house, told him he didn't have the damn thing on him. What fucking luck. He caught sight of Nicky, who'd jumped up to look into a back yard. "Hey! Nicky!" Good thing, since he'd bolted out of the house without the key Nicky gave him.

"What?" Nicky started running in his direction. "Find her?"

"No." Still running, assuming Nicky was following, Brandon

rounded the corner for Nicky's block. "Get your keys. The child locator."

"Holy shit!" Nicky footsteps pounded after him.

Brandon skidded to a stop on the porch with Nicky not a minute behind him. The moment Nicky unlocked the door Bandon pushed into the dim house. "Wait, where the fuck did I leave it?" He spoke more to jog his own memory.

"Luggage?" Nicky spun first in the direction of the bedroom. "Ah, maybe," he turned toward the front room where Shayna'd been sleeping, "Shayna's bags?"

"No." Brandon held up his hand to stop Nicky from talking, messing up his own thoughts. "Where the fuck did I leave the babysitter's remote?" Maybe if he verbally went through last night, he'd remember. "We came home. I had it in my pocket."

Nicky headed off toward the bedroom. "Where's your pants from the other day?"

No, the last place Brandon had it was in his jacket pocket. "We got into the kitchen…" That was it. Brandon bolted through the swinging doors into the kitchen. A pile of his stuff, mixed with Shayna's stuff, still sat on Nicky's table. "Crap here." Brandon dug through the junk he'd emptied out of his pockets the other night. In amongst Shayna's purchases from Libby Girl, Brandon spotted the putty colored remote. "Fuck! Fuck! Got it." Most kids Shayna's age, if they didn't come home, it was because they were hurt and couldn't answer: trapped in a basement where they'd followed a kitty, knocked out by a swing in someone else's backyard, hit by a…Brandon stopped that thought.

"How's it work?" Brandon looked up at the sound of Nicky's voice. He hung on the bar style door with one hand and panted.

"Okay," Brandon swallowed and forced himself to calm down. "Dian said like a metal detector…sort of." Another deep breath and Brandon opened the case. "Flip it open, hit the red panic button and start kinda moving it in all directions." As he spoke, Brandon mimicked the moves. A series of fast electronic beeps, like a piece of heavy machinery backing up, sounded out of the tiny speaker.

"Holy shit that's loud." Nicky stepped up and put his hand on Brandon's shoulder.

"It's like sonar." Brandon swung the remote in an arc. As he passed the general direction of Miri's house, the pace of the beeps increased and then dropped as he kept swinging. "Okay, loud fast beeps good, low slow beeps bad." Brandon headed back to the front door. "We just have to follow the beeps." Brandon kept talking just to have something reasonably constructive to do. "If she's hurt or something, it'll take us to her." That was said more to reassure himself than anything. "She's in range, so maybe she's just not able to call out."

"But we've been that way," Nicky reminded him and Brandon wished he hadn't.

The pace of the beeps kept increasing as they walked the way to Miri's house. They weren't even all the way down the block when the beeping became a long continuous tone and the screen turned blue. Brandon looked around. They were on the sidewalk. Nothing was near them: an open front yard to the left, the street to the right with the sidewalk ahead and behind. By what the locator said, Shayna should be within five feet and that meant he should be able to see her. She wasn't there. Brandon hunkered down to sit on the curb, dropped his hands between his knees and just stared at the street. What was he missing? Frustrated, he picked up a rock and chucked it onto the asphalt. It wasn't where the rock bounced, but stilled that focused Brandon's attention closer to his feet. He rocked forward onto his knees.

"What," Nicky stepped off the curb, "what did you find."

"The pendant." Brandon could barely speak. No, just no. "It's broken." About two feet into the street, Shayna's locator fob lay on the pavement. The catch still looked intact but the cord had snapped. No blood, no broken glass to indicate a hit and run. Relief washed over him and then funneled back. If she hadn't been hit, but the fob was broken...it meant someone took it off her.

"Oh fucking Christ," Nicky hissed.

"Call 911 Nicky." Brandon resisted the urge to reach out and grab it. Instead he killed the alarm on the remote. His hands shook. "Something's happened to her, someone's got her."

Nicky knelt next to him. "How do you know?" He reached out toward the gray bit of plastic.

"Don't." Brandon grabbed Nicky's wrist to stop him. The cords in his wrist almost popped with the strain of his own grip and Nicky hissed. Brandon had to will his fingers to release one at a time. "Let the police see it like this." The only real scenario chilled his guts. "She wouldn't have taken it off. Not without fighting. Dian has her so programmed."

"How would anyone have known it was there?" Nicky fumbled with his phone.

"Panic button." Trying not to completely lose it, Brandon sat down in the street. "She probably was going for the panic button. If she'd been able to hit it, damn remote would have started wailing."

"I've got the police on the line...what do I say?"

"Give me the phone." He held out his hand and when Nicky passed the phone over, brought it to his ear. "Hello dispatch?" His voice cracked. "This is Detective Brandon Carr, Riverside, California PD. I have good reason to believe someone's taken my daughter."

clickjacked.blogroads.net—Private Post Dec. 29, 12:05pm

Why wouldn't the damn thing shut up? Yap, yap, yap. Like a puppy, but more annoying. Even the radio couldn't drown the sound. If it just stayed quiet everything would be fine. Everything would be fine. It could fit in the picture if it would only be quiet.

Pretend it didn't exist, don't listen and drive. They needed to get out of town. Then it would be taken care of, wouldn't hear the whining anymore. Shut it out, keep it out. Out long enough, and, and, and, and that other problem, it'd be gone, too.

CHAPTER 9

Brandon relayed the confusion of the last half hour as concisely as he could manage. Procedure, stepping back into rote patterns of police work, allowed him to focus and keep terror caged in a little corner of his mind. The emergency operator, efficient and reassuring as possible, passed the information on to Vegas Metro PD and asked Brandon if he wanted them to stay on the line. Brandon declined, but told her he'd wait right where he was for the cops to show. Then he sent Nicky back to Dennet's place telling him to have Miri get names of the kids who'd been there and take her boys home. The cops would need to interview them all.

He should have pushed, not let Nicky and Miri talk him into leaving Shayna. He's over at Nicky's getting his rocks off and some creep snags his kid. Thinking with his dick, that's what always got him in trouble. Brandon laced his hands behind his skull and dropped his head between his knees. Shakes grabbed him like a pit bull and shredded his nerves into a jangling mess. How could he have done it? He should have known something like this would happen. Leaving a nine-year-old kid with people he barely knew in a strange city. Fucking stupid. Brandon didn't really even know Miri, not well. Not well enough to leave Shayna. Yeah she was Nicky's best friend, but what the fuck did Nicky know about who was responsible with kids?

Enough time passed before a squad car and an unmarked pulled up across the street to allow *what ifs* and *whys* to swallow Brandon. He looked up to watch a plainclothes detective clamber out of the big American made sedan. Orozco. Brandon recognized him from an investigation where a former Nevada Gaming Control agent and colleague of Nicky had gotten himself whacked. That's what the guy got for getting involved in a Mexican Mafia money-laundering scheme. Of course, that investigation had nearly resulted in Nicky getting offed as well.

Orozco had been lead Vegas homicide on part of that. "Detective Carr." Orozco ambled over, his round brown face and white handlebar mustache somehow comforting. "So sorry to be reacquainted under these circumstances." Probably, Brandon figured, just the fact that his was a kinda familiar face helped. "You might, however, want to get out of the middle of the street."

Brandon stood and held up his hand...not for a shake but to stop him. "Wait. Don't move." Again, he pushed his terror, guilt, all of it down. They had about twenty-four hours to get Shayna back in any condition. After that recovery odds dropped to near zero. If he was going to help, Brandon had to stay calm.

"What?" Pausing, Orozco held his arms out to the side halting the progress of the uniformed officers a few steps behind him.

Focus, he reminded himself, like it's a case, not your kid. "That," Brandon pointed to the one little link to Shayna in the street, "It's my daughter Shayna's. A child locator." He held up the remote. "It reacts to this. Looks like someone ripped it off her neck. It's why I called. She's not lost. She didn't run away." Those were the first two assumptions made in any child missing call. Brandon had to make sure they understood that: get the alerts out quickly to up recovery odds. "That, I think, says someone took her."

"Jefferson, Mully," Orozco instructed the officers. "Block off the street to traffic. Call in someone to process the scene." Orozco looked up, "Ah, Agent O'Malley." He called out as Nicky jogged up. "We meet again, in as miserable of a situation as the last time."

"Yeah." Nicky moved close to Brandon, put his arm around his shoulder. Brandon didn't shrug it off. Orozco knew about them, all about them. "Miri's gone back to her place, okay?" That strong, comforting grip, as Nicky told him, helped some. Still, somehow he'd slipped into this vortex where he couldn't really even feel his own body. There was a distant roar like an army on the move over the horizon in the back of his brain. Then Nicky looked up at the detective. "I thought you did Homicide?"

"Major Crimes." Orozco smiled, but it wasn't happy or reassuring. "At Metro we're going to treat the disappearance of a cop's kid as a major crime. Not like we don't always. But I heard the name, I know Detective Carr isn't from here and that means his little girl isn't hiding with a friend or relative. She's lost, hurt or something." Brandon knew that something meant taken…and stranger taken. Shayna's odds of survival dropped from somewhere around 70/30 to close to zip with that fact. The information swirled in the void inside him. Orozco's pained expression confirmed Brandon's own thoughts. "Okay, I don't have to go through the intro drill with you, detective. Do I?"

"No." Brandon shook his head. The cops didn't need to sugar coat or apologize for digging into his past, present and everything else. "Ask what you need to. Then get on the streets and find her and the bastard that did this to her." It would be a him and, if they found her, Shayna'd be broken at best, but probably it wouldn't be best. That's what training told him. The thought drifted away as though Brandon's mind had no way to pin it down. It was like watching some movie play out, not his life, not his daughter.

"We will." Orozco gave a few more instructions to the patrol officers. Then he steered them off toward Nicky's house, relaying more instructions over the radio as they walked. "Shayna Carr, is that her name?" Like any good officer, Orozco took out his note pad and pen, ready to jot down anything he might need. "What does she look like?"

Brandon blinked. He had to think a moment. "Shayna Carr, yeah." Nicky opened up his house again and ushered them inside while Brandon rattled off Shayna's stats. "She's about three-foot-nine inches and maybe fifty-five, sixty pounds. Skinny." Collapsing into a corner of the couch, Brandon kept up the description. "Blondish brown hair with blue eyes. It's kinda frizzy, curly down below her shoulders. She looks like a pixy doll."

"What was she wearing today?" Orozco settled into one of the other chairs. Fuck, Brandon remembered him exactly in that spot back in June. He could almost swear Orozco'd been wearing the same tie as he sat in one of Nicky's red velvet arm chairs and interrogated Nicky mostly, but Brandon as well, about the other agent's murder.

Brandon thought hard, trying to dredge up the fight about clothes this morning. "Pink top...one of those little halter things over a white long sleeve T-shirt and sleeves that came to about here." Shayna'd wanted to just wear the halter. Brandon knew Dian would roast him if he let her, plus it was fucking freezing. "These, like, legging things, with pink hearts and rhinestones on the leg. With a skirt over it. I don't remember the skirt." Since they hadn't argued over that, Brandon just couldn't picture it. "The little Chinese or Indian slippers that they sell all over... shiny pink with stitched flowers and little beads on them. We bought them last night. Pink...lots of pink." Brandon spaced. The memory was right there and then it just wasn't. "Her jacket, what jacket was she wearing?"

"The one with the rabbit fur." Nicky perched on the arm of the couch. "Pink parka, all fake fur."

Orozco jotted that all down. The detective's radio crackled about the time a knock sounded at the door. Nicky jumped up to open it and let in a female officer. Brandon vaguely registered a fairly muscular but small Hispanic woman in a uniform. "Do you have a picture?" Brandon's attention swung back to Orozco. "We should get one to the press right away. To go out with the Amber Alert."

"I don't know." Brandon rubbed his hands together. Maybe his wallet? Brandon fished it out and dug through the credit cards. Fuck, he must have taken Shayna's photo out the last time he cleaned out his billfold. He remembered it had been pretty ratty. He needed a new one. "Not here. Riverside."

"Yeah, we do." Nicky yanked his phone out of the holster on his hip. "My cell phone. When we were over on the strip." He pointed back toward the office. "I can print one out."

"Okay, Myestas," Orozco used his pen as a pointer, "go assist Agent O'Malley." Brandon knew, even if Nicky probably didn't, that the cops didn't want them off alone in the house until they'd had a chance to search it for evidence. "Now, Detective Carr, take me through everything that happened today."

Brandon dredged up the morning's events—viewing all of it through a fog. "We went to Miri's for breakfast this morning. You know to, I guess, do our Christmas. She's Nicky's best friend, lives a few blocks over. Shayna stayed to play video games with Miri's kids, and Nicky and I came home to you know..." God he didn't want to say it, but because of the other investigation, Orozco already knew about he and Nicky even to the point of them being in the bondage scene, "have some adult time, us, you know?" He rubbed his temples and rushed on, "Then we called Miri about one-ish, told her we're coming over. Maybe take all the kids for burgers or pizza or something. Miri told Nicky that the boys had left with Shayna about half an hour before."

After more notes, Orozco prompted, "Okay, and then what?"

"Well, Nicky and I, we headed toward Miri's and she headed toward us. We found the boys at one of their friends. Shayna wasn't there. The boys said she wanted to walk home by herself, because it wasn't that far. That's when we started to search, 'cause we hadn't seen her on our way over. And one of the other boy's fathers, Dennet I forget his last name, there was a whole group of kids, he helped." Brandon thought for a moment. He wanted to provide Orozco with as accurate a time line as possible. "Maybe that took another twenty minutes of time. Then I remembered about the child locator that Dian, my ex, bought. So I ran back here. Turned it on. And it led me about a block down. Where I showed you. That's where we found the broken fob."

"How was she acting when you left her with Miri?"

These were the questions that Orozco had apologized for out in the street. The inevitable prying and poking. "Fine." Brandon knew that they had to go through it all. And he was the distraught parent here, there might have been something in Shayna's behavior he missed. "Blowing shit up on video games." Brandon tried to think of anything that might have been an issue. "We fought some this morning about her clothes, but nothing big."

"Has she ever talked about running away?"

"No."

"Has she ever been in Vegas before?"

"Not as far as I know."

Nicky and Myestes walked back into the room. "Here's the picture." Nicky held out a still wet color print of Shayna's face. It looked cropped from the picture of the three of them in front of the penguin display. "Will that work?" Orozco nodded and Nicky handed the photo to the officer. As he walked around and settled on the couch next to Brandon, Nicky volunteered, "Other than she's been hanging out with Miri's kids, this weekend she's been here with her dad and me."

Orozco let the interruption slide. "Are there family problems? Things Shayna might be reacting to?"

"Yeah, I mean..." Brandon shrugged. The divorce had happened long before Shayna could even walk. Still, you never really knew how things like that affected kids. "Dian and I have been divorced since she was little. So she's used to that. But, other than a day here or there, this is like the most extended visitation we've had." Just the break in her routine might have set her off, made her do something stupid, talk to someone she shouldn't have. "She met Nicky and it seemed to go well. Although she did mention that the whole Goth, you know, decorations and stuff weirded her out a little. I figure if she talked about it, then it wasn't major."

And then he'd gone and left her with Miri. *You barely know me, let me dump you with a stranger.* The big chasm opened up in the floor of his gut again. "It's been going well." Brandon managed to get it out without losing control of his vocal cords. "Day after tomorrow we were going to drive home. And hell, if Princess said 'boo,' Dian would have dumped everything and come and got her. There wasn't any reason for her to take off."

"Is she using drugs or drinking?"

Taken aback, Brandon sputtered. "She's nine!" He knew the question would come and still it hit him raw and wrong.

"You work Vice, detective," Orozco's chiding backed him down.

Nicky put his hand on Brandon's thigh, comforting him with the touch. Brandon covered it with his own and squeezed trying to tell Nicky how much he appreciated him there. "Not that I know." He'd busted kids as young as eight for possession. Most were street rats, but not all. Middle class drug use started fairly young. Orozco's question wasn't unreasonable under the circumstances. "Nothing I can see or smell."

Orozco nodded. "Who would she call if there was a problem?"

"Her mom." Brandon realized he knew so few of the people in Dian's circle. "Maybe, her Bubbie, that's Edith, my stepmom. Her friend Beth, in Grover Beach. Other than them, I don't know."

"Has anything like this ever happened before?"

"No." Dian never mentioned anything like Shayna running away or getting lost. He and his ex didn't see eye-to-eye on ninety percent of shit, they didn't talk much, but Brandon figured she'd have told him if there'd ever been a problem that big. "Not that I can think of."

"You said this was the first extended visitation you've had." Orozco flipped back to an early note. "Have there been any problems?"

"She's been a little mouthy," Brandon knew covering up, sugar-coating his relationship with his daughter wouldn't help, "but that's because she's not used to having me around telling her what to do. I mean usually I'm the guy she just gets to hang around with, have fun with. I'm not usually the punisher and I've had to set down the law a little—bed-time, brushing teeth, clothes and that shit. But nothing that might...nothing that would cause her to go."

"Look," Orozco's stare hit Brandon hard, "you're a cop. What do you gauge her chances at?"

"She's fucked." As Nicky started to protest the finality of the statement, Brandon cut him off. "We're talking a sheltered little girl who goes to a tiny public school in Grover-fucking-Beach." He swallowed against the rising tide of panic. Saying it, laying out the odds, made the situation real. "The place is like it got lost in the fifties. Dian wouldn't even let her take karate 'cause it was too violent." The empty space inside him coalesced into something so palpable Brandon could reach down and touch it. "And she's grabbed in Sin City?" Resting his elbow on the arm of the couch, Brandon put his face in his hand and tried to massage away the budding headache. "Fuck!" Worming through his system...soon that emptiness would suck him inside out.

"Anyone suspicious been hanging around?"

Nicky answered that one. "No, not anyone I could pick out. I mean it's not the greatest neighborhood in the world." He looked about as terrified as Brandon felt. "I haven't noticed anyone, but I wasn't really, you know, studying everything."

Orozco seemed to expect that response. Brandon would have as well. Most people didn't log everyone and everything that happened around them. "Any reason someone would want to get back at you?" Brandon knew which *you* Orozco meant. "Anyone you can think of?"

Brandon laughed. It came out dry and soulless. "You mean, other than anyone I've ever put away?"

"Anyone who comes to mind beyond the normal? Anyone make threats?"

"No," Brandon shook his head, "just the run of the mill jerks and perps."

"Is there anyone or anyplace in this area that children fear? You know, the creepy neighbor? That kind of thing."

Brandon had no idea on that one. "Nicky?"

"I don't know." Nicky shrugged. It was a bit below his age group that that information would circulate. "You can ask Miri's kids. They'd be able to tell you."

"Look, Agent O'Mally, Nick." Orozco's smile seemed pained.

"I know you have a computer. Can we look at it? Can we search the house?"

Yeah, Brandon understood. Just because it looked like someone took Shayna, didn't make it so to the cops. He could scream and yell and tell them it wasn't him, it wasn't Nicky and they'd dig the same places…it would just take longer. Sixty percent of the time, in a missing kid case, one or both parents were involved. The rest of the odds spread…that was taken up by boyfriends, girlfriends, aunts, uncles—people who knew the child. Stranger abductions were so rare as to be almost legendary, despite what the news reports said. That meant both he, and Nicky, were suspects.

"Anything you need to do, Detective Orozco." Nicky squeezed Brandon's thigh. "Just do it. Find her."

Brandon huffed. He didn't want to say it with the other officer there, but letting things go and someone stumbling on toys or shit would be worse, derail the search into areas that didn't solve anything. "Detective," he took a deep breath, "You understand some stuff about Nicky and I, right?"

"Depends on what kind of stuff." Orozco sucked on his mustache a moment. "I know you're a couple. I know you have some, well, you used the word kinks I believe."

"Oh." Nicky's eyes went a little wide. Yeah, Brandon figured he hadn't thought through it all. "You could say that."

"What am I going to find?"

"Besides the sex toys?" Orozco's smile went tight at Nicky's answer. "Rope, bondage equipment. Computer too, huh?"

"Yes."

Nicky's explosion of breath ended in a, "Wow. Some hardcore S and M chatting. Pics and the like. Nothing illegal, although if you're not into waterworks and fisting it might push your buttons."

Brandon kept Myestes in view out of the corner of his eye. She didn't even blink. "The porn shit should all be gay. But," Brandon swallowed, "you're going to find a lot of rope and handcuffs."

"Floggers, whips, paddles, clamps—"

"Nicky." Brandon cut him off with a growl. There was a difference between letting the cops know what they'd turn up and giving them an inventory of their sex life. What rumors wound their way back to Riverside would be hell enough. The worst, 'cause it would come out, Brandon getting fucked up the ass while some perv took his kid. All those thoughts dropped off into the still growing bottomless pit to the point where he couldn't even care.

Orozco looked up at the uniformed officer. "Okay," he huffed, "we treat this like any other scene. But, let's be discreet. We're dealing with another officer. Get me some guys who will be thorough, but keep their yaps shut. We don't need anyone who doesn't have a real reason to know getting a hold of this."

"Yes, sir," Myestes acknowledged. "I'll hand select the team for the initial search." She keyed her mike and headed out the front door. By now Nicky's street had to be crawling with uniformed officers. In a little bit, Nicky's house would be, too. Almost clinically detached, Brandon wondered if Nicky really understood the complete blue invasion that was about to be unleashed.

"Thanks." Orozco did a quick rundown of his notes. Brandon knew there were a lot more questions that needed answering. Still, Orozco balanced the need for information with the need to get out and start looking. When she'd shut the door, Orozco heaved another sigh. "Myestes, she's on the Gay and Lesbian community taskforce. Asked for her when I got the call. Figured someone from your people…" Letting the thought trail off, he stood. "Look, I'll go back into the bedroom with you. You should both get some clothes and be prepared to be out of the house all night. Show me anything you got hidden back there, okay."

"All night?" Nicky turned to Brandon. "Really?"

Brandon nodded. "Yeah." Then, he added, "Shit, I'll pay for Miri's family's as well. Let her know, okay?"

"They're going to be kicked out of their place?"

"It might not take all night," Brandon shrugged, "but, maybe, yeah."

Orozco jumped in. "Look, it's procedure." He explained what Brandon already understood. Police investigations equaled invasive, frustrating and messy. "We have to document who came in contact with Shayna in order to rule them out. That means fingerprints, collecting trace, all that. And that," Orozco grimaced, "takes time."

"Fuck." Nicky banged his head on the spine of the couch. "Miri's going to kill me."

Brandon might have been mad...Shayna was gone and Nicky was worried that his fag-hag might be inconvenienced, but he knew big pictures were hard to focus on. The petty shit seemed easier to handle. Brandon started to say something, but his phone began to scream in that discordant, cartoon voice. "Fuck." He echoed Nicky's earlier expletive. Orozco stared at him, not comprehending but somehow understanding that it meant issues.

Almost on top of each other, he and Nicky spat out, "Dian."

That seemed to clue the detective in, "Your ex-wife?" When Brandon nodded, Orozco coached, "Answer it. Be calm. Non-committal. Make sure she's in a safe place."

Brandon pulled the phone out of its holster. His gut filled with dread as he flipped it open. "Hey." He managed to get that single syllable out without too much strain.

"Hello, Brandon." Dian sounded wary. He must not have come across too well. "Everything okay?"

He couldn't answer that. Instead, Brandon asked, "Ah, where are you?"

"At break," Dian said it slow. "At the training. What's wrong?" Repeating herself, okay, Brandon figured she clued in fast that everything wasn't right.

Still he had to make sure she wouldn't wreck or something.

"Are you driving? You alone?"

"No and no." Rising panic swept through her tone. Dian's voice cracked over the connection as she almost screamed in his ear, "What's wrong?"

Fuck, he couldn't tell her. All his training, it never included how you broke this shit to your own ex-wife, the mother of your child. Every class Brandon had ever taken, every post-training seminar he attended; they all failed him at the exact same moment. A big old wave of terror came rushing up from inside. He was left swimming in fear like any other victim. He swallowed, "Ahh…I'm going to have you talk to someone." In a panic he shoved the phone at Detective Orozco.

Calm, serene and able to be removed from the moment, Orozco took the phone from Brandon's hand. His frown told Brandon he understood…and somehow Brandon knew Orozco had sat where Brandon sat and listened to some other officer wade through lines he knew by rote and could quote the subtext chapter and verse. Orozco closed his eyes and asked, "Is this Dian?" After she must have answered, he continued, "My name is Emanuel Orozco with the Vegas police." He paused as if in response to something Dian said. "No. She's missing." Another pause. "Is there someone there who can help you? You'll probably want to come out to Las Vegas." His words echoed with the *calming* tones all cops learned early on. "I'd feel much more comfortable telling you everything personally. Have someone drive you to the airport. My department will work with the airlines to get you on the first stand-by flight, okay? Here's my info," Orozco rattled it off and repeated it probably four times before he hung up the phone.

A deep, heavy sigh sounded as he passed the cell back. "Detective?" Orozco let his grip linger on Brandon's a moment as they transferred the phone between them. A fatherly, brotherly gesture and Brandon damn near lost it with that. "Is there anyone else you want me to call?"

That second, that question, thrust Brandon all the way back to being ten. He'd sat on the porch of his home in Grover Beach staring out at the surf, with some uniformed cop who'd finally responded. Brandon's mom, Shayna, who his daughter was named after...Brandon had found her on the floor. He knew she'd been sick. Really sick, in the hospital a lot. But, this time, he shook her and she just wouldn't wake up. The cop, who probably hadn't been twice Brandon's age, settled on the step next to him, picked at his own hands and mumbled, *Is there someone I should call?*

The same answer bubbled up from the past. "Edith. She'll tell my dad."

CHAPTER 10

"Why are you talking to me and not out there finding Shayna?" Nick slumped in the hard metal chair in a room barely big enough for him, the detective and the small table. Each of them occupied the three corners of the room not taken up by the large metal door. Real life never equaled the glamour of TV shows and their producers' ideas about what things should look like.

"We are out there Agent O'Malley." The detective, Decker, if Nick remembered right, rested his left elbow on the table and his head against the wall behind him. "The FBI's been contacted." Orozco had introduced Nick to a different detective earlier, said she'd be doing the interview. "We've had dogs in the neighborhood. Going door to door and asking questions." Then Decker showed up and mumbled something about a murder at a liquor store and he was filling in. "But we have to talk to everyone about what happened." Decker huffed and ran his other hand across his thick face. "The best time to do that is right now, while everything is fresh in your mind. You can't go back to your house right now, so we might as well get this over, right?"

"I guess." They'd been at this for a good hour or more. "Orozco's not putting Brandon through this, is he?" Being shut up inside a tiny, gray windowless room with a large, humorless detective wore Nick down, frustrated him, and Shayna wasn't even his kid. He could imagine how the whole situation was tearing Brandon apart.

"Why do you ask?"

Nick's stomach rumbled and he ignored it. "Because he's freaked out." He and Brandon had been on the go since the police showed up at his house hours ago. "This is hell on him." The most he'd eaten since breakfast was a pack of stale peanuts out of the vending machine.

"I'm sure the detective understands why we have to go through this." Decker flipped back through the notes he'd been jotting on a legal pad. "So, you left Shayna at your friend Miri's house and you and Detective Carr went to your home. What did you do next?"

They'd been over this ground fifty times at least. "We, Brandon and I, spent some time together." Brandon told Nick to be honest with the police. Still, Nick didn't know Decker and it wasn't his place to tell him about Brandon. "A couple of hours." Brandon was out now, sort of, but not in big public way.

Another huff. "Doing what?"

"What do you care?" Nick added his own frustrated sigh.

"Just answer the questions," Decker snapped at him, "it'll make it easier. Or is it that you had something to do with this? That why you keep avoiding this question? A single guy. Cute little girl in the house. Maybe you did something you don't want your friend to know about and she was going to tell daddy."

"That's disgusting!" Nick almost gagged on the statement. The only thing sicker than what happened to Shayna was the detective's insinuation. "I'd never do anything like that to anybody."

"You've got a history of violence. Some guy named Jake Ralin made a complaint that you totaled his car during a fight." The detective sneered. "You were a suspect in a murder investigation of another GCB agent. That one's never been formally cleared."

"Mike Ducmagian. He'd left the GCB by the time the Mexican Mafia killed him." Nick had nothing to do with Mike's death other than he held the only piece of evidence linking that agent to a massive money-laundering scheme. "And I was cleared…you know since they tried to kill me too. The whole being kidnapped, tied up and having to jump out of a moving vehicle to escape." The other incident, well Decker nailed him on that. He had totaled Jake's Miata: intentionally and with inordinate amounts of satisfaction. "Jake never pressed charges." Especially, not after Orozco had a little talk with Jake about the sexual assault on Nick that happened before the fight.

"Yeah real convenient how you managed to get a victim to

recant like that."

"I didn't have anything to do with him dropping the matter." Nick wanted to tell Decker to go discuss the issue with Orozco, but that might get the other detective in trouble.

"They pulled all sorts of crap out of your house." Decker leaned across the table and glared. "Ropes. Whips. You're a real pervert."

Orozco said that information would be kept down—need to know only. "That has nothing to do with Shayna!" Now here this asshole twisted everything. Had he even talked with Orozco? "I was with her dad when someone took her!"

"That's what you say. The evidence, what's that going to say?" Decker pounded the legal pad with his index and middle finger. "We going to find her DNA and shit on your bed? Or yours on hers?"

"You're fucking sick!" Nick spat. "I would never hurt her like that!"

Decker came up out of his chair and leaned over the table. Nick smelled onions and cheap cologne. "Yeah that's why you have rope and handcuffs in your bedroom."

"No!"

"Like to hurt little girls?"

Nick snapped. "You know what I use that crap for?" Brandon didn't need this idiot searching in the wrong dark corners. The clock was ticking and they needed to find Shayna, not pry into his and Brandon's lives. "I had Brandon tied up to the bolts in my wall while I was fucking his brains out." Nick managed to get right back in the detective's face. "Then I sucked him off. Took a shower afterwards to get the shit off my dick. That pretty much ate up the whole time between us leaving Shayna at Miri's and then realizing she was gone." Rocking back in the chair, Nick glared. "That account for my time enough?" He'd apologize to Brandon later for laying it out like this. "And by the way, if you need proof, test the sheets. You'll find both of us on there...you know, DNA and shit."

The rest of the interview—interrogation—whatever it was went smoother after that. Mostly, Nick sensed, because Decker couldn't seem to find space far enough away from him in that cramped little room. Nick left the interview rubbing his temples with the butt of his palms. Somewhere along the line he'd picked up a bit of a headache.

Brandon sat across the hall on a bench, near the corner where various corridors intersected. His whole body sagged, arms resting across his knees and hands dangling between them. When he saw Nick, he stood up and shoved his hands in his pockets. "Hey, how'd it go?"

"Not so good." Nick shrugged and looked off to where Decker had disappeared down one of the halls. Finally, he turned his attention back to Brandon. "I guess. I, ah…well there's a Vegas cop who knows I tie you up…sorry." He tried to smile and couldn't even dredge up the energy. "I got pissed. He was being, disgusting, you know?" Nick didn't ever want Brandon to know what that ass had insinuated. "The shit he was saying."

Brandon, looking tired and resigned, shook his head. "Don't worry about it. Nothing matters." Even his voice seemed sucked of will. "Finding Shayna, that's all that matters." Brandon pulled his hand from his pocket and reached up to grip Nick's shoulder.

"I know, baby, I know." Nick stepped the extra inch in…not touching, but being there.

After a bit, Brandon stepped back. "I'm gonna hit the head. I think I drank my weight in coffee. Then we'll go see about a place to crash tonight."

"Okay." Nick nodded. "I've got a couple offers from friends with spare rooms, but I think a hotel might be better." His friends would all want to be helpful, do something, say something and probably end up doing or saying the wrong thing. Someplace reasonably quiet would be best for their frayed nerves.

"Yeah." Brandon almost smiled as he walked off toward the can.

Nick watched him go. The slump in Brandon's shoulders, the way he dragged his feet like it was hell just to move…it tore Nick up. God, he wished he could just turn back time, make everything better. Even though he really wasn't hungry, and even though the crap in the vending machines hardly rated as food, Nick wandered over to peruse the candy and chips. Mostly, it gave him a direction to walk and something to do besides stand and wait.

All he could think about was how much he'd let Brandon down. After all, he'd been the one pushing Brandon to leave Shayna at Miri's. Brandon had to blame it all on him. He fed a buck into the machine and chose a pack of Pop-Tarts. Hopefully, they weren't half as stale as the peanuts. Taking a bite of one, Nick barely tasted it. What was happening to Shayna? He couldn't let his thoughts go there. It was too much, too deep a pit of horror to even think about it. Every time he started to, his stomach rolled. And even, even if Brandon didn't blame Nick… Nick blamed himself. Shit, he'd have to figure out a way to let Miri know he didn't blame her…none of them could have seen this going down. Unthinkable. Totally unthinkable.

As he drifted aimlessly back down the hall, Nick heard Orozco say the name, "Mrs. Lippincott, okay if I call you Dian?" It hung him up in midstride. Brandon's ex-wife, had to be…Nick's gut frosted over. Besides all the awkwardness of he and Brandon and her, what could he possibly say to a woman whose kid had been taken? Especially since he felt so responsible. He licked his lips and slowly moved the few inches to the corner so he could see down the other corridor. Orozco, his face in the mask of sympathy he'd been wearing most of the day spoke to a tiny, trembling woman.

Pretty, delicate features marked by the strain of holding her terror in check. She rubbed at her arms where the long-sleeve T-shirt, not to tight, but flattering, had been rucked up. If she hit five foot even, Nick would have been amazed. Thick, long and from what Nicky could tell curly, light brown hair was caught up in a woven hair net, which she kept tugging at.

That was the woman Brandon had been married to…Shayna's mother.

A hand landed on his shoulder, "Hey." Nick started, stepping all the way into the intersection of halls. When he twisted around, he caught the look in Brandon's face. By his expression, Nick came off as startled as he felt. "What's up?" Nick couldn't think of a thing to say, he was just glancing back down the hall at the woman who'd once slept with his lover, given birth to their child. Brandon's gaze tracked Nick's down the corridor. He swallowed and breathed out, "Dian. Oh, shit."

Dian looked up and must have seen them. One shaking hand came up to cover her mouth. She almost screamed, "Brandon!" through her fingers.

"Oh, fuck," Brandon hissed under his breath, then louder, "Dian." Brandon headed down the hall and Nick followed.

"How could you?" She shook, screaming through her hands clamped across her mouth and her eyes scrunched shut. "You lost my baby! You're a cop, a stupid cop, how could you lose my little girl?"

"Dian…" Tentative, Brandon reached out and tried to touch her arm.

She swatted his arm away. "I trusted you not to screw this up!" Then with the open palm of her hand she slammed his chest. "I don't know why." Her other hand balled into a fist so tight her fingers went white. "You've screwed up everything else in your life!" Each word was punctuated by a blow on his shoulder or chest. Brandon attempted to catch her flailing arms. "You screwed up our marriage. Maybe I thought, you know since she's YOUR DAUGHTER, you might be able to handle this!"

"Okay, whoa, folks." Orozco stepped in, pushing Brandon back with his frame and grabbing Dian's shoulders.

"Why didn't she have her cell phone?" Dian almost collapsed into Orozco's body. "You ever charge it?" The strident tones mixed with sobs. "Maybe she could have called someone, anyone. How could you let her walk in a strange neighborhood?"

"I thought'd be okay." Brandon's emotions seemed only slightly more in check. "She was with Miri's kids. It's not like I threw her out of the house and told her to walk to the park or something."

"Why did you leave her with this Miri person?" Dian pushed Orozco away. "Who is she?" Nick could see the tears welling up. "How do you know her?"

Brandon half turned toward Nick. "She's Nicky's best friend." Then he held his hands open like he presented her with the explanation. "Look, Princess was having fun playing video games with Miri's kids. It's only a couple blocks away from Nicky's house. It should have been okay."

"But it's not okay," Dian's voice cracked. "She's gone." She advanced on Brandon, this time balling her long skirt into her fists, her knuckles going white around the fabric. "Why didn't you stay there with her? Why did you leave? What were you doing while someone was taking my baby?"

"We were just at Nicky's." Nick could tell, from Brandon's voice, he didn't buy the excuse any better than Dian. "We weren't doing anything, just hanging out with my best friend."

"How could you? Just how could you? You're a cop you should know better."

clickjacked.blogroads.net-Private Post, Dec. 29, 9:05pm

Why is there so much noise? All over the TV. You can't change the channel without running into more noise. At least it's out with the others now so that noise is gone. But people need to stop talking about it. Just everyone be quiet so what needs to be done can happen.

CHAPTER 11

Settling down heavily on the edge of the bed, Brandon flipped on the TV. He needed the noise to fill the black emptiness in his head. Everything jangled. It was like his thoughts were puffs of smoke and each time he reached for one it just dissipated under his touch. They were there. He could sense them. He just couldn't mesh together anything coherent.

Not that he really wanted to. Brandon fished the last cigarette out of his pack, lit it, inhaled. Haunted, dark memories of every missing kid case he'd ever worked skulked about his brain. Parents sinking into absolute hell as any hope slipped farther and farther out of the range of possibility. The brutality visited on small bodies and buried by police jargon in reports so that family never quite got the full gut blow.

Sirens wailed outside and the ever-present glow of neon seeped through the blinds. The motel equaled about one step, maybe two, over total flophouse. They could have gone onto the strip and found something decent…but this dive was close to both the station and Nicky's place. Orozco mentioned they hadn't popped anyone for narcotics, prostitution or assault on the premises in a good thirty days. For Brandon, it worked.

Orozco promised to shelve Dian somewhere more upscale for the moment and leave a uniform with her for the time being. The department was also sending over a Trauma Intervention Program volunteer to stay with Dian overnight and help her out. Tomorrow, sometime, her husband Frank would hit Vegas from the east coast—he caught the best flight he could, given winter weather and timing. Hopefully, wherever Dian was had room service, 'cause he'd hate for her to be out on a burger and smokes run like Nicky was. If her nerves jangled like his, however, she wouldn't want to eat anyway. He'd only given into the suggestion because he knew Nicky would keep on him until he did. Now he just needed distraction from his own dark thoughts until Nicky came back.

Of course, when Brandon channel surfed, what he landed on was the Eleven O'clock News. Even if he knew he shouldn't, Brandon couldn't tear himself away from watching. He took a deep drag of nicotine and studied the female host. "Tonight, our top story," vaguely Hispanic heritage, but all bright TV teeth, she intoned in a downplayed dramatic dirge, "police have issued an Amber Alert for missing Shayna Carr." The newscaster's face went tight in scripted sympathy. "Shayna and her father, Brandon Carr, were visiting a friend in Las Vegas when she was apparently abducted while walking home and becoming separated from a group of children. Police have released this photo of nine-year-old Shayna." The picture Nicky'd given Orozco appeared in the top left corner of the screen. His daughter's smile accused him of abandoning her from the TV, raking little fingers across the inside of his chest. "Reporter Jacob Rains joins us live from the search for missing Shayna." The view split from the newsroom to a street side view of Nicky's place. "Jacob do they have any idea what happened to Shayna?"

"Rita," as he spoke, Jacob's local bled over so the full view of Nicky's dark street spread behind him, "at this point the police have no idea what happened to Shayna, but they say they have every reason to believe she was taken by someone." He motioned behind his camera position to where officers could be seen wrapping up the search of Nicky's house. "Although her parents are divorced, the police say Shayna's kidnapping has all the markings of a stranger abduction not a custodial dispute." Brandon, after nine years on the force, knew this was the tail end of it. A uniform by the door and no parade of technical personnel, the major work had been done.

"As you can see police are still in the residential neighborhood off Desert Inn Road conducting a search and doing everything that they can to find her." The camera cut back to a close up of the on-scene reporter. "Of course, one of the twists in this case is that Shayna's father, Brandon Carr, is a Riverside, California police detective. Police are investigating whether this abduction may have been motivated by revenge against her father."

The broadcast cycled to an earlier clip of Orozco, late winter sun casting heavy shadows across a worried, lined face, with the preliminary news briefing. "We take every disappearance and abduction seriously. Although Detective Carr is not a member of our force, he is a police officer, and we take this one personal. We are looking at every lead possible and we will find Shayna."

Again the scene changed: he and Dian at the station. Together, but not, they stood next to each other. "I don't care who you are, just let my baby go." Dian seemed so drained as she pleaded, "Please give Shayna back to me, she's only nine. Shayna, Mommy loves you, Daddy loves you. We all love you and we're looking for you."

Brandon's own two-second sound bite clawed his gut again. He watched like it was some other person, some other guy with dyed black hair, blue eyes and the tats and piercings that rubbed his hands over his skull. "She's my daughter, I want her back." That other Brandon huffed, "What else needs to be said?"

"Although police have not released all the information surrounding Shayna's disappearance, they do say that it appears that Shayna may have been taken from the street in front of the house of her father's friend, Nicholas O'Malley, an agent for the Nevada Gaming Control Board. It's estimated that the abduction occurred at a little after noon. Police have interviewed family members and are looking at registered sex offenders in the area. Jacob Rains for Channel Five News."

He signed off and the broadcast cut back to the studio shot. "I can tell you Jacob a lot of people are praying for Shayna and that they find her soon." The female anchor's face faded under a blue screen with Shayna's picture and stats. "Now take another look at this picture. If you have seen Shayna at any time today, or anything suspicious in the area around El Camino Real and Antigua, please contact the Las Vegas Metro Police."

As the anchor moved onto other news, Brandon's phone rang. Brandon grabbed it off the nightstand and looked at the number. Then he put it back without answering. Half the detectives he worked with had called—shit was already filtering back to them. The only ones he'd bothered to answer were his sergeant and his partner Jeff Weaver. Vegas Metro'd called them up sometime during the day. Weaver was going to cull through all their old cases and see if anyone looked good for this crime…especially some of the *Khát Máu* gangbangers they'd put away that summer. Good old fashion gang payback; you bust our lucrative prostitution and gray-market computer rings and we'll take something of yours away in return.

If that was what happened—God the idea alone twisted his gut. The best case scenario was if they killed her quick. Of course, the alternatives were just as bad. Every scenario was too horrible to think about.

The sound of the key card in the lock interrupted the downward spiral of Brandon's thoughts. Brandon hit the button killing the TV. Nicky pushed the door open with his shoulder and edged through carrying a plastic bag. "Hey." Nicky attempted a smile as he set the bag on the long dresser next to the TV. "Got sandwiches." Pulling two unappetizing hunks of shrink-wrapped food out of the bag, Nicky asked, "You want ham or roast beef?" He held both out.

"Save 'em." Neither looked vaguely edible. "I'll eat later." Brandon figured he wouldn't, but he didn't want to get into it with Nicky. After he ground out the butt of his cigarette, he held out his hand. "Toss me a pack of smokes." While Nicky dug it out, Brandon glanced at the clock. He sighed long and hard. "Should be getting a call soon."

Nicky tossed the pack on the bed next to Brandon. Then he unwrapped one of the sandwiches and took a bite. After chewing a moment, Nicky's face went sour and he folded the plastic back over the food and dropped it the bag. "About what?"

"Watched the news," Brandon opened up the pack and pulled a cigarette out with his teeth. As he fished out his lighter, he mumbled around the smoke, "Looks like they're about done at your place. They'll probably release the scene soon." He lit it and took a drag.

"You shouldn't be watching the news." Nicky wandered over to the bed and sat down next to him. "Just make you relive it." Then Nicky leaned over and grabbed the pack of cigarettes from where Brandon dropped them on the covers.

"I'm reliving it up here," Brandon tapped his temple with his middle finger, "since it happened." As Nicky put the cigarette to his lips, Brandon flipped open his Zippo and lit it for him. "Seeing it on the boob-tube doesn't change that. At least I know the word's getting out. It's the only way we'll catch the bastard."

"Somebody saw something." Nicky rubbed Brandon's thigh. "We'll get her back. You'll see."

All Brandon could do was shrug. "Yeah." Obviously, Nicky was trying to stay positive, but he just didn't understand the true odds. Maybe seven or eight percent of abducted kids were taken by people the child didn't know and most of those, their abductors abused them and then let them go within an hour. Shayna, she fell into that horrible one percent. Those were the kids who never came home...alive. If they were lucky, if the police caught a break, they'd be able to punish the person who took her. A lot of times, the police didn't catch that kind of break.

Nicky's cell phone rang and startled Brandon out of his thoughts. He palmed his face. "I bet that's Metro."

Dragging the phone out of the holster, Nicky tapped the talk icon. "Hello." He paused for a moment then added, "This is Nick." A longer pause, while Nicky nodded his head as if listening to a string of instructions. Finally, he responded, "Okay, we'll be there in a bit." Nicky slipped the phone back on his hip. "You were right. They say a detective will meet us there and release the scene." He turned to Brandon and chewed his lip. "We could just stay here tonight, sleep and get the key back in the morning."

Brandon stood. He didn't want to stay at the hotel. Where he was wouldn't change the facts, but at least he wouldn't feel hemmed into a twelve by twenty box. "I'm not going to sleep anytime soon." At Nicky's he could find someplace to be alone. "Let's go back to your place."

"Okay." Nicky crushed out his cigarette. "Let's blow this taco stand then."

It took longer to check out then it did to drive back to Nicky's place. A chill slid down Brandon's back as they turned onto Nicky's street. It was the last place where he could say for certain that Shayna was alive. Beyond that nothing seemed certain except that she was gone. Brandon parked the van at the rear of the drive. Then he just sat for a bit, waiting as Nicky jumped out and walked over to a plainclothes officer who came around from the front of the house. There were probably a few uniforms lurking around as well.

As much as he hadn't wanted to hang out at the hotel, Brandon didn't really want to go inside either. Shayna's stuff still sat in Nicky's office. He'd given some clothes to the cops for the tracking dogs and her toothbrush so they could generate DNA exemplars. But all those stuffed animals they'd won were still cluttering up Nicky's living room. Her sleeping bag still rested on the cot. Brandon wasn't sure he could even look at those things and not lose it.

Brandon looked over when Nicky tapped the driver's window. He took two deep breaths and then got out of the car. Sooner or later he'd have to face things. It might as well be sooner. They didn't talk much as they walked through the backyard and up the rear steps.

Nicky opened the back door and Brandon walked through the small laundry room, into the kitchen and flipped on the light. The blue-green tile of Nicky's countertops was streaked with swaths of black powder. Every drawer and cabinet was opened. More powder coated the handles and knobs. All the cleaners and crap from under the sink sat in a jumbled heap in the middle of the kitchen.

"Holy shit," Nicky hissed as he came in behind Brandon. "My kitchen. It's a disaster."

Who the fuck cared what happened to his kitchen? Shayna was gone. Brandon blew out a breath, reminding himself that people, people like Nicky, focused on the small shit when the big shit was too much to process. He shrugged and muttered, "I've seen worse."

"Worse?"

"Yeah," Brandon dredged up a snort, "they didn't take chunks of the wall or floor."

Nicky stepped over to the counter and brushed his hand through a black streak. "What's all the dust shit?"

Brandon wandered over to the fridge. After snagging a beer, he answered, "Fingerprint powders." Too bad there was only three left in the six-pack. Maybe if Brandon got really plastered he'd pass out and not think for a while. Brandon turned around as the fridge door swung shut and propped his butt against the counter.

Nicky stood there, one hand mussing up his hair the other on his hip. He looked up at Brandon like he searched for someone to make things right. "Who's going to clean this shit up?"

Who the fuck do you think? He glared at Nicky for a bit. "You are." Brandon twisted the cap off and tossed it in the sink. "Or you can find someone in the phone book tomorrow." He took a swig. "There are companies that do it for about two-hundred an hour."

"I got to clean this up." Nicky looked as overwhelmed as Brandon felt.

Not wanting to deal with Nicky and cleaning and really anything, Brandon tried for a little reasonable thought, "Why don't you wait until tomorrow?" Nicky just stared at him. Brandon stared back. Then he gave up. If he gave Nicky something to do, maybe he'd leave Brandon alone and let him be. "Never mind." Brandon pushed away from the counter. "I'll go get the auto cleaner from your garage."

"What?"

Brandon used the beer bottle as a pointer, waving it around the kitchen. "Normal household crap don't work on this shit." As he walked past the pile of cleansers and rags, Brandon bumped a yellow aerosol can with his boot. "Use the spray furniture polish to pull the powder off TVs and electronics." Another huff and another swig, before Brandon added, "Auto detailing cleaner for everything else, except for carpet, then you'll need that foaming bathroom shit." He stopped next to Nicky who alternated between shaking his head and palming his face. Irritating as it was, the fretting was Nicky's way of dealing with the tension. Probably, in light of everything, a more healthy and more productive idea than Brandon's plan to get shit faced. Leaning against Nicky's frame, Brandon drew as much comfort as he could from Nicky. "It's going to be a long night."

CHAPTER 12

Nick shuffled toward the door in a sleep-deprived haze. He'd finally passed out sometime around four just to be woken up too early by someone at the door. The sound of the bell cut like a dull knife across his nerves. If it was someone stumping religion, he was going to be righteously pissed off.

He opened the door and blinked under the onslaught of morning light. An older woman, thin, with brown hair showing some gray stood on his doorstep. An overly large shoulder bag rested at her feet. If it wasn't for the upscale navy suit, expensive coat and chunky gold jewelry, Nick might have guessed she was handing out religious tracts. Nine-ish on a Sunday morning equaled the right time of day, but she added up to the wrong kind of person, at least in his neighborhood. "Yeah?" he growled out. Reporter, maybe, or another detective.

She touched her lip with her right hand and studied him for a moment. "I'm looking for my stepson?" Her voice was rich and confident even in a question.

Nick scratched his chest, up under his ratty T-shirt. Ripped up, stained jeans and bare feet, he'd crashed in the clothes he'd been cleaning in. "Who?" Given how little he'd slept, he probably looked like some crack addict and he didn't much care at that point.

"My stepson," her smile went a little tight, "Brandon."

"Who is it?" Brandon's hoarse voice caught Nick by surprise.

"What?" Nick looked over his shoulder to see Brandon, still in last night's rumpled clothes and with a cigarette hanging from his lips. Too little sleep, too confusing a concept, Nick's brain couldn't process anything coherently. He managed to mumble out, "Your stepmom is here." And he knew he should be more polite, but fathoming the next step fuzzed out into a gray haze.

Brandon came up to lean on the doorframe next to Nick.

After taking a deep drag off the smoke he added, "Hey, Edith." For a bit he smoked and stared at the woman on the porch. Finally, he grumbled, "What the hell are you doing here?"

"What?" Edith reached out and brushed Brandon's cheek with her fingers. "I should leave my husband's son to suffer?" Then she stepped in and hugged him. Brandon held himself stiff until she pulled away. "Your father, once I got a hold of him, well, we both thought I should come and be with you." She bent down and retrieved her bag, then handed it off to Nick. He was so startled that he just took it. "At least until he can get here from overseas. Problem with the Doctors Without Borders program is they tend to plunk you down in inaccessible places." Without being invited, Edith pushed between them and walked into Nick's living room. "We don't think you should be alone, not right now."

Brandon rolled his body so that his back was against the doorjamb. "I'm not alone. Nicky's here." He took another deep drag and then flicked the butt back through the door. "Shit, Edith," with a wave of his hand he made introductions, "this is Nicky. Nicky, my stepmom, Edith."

"Hello, Nicky." She smiled. It was strained. "You both look exhausted. You haven't slept, have you?" The barest hints of purplish skin were visible under her eyes. Makeup might have concealed the stamp of Edith's own exhaustion in her face, but it couldn't hide it.

"No," Brandon acknowledged the obvious. "Not much."

Edith glanced around the living room until she seemed to register the swinging bar-style doors that led into Nick's kitchen. She turned and headed through the small dining area. "Let me fix you something to eat, Brandon." As she walked, she spoke over her shoulder. "You'll at least feel better with food."

"Look," Brandon pushed away from the wall and followed her. "You didn't have to come." Nick dropped the bag on his couch and drifted along behind them into the kitchen. "Not for me."

"All right, Brandon, not for you, but for me. Even if she's not my blood, Shayna's my granddaughter. I love her as much as any of Jacob's or Ben's kids." Edith shrugged out of her jacket, folded it neatly and draped it over the back of a chair. "Let me fix you something to eat. You boys sit down, I'll get started."

Brandon caught another chair with the toe of his boot. Pulling it out from the table, he dropped heavily into the seat. "I don't want to eat, Edith."

"Nonsense." Again, she flashed the strained smile. "You have to eat. Plus, it gives me something to do." She dragged in a deep breath and then looked puzzled. Turning to Nick, she asked, "Why does your house smell like lemons?"

His house didn't smell like lemons…it reeked of them. Nick grabbed another chair and sat down before responding, "Because that can of *Tuff-Stuff* auto cleaner was the only thing that got the fingerprint powder off the walls and counters." Lacing his hands over his head, Nick studied the ceiling for a moment. "That junk was everywhere," he griped to Brandon's stepmom since Brandon made it clear he wasn't going to listen or help. "I made Brandon wipe down the electronics with *Endust*." Lot of good that had done…he basically ended up with streaks of powder instead of dustings of it. "We've been cleaning all night."

"Don't the police do that?" Edith echoed Nick's question from last night. "And why did they fingerprint your house?"

"No," Brandon growled, "cops aren't paid to clean up. We finish. We go home." Almost angrily he added, "And, it's standard procedure. You have to eliminate the family and those close to the victim as suspects. So they took saliva swabs from both of us, hair samples, our fingerprints and they took Shayna's hairbrush and toothbrush. That way, if they find her, they'll be able to identify her and rule us out from any other trace evidence they find."

"But," Edith's eyes went wide and she stuttered out the rest, "she'll just tell them who she is when they find her."

Brandon stared at his hands for awhile. Finally he huffed

and looked up. "I'm not hungry, Edith." Rocking his chair onto the back legs, Brandon rubbed his face with his hands. "Look, Frank's flight gets in sometime around nine or so." Nick vaguely remembered Brandon mentioning a phone call last night from Dian and something about airlines. "He and Dian say they want to come here, check in, you know." He glanced over at Nick. "Nicky, why don't you try and get some sleep?"

Nick leaned over the table and ran his knuckles along Brandon's arm. "You should, too." Chain-smoking, drinking and pacing…every time Nick encountered Brandon last night he was engaged in all three. He'd put Brandon to dusting just to give him something constructive to do with his agitation. Hadn't worked at all.

"Later." Brandon pulled another cigarette from the crumpled pack. After lighting it and inhaling, he grumbled, "Edith, how did you get here?"

"The nice detective gave me the address." Edith busied herself in Nick's fridge. Nick could have told her what she'd find, but he didn't have the energy to comment. She rushed through her words like she needed the distraction, "I knew you'd need me, but you'd never *admit* you needed me." Fussing with moving eggs and turkey bacon from refrigerator to counter, Edith kept up the patter. "I drove to San Luis Obispo last night and flew in this morning first thing. Then I took a cab." She paused and turned. "I, ah, had the home phone forwarded to my cell phone." It was as if she sought confirmation from Brandon that she'd done the right thing. "You know, in case Shayna calls."

Brandon stood and took another drag of nicotine. "Yeah," he shrugged and snorted, "in case she calls you, Edith." It was as if he didn't believe there'd ever be a call.

"What do you mean by that?" Edith must have caught the tone, too.

He shoved one hand in his pocket stowing the lighter he hadn't put away. "By what?"

Massaging one hand with the other, she stared at him. "The

way you said it, Brandon." Nick could almost feel her worry in his body. It probably echoed similar to his own...with a higher level of angst. Not that Nick wasn't terrified, but Shayna wasn't his daughter or granddaughter; that personal connection to make it sting even worse.

"It's nothing." Brandon shook his head. "I'm just tired." Nick knew Brandon well enough to know that was a bullshit excuse.

Edith seemed to buy it. She turned back to the counter and pulled the bread from the box. "I'll make you boys some breakfast. You should eat."

"Whatever." Brandon shrugged again and headed toward the back door. "Knock yourself out, Edith. Going for a walk, I need some air."

Nick just stared after him. Yes, he was anxious and rightly so, but being rude to his stepmother wasn't cool. She had to be as terrified—no more so—than Brandon. Brandon was a cop. He knew what the police were doing behind the scenes. The rest of them, his family, were left to guess. "Ah," he knew he ought to say something to Edith, he just couldn't quite put his finger on what. "It's been a long night for everyone." It was a lame excuse, but the best one he managed to dredge up.

"It has," Edith agreed. She paused and looked over her shoulder. "Why don't you let me keep busy and make you some breakfast? Go lie down on the couch. You both look like death warmed over."

Edith didn't look all that much better. "Are you sure?" If she got much sleep last night herself, Nick would be surprised.

"Please." She stifled the hint of a sob. "It gives me something to do. Go, it'll be a few minutes."

"Okay," he conceded. While Nick wasn't too keen on having a strange woman, even if she was Brandon's stepmom, messing around his kitchen he didn't have a clue what to say to her. "I'll go watch some TV or something."

She just nodded as he walked out. Nick stumbled over to the couch and sat down. He felt like he was stuck in some daytime movie: a really bad one with overwrought drama and unbelievable story lines. Lying back, Nick tried to think the horror away. Maybe, if he closed his eyes and clicked his heels he'd be back in Kansas or at least a Vegas where little girls weren't kidnapped off streets. Being a *friend of Dorothy* ought to count for something after all. He'd never felt so drained. It wasn't just lack of sleep. He'd hit the bottom of the emotional well about dinnertime last night. Right now, he was running on fumes. Nick covered his eyes with his arm and yawned hard.

The rattle of the front door snapped him awake. Nick blinked. His neck and back felt stiff. The ache in his bad shoulder stung his nerves. Holy crap he'd actually fallen asleep on the sofa. He yawned and palmed his face.

"Sorry." Edith standing at the arm of the couch came into focus. "I didn't mean to wake you up," she whispered.

Nick sat up. "That's okay." Another yawn caught him off guard. Then he asked, "Where's Brandon?"

"He's in your bedroom." Edith moved around to sit down next to him. "Went in there to watch TV so he wouldn't wake you up." She patted his thigh. "I went in to check on him and he's out." For a few moments they sat together silently sharing mutual pain. Well, it was more hers than his, but Nick was caught up in the situation as much as anyone. Then she patted him again and stood. "Let me get you your eggs. You both fell asleep before I was finished." She kept talking as she walked. Nick pushed himself off the couch and followed. "Frank called me, on my cell. He's still stuck back east at that stupid company meeting—snowstorm."

He walked into his kitchen to find his old table set with plates, glasses and proper silverware. Well, if it helped Edith deal with the anxiety…more power to her. He sat down at one of the places and listened to her ramble.

"The police took Dian over to a news station for an interview, then they're going to bring her around later. The police came by here, while I was outside getting some air, but they said not to wake Brandon. They just wanted to let us know they set up a command center about a mile from here at a community center." She grabbed a potholder and pulled a covered plate out of the oven. "I didn't think to ask before I made them, is scrambled okay? If not I can make more."

"Yeah, that's fine." Since he hadn't checked the clock, Nick had no idea how long the food sat waiting. Didn't really matter, he doubted he'd taste it anyway. "The police have any news?"

"No," her voice almost cracked on that one word, "but I've got directions to the command center the police set up." She walked over. As she dished out a serving she mumbled, "When Brandon wakes up, they said to come over. They want to hold another press conference around one or so."

He lifted a forkful to his mouth. "Maybe they'll have news then." Nick shoved the eggs in and tried to eat.

Edith sighed. "Let's hope."

clickjacked.blogroads.net- Private Post, Dec. 30 10:05am

Crazy. Everything was going crazy. Didn't think it through, not at all. Thinking and not thinking. No sleep at all. All the howling and screaming. Couldn't sleep with that, nobody could.

Now there was too much attention. All the TVs talked about it. Too messed up, because didn't think it through. It almost ruined the whole plan. Regroup, it was time to regroup and try and salvage the plan. Make things happen like they were supposed to happen.

TVs talked about it, but talked about nothing. Same words over and over. There had to be more to know. Need to find out more about it.

CHAPTER 13

Nick pulled the minivan into the lot off McLeod drive. It took a bit of finesse to find a space between the crowds gathered for Sunday afternoon activities at the community center and the news vans setting up for the press conference. The spot the van occupied earlier that afternoon had been lost when he headed back out after dropping Brandon and Edith off. He'd gone in and come back out with a list: aspirin for Dian's headache, a carton of smokes for Brandon and coffee for them all. Nick clambered out of the van, tucking one pack of cigarettes into his jacket pocket and balancing a cardboard drink holder with four cups of coffee and small bottle of pain relievers sandwiched in the middle. At least being a gofer gave him something to do.

Walking across the lot, he caught sight of Edith huddled into her long coat on the lip of a brown concrete planter in front of the building. So far they'd both managed to avoid the scrutiny of the press. Nick figured his anonymity came from not being family…just a friend, another faceless guy in the background offering support. Edith, well, she probably ought to enjoy it while she could since, after this press conference, everyone would know she was Shayna's grandmother.

Nick almost made it over to Edith when a high pitched, but still male, "Oh my God, Nick," cut across the parking lot. Nick stopped and looked toward where the voice came from. "Baby, we heard and we came." A too thin blond with perfectly spiked hair waved at Nick as he hurried over. "Steve and Jayce, Miri told them what happened and they spread the word. A bunch of people are headed over and they'll do whatever you need." A powder blue T-shirt set off his eyes. Matt's bleach stained jeans and a pea coat with a wool scarf conceded the cold of a Vegas winter day. "Just tell us and we're there. Give us posters and we'll paper the Fruit Loop for you." His flip-flops conceded nothing.

Behind him, a slightly more muscular and older brunette

wearing a tattoo T-shirt and low rise jeans kept his hands shoved into the pockets of a designer jacket. "Hey, Nick." He sauntered up behind Matt. "Sucks what happened." Frederic, Matt's dating flavor de jour, smiled his sympathy as Matt pulled Nick into a quick hug. It took a bit of juggling for Nick to not wind up with hot coffee all over his clothes.

After releasing Nick, Matt leaned back against Frederic and covered his mouth with his fingers. "I talked to my boss at the bookstore at the mall." He spoke and played with his lower lip at the same time. "He says they'll throw flyers in all the bags, got a few other of the bars and such that are gonna put it up on their websites." Matt prattled on as though the world centered on him. "I figure the more you get that face out there the more likely someone who saw something will see it. 'Cause, you know, a lot of them are nearby here." Matt circled his hand in the air as though reminding them all that Nick lived in close proximity to the cluster of gay bars off the strip. "I've been working it for you." Then he reached out and brushed Nick's shoulder with his hand. "You just hang tight. We're all here for you. 'Kay, baby?"

"Yeah, thanks guys." Nick knew Matt from the leather scene. Cute little sub, but way too into poppers and harder recreational substances for Nick's tastes. "Appreciate the effort." His heart seemed to be in the right place most of the time—always the first to pitch in on charity walks or start collections...and the first to remind you of that fact. "Thanks for pitching in."

"Gotta be rough on poor Brandon." Frederic wasn't as familiar. Nick'd met him a few times around, some when Brandon was with him. He always seemed a little standoffish with the both of them...actually just with Nick. Frederic and Brandon seemed to get along the few times they'd run into him. "You two holding up okay?"

Nick shrugged. "As good as we can." That bodily connection never bothered Nick, but something about Frederic's personality just rubbed him wrong.

"Where is he?" Matt pouted and huffed. "We want to tell him we're here for him."

"He's in getting briefed by the police for their press conference." Nick brushed them off with a tense smile. Brandon wasn't up to dealing with an overzealous twink combined with a past hookup. "I'll tell him." Walking backward toward where Edith sat, Nick reiterated, "I promise, I will."

Nick turned to find Edith standing at the lip of the sidewalk. "Your friends?" she asked as he walked up. Then, when he nodded, figuring it was the safest non-committal response, she held out her hands for the coffee. Instead of passing the whole tray, Nick pulled one cup out and handed it over. As she took the cup, Edith innocently asked, "What's the Fruit Loop?" At least it sounded innocent.

Holy crap...how to explain the imaginary boundaries of the gay cruising scene in Vegas without using the words *gay* or *cruising*? Nick stammered a moment before hedging, "A business area with a lot of alternative night clubs and such." One of the reasons he stayed in the house he'd inherited from his Gramps was the ten-dollar-cab-ride-closeness to old-school queer staples like the *Backdoor* and *Freezone* and not too far off from the new Goth/Gay—depending on the night venue on Sahara.

"Oh," blowing over the coffee she paused, then added, "the types of places singles go to meet people?" Edith sipped her coffee for a while. Nick didn't bother to correct the assumption with an answer. Finally, she heaved a sigh and changed the subject. "After this, Dian and I are going to go meet with a rabbi here in Vegas...just to talk. He's getting together some of the ladies from the Jewish Family Services." Staring off for a moment at the traffic, Edith added, "Do you and Brandon want to come?"

He had no clue how to respond to that. "You know, you'd have to ask him." As far as he knew, Brandon wasn't religious. Being marginally Catholic, Nick couldn't fathom why he'd want to talk with a rabbi. "You all are family, after all." Still he tried to be reasonably nice when dealing with Brandon's stepmom. He didn't tell her to *blow it out her ear.*

"Hey, Nick." Another voice, this one female, startled him out of his thoughts.

Nick spun around, again narrowly avoiding drenching himself with coffee. A non -descript woman in too big of a coat stared at him. "Do I…" he started to mumble out a question and then recognition hit. "Jen?" Nick couldn't recall ever interacting with Jen outside the walls of the GCB. "What are you doing here?"

"I saw the news last night." She didn't seem fazed by his stumble. "I kinda recognized your friend on TV…you know 'cause he came by the Board the other day. I saw you all in the reception area. And then I saw you on the TV with him and they mentioned you. So I knew it was your friend." She shuffled her feet. "So I decided to come around to see if you needed help."

"How'd you know where I lived?" As far as Nick knew, she didn't have access to employee address lists.

"Ah, uhm, I didn't really." More shuffling, but this time Jen punctuated it with a small shift of her shoulders. "But the morning news said they were setting up a volunteer center here… so I came."

"Oh," probably everyone he knew in Vegas found out the same way. "Well thanks. I appreciate it." He felt Edith's hand on his arm. When he looked at her, she nodded toward the door of the community center. It was getting about that time. "Look I got to run." He turned to follow Edith into the building. Speaking over his shoulder, he let Jen know where to check in. "If you go in, head right, there's a place where the police are wrangling volunteers."

A meeting room had been pulled into service as the command center. Nick glanced through the open double doors on his way past. A card table already held stacks of flyers. He'd printed them up this morning and had Miri head over to the local copy shop to run them off. Two teenagers from the Police Explorers checked IDs, jotted down names of search volunteers and passed out orange and yellow safety vests.

Since it appeared someone snatched Shayna off the street, the cops decided to beat the bushes in the parks, vacant lots and brush filled arroyos surrounding the area. Any of which would have made a convenient site to leave Shayna. If she was hurt or…well Nick didn't want to think on the other possibility…the searchers would find her. He'd gotten that bit of information before taking off earlier.

The volunteers clustered in knots around uniformed officers and off-duty fire personnel who would act as coordinators for the searches. They listened to instructions on how to look and what to keep their eyes open for. Nick vaguely recognized a few people, but decided against saying anything to them. Most of these people Nick had never even met, yet here they were to help. It just floored him.

Nick pushed through the gaggle of reporters and their attendant equipment clogging the hall. They all jockeyed for position as the cops directed them where to set up in the small auditorium they'd opened up for the press conference. Nobody paid him or Edith much attention, other than to grumble about them getting in their way. Once they made it past the obstacle course of audio/visual equipment, they headed over to the lone uniformed cop barring the backstage door. After verifying who they were, she let them through.

For privacy and a little quiet, the cops stashed Brandon and Dian in the small dressing rooms. Edith turned around when they'd almost made the doors. "Why don't you give me the things for Dian?" She shook her head and offered a tight smile. "It wasn't going too well, having them both in the same room. So Brandon's on the men's side, Dian the woman's." As Nick handed over the cardboard tray, Edith added, "I shuttled between them for a while…and then Brandon needed a cigarette and Dian the ladies' room so I took the opportunity for a little air."

"Yeah," Nick took the coffee for Brandon and himself. "I don't think Dian would be comfortable with me." He knew he wouldn't be at all comfortable with Brandon's ex-wife at this point. Beyond the simple awkwardness of the ex-wife issue, Nick harbored a gnawing guilt in his gut. He wished he hadn't pressed Brandon into leaving Shayna. Seriously, what did he really know about kids and how to take care of them? The whole thing was a nightmare. If there were any way to turn back time and fix it…

well Nick would give damn near anything to be able to do so.

He pushed into a room of counters, cabinets, and linoleum flooring. Except for an overabundance of light bulbs and smaller proportions, it looked identical to most of the public spaces in the community center. Brandon sprawled on a couch that had seen better days, one arm draped over his eyes, his right boot on the floor. It ate Nick up inside to see Brandon so devastated.

Using his knee, Nick bumped Brandon's other foot. "Got coffee and more smokes."

Brandon rolled his arm up to peer at Nick. "Thanks," he mumbled. "Just set it on the counter."

"Okay." Nick set the cups down and then grabbed one of the plastic chairs and dragged it over to sit next to Brandon. "It's crazy out there." He didn't know why he brought it up. Maybe just so they wouldn't have to sit in silence and he wouldn't have to think about what happened.

Brandon shifted and rubbed his temples with one hand. "It's crazy in here."

Yeah, being with his ex-wife, the cops, and public liaison officers who swarmed around before Nick left, would be crazy. When Brandon didn't jump in with anything else, Nick tried for a different line of conversation. "So what do the police know?"

"About the same shit they knew yesterday afternoon." Brandon sat up and, leaning forward, rested his elbows on his knees. Every move seemed almost more than he could manage. "Several people reported seeing a blue minivan they didn't recognize in the area these past few days."

The obvious occurred to Nick. "You have a blue minivan." And they'd been driving it around.

Brandon snorted. "Yeah."

"So they have no real leads." He'd hoped, they'd all hoped Nick guessed, for some positive news. People reporting sightings of Brandon's own vehicle was almost worse than no leads. It meant the police would be chasing smoke.

"Nope." Brandon leaned back. Frustration came out in restlessness—obvious in how Brandon's left leg jiggled, how he couldn't stay in one spot for long. "Frank called." Brandon stared at the ceiling. "They're going to open up the airports. If everything goes okay he'll get in around midnight or so. He has a cousin, or something, that lives in Green Valley. He'll go there. Dian wants to stay at your place tonight."

Why the hell would Dian want to be anywhere near them? "Why?" To say that her attitude when forced to be around them, like the press conferences and such, was cold did not even begin to equal the ice in her demeanor. "She hates us right now."

Another humorless snort of laugher echoed Nick's sentiments. Brandon explained, "Because the crisis volunteer that's been with her, she has her own life to get back to, so Dian would be alone most of the night. At your place Edith is there and I guess I am, too. People she knows. Plus it's the last place Shayna really was."

"She blames you!" She pretty much blamed Brandon and by association Nick for her present hell. "Why would she want to be in a house with you...in my house with you?"

"Better the devil you know," Brandon shrugged, "than being alone in a hotel room, I guess."

Christ, Nick's house was barely big enough for one person, let alone four. He snapped, "So when are Dian's parents coming so I can fit more people in my house?"

"I doubt they will." Brandon's attitude didn't change from exhausted and beaten down. He just mumbled out, "Dian's mom has advanced RA—rheumatoid arthritis. She can't travel well. With her it's not just pain and the joint stuff, but it hit her organs, too. And Dian's dad wouldn't leave her mom alone like that."

"I'm sorry." Nick wished like hell he could take back those last words. Everyone was frustrated, himself included. "I mean, but, holy crap." Frayed nerves and lack of sleep kept them all on edge. "I'm just really tired. I know you are, too."

"Look," Brandon shifted again, one arm across the back of the couch, the other hand on his thigh. "Tonight give Edith and

Dian your bed. I'll sleep on the couch, you take the cot." He reached out with his foot and bumped the toe of Nick's boot with his own. "I'm sorry, Nicky."

"No, I'm sorry." Nick stared at his hands. They shook just a little. "I shouldn't be pissy." Really, he didn't mean those things. He just wanted to be able to hold Brandon, let him know he was there for him. But Nick couldn't, not while Brandon's family was there...because they didn't know about Brandon and about them. And that hurt, not being able to be there for Brandon. "It's a crisis. We'll get through it." If he said it enough, Nick figured they'd all start believing that. "We will. Just, nothing in my life ever prepared me to deal with something like this." Nick looked up as he ran his hand over his face. "I'm not you, after all."

Brandon huffed. "What do you mean you're not me?"

Nick stated the obvious. "You're a cop." This kind of thing, this was what cops dealt with day in and day out. "You're trained to handle this shit, you know."

"No, I don't know," Brandon snarled. The first real crack in that hard shell *I got it covered* façade Brandon maintained appeared. "I'm not trained to deal with this, Nicky." Running his hands through his hair, Brandon stood and began to pace the confines of the tiny room. "I'm trained to deal with other people's problems, not mine." The tension and the volume of his voice ratcheted up with each word. "Not like this! Some asshole took *my kid!*" He punctuated the statement by slamming his fist against the wall. "I haven't been much of a dad, but goddamn it she's my flesh and blood. My little girl. I swear, if I get to whoever did it before the Vegas cops do they will *never* find the fucking body! I will rip them to pieces. Make them suffer."

"Okay, okay." Nick scrambled out of his seat and grabbed Brandon's shoulders. "Just take a deep breath, all right?" He said it as much for his own benefit as Brandon's. "Calm down."

"I don't want to be calm." Brandon's body vibrated under Nick's grip. He wrapped his hands around Nick's forearms and leaned in slightly. "I want to hurt somebody!"

"Just chill." Nick pulled him in close. Fuck if anyone saw… how could they interpret it beyond just a friend comforting a friend anyway? Brandon buried his head against Nick's shoulder. "You can't be all upset like this in front of the press…I mean, upset's fine…punching walls not so fine on camera."

"What the fuck am I going to do, Nicky?" Nick couldn't tell which of them shook more. "I can't take this."

"It'll be okay." Nick tried to keep his tone positive. "I'm right here for you. Take a deep breath," he instructed and, when Brandon complied, added, "Do it again." Then he pulled back a little so he could look in Brandon's eyes. "All right, you gonna maintain?"

"Yeah, I'm good." Brandon looked anything but good. A knock on the door forced them apart…almost instinctually Brandon reacted before Nick really even processed what was going on. Brandon shoved his hands in his pockets and barked out, "Yeah?"

"Brandon. Nicholas," Orozco greeted them as he opened the door and held it. Dian, Edith and another police officer, Rene Escamilla filed in. Escamilla wore the uniform of Vegas Metro: dark green shirt, tan tie and slacks. Nick met her that morning. She'd been assigned as the senior media relations contact for the case. "They're going to let us use the theater for the press conference." Orozco, dressed in his standard suit and tie, pulled the door closed behind him. "Ten minutes, folks, and it will be show time." It'd taken Nick's involvement in a Riverside PD investigation to understand that whether a cop wore a uniform or not had little to do with their rank within a department. Brandon's status as a Police Officer III wasn't mutually exclusive of his Detective I designation. The first related to time on the force, the other indicated a prestigious assignment.

Orozco stepped over and patted Brandon's shoulder with one big paw. After, Edith and Dian settled onto the couch, Orozco continued briefing them, "And just to let you know, we're not going to be saying anything about the locator fob." His voice was somber. "The average person doesn't need to know that she was wearing it. That way, if we find someone who looks good for this, we have something to verify their story with."

"After this, there's probably going to be a lot more influx of people who want to volunteer," Escamilla chimed in. "Anyone who approaches you and offers to help, direct them here."

"Why?" That question came from Dian.

Patiently, like she'd been through this a thousand times, Escamilla explained, "So we can take down address, verify ID and the like."

Dian repeated. "But why?" Nick was as confused as Dian sounded.

"Because it's highly likely that whoever took Shayna wants to know what's going on." The officer spread her hands. "Easiest way to find out is become part of the search."

"Get in early." Brandon sat down heavily in the chair Nick had vacated earlier. "Be a big part of it so that you become a coordinator and can learn what the cops know. They can mess in the investigation, you know, send them off in the wrong direction."

"Unfortunately, it's true." Orozco leaned against the wall. His genteel, mustached face, folded into a mask of sympathy. "Over and over, your major suspects in an abduction were there at the beginning beating the bushes right along with everyone else."

Dian slumped against Edith. "That's disgusting."

Wrapping her arms around Dian, Edith echoed Dian's sentiment. "Why would they do something like that?"

"For a lot of perps this is their big moment of glory." Brandon seemed resigned to the horror of it. All the anger and agitation from moments earlier seemed to have evaporated leaving a worn shell behind. "What they live for. Getting inside the investigation, patting you on the back and holding your hand while you cry… they get to relive their jollies through our pain."

"So you mean we can't even believe in the decency of people?" Dian hissed the question to Brandon. "That they just want to do something good?"

As though he sensed the landmines between Brandon and his ex-wife, Orozco broke in with the answer. "Most of them do." Of course he'd witnessed that last encounter at the police station. "But, yes, you have to keep one eye open at all times."

"Let me also remind you that Shayna's abduction is getting a lot of press." Escamilla tried to throw a positive spin into the otherwise depressing conversation. "That's a good thing. Our best hope to bring her home is someone, somewhere saw something. The more folks hear about it the more likely they are to come forward." As if to focus their attention on her, Escamilla took a deep breath before continuing, "But, this also means you all will be under a lot of scrutiny. I don't want you to worry about it, just be aware." She hit Brandon and Dian with an intense gaze. "There's going to be trash reporters digging into your divorce and all your dirty laundry. You can't change it. Just be ready when it comes up." After letting it sink in, Escamilla checked her watch. "You folks ready?"

Brandon stood and offered his hand to first help Edith and Dian off the couch. "As much as we can be."

Officer Escamilla led them out into a small hall area and then through a door into the black painted expanse of the stage. For a moment the curtains blocked the view of the audience although Nick could hear the restlessness. At the edge of the small sound wall, Orozco pushed the thick drape aside. A row of wire frame chairs sat waiting for them...well the family them. Nick propped himself at the edge of the wall while Dian and Edith settled into the seats. Brandon, his hands shoved into his pockets and his face drawn, stood behind them. Nick wished he could reach out, touch him, hug him.

Escamilla moved to the podium at center stage. Without preamble, she started the news conference. "As you are all aware, yesterday morning between approximately eleven-thirty and noon, Shayna Carr was abducted while walking back to the residence where she was staying with her father and a family friend." To the officer's left a large photo of Shayna was propped on an easel. A blown up version of Shayna's school photo from Dian's wallet… it was far better quality than the one off Nick's phone. "Officers have been conducting an intensive search in the area which, as of yet, has turned up very few leads. We're asking the public to come forward with anything they might have seen."

Glancing at her notes and then back out at the assemble reporters, Escamilla brought the press up to speed. "Vegas Metro is working closely with the Vegas FBI Field office and their Child Abduction Rapid Deployment Team which has offered the assistance of behavioral analysis experts, witness and victims' resources as well as their full cooperation and support in the joint investigative efforts." Escamilla held her hand out to Orozco. "I'm going to turn the conference over to Lead Detective Emanuel Orozco. Both he and I will be available for questions at the end of the briefing."

Orozco took her place at the podium. As he started in on the facts of the case, the ones the police wanted the press to know, Nick's attention drifted across the crowd. At the back of the room a scattering of people who had nothing to do with the press gathered. Among them, Nick sighted a few of his friends from the Goth scene. Jen was there too, but he didn't see Matt or Frederic. For a moment he wished Miri would show, although he knew she wouldn't. She'd already called to apologize. Given the intrusiveness of the media and volatile nature of her current boyfriend in the wake of having their house torn apart, she'd grabbed her kids and headed for her mom's place in Pahrump.

A shift in the people on the stage brought Nick's focus back to the podium. Brandon moved up next to Orozco. After seeming to think a moment, he spoke. "I'd just like to say to whoever took Shayna," Brandon's normally deep voice was ragged from chain-smoking and exhaustion, "I don't know who you are, she's only nine, so if you're watching, let her come home." He paused again and chewed on his bottom lip. "I swear, I will spend every last minute to find her." Nick hoped the threat under his words didn't carry over TV very well. The last thing they needed was for Shayna's abductor to freak out and do something final.

Dian took Brandon's place at the mike. "We're doing everything we can, Shayna, to find you. I don't know if you'll hear this, see this, but just in case, just know how much we all love you." Tears streaked her face. "Lots of people are here for you. Me, your grandparents, Daddy and Brandon." She drew in a ragged sob. "We're doing everything for you, Shayna." At that she turned and almost fell into Edith's arms. Edith was supposed to have said a few words, but with Dian sobbing against her there was no way she could. For a moment Nick wondered what he should do.

"Someone knows what happened to her." Orozco jumped in to fill the vacancy. "Someone saw something." As Edith led Dian off the stage, Orozco ended the more formal part of the briefing. "That person has it within their power. I just ask somebody to come forward and let us know." Brandon edged back to stand between Nick and the podium. When Nick sensed Brandon's attention on him, he gave a small jerk toward the door behind the stage. Like he sensed the question implicit in the gesture, Brandon shook his head in a negative response. Then he folded his arms in front of his chest. Apparently, Brandon wanted to wait and hear the questions the press had and what answers the police would give them. Nick shifted and settled in to wait.

CHAPTER 14

Brandon turned onto Nicky's street. The whole neighborhood seemed weighed down with the hell of what happened. Christmas lights looked tacky, not festive and the wan yellow pools of the streetlamps barely kept darkness at bay. In the passenger seat, Edith gazed out the window. A quick check in the rearview gave Brandon a half view of Dian staring at her hands.

Silence clogged the interior of the minivan. None of them had spoken much beyond Dian's request that Brandon stop by a discount shop on the drive back. Brandon wished he, like Nicky, could have begged off the whole ride to the Jewish Family Services place, but Edith and Dian expected him to play chauffer. They'd dropped Nicky off at his house a few hours back, and then headed over. Most of the time the women spent inside doing whatever, Brandon had spent outside; pacing, chain smoking and huddled into his leather jacket fighting a winter night in the Nevada desert. At one point a rabbi, a guy younger than Brandon, came out and tried to talk. What the hell was there to say? Brandon nodded, promptly forgot most of the conversation and tucked a card with the rabbi's number into his pocket with an empty promise to call if he felt like talking.

Brandon looked up and realized he'd negotiated the route into Nicky's drive on autopilot. The last twenty-four hours felt like he was a robot…moving, doing what was needed, but not even being conscious of why. Brandon killed the engine and sat with his hands on the wheel. It registered with some part of his brain that the doors opened, the dome light went on and then slowly faded. A tap on the driver's side window pulled his attention to where Nicky stood just outside the door of the van.

Well, he couldn't stay in the van forever. Brandon popped the door and, as Nicky moved back, hauled himself out.

Nicky wrapped one hand around Brandon's bicep, patting his shoulder with the other. "You look tired." A bleak smile flashed across his face. Brandon took the thin comfort both gestures offered.

"We're all tired." Brandon shrugged. "Been a long couple of days." Dian and Edith stood toward the back of the van as though waiting for him. Shit, they probably expected him to take charge or something and he just wasn't up to it. After a moment of staring at them, Brandon shook it off and mumbled, "Dian, Edith, why don't you head inside?"

"Yeah, back door's open." Nicky stepped back and shoved his hands in his jeans pockets. "I'll help Brandon get Dian's stuff out of the car." Nicky shuddered slightly as they watched Dian and Edith head up the back steps. Another shiver out of Nicky accompanied the hiss of indrawn breath. About that time Brandon realized Nicky wasn't wearing a jacket. Nicky jerked his chin at a pile of luggage on the floor and open topped boxes and plastic grocery bags on the seat. "What's all this crap?"

Brandon reached in and pulled out Dian's large bag and set it on the concrete. The smaller one he swung the strap over his shoulder. "Dian's suitcases." He grabbed the box and handed it over to Nicky. "Food." A faint warmth drifted off the bottom of the cardboard. "Lots and lots of food." Once he was certain Nicky had the box, Brandon reached for the plastic bags. "And a couple of plates we picked up."

Nicky shifted the box to cradle it in one arm then he grabbed the handle on Dian's rolling suitcase. "I have plates."

Shit, how to say it so as not to piss Nicky off. Brandon's brain tried to process the options and just couldn't. He huffed out, "Yours aren't clean."

"Of course they're clean." Even in the dim light spilling from the windows onto the drive, Brandon caught the glare. Then Nicky blinked. "Oh, you mean, like, the whole kosher thing."

Just assuming Nicky would follow, Brandon turned and trudged toward the back door. "Some cheap ones from the discount store." Dian mentioned something about having to boil them and Brandon hadn't cared enough to inquire past the volunteered information. He did care enough about Nicky's attitude. Brandon paused on the first step and waited for Nicky to come up beside him. "Don't take it as an insult okay? Just for tonight so I don't have to deal with obsessing about that on top of all the other shit that's happened."

"Okay. Whatever." Nicky snorted out a not quite laugh. He sounded as drawn out and tired as Brandon. "Your stepmom bleached and rearranged my fridge this morning. I guess I can deal with new plates too." Shaking his head, Nicky headed up the stairs. "I thought, I mean from just some comments, that she didn't go the whole nine-yards with the food thing." He juggled the box in his arms to get a hand free to open the screen.

"No, honestly, that's not why." Brandon waited. There wasn't enough room on the stoop for them both. "When my mom died...Edith, she'd come over to my dad's place like once every other week and just sanitize it." The screen door opened and Nicky pulled it back with his ankle. Brandon stepped up and pushed the back door open. "It needed it 'cause I was pretty young and dad stopped caring about stuff for a while." He had to blink as the brighter light spilling from the kitchen into the small porch caught him off guard. "Fuck, I ate dinner at her place more than mine right after." Brandon huffed out the last low enough that just Nicky would hear. "But, that's her way of dealing with emotional shit."

"You boys hungry?" Edith's voice greeted them as they stepped through the laundry area into the kitchen. "I'll warm up something." She stood and ran one hand through her hair.

Dian sat at the table, her hands folded on top of the scarred surface. She stared vacantly out the kitchen window. Not that there was anything out there to see...a dark driveway and the concrete fence of the neighbor's yard. Brandon wondered if he looked as lost and drawn as his ex-wife. If he did, well then they both looked like hell.

"I'm not really hungry, Edith." What he needed was a stiff drink and another smoke. Brandon slid the plates onto the kitchen table before dropping Dian's suitcase against the wall.

Edith directed her attention to Nicky who was easing the box onto the top of the stove. He'd already propped the other bag next to the door. "Nick?" A few steps and she stood next to him.

Nicky looked over his shoulder at Brandon and shrugged. "I don't know."

Pawing through the box, Edith recited the contents. "Chili-cornbread casserole, cake, cookie bars, cheese kugel, ziti, some squash dish, baked broccoli, glazed carrots." She looked up, her expression hopeful—like maybe they'd give her something to do so she didn't have to think. "Anything strike you boys as what you want for dinner? The ladies showed up at the center with enough food to last us a month. You all need to eat."

Why did they all keep turning to him? Even Dian sat there, stared at him as though she waited for some kind of instruction. Instead of responding right away, Brandon headed to the cabinet. He yanked it open, pulled out a glass then he rummaged in the next set of shelves until he found the bottle of Jack Nicky kept there. After pouring a belt, Brandon turned around and propped his butt against the counter. "You know," Brandon muttered as he downed the first shot, "Edith, why don't you choose whatever seems good."

"All right," Edith nodded and reached into the box. "Dian, why don't you let Brandon show you where the bedroom is?" She paused and turned back to where Dian just sat, as if waiting for something to happen. "You should lie down. I'll warm up one of these casseroles and a veggie."

Like it almost took more will than Dian had, she stood. "Okay."

Nicky rushed forward and grabbed Dian's bags. "I ah, changed the sheets on the bed." He backed out of the kitchen pulling the rolling suitcase. "Cleaned up the room for you while you all were out."

When they reached the living room, Dian hesitated. Almost embarrassed she turned to Brandon and whispered, "I could use the lady's room."

"It's right there." Brandon pointed toward the arch separating the short hall between front and back bedrooms. The bathroom door was square in the middle. "We'll put your bags in the room." Brandon called after her as Dian hurried through.

At a more sedate pace, Nicky headed in the same general direction. Instead of going straight he turned right toward the rear of the house. "I put Edith's stuff in there earlier." He rolled the bag into his bedroom and settled it near the foot of his bed. In a quieter voice he added, "Also figured I should do a little camouflage, you know, in the corner."

Brandon wasn't sure what Nicky meant. "The corner?" Hesitating at the doorway, Brandon tried to figure out what corners had to do with anything.

"Yeah, you know," Nicky jerked his chin in the direction of the head of the bed and the play space behind it, "the *corner*."

Brandon hissed, "Fuck." He hadn't even thought that through. Thankfully, Nicky had.

"Yeah," Nicky leaned against the thick uprights supporting the canopy structure of his bed. "Don't be surprised to find a bunch of my extra bike gear back there." Running both hands over the top of his head, Nicky brought Brandon up to speed in a low toned whisper, "Stretched one of the bungee nets between some of the eyebolts and tossed my rain gear in it with extra goggles and gloves and shit. I hung my old helmets and summer weight gear off the bolts, too. Just piled my long haul gear—saddle bags, tail and tank bags, backpack and a bunch of other crap—on the floor." He snorted and folded his arms over his chest. "It was the best I could figure out on short notice."

Scanning for any evidence of bondage gear, Brandon stepped into the room. "What about, you know," Brandon knelt down to peer under the bed, "the *other* gear?" The space underneath was dusty, but empty. Thank God, Nicky was clearheaded enough to think about those things beforehand.

"Took the fun stuff and tossed it in the tool cabinet in the garage…you know, where I normally keep the extra bike shit." Nicky explained as Brandon stood. "Figured they won't stumble upon it there." It looked like Nicky was going to say more, but he stopped and glanced at the door.

Brandon tracked his gaze. Dian, one hand on the doorframe, paused at the edge of the room. "Hey, Dian. We'll get out of your way."

Her other hand massaged the fabric of her skirt. "This is an interesting room." Dian released the lintel, reached forward and rested her hand on Nicky's old deco dresser, before moving into the room. It was as though she needed the physical support. "Interesting bed."

"It's custom built." Nicky offered the explanation as he slid past her into the hall. "Like an art piece."

"Oh." It sounded like Nicky's words didn't really register. "The room smells strange."

"It's the protective coating on the nylon…my bike stuff." Nicky stood in the doorway with his hands in his pockets. "I store it in the corner." Dian didn't even look at him as he spoke. "That and all the cleaner we used after the cops searched."

Instead, Dian turned to Brandon. "Why did the police search this house?" Suspicion wound under her tone and coiled about Nicky…and Brandon.

"It's routine procedure, Dian." Brandon tried to keep his response measured, defray the implication with logic. "They take samples of all the fibers and fingerprints and shit from this location so that whatever doesn't match up, well they know that came from someplace else." Still, it made him angry that Dian might think Nicky was involved. "You know, like all those investigation shows…there's no beige carpets here. They find beige carpet fibers on Shayna's clothes it rules out here and puts her somewhere else."

"Oh." She didn't sound convinced. "Where did Shayna sleep? Not here."

"No." Brandon really didn't want to be dealing with Dian's

questions. "We set up a cot in Nicky's office, I took the couch." Slowly, so hopefully Dian wouldn't reel him back in, Brandon backed toward the door. "We'll call you when dinner's ready." A siren's wail at his hip saved him from further interrogation. "Hold on," Brandon spun as he grabbed his phone out of the holster. Dodging past Nicky into the hall, he yelled over his shoulder. "I got to take it. It's Jeff Weaver." Then he flipped the phone open and brought it up. "Carr here."

"Hey, Baby D," Jeff's gruff voice sounded comforting… maybe because he was a line to information. "How you holding up?"

"I'm not in a rubber room." He may have been in hell, but it wasn't one with guys in white coats and little blue pills.

"Look, got some info for you." Brandon shifted the phone to his other ear as he perched on the arm of the couch. "Passed it on to Metro already, but thought I'd bring you up to speed." Weaver's long, drawn out huff steeled Brandon for things he didn't want to hear. "There's bad news, and even worse news. The bad news is: we don't have anything solid."

At the edge of his vision, Brandon caught Nicky standing in the archway to the hall. "The worse news?" Brandon really didn't want Nicky to hang around, but he lacked the mental energy right then to tell him to go pound sand.

"First," Weaver growled, "let's talk about how you've been holding out on me…how the fuck do you know the LAPD Spooks?"

What the hell was wrong with Jeff? How did that have anything to do with Shayna and what Jeff discovered? "I have no clue what you're talking about," he snapped.

"OCID," Weaver used the acronym for the Organized Crime Intelligence Division—LAPD's hush-hush cop squad. "Got a call from some Detective Bryant who said he owes you one." A heavy pause lingered over the line. Then Weaver barked out, "How the fuck they got wind of your situation, who the hell knows. 'Cause they called me and seemed to have the whole story, parts I don't even have."

"So?" What did it matter? That was his problem not Jeff Weaver's.

"How do you know them? If you want me to trust you to handle the info I got," Weaver growled over the line, "you've got to trust me. I'm your partner. Don't hold out on me and expect me to come clean with you."

Brandon didn't have time for this crap. The suck ass thing of it all was Weaver held the cards. If Brandon didn't tell him, he'd never give up what he found. "You know that big meth bust back in June, the one we tied into *La Eme* and the Nevada Gaming Agent that got popped?" Brandon glared at Nicky...not that he'd even moved, it was just that Nicky stood five feet away and Weaver sat on his butt in Riverside. "OCID was watching the dead guy." Nicky flashed him a look like he wondered why Brandon explained past history. Brandon brushed him off with a flip of his hand. "I did a look-see on the system, the guy's account was flagged so my search popped up on their radar. Then they came and had a chat with me. We played a little give and take. And I've played straight with them whenever they asked me to check on something since then..."

"You're one of their informants?" Jeff spat the question like it tasted bad.

Brandon growled back, "Jeff, I don't have time for this twenty questions shit." If Weaver had been within arm's reach, Brandon probably would have slugged his partner. "Tell me what you got and I promise when this is all over I'll tell you everything, okay?" Instead, the situation forced him to play nice or he'd never learn what Jeff knew. "Deal?"

Jeff made him wait until Brandon contemplated chucking the phone across the room in frustration. Then Weaver huffed, "Look, apparently there's a big contingent of *Surenos* out in Vegas now." Jeff used the nickname for the Southern California arm of the Mexican Mafia. "They say there's some chatter out here that players in La Eme out there might know a little more than they should."

"Who?" That equaled someplace to start. "How do I find them?"

Weaver killed his hope with his answer, "They didn't tell me. Bryant just said you and Nick ought to watch your backs. They're on it. They say they'll pass what they find to Metro if it's warranted."

"Fuck!" Brandon slammed his free hand against the back of the couch.

"Yeah, it does sound like classic Mexican Mafia payback." La Eme was brutal. Most of the big, old school gangs kept family out of their wars, unless they sprouted up unexpectedly out of the shit—where the term *mushroom* for collateral victims came from. "They've probably been watching you since you guys tore a hole in that whole slot rigging scheme they had going on." Everyone and anyone attached to someone *La Eme* wanted to hurt equaled fair game. In fact, there were times when the gang preferred to target family. It made the true victim pay with their heart instead of their life. "Bryant says, if it's them, be prepared for some kind of message."

If *La Eme* took Shayna it was long past over for her. "I'll kill 'em." Brandon wouldn't just kill them; he'd tie them down and cut one inch squares out of their bodies with a dull box cutter for payback.

"Look," Jeff wrested Brandon from dreams of revenge, "there's also a few guys on our end who've popped up active. A couple of the *Khát Máu* members we didn't manage to tag-and-bag in that prostitution/computer fraud sting you and Nicky played in." The Vietnamese gang they'd bagged that summer, brutal fuckers. What the *Khát Máu* members might lack in style, they more than made up for with balls. "They've shown up in Sin City as well." It sounded as if Jeff read from a list. "One of the big-daddy skinheads you put away while you worked undercover Narcotics…he's out and paroled in Vegas." He snorted. "Along with about half the junkies, pimps and prostitutes on our regular roster…like everyone else, the lowlifes have moved to Vegas for the easy money."

Brandon jammed the phone between his shoulder and ear. "Just fuck." Then he pretended to write across his palm with an invisible pen. Apparently not comprehending, Nicky stared back. Since subtle didn't work, Brandon covered the phone's face and snapped at Nicky, "Get a pen and paper!" Nicky rolled his eyes and headed toward his office in the front bedroom. "Give me their last known addresses and associates." A shitload of suspects dumped in his lap. Brandon would have to start at the basics and eat that elephant of information one bite at a time.

Weaver didn't even hesitate before responding, "No."

Brandon's eyes bugged out of their sockets...he could feel it. "What the fuck do you mean, no?"

"No, I gave the stuff to Metro." The hell with the bangers, Brandon was going to kill Jeff. "They'll follow up on it."

Jumping off the couch, Brandon screamed into the phone. "Give me the fucking info, Jeff!" That brought everyone in the house running. Nicky almost slammed into Dian as they ran out of opposite ends of the short hall. Edith rushed from the kitchen with her hand on her chest.

Oblivious to the chaos erupting around Brandon, Jeff repeated. "No." Brandon had to stick his finger in his free ear just to shut out the questions from Nicky and the women. "I'm not going to help you go cowboy." The tough vice detective attitude slammed down in Jeff's voice. "I wouldn't want Vegas to hand me a rogue cop. I'm not going to fuck up Metro's investigation by letting you go off."

Brandon shook off Nicky when he tried to grab his arm. "Goddamn you!" Jeff wouldn't give him the information. Without that Brandon was stuck, powerless. "She's my fucking kid, Jeff." Jeff couldn't leave him hanging on this shit. He had to do something. "Help me out here!"

"Brandon, don't make me regret keeping you in the loop on this shit."

The only response Brandon could dredge up was to yell, "Just fuck you!"

"Go cool off," Weaver barked. "Think like a fucking cop!"

He was thinking like a cop. "Screw you!" Cops solved cases. They didn't lose their own daughters.

"I'm hanging up, fuck off." The connection died.

Brandon roared out his frustration. He hauled back to chuck the phone. The only reason he didn't was because Nicky grabbed his arm. Brandon jerked. The momentum sent Nicky sprawling backward. He tumbled into one of the heavy, Victorian armchairs. Although it rocked, the weight kept it, and Nicky, from going over. Brandon could only stand and shake.

Finally, nerves hit him so hard that Brandon's knees went weak. "Shit, Nicky." Brandon managed to sit on the coffee table rather than fall on his ass. His hands trembled as they rested on his thighs. Swallowing, Brandon looked up at Nicky. "What's happening to us?"

"We're dealing." Nicky panted as he swung his legs to the floor and sat up. "That's what's happening." Reaching out, Nicky ran his fingers across Brandon's cheek. "We'll get through it, I promise."

"Brandon!" Dian's broken sob reminded him that his stepmom and ex-wife were still there. "What's going on? What did he say?"

Edith held Dian over by the TV. Things happened so fast he hadn't seen them move. "Nothing." Brandon pulled back. "It's okay."

Dian broke from Edith and screamed, "It's not okay."

"Just relax." Nicky clambered off the chair to put himself between Brandon and Dian.

"No!" She shook off Edith who tried to pull her back and pushed Nicky to the side. "Don't tell me to relax, or it's okay. My little girl is gone and it's your fault!"

Edith tugged at her arm, trying to pull Dian back. "It's nobody's fault," she reasoned. Even Brandon didn't believe that.

"What kind of place is this?" Tears streaked Dian's face.

She pointed back to Nicky's bedroom. "There's a mirror on the bedroom ceiling! That's disgusting! What kind of place did you bring my daughter to? What kind of friend is Nick?"

Brandon scrambled off the table putting the small piece of furniture between himself and Dian as he stood. "What do you mean?"

Her hands fluttered in front of her chest. "There's condoms and massage oils in the nightstand!"

Nicky stuttered out, "You went through my bedside drawer?"

"I looked," she spat back.

"Shit!" Brandon grabbed his skull to keep his brains from bursting out his ears. "Nicky didn't you get rid of that stuff?"

"Get rid of that stuff?" Wide-eyed, Nicky turned on Brandon. "That's my fucking private space." Then, one hand on his hip, the other gripping the back of his neck he swung to confront Dian. "What the hell were you doing digging in my drawers?"

"Stop," vainly Edith pleaded with them. "Everyone, please stop yelling. Calm down."

"Calm down!" Hissy pissed-off Diva Nicky surfaced in those two words. "She's digging through *my* things. Like it wasn't bad enough the cops did!" He rolled his shoulders and flung his arms up. Two fingers pointed at Dian, he hissed, "You do *not* have a *right* to go through *my shit.*"

"It's nothing, okay." Brandon stepped over the coffee table, moving between Nicky and Dian. "Nicky's responsible about his sex life. It's nothing."

"Do you go out and pick up women together?" Dian hauled back and slapped him. The blow stung him to his soul. "Is that why you come here?" Brandon was so shocked he couldn't even react. "Cruise the strip for loose women, strippers, cocktail waitresses? That's what you used to do when we were married, wasn't it? Why did I ever think you'd change?" Trying to yell through her sobs, she could barely get out the accusations.

"Irresponsible then. Irresponsible now."

"Dian, it's not like that. Nicky's not like that."

"Then why is his bedroom set up like some kind of sex palace?" When she raised her hand again, this time going for Nicky, Brandon grabbed her wrist. "Red velvet and purple walls... what kind of man has a bedroom like that? And that monstrosity of a bed." Dian yanked away. "I need some air." When Edith tried to intercept her, Dian dodged her hug. "I need to take a walk."

"I wouldn't go walking," Nicky sagged against the high arm of the chair, "around here at this time of night."

Almost incredulous, Dian snapped, "What?"

Nicky shrugged. "It's not really safe for a woman to walk around this neighborhood at night, alone."

"It's not safe for me." Dian looked from Brandon to Nicky and back again. "But it was okay to let my daughter walk by herself?"

That wasn't what happened. That's not what he and Nicky had done. Once again Brandon explained, "She was supposed to be with Miri's kids."

Like she was trying to banish a chill, Dian rubbed her arms with her hands. "Who is this Miri person?" Edith leaned against the mantel, her hand over her mouth, looking at a loss for what to do or say.

"She's Nicky's best friend." It was the only excuse Brandon had to offer.

"Married women," Dian glared at him, "do not have single male friends."

Before Brandon could respond, Nicky interjected, "Miri's not married."

This time, Dian's ire was directed straight at Nicky. "So you left my daughter with your slut of a girlfriend?"

"She's not my girlfriend, we've known each other since high

school." Nicky sputtered. "And how dare you call her a slut." His anger tensed his neck as he hissed, "I don't care what shit has happened in your life, that's just bitch nasty!"

"What am I supposed to think?" Dian spat her own rage back. "Just look at this house." She swung her arm out indicating the small confines of the living/dining area. "Some freak show bachelor pad. Skulls and coffins all over the place." Again she glared at Brandon. "This is not where my little girl should have been."

"Where should she have been?" Brandon gave her the most reasonable response he could. "In my little one bedroom apartment in Riverside? 'Cause I don't even have doors on my bedroom there." Problem was, even he didn't really buy it. "Is that better?"

"You were supposed to look out for her." Dian went straight for the gut blow. "She's your daughter. You're a cop! How can a cop lose their only child?" As if she had to remind Brandon of that fact. "How could you so royally have screwed this up? I may never see my baby again and it's your fault!"

God, did he ever understand that. "Don't you think I know that?" More than any of them could ever comprehend.

"I hope you do." Finally, Dian let Edith embrace her, pull her back toward the bedroom. "I hope every single breath you take reminds you, big shot cop, how you destroyed our daughter's life, my life." Edith whispered something in Dian's ear and Dian sobbed. With one last, hate filled glare, she let Edith lead her away.

Nicky's hand touched Brandon's arm. "Don't listen to her." When the sound of the bedroom door shutting echoed back to them, Nicky pulled him into a rough hug. "It's not your fault."

Brandon wished he could believe Nicky. He couldn't. No matter what, it was his fault. He should have been more observant, more careful. His own lack of willpower caused this horrid chain of events. If he'd been a stronger man, a more responsible man, he wouldn't have let Nicky talk him into fooling around. He couldn't even shove off part of the blame to Nicky. What did Nicky know about kids and keeping them safe? That…that was his job.

And he'd blown it.

CHAPTER 15

Another night of barely any sleep grated raw across Nick's nerves. The couch at his place really wasn't meant to be slept on—somehow he'd ended up there while Brandon got the cot. Nick settled down at his workstation and tried to make sense of the jumble of slot parts and equipment cluttering the surface. There were things he needed to work on, but he just couldn't wrap his mind around what he should start with.

Beyond the physical discomfort of hard cushions and not enough leg room, the fact that he couldn't be with Brandon, hold him, tell him it was okay, kept him tossing. Nick wanted to be there for him, especially after the throw down with Dian, but Brandon just pushed him away. It was almost as if, with his turning away from everyone, Brandon believed what Dian said.

What she said wasn't true.

"Morning." A touch on his shoulder startled Nick. "I'd say Happy New Year, but it just doesn't seem appropriate. Although I'm surprised to see you at the office." Ada's sympathetic smile backed up the gentle compassion in her tone. "I saw the report on the news, Nick." She pulled over another chair to sit down. "It's so horrible. I can't imagine it with my kids. My brain just shuts down at the thought. I'm praying for Shayna. I only met her once, but such a sweet little girl." Every so often she'd touch his knee or arm. That little bit of contact let Nick know she was there for him. Nick appreciated it more than he could really express. "My whole church is praying for her." The outpouring of good thoughts from strangers stunned Nick. "You'll let Brandon know, won't you?"

"Yeah, I will." He wished he knew what to say. The only thing he could manage was, "Thanks."

A clatter by the door caught their attention. Jen stumbled in carrying a bundle of large envelopes. "Agent O'Malley." A hesitant smile blew over her face. Jen paused and clutched the envelopes against her chest. She chewed on her lower lip. "I brought you your mail."

"Thanks, Jen." Nick motioned her over. "You didn't have to." Since she seemed hesitant, Nick added, "Thanks for coming by the command center and offering to pass out flyers. You didn't have to do that." Not that he could really tell, since she'd been wearing a large coat, but it seemed like Jen still wore the clothes from Sunday—rumpled and messy. 'Course for Jen, Nick reminded himself, rumpled and messy equaled par for the course: her daily attire. Nick wouldn't even have remembered at all except that Jen was one of the few people he knew who showed up to the briefing. That made a rather vague impression.

"It's okay." Swallowing, she ducked her head and shuffled her feet. Her too big coat sagged about her shoulders. "I mean I saw it on the news and recognized your friend." Then she edged around the worktables. Holding out the envelopes, she kept a bit of distance between them. "I wanted to help, somehow."

As Nick took the packet of mail, Ada peered at Jen. "You don't look too good." With a motherly gesture, Ada reached out and pressed her wrist to Jen's forehead. "Are you okay?"

Jen backed away from the touch. "I haven't been feeling well."

"Oh." Nick hardly cared about Jen having a cold. Maybe that made him callous, but his current home life equaled a hell of a lot more pain than a stuffy head. "As my mom used to say, *drug-up, move on.*" Sliding into his workspace, Nick fished for a way to get rid of Jen. Not that he really wanted to ditch anyone, but he mostly wanted to be alone…with the offices as empty as they were on New Year's Eve day, he should be able to manage. Nick pushed a stack of paper aside to make room for the mail. That gave him a solution. "Look, can you do me a favor?" Nick fingered the reports. "Feel up to it?"

Her mood seemed to brighten at the offer. "Anything you need." It fit what he knew of Jen, about the only way to engage her was work.

"I've got this stack of reports here. Another batch is on the way." Nick picked up the mass of printouts. "I was going to do it myself, but I just can't concentrate right now." Turning to Jen he explained the minor project. Minor…but necessary. "We've got to cull through and see who's using time on what databases—you know-Admin, Investigations-break it down by department. It's not even code-monkey work. Do you think you could handle it for me?"

"I would love to." She beamed and took the reports. Clutching them like she had the mail earlier, she backed toward the door. "You won't be disappointed. You can have complete faith in me."

"Thanks a bunch." He gave a Jen a thumbs-up. "I need it by Wednesday. I'm supposed to pass out the data to some of the contractors and I'll need to get that integrated into the other reports." That was the essentials of the basic project. "Still okay with it?"

"Thank you for trusting me."

Taking that as a yes, Nick dismissed her with a, "No problem." Well that got one of a thousand things off his plate. Now to figure out how to get through the other nine-hundred-and-ninety-nine.

Ada stood as Jen scurried out of Electronic Services, and then sat back down. She leaned in. "Why are you here, Nick? Shouldn't you be at home with Brandon?"

For all of her issues with his life, Ada just accepted that he and Brandon were a couple. Somehow that meant more to Nick than any card or hug. "Yeah," he huffed out, "I should." She put her hand on one of his and squeezed. "I tried to call in this morning. And the Lab Manager…he's sympathetic, but between my injury and all the time off to get my car back I'm out of sick time, vacation time and since she's not my kid I don't even qualify for any unpaid time off." Shaking his head, Nick added, "So I sucked it up and came in."

At least his manager hadn't said anything about Nick's loose interpretation of business causal that morning: black jeans, combat boots and an un-ironed club shirt. Basics out of the dryer that morning. Since Edith and Dian camped out in his bedroom, his closet remained inaccessible. He'd made the call, thrown what he could on and, after leaving a note for Brandon, took off to work. Nick passed the lab manager in the hall, got a hard once over, then the man merely shook his head and walked off without speaking.

"What about crises time?" Ada patted his arm. "I read something about that in the employee handbook. I'll donate some of my vacation hours to your account. I'm sure there are others here who would, too."

"Still the problem of Shayna not being related to me by blood or marriage." Heck, even if they were a regular couple, under Vegas' rules he wasn't sure they'd give him the time. "I appreciate the offer, but there's no way I can take you up on it."

"Okay. That's too bad. I didn't realize…" Now Ada got up. "If there's anything you need just let me know." Patting his shoulder, Ada headed back toward her department.

Absently, he mumbled, "Thanks, I may take you up on that," as she walked off.

Most people didn't *realize*…not that Nick would be entitled to comp time or leave time at this stage if Brandon was a gal. Heck, even if they registered as Domestic Partners in Nevada, Nick wasn't sure if he'd qualify. The last policy statement out of the state was that DPs might be covered by their partner's state health plan…if the state ever came up with the money to fund it. Political injustice made his head hurt, especially when everything else in his life spun out of control. Nick needed to start with the small tasks and try and make it through the day without losing it.

Nick picked up one of the few envelopes that wasn't interoffice mail. Grease darkened one corner and something that looked like ketchup dotted the back. God, someone needed to have a talk with the idiots down in the mailroom about eating and sorting at the same time.

Nick didn't get much outside mail, so he double checked. Yep the address for the building and his name: Agent. Nick O'Malley typed on the print and peel label. Since whoever sent it used his title but not the full version of his name—Nicholas—it indicated familiarity instead of formal business correspondence. No sender's name but a return address in Connecticut and stamps instead of a metered strip. Packing tape sealed the flap closed. All rang a little odd, he thought as he slit the top. Maybe someone he met at an industry conference or something. He often traded business cards and exchanged promises to forward interesting info. Most people never followed through.

Nick dumped the contents across the only clear space on his workstation. A pile of inkjet printed photos spilled over the surface. Partial profiles and blurred shots caught the light. Nick. Nick and Shayna at the merry-go-round. Brandon and Nick together in front of that glitzy girl store. All three of them playing games and walking on the strip. Nick started shaking. "Holy fuck!" He almost fell over his chair trying to back away from the massive invasion of his life laid out in pixilated color.

"What is it?" Ada rushed back toward him from the hall.

Nick realized he must have yelled. "Photos." Nick stepped in front of Ada before she could reach his station. "It's got pictures of me and Brandon and Shayna in it. Like just before she was taken." What little training he had in evidence handling kicked in. A million people had probably touched the outside of the envelope, but whoever sent the pictures was the only person to handle those. "Don't touch!"

"Oh no." Ada stepped up and hugged him. "You okay, Nick?"

Nick pulled back. "Somebody mailed it. It came in with my mail." Brandon mentioned a threat might come if someone had taken Shayna to hurt Brandon. Nick just hadn't expected it to come to him at work. "Get Enforcement in here, please." Palming his face, Nick perched on the edge of his chair. "Have them call Detective Orozco at Metro. Holy fucking shit," he hissed out, not really conscious of Ada's presence. "Holy, motherfucking shit."

He was still repeating it when Enforcement hustled in. They cordoned off the area and then parked him in the lab manager's tiny office.

Fifteen, maybe thirty, minutes later an enforcement agent ushered Detective Orozco into the office. After a few brusque pleasantries about coffee and how everyone was holding up, Orozco perched on the edge of the desk and pulled out his note pad. Nick had to bite back an inappropriate snort of humor. Almost six months earlier they'd occupied the exact same positions in this office while Orozco interrogated him about the murder of Mike Ducmagian, a former co-worker of Nick's at the GCB, and a guy who turned out to be a money launderer for the Mexican Mafia.

"Agent O'Malley," the detective's tone seemed far more gentle this time around, "has anything strange been happening recently?"

"You mean other than Shayna getting taken?" Nick rubbed his hands together and tried to think. "I don't know."

"Look, when we were out at your house the focus was on Detective Carr." Orozco crossed his arms over his chest and sucked on his mustache. "His daughter, he's a cop, most logical assumption was that if it wasn't random, it was because of who he was. But, this says, we might be wrong." He blew out a long breath. "Whoever did this sent the stuff directly to you, not him. One of the easiest ways to hurt you is to hurt him. And vice-versa." Orozco knew pretty much everything there was to know about Nick and Brandon's relationship. "Think, Nicholas, anything strange."

"I don't know," Nick shrugged. "Ah, I've been getting calls on my cell phone from an unlisted number." He hadn't really thought much about that until Brandon pegged it as odd. Maybe it might mean something to Orozco. "First few times I picked it up and nobody answered, so now if I don't know the number I just let it go to voice mail. If it's somebody who needs me, they'll leave a message, you know?"

Orozco jotted some notes then looked up. "How long has

this been going on?"

Nick tried to think back. "Three or four months, maybe." It was hard to recall precisely when, since at the time, it didn't seem much of anything. "I don't remember exactly."

"Could be tracking you. Trying to see if you'll answer and if you're someplace public or not." Tapping the pen against the paper, Orozco seemed to think for a bit. "Give your cell phone number out a lot? How might someone have gotten a hold of it?"

"Fuck I don't know. It's on the employee phone tree list. People take them home, keep them in their cars." After a moment he added, "Could have ended up on some volunteer lists through a couple of AIDS support charities and the local rainbow teen center—I don't have time to do much, but if their computers break down I'll run over and fix them for the cost of the parts. So, God, could be tons of people who had it out where someone else could grab it."

Nodding, Orozco followed up with, "You're on line a lot, tech geek and all. Anything there?"

"Nothing major I guess." Well, yeah, he remembered the emails. "A guy who's just bugging me on emails and forums and shit." Really, couldn't be connected, but then again, it might be something. "That's nothing right?"

"You never know. We'll look into it." Orozco motioned to someone at the door. Nick twisted in his seat to see Ada there with a cup of water. "What about here?" The question refocused his attention on the detective. "Weird calls? Strange emails to your office account?"

"Nothing," Nick reached for the water with a mumbled, "Thanks." After a sip, he repeated. "Nothing I can think of."

Ada started to back out the door and then paused. Like she wasn't sure she should break into the conversation she tentatively asked, "What about all that stuff that keeps showing up on your workspace?"

Orozco studied her. "What stuff?"

"Pens. Calendars. Mugs." She ticked the items off on her fingers. "We were starting to tease Dracula that he's going klepto because some of it belonged to other people."

"You know, that's people just forgetting where they left stuff," Nick minimized it. That didn't have anything to do with Shayna. "Walking around with it and setting it down. They walk away and forget. I do it a lot, too. Keep losing pens, my favorite coffee mug-with skulls on it-has gone missing." Nick rolled his eyes. "Probably left it in the planters when I went outside for a smoke or something."

"Nick," Ada chided. "Your workstation is not in a traffic area, even for ESD." Looping her arms in front of her stomach, she added, "People have to go to it. You're off in a corner."

"Okay, but that stopped like last month."

"Well, we'll follow up on it just in case." A few more notes went into the book. "Anybody fired in the last month? Someone who might have resented you?"

"This is state employ." Nick didn't bother to stifle the derisive laugh this time. "You know how hard it is to fire people?"

"Transferred out, resigned, retired, vacation?" Orozco listed alternatives. "Think, Nicholas."

Nick thought back. As far as he could remember they hadn't lost anyone recently. "Not that I know of." He looked over at Ada. She spent far more time in the office than he did. "You know of anyone?"

"No." She looked as perplexed as Nick felt. "Not that I can think of."

"So what happened last month?"

Nick explained what little there was to explain. "First, I got teased by the lab manager for it. Then my boss realized shit was happening when I wasn't around, so we figured it might be someone who had a problem, you know with me."

"Like what kind of problem?" As though he realized what he just asked and how obviously inane the question was, Orozco held up one hand. "Oh, yeah, that."

Nick sneered. "Yeah, that." A little more reasonable, he explained the repercussions of the incident. "So, a meeting, and a memo about harassment."

Ada chimed in, "The chief told everyone that if someone was caught, heads would roll and it stopped."

"Did they ever figure out who it was?"

"No." Nick shook his head. "But it stopped. Come on though. That was pissy shit." Minor stuff like an errant pen did not escalate to kidnapping his lover's kid. Especially since, beyond Ada, only a few people at work knew anything about his and Brandon's relationship. "Petty crap and it stopped."

"Okay. I assume enforcement looked into it?" When Nick and Ada nodded in the affirmative, Orozco jotted that down as well. "I'll see about getting the investigation they did."

"I don't think it really means anything." How could it?

"We look at everything." Orozco made a few more notes then flipped the pad shut. "Do you have the emails that you got?" He tapped the pen against his thigh. "I'd like to see them."

"No, I just deleted those." Although it seemed like a good idea at the time, Nick wondered if he should have trashed them. "Really, it was just annoying junk. 'Look at this penis cannon shooting snowballs'" He caught Ada's hiss and winced. Damn, he'd forgotten she was there. Almost apologetically he added, "Stuff that was funny the first fifty times I saw it."

"You know." Ada backed out of the room. "I think I have work calling me."

Orozco nodded and touched his forehead almost like he tipped a hat. "Thanks for your help."

Once Ada had gone, Nick blew out his breath. Usually, he didn't talk about stuff like that in front of Ada. "If you think it's necessary, I can pull down some forum posts."

"Okay. Let's do that." Standing, Orozco held his hand out and indicated the door. "Why don't you come with me to our crime lab?" Not knowing what else to do, Nick stood as well. Then he let Orozco steer him out of the office and into the hall. As they walked, Orozco explained, "You can pull the forums up, show us the posts. Fill out consent to pull your phone records and we can get a warrant for the unlisted numbers. It may take a few days to get the information. Then my guys can start the magic."

"The forum stuff is all just geeks talking to each other about tech."

"Nothing spicy?" Orozco teased. "I won't tell Brandon, promise."

"That?" Nick thought for a moment. "No all that contact's been under my *2TechNick* alt. Brandon knows about the other stuff though," Nick coughed into his hand, "my gonzo accounts."

Orozco paused. "Gonzo accounts?"

"Accounts I use when I'm on dirty chats and BDSM forums and such. *Disdain99* is for tame, more social, dating. Really intense crap," Nick dropped his tone to a whisper, as they passed through admin. A smattering of technical and data processing personnel bent to their tasks—anybody who couldn't manage to take the day off. Jen sat off to one side flipping through the reports he'd given her. Nick flashed a half-ass smile in reaction when she looked up. Then he gave his attention back to the detective. "That's *LeatherGothBoi*." Last thing he needed was people like Jen and her co-*irkers* knowing about his cyber-sex life. "But I've never seen that guy show up on any forum where I use those. I don't know why this is important."

"It may not be Nicholas." Orozco ran one meaty hand over his mustache. "But there's a little girl missing and someone just sent you a pretty clear message. We can't afford to ignore anything."

A couple hours later, a little after lunch, Nick finally hit home. Nick had called back into the office, but his manager told him to just go home as they were probably going to shut down early anyway.

An empty driveway—no minivan—and a cold dark house greeted him. Nick grabbed a banana for lunch on his way through the kitchen. Brandon had left a note taped to his TV about driving Dian over to Frank's cousin's place and some more press interviews they'd committed to. Nick wasn't sure whether he should be grateful for the relative peace or disappointed in not seeing Brandon. He wanted to talk about what happened... be with Brandon.

Several times throughout the morning he'd called Brandon's cell, but it went straight to voicemail. Brandon was as bad about charging his own phone as Shayna's. Or maybe he was on another line. Nick didn't want to leave a message about the photos beyond, *hey, call me.* That would just freak Brandon out more. Last thing either of them needed was more of last night.

Nick flipped on the idiot box and switched over to the History Channel for background noise then headed to his computer. Orozco asked him to search through his email for any of the messages that he'd downloaded to his desktop client and that might not have been permanently deleted. Those he'd forward on to the AV guys at the crime lab. Thankfully, no new messages, other than spam and RSS feeds, appeared in his *2TechNick* account folder. Nick shook out the tension in his hands...the stuff he hadn't realized was building there.

That done, Nick typed in a search based on Shayna's name... time to see what the media buzzed about and what they could do to get more attention to her disappearance. The links were there, but random and disorganized bits of data. Someone, at one of the many meetings, briefings or whatever suggested a web page to consolidate information. Nick might not be the most kick-ass web designer, but he figured his rusty CSS skills and an all-in-one cheap hosting site should be up to the task. The project would kill time productively and hopefully be useful.

clickjacked.blogroads.net—Private Post, Dec. 31, 2:00pm

Things were happening now.

All the buzz about it sent nerves jangling. Constant net surfing pulled the details in. Alerts and feeds collected and combed through. What they knew. What they didn't. Pictures. Stories. Feelings. Video. Blogs. News Feeds. They all fed the need to know and see.

It was taken care of for a while. Toss some crumbs and watch the ants scramble for tiny bits.

The whole thing in motion, rolling. Soon, he'd realize what needed to take place. All the little bits…picking and poking…paying off. It'd click and he'd know. He'd see. And it'd all be like it was supposed to be. 'Cause he'd have to understand by now.

He knew.

He saw.

All the puzzle pieces were there. Just fit them together and…

Boom.

CHAPTER 16

Brandon shucked his jacket on the way through the house. Between the chatter from the television and the bike in the garage, Brandon figured Nicky had come home...maybe for a late lunch. "Hey, Nicky," he called over the sound of the TV. Nicky'd left the idiot box tuned to the WWII channel—at least that's what programs they seemed to be running every time Nicky flipped it on.

"Hey, yourself," answered him from the computer room. "I'm in the office."

Brandon tossed his jacket onto the couch as he passed. "Edith wants to know if chicken enchilada casserole is okay for lunch." Late lunch or early dinner, but they hadn't stopped to eat since leaving that morning. "One of the gals from Jewish Family Services brought it by as we drove up." Stepping into the doorway of the front room, Brandon scowled as Nicky spun his chair around to face Brandon. "I quote, 'it's chicken, it's hot,'" the moment they hit the driveway Edith started pestering him about eating; "'we should eat it now.'" Brandon couldn't really even begin to look toward a meal. Minutes into the future seemed beyond his grasp, much less eating and bed and waking up tomorrow. "Is that okay with you?" With Nicky home, Brandon could pass the decision off to him.

"If you like it, I'll eat it," Nicky waffled.

Brandon needed Nicky to tell him which options for day-to-day living—the small picture—would work. He had, because of his training, a decent grasp of the big picture, like getting Shayna's name and face in as many places as possible. That would, someday, bring her tiny, violated body home. Inevitable as that outcome was, Brandon had to somehow figure out how to put one foot in front of the other. Little things, such as whether he really needed a shave or when to shovel food into his mouth, just escaped him; unraveling into a thousand strands of options he couldn't get a hold of. Finally, Nicky nodded and Brandon took that as an okay, so he yelled back toward the kitchen, "Edith… casserole is fine."

"You look beat."

"I am." If he looked as worn out as he felt, Brandon figured he looked like absolute shit. "Amazing how much doing nothing wears you out." It took all of Brandon's mental energy to deal with Shayna's disappearance. What little was left he used to force himself to put one foot in front of the other and attempt sleep. After that, a hollowed out shell encompassed his being. Brandon wished he could care more about Nicky, or his job, or fuck, even Edith and Dian.

"So, what are you doing?" He could mouth the words right now…spit out lines pretending at interest. Maybe, someday, actual feelings would back them.

Nicky turned back to the computer. "Putting together a website." He moused around the screen changing colors and moving objects.

"For what?" Brandon came around the end of the cot and sat down. He picked up Shayna's pillow and clutched it to his chest, turning his chin down into the end. A faint ghost of strawberry mixed with Shayna wafted up and smothered him. Brandon shuddered and tried to breathe through the shock of it.

"To focus the information." Nicky didn't seem to notice. "It's got links to the news articles and viral vids of the press conferences." As he talked Nicky messed with the elements on the screen—first in plain view and then he'd hit a tab, which took him to lines of code. None of it made sense to Brandon.

"I also talked with some of the FBI guys and Vegas lab people today, 'cause, you know, I thought this could be something I can do to help. I'm setting up a comment board that they're going to monitor. People have to leave an email, which they could fake, but it'll log IP addresses," Nicky sighed. "So, if someone starts talking about more than they ought to know…it'll be there."

Brandon managed to dredge up a response, "You've been

busy then."

"Yeah, I guess." Shrugging as he turned back around, Nicky asked, "What about you?"

"It's been hectic." Brandon gripped the pillow to his chest. "Took Dian over to the station first thing, met Frank there. And then I spent the good part of the morning dealing with them and the Metro detectives."

Nicky leaned forward, resting his elbows on his thighs. "What do you mean?"

"Yeah, well," Brandon snorted, "I keep having to tell Dian it's okay that the police want to give Frank and you and everyone else in the world a polygraph." They'd gone round and round about it. She just couldn't seem to grasp the concept of using a lie detector to exclude people from the millions of possible suspects. "Had to damn near freaking hold their hands the whole time."

Everyone kept turning to Brandon, like he knew what was going on. Well, he did, sort of, but it wasn't like Metro felt they had to give Brandon any more information than they'd provide anyone else. They just extended a little more courtesy in keeping him in the loop and not dumbing it down. "And some numb-nuts reporter outside the station caught me having a smoke. She's all like, 'does it bother you to have a polygraph test?' 'Cause they all have gotten the press on that."

Shifting so that their knees touched, Nicky asked, "What'd you say?"

"I told her that if cutting off my dick without anesthesia would bring Shayna home, I'd let Metro do it."

Nicky gaped, "You didn't?"

"Yeah." Brandon's normally low tolerance for dealing with people had sunk to around zero. "Orozco got on my ass about it...wording wise." And tone wise. The question hadn't been obnoxious; in fact Brandon expected to field the routine junk that reporters always asked. Being prepared for them didn't make it any easier to answer. "Not much because he had to run off to another call."

"Oh." The sound was long and drawn out.

Not particularly paying attention to Nicky's interjection, Brandon rambled on, "So I spent the rest of the morning on the phone with my lieutenant, my sergeant, Weaver and the OCID detectives." At least his own people didn't shut him out—as far as he knew. If they had something, they shared it. Mostly, though, nobody knew squat.

"No one's got anything more concrete than what they had last night. The Blue Knights, several other officer associations in California, all have already volunteered to cover costs and pony up for a reward. My own department is taking up a collection to help. Spent some time on the phone with a couple of national TV programs, getting them info." Doing things kept his mind quiet. Brandon wasn't certain how productive it all was, but he kept busy.

Keeping one arm wrapped about the pillow, Brandon palmed his face. After a moment of feeling small and overwhelmed, Brandon managed to continue, "Got some more flyers run off and took those back over to the Jewish Community Center and the command center." Not sleeping much at night and running around like mad during the day, God he felt like shit. "'Course when I went to drop off…both those places I get caught up talking to people." As well meaning as they all were, Brandon couldn't stomach hearing any more platitudes and hope. Especially with his nerves frayed to the breaking point.

The hope hit him the hardest. The world was clueless. The abduction had long since slid past the catch-and-release of small time rapists or molesters. Every minute now it inched closer to the forty-eighth hour when the chances of even figuring out what had happened to Shayna would drop exponentially. "Had to call Shayna's doctors and dentist to get her records sent over to Metro…Dian was a complete basket case with that. Pretends like if she doesn't do it, she won't need it."

Nicky stood, twisted and sat down on the cot next to Brandon. "I can't imagine how hard it is for you." He slid one arm around

Brandon's shoulder, the other hand landed on Brandon's thigh. "Either of you." A gentle tug pulled them close.

"It's insane, Nicky." The touch drained Brandon and he sagged against Nicky's body. "It's just insane, getting calls from reporters all the time." He wanted to just bury himself against Nicky, lose a sense of time and place, and he couldn't. "I don't want to talk to them anymore." Brandon swallowed. "But I also get that one of the reasons that the media is still paying so much attention is because of what I do." He hugged the pillow tighter and breathed in the fading scent of his daughter. "They want to talk to the cop who was such an idiot that his kid got snatched."

"You can't think like that, Brandon." Pressing his forehead against Brandon's cheek, Nicky whispered, "It's not your fault."

"Dude, I'm a cop." Of course it was his fault. It all came down to Brandon blowing it. "I should have known where she was." He shouldn't have been screwing around with Nicky. Not that it was Nicky's fault...no, he owned it. He'd given in to his dick and now he paid for it. "That's my job. I know the hell that's out there. I'm not walking around blind like all those civilians out there." Acid bubbled in his gut and threatened to break out as a scream. Brandon shoved it down with a few sharp breaths. "And if, fuck, someone did it because of what I do..."

Nicky pulled back. "It's not because of you."

He wished Nicky would stop trying to lie to him. "Yeah, right." That just hurt. Not like Brandon was stupid. He knew.

"No." Nicky stood and hooked his thumbs in his back pockets. "I've been trying to call you all morning." After taking a few steps, Nicky turned back to Brandon. "See, this morning, Orozco came to see me." He tapped his chest. "I got a package at the office."

Brandon didn't hear that right. "What?"

"I got a package. Addressed to me, at the office. It was full of photos." Nicky took a deep breath and then rushed through the next sentence, "Most of them over the last few days. Me, you and me together, the three of us at the casinos and the mall. I think a few of them may have been taken before you got here." The importance of that fact dropped a bomb into Brandon's brain. Everything he thought he'd figured out about this whole situation blew away in tiny, torn up pieces. He barely heard Nicky's next words. "I'm not sure. I didn't look close. They're processing them, the envelope, all that. Orozco and his guys are thinking Mexican Mafia...something about their style."

Brandon felt shaky. He looked at his hands expecting to see tremors, but nothing. "Why the fuck didn't you tell me?" Brandon hissed out the question through clenched teeth. It was as if his body knew if he let go for one second, gave into the rage boiling up in his bones, the semblance of calm and the thready sanity it carried with it would vanish. Every time he cracked it became harder to lock his emotions back down. Eventually, like a puff of smoke, his ability to hang on would escape his control and there'd be no way to recapture the outward stillness.

"I've been calling you all morning." Defensive, Nicky laced his arms over his chest and leaned against the lip of the desk. "You haven't been answering. Your phone rings and rings or goes straight to voicemail whenever I called. Either way, I didn't just want to leave a message about it."

Heat welled up in Brandon's chest and pulled the tendons taut. Every muscle in his neck, legs and face wound so tight they felt like they were ripping off his bones. Brandon strained to keep himself sitting on the cot. "You should have fucking found me!" The roar that came out of his throat surprised even him.

"I was fucking trying to!" Nicky bellowed back.

The pillow hit the floor as Brandon shot off the bunk. "You should have tried harder!"

"Brandon, Nick..." Edith's voice broke in before she reached the door. "What's the matter?" She panted as she leaned against the frame.

"Nicky's fucking holding out on me!" He spat the words like they tasted bad. In a way they did. How could Nicky not tell him? Like the moment it happened? Nicky owed him that.

Edith pressed her hand to her chest. "What?" She sounded confused.

Brandon couldn't deal with his stepmom right then. He turned on Nicky. "You're fucking hiding things from me!"

"Anything but..." Nicky protested. "I tried to reach you!"

Brandon didn't want to hear his excuses. "I need to know these things." He needed to solve this, figure it out. If Nicky kept him in the dark...time slipped through his fingers so fast, there wasn't a second allowed for delay. "How else am I going to find the asshole who did this...if you don't tell me?"

Nicky stammered, "I tried to call!"

"You should have found me!" Brandon slammed his forehead with the butt of his palms. "Left me a message!"

"What?" Poison seeped through Nicky's tone. "Some asshat mailed me pics of us and Shayna? No. That's not what you leave in messages! I tried to get you...you didn't answer."

Brandon dropped back on the cot and pounded his thighs with his fists. "How am I supposed to do anything if you don't keep me in the loop?"

"What do you mean, 'do anything?' You're not the police in this." Nicky pressed his palms against his temples. "I gave it to Orozco. It's his investigation...not yours."

"I have to find her!" Nicky didn't understand. "It's my job to find her!"

"No, it's not," Nicky gaped at him. "It's the police's job to find her. Stop acting like you can solve this." Rubbing his face with his hands, Nicky muttered, "You're just her dad here. You're not super-cop!"

No! Brandon wasn't just a victim. He was a cop. Cops didn't suffer crimes they solved them. "Fuck you, Nicky!" Brandon bolted off the cot, got tangled in the legs and sheets. "Just fuck you!" Managing not to trip as he sputtered it out, Brandon headed toward the door.

Edith caught his arm as he tried to pass her. "Brandon, where are you going?"

"Out." Brandon jerked away from the touch. "For a walk." He managed to huff through his rage. "Something."

Nicky'd just shredded everything he understood about the case...about his daughter and her odds. If they were after Nicky, then the whole thing equaled dishing out pain. No one wanted ransom or concessions from Brandon. Strike at the heart and dig deep...Fuck! Stumbling through the house and toward the front door, Brandon forgot his jacket. The biting Nevada winter afternoon, as he hit the front stoop, drilled into his bones and kept him moving. Pain from the cold focused him on something beyond his thoughts. If he stayed in his own brain...well, Brandon didn't know how much longer he could keep going.

CHAPTER 17

Nick edged through the open door to his bedroom, trying to be as quick and quiet as possible. Edith lay on his bed, her arm over her eyes. "Sorry, Edith, I just wanted to get my old jeans and a T-shirt out of the drawer." After Brandon stormed out, Edith had complained of a headache…and headed toward Nick's bedroom as though it was hers. In a way, Nick guessed it was. "I thought I'd work on the hearse some." Since he'd given his bedroom over to Edith and Dian, Nick realized he needed permission to enter his own room and get his own stuff. "If that's okay?"

"That's okay." Edith sat up. "Although, I thought you might have gone after Brandon."

"No." God he didn't want Edith to think he didn't care. Nick cared more than she'd ever understand. "I mean, if he's not back in twenty minutes I'll go look for him, but sometimes Brandon just has to step away from things before he can process it."

"I know." She fussed with tucking strands of her hair behind her ears. "Remember, I had to deal with him in that whole pre-teen through teenager tormented period."

"I'll be quick and get my stuff. Then you can relax." This was so hard having his house, his life, taken over by Brandon's family. "Wanted to do it now," he buried his irritation and tried to be polite, "before you got settled for a nap or something."

Strange people slept in his bed. Nothing was put back where it belonged. He'd been invaded by the cops and then by these people he didn't know. If it didn't end soon, he'd freak. God, Nick so did not want to feel that way. Still, he wanted things back to normal. He wished it had never happened. He wished he'd never been so insistent with Brandon. Maybe if he tore into the carburetor on Querida he could work through it all and be somewhat rational by the time Brandon came back.

She smiled at Nick. "Call me mom." Holding her hands out

to him, "All my kid's friends called me mom. Especially the ones that hung around a lot, you know the best friends, girlfriends. Between my two boys and Brandon I was probably 'mom' to twenty kids at one time."

"I'm hardly a kid, Edith." Nick stayed put and hooked his thumbs in his back pockets. He wasn't sure what she was fishing for.

Not seeming to notice, or just being polite about his reluctance, Edith let one hand drop into her lap. Leaning over, she reached out and picked a photo frame off his nightstand. Edith glanced at it as she sat back. Then she flipped it around, holding it against her chest. "You're hardly just a friend either."

"What, that?" Defensive, Nick crossed his arms and leaned against the dresser. As casually as he could manage he minimized, "That's out at Red Rock. We went hiking up there with Miri and her boys."

"Oh." Edith flipped the frame again, studying the picture. "I see." Nick knew it by memory: Brandon and Nick leaned against Brandon's Harley. T-shirts and jeans for both, Nick wore his gramps' battered old cowboy hat pushed back on his head. They posed closer to each other than most men would. If you looked real hard you could just make out Nick's right hand in Brandon's right back pocket.

Edith was looking real hard. "Well, most men I know don't keep photos of other men in their bedroom. Especially not next to their bed." With a sad smile, the photo went back on the nightstand among a group of others. A small pewter frame in the shape of bat's wings held a snapshot of Nick and Brandon on their first date at Hugo's. The largest, a portrait of Brandon— shirtless from the portions of his tattooed shoulders visible in the shot—glared out of a plain black frame. Edith fingered them all before turning to Nick. "So how long have you been *just friends?*"

Nick swallowed, "April."

"Good friends, huh?" Edith perched on the edge of his bed.

Patting a spot on the covers next to her, "Come. Sit down and talk to me. I like to know about my sons'…friends." When Nick hesitated, Edith leaned forward and swiped at Nick's thigh. "I don't bite. I promise." Slowly he eased over and settled himself on the bed next to her, his hands tense on his thighs. Edith covered one with both of her own. "So tell me how you two met."

Oh God. Nick flashed back to their first night together. They'd picked each other up at a club event. Edith didn't need to know that. He stammered as his cheeks grew hot, "We met at a conference of sorts; a weekend of bands and parties." Two days spent more in than out of bed. Nick shifted as a rush of chills hit his body with the memory. It had been intense. It still was intense.

"That's nice, so you share a lot of the same interests?" Nick just nodded in response. "And what do you do together?"

"Work on Querida, the '68 Cadillac hearse I'm restoring. Sometimes we watch movies or go to clubs, take the bikes out on the road." He shrugged, "You know, guy stuff." Nick picked at his cuticles. Somehow he doubted Edith would buy that. "Brandon helped me out, took care of me after my accident." Calling falling out of the back end of a hearse doing sixty on the Grapevine an accident was a lot like calling a plane crash a mishap.

"Accident?"

"I worked this case for the State, you know as a gaming control agent. My investigation stumbled onto something a lot bigger than we anticipated. Basically I had to jump out of a moving car to escape." He didn't want to tell Edith everything, but he figured she ought to have some of the reason Nick felt obligated to help out as much as he did. "Messed up my shoulder, ribs, broke my butt. I was a mess. Brandon…Brandon got me home and got me through it. At least until I could manage on my own." Of course it didn't explain why Brandon would have done that for Nick. He'd leave that for Brandon to field. "I owe him a lot."

"Sounds like he cares about you."

Another shrug. "Yeah, I guess." Sometimes Nick wondered

about how Brandon really felt. Whether he cared at all or if it was just fucking around for him. There were occasions where Brandon rated as a class-A jerk. Then he'd turn it around and be wonderful. Emotional roller coasters didn't sit well with Nick. He wanted Brandon to suck it up and commit to him.

And Nick hated being so self-centered about that at a time like this.

"Can I tell you a story about Brandon?" Edith took both his hands in hers, breaking Nick out of his thoughts and forcing him to turn toward her. Nick's mother did the same thing whenever she had something really important to talk about.

"Sure."

"For the longest time, after I married his father, I thought that Brandon didn't like me." She smiled and looked back at the portrait of Brandon. "He was just this quiet, stoic kid who read all these true crime books." A small, almost embarrassed, laugh broke from her at that point. Edith shook it off and returned her attention to Nick. "And let me tell you what fits that gave me. I thought I had inherited a potential serial killer. Dressed all in black. Posters of this band. All these big scary guys with tattoos and long hair…Blood Type something."

Nick laughed, "Type-O-Negative. I like them a lot."

"So, anyway, I was going to put a rose garden in the backyard. Brandon was probably sixteen." She sighed then smiled. "I had it all marked out with plans and everything. Well I threw out my back trying to dig out this stone. I spent a week in bed, zonked out on pain killers. When I'm good enough to walk I go out to the back yard and it's done. First I hit up my boys and no it wasn't them. Then I was all over Robert, Brandon's dad, and he kept denying it. So then Brandon comes in, headphones on, totally oblivious." She mimicked yanking a pair of ear-buds out of an invisible set of ears. "So I unplugged him and asked, 'do you know who did that?' He says, 'yeah.' Then I asked, 'who?' And he says, like it's nothing, 'me,' and walks out." Nodding, like something made sense to her, Edith asked, "You know what I learned about Brandon that day?"

Nick couldn't fathom what she was getting at. "That he's good at landscaping?" A stupid, snide statement and Nick cringed a little the moment it came out. He shouldn't let his irritation with Brandon roll over onto Edith.

"Cute." Edith seemed to not take offence at his tone. "No, that Brandon doesn't use words to tell people he cares about them." Patting his hand again, it was like Edith tried to reassure Nick that things would be okay. "Never has and never will. But when he really cares about someone they are the world to him and he'll do just about anything to see that they're happy."

Nick huffed. "I don't know about that, sometimes." He really didn't. It was as if Brandon walked around in this oblivious haze. He never wanted to take the next step. If Nick didn't push, they'd never move forward.

Instead of commenting on his doubt, Edith changed the direction of the conversation. "It's a good thing he has a friend like you." She reached up and moved a strand of hair off his face. One of those motherly gestures, "There aren't many friends who would just let their house be taken over like this. Sleep on the couch…it could be a long wait and you just smile and let us disrupt your life."

"Well, I ah, kind of feel responsible." Nick felt more than kind of responsible. This whole disaster was set in motion because of him. He insisted Brandon come even if he had to bring Shayna. He insisted that that Brandon leave his daughter with Miri. "You know, with the photos and all." Then, to find out, someone targeted him and used Shayna as the weapon; if anything happened to her Nick didn't know how he'd survive the guilt.

"You didn't know that until this morning," Edith reasoned. "How do you feel about all this?"

Why was she being so nice to him? "You don't need to hear my troubles." It wasn't like she didn't have a boatload of pain of her own. Shayna was Edith's granddaughter. From comments Brandon made over the time they'd been together, Edith treated Shayna as her own flesh and blood. "You have plenty of things on your mind without listening to me."

"Look, Nick." Like she might with her own sons, Edith slipped one arm around his shoulders and squeezed a little. "Dian can cry on my shoulder or lean on Frank. Brandon can cry on my shoulder—not that he cries, but I'm there for him. I can hug them both and cry my heart out. The one person who seems to be getting shut out of all this is you." Another gentle hug came with the statement. "And no matter what Brandon wants to pretend," she held up her hand stopping Nick before he could protest, "you're more than just friends. I may not have given birth to that boy, but I've known him since before he could talk. His mother was a good friend of mine...I was there at Brandon's bris. She was there for my boys. We were family."

Edith paused and let that sink in before she continued, "And I watch you two together, and I just know, because I know him. He keeps turning to you, leaning on you. And I'm glad you're there for him. But right now he doesn't have anything to give back. So come on...mom's offering."

"I feel so guilty." The words came out in a rush, "I feel like it's my fault. I don't know why you all don't just hate me." Because he didn't want to throw his burdens on top of their own considerable ones, he'd held it all inside. "If it hadn't been for me, none of this would have happened. I'm so sorry."

Edith pulled him against her in a fierce hug. "Oh, Nick, you know that's not so. You couldn't have known this was going to happen."

"But whoever did this did it to get back at me." He pulled back. Rubbing his face with his hands, Nick tried to regain control. "And...and..." he could barely get the words out, "I don't want her to get hurt. I don't want Brandon to be hurt. And I hurt them both because some idiot wants to hurt me. If anything happens..."

"You can't blame yourself for the actions of some other person."

"Brandon blames me." God, did he ever. Every time Brandon

looked at him, Nick felt that blame.

"No he doesn't," Edith tried to deny what Nick knew, "not in his heart. And neither do I."

"Dian does." There was no way Edith could refute that. "What she said last night."

Instead of contradicting, Edith gave him an explanation, "Dian's hurting and she's lashing out. And some of it is trying to get to Brandon through you." That theory, Nick could buy. "It's not fair and it's not right, but she can blame him for not being there and absolve herself of the guilt of not being there. But we talked last night and this morning."

Edith took a few deep breaths, and stared off across the room for a moment. When she turned back to Nick, a tired sad smile was for him. "Oh God, when Brandon called us and told us they'd gotten married because Dian was pregnant...I started putting up the storm windows. You just knew it was coming. Dian is a lovely woman. Brandon can have some not so nice moments." At least she wasn't blind to Brandon's faults. "But his heart is always in the right place. The two of them was like throwing gasoline on a fire, it just spelled disaster. Neither one would give an inch to the other. They were never meant to be together."

What Nick seemed to get from the way Edith said it, was Dian and Brandon weren't meant to be, but maybe Nick and Brandon were. "However, they are tied together through one small person. And she needed her daddy. Frank just is not Brandon." Again she smiled and this time it was stronger.

"Somehow I think that this move to be more involved with Shayna was your doing and that was a good thing. It's going to turn out all right. It has to turn out all right." A ragged breath brought a hint of tears to Edith's eyes. "But even if it doesn't, he needs you there." Edith squeezed his hand tight. "More than anything he wants you there."

"What," Brandon's voice at the door startled Nick, "are you talking about?" He turned to look and could almost feel the guilt painted on his face.

"You have a nice walk?" Edith didn't seem fazed.

"If you mean did I cool down?" Brandon leaned against the doorframe. "A bit, but I forgot my jacket and it's freezing outside." Then he glared at Nick. "What are you two up to?"

"Nothing," Nick managed to stutter out. "Just talking."

Edith patted Nick's thigh as she stood. "Talking about you and Nick." Oh Christ, Edith blew that. Brandon still wasn't comfortable with the two of them as a couple. The way he acted around Nick screamed it. And if he thought Nick might have inadvertently outed him...Nick didn't want to think about that.

"What about?" Brandon added a growl to his glare.

"Really, nothing," Nick insisted.

"You know, Nick." Edith added a glare of her own. It was far less scathing than Brandon's. "You're a worse liar than he is." Returning her attention to Brandon, she took a hesitant step toward him. "Don't worry, Nick hasn't said anything." A little more sure, she walked to him and put one hand on his shoulder. "It's what he hasn't been saying, what you haven't been saying and what I've been reading between the lines. And I'm going to take a wild guess here. You didn't just bring Shayna out to Vegas because of your tiny apartment. You brought her here to meet Nick."

Brandon shuddered. Mouth hardening into a tight line, he looked past Edith at Nick. "What would give you that idea?" Nick figured Brandon thought maybe Nick gave it to her.

"The way you are together." With a light touch, Edith drew Brandon into the room. She led him over to where Nick sat. "Some of Nick's, and your friends who came by the command center on Sunday."

"Who?" Brandon demanded.

Uncomfortable and on the spot, Nick looked up at Brandon. "Ah," Nick ran his fingers across his scalp. "Matt and Frederic." If he could figure a way to jump into a black hole and vanish, he would have.

It looked like the wind had been kicked out of Brandon. He sagged, turned and sat down heavily on the bed next to Nick. "Oh great, tweaker-twink and his lecher pal."

"I'm not sure what that means, but they seemed very nice." Edith spread her hands slightly. She pointed to the nightstand. "Then there's the photos Nick has of you here, in his room." After a pause she added, "A very interesting album on the bookshelf in the living room."

Nick's jaw dropped as he stared up at her. "You were looking at my photo albums?"

Brandon grabbed Nick's arm. "What photo album?" He growled out the question as he pushed Nick to look at him.

"I've had a great deal of time to fill. Trying to distract myself." The tone of her voice seemed calculated to calm them both down. "I assumed they were family photos. The first two seemed to be, family and friends. The next one…I opened it up and then shut it very quickly."

Brandon dropped his face into his hands and spoke through his fingers. "Nicky, you said you put shit away."

"I thought I did." Fuck, he sounded whiny. "What kind of picture did you see?"

Edith coughed into her hand. "Brandon, wearing his tattoos and nothing else." When Brandon jerked up to stare at her, she minimized, "Don't worry, it only showed your backside. But it was a little more of you than I was prepared to see."

"Aw, crap." Brandon retreated to speaking into his palms. "I, ah. Fuck."

Nick flopped back on the bed and stared up at the mirror bolted to the ceiling. "I didn't realize that album was out there." Not only did he get to feel like an idiot, he got to watch himself look wretched. "I'm sorry, Brandon."

"Of course you didn't." Brandon looked like he used his hands to keep his brain from exploding out his skull. "You don't think, Nicky."

"Don't get on Nick," Edith scolded him. "I guess I was snooping." She crossed one arm over her chest, rested the elbow of the other on it and her chin on that hand. "It wasn't like he left it out on the coffee table. Besides, I really barely glimpsed that one picture." Then Edith crouched down and put her hands on Brandon's knees.

"Like I said to Nick, though, those aren't the kind of mementos men usually keep of other men." She smiled up at him. "So no one told me, Brandon. I made a few educated guesses and Nick danced around my questions." Using her grip on Brandon, Edith pushed herself up enough that she could turn and sit on the bed next to him. Nick figured it was best just to keep quiet and let them talk. "When were you planning on telling your father and me?"

Brandon sounded like he'd been kicked. "I don't know."

That resigned, defeated reaction was at odds with everything he knew about his lover. Nick expected explosions and denial out of Brandon when confronted like that. Anger. Yelling. All that surfaced was defeat. As if Brandon had given up on fighting anything. Maybe the lack of sleep and the emotional rollercoaster lately seeped the fight out of him.

Although he wasn't about to open his mouth, Nick could still prop Brandon up. He reached over and ran his fingers over Brandon's back. That small touch to let Brandon know he wasn't alone. Nick would stand by him; shore him up, no matter what. Trying to convey that through gentle strokes and contact, Nick rubbed the small of Brandon's back.

"I never actually thought about it, not really," Brandon huffed. "I mean…dad hates everything I've done in my life." Reaching out, Brandon ran his hand along Nick's leg. "He hates that I'm a cop and not a doctor or lawyer or stock broker like he kept pushing for. He hates that I married Dian. He hates that I bailed and divorced her when we had a kid. If I tell him about me and Nick, he'll hate me even more."

"You know what he hates?" Edith snorted. "Those tattoos, the earrings and metal in your eyebrow." She shuddered, although

Nick sensed it was more for emphasis than horror. "I know, because he says, 'How is my son, Brandon, the cop, supposed to get any respect looking like a Hell's Angel?' He worries about you." Patting his thigh more, Edith rambled on, "He wants you to be happy. That you're with Nick," Edith smiled over Brandon's shoulder at Nick, "this brave, strong, person who obviously loves you back—that he wouldn't care about, not like that. Not that Nick is a man. Your father will always love you."

"He'll be so ashamed."

Nick could tell, by the way Brandon spoke, how he held himself, that he didn't believe his stepmother.

"No he won't." The pat on Brandon's leg was more forceful this time, as if the contact would convince Brandon where words didn't. "You have no idea how proud he is of you. Don't tell anyone, but he has the Riverside papers delivered to our house, all of them, in case you get mentioned." Edith sounded as impressed as she made Brandon's father out to be. "He keeps a scrapbook in his office with everything you've ever been mentioned for: high school baseball, all your graduation photos, the little announcement they sent when you graduated the academy." After a moment's pause, Edith added, "That photo of you in your uniform is framed on his wall. He shows it to all his patients. Tells them, 'There's my son, the detective.' He's so proud of you."

Brandon hardly sounded convinced, "This would ruin that."

"How so?" Edith pushed Brandon's hip with her palm. Physical contact to drive home the tone and importance of her words. "I'd be proud to have someone like Nick as my son." That one sentence swelled in Nick's chest more than anything he'd ever heard. Except maybe when his own parents said they loved him no matter what. "I can tell you, with knowing your mother since we were little girls; she would have adored him, been so happy for you." That thought added another layer of comfort to Nick's pride. Someone who knew Brandon's mother, really understood her was telling Brandon she'd think it was okay… Nick knew Brandon needed to hear that. "Robert loves you no matter what."

"Yeah right," Brandon growled. "When I joined the academy, he threw me out on my ass." With a shake of his head, Brandon added, "It wasn't until three months before Shayna was born before he'd even speak to me."

"I'm not saying it's going to be easy," Edith conceded. "We all know where your stubborn streak comes from." God, if Brandon's obstinate personality had roots in his dad, Nick could see where the fear and doubt came from. "It'll take him some time to adjust."

"It would take a nuclear bomb to make him adjust."

"Don't sell your father short." Chiding him, but reassuring at the same time, Edith ran her hand down Brandon's arm. "It won't change that he loves you."

"It'll change things," Brandon huffed.

"It doesn't change who you are: strong, independent, sure of yourself. You work so hard to keep the balance tipped for the world in the good." Sliding her arm around Brandon's shoulder, Edith tried to reassure him. Nick understood how futile that could be at times. Brandon believed what he believed and would go down fighting to hold onto his view of life.

"Your father knows that you are working for the good of the whole…I remember that fight you had. You told him it was your fate to protect people to make sure justice prevailed. And he was terrified for you. Robert tried to talk you out of it because he was afraid he'd lose you. You defied him." Another low-key laugh sounded as Edith shook her head. "He thought you'd come crawling back to him and you didn't. You made your own way."

Nick felt Brandon tense under his touch. "It pissed him off."

"No," she corrected. "It made him so proud that his son had such purpose in his life."

"But I failed." Now Brandon just sagged, even his hand on Nick's leg went limp. "I couldn't keep Shayna safe. I shouldn't have ever brought her to meet Nicky."

"Oh, Brandon, no." She squeezed him tighter. "You did the right thing. You came back to Shayna and tried to make her part of your life. Your life, I think a big part of it is Nick. This thing that happened, we don't understand what the plan is. We're small." Her voice drifted soft, like she tried to put it in perspective for herself as much as for Brandon. "Maybe the plan for Shayna is bigger than us. God sees the forest, the trees and each individual leaf. We only see the leaves on our own branch so how do we know what the tree, the forest needs?"

After a moment, Brandon sputtered, "What the hell are you on?"

"Look, grieve, rage, suffer as we wait, but believe in God. We wouldn't have been given these emotions if we weren't meant to experience them. But ultimately we have to trust. You have to go on...for her sake, it's the only way to find her."

"No." Brandon pinched the bridge of his nose like he was trying to drive away a headache. "The only way to find her is find the asshole who took her."

"God will lead us to her." Edith sounded so sure. Nick wished he had even half that much faith. "We have to trust in him."

"If anybody, I trust the police," Brandon huffed. "They're the ones that will bring her home." Every time Brandon said those words, *bring her home*, Nick shuddered like ice dripped down his back. Something in Brandon's tone said he held no hope in that statement. All it seemed to speak of was closure...and not the good kind.

"And you and they are God's hands on earth."

"I don't understand you, Edith." Brandon looked devastated, lost.

Edith appeared only slightly less distraught. "To completely misquote some poem I half remember: 'When I asked God for wisdom, he gave me problems to solve and when I asked him for strength he gave me burdens to bear and when I wanted truth, he showed me where I lied.'" She seemed to have faith...that probably gave her something to fall back on.

"What do I do?"

Nick wasn't sure whether Brandon meant about trying to live through this or telling his dad or both.

"You want your stepmother's two cents?"

"Why not?" Brandon's laugh sounded hollow. "You'll tell me anyway."

"Get rid of the tattoos." After another hug, Edith looked over at Nick and smiled, "Keep Nick," then her attention focused back on Brandon, "and just keep putting one foot in front of the other." Standing, Edith smoothed her skirt. The fussing seemed more nervous energy than anything. "I'm going to go warm something up for me. Maybe you two ought to get out of the house for a while. It's New Years Eve, you could go have dinner or a drink somewhere."

Brandon collapsed back on the bed next to Nick. "I'm not up for a party, Edith."

"Not suggesting you were." Edith smiled down on them. Like everyone in the room, her face was drawn with tension. "Spend a little time with Nick. You've been tripping over us and not feeling like you could be with him. You need him. You don't have to be out late, but take some time together."

"What if someone calls?" Brandon sounded desperate. "I need to be here if anything happens."

"You're out and about at the command center or the police station," Nick jumped in. "You don't worry about getting calls then." Maybe Brandon really didn't want to be alone with Nick... still blamed him.

Brandon twisted around. "That's different. I'm there where I can do something."

"Listen," Edith's reasonable tone drew their attention to her, "keep your cell phone handy and I promise, Brandon, if anything happens I will immediately call you." She reached out and brushed his knee with her fingers. "Please, for your sanity, get out from looking at these walls. Have some time with Nick this afternoon.

I'm going to call your father anyway." When the panicked look struck Brandon's face, Edith added, "I won't say anything. That's between you two. But, I need to hear my husband's voice as much as you need to be with Nick."

CHAPTER 18

Brandon slid into the front seat of Querida as Nick turned the key in the ignition. Over the roar of a V-8 hemmed in a garage, Nick asked, "So what do you want to do? We could go lose ourselves in a movie." He waited for Brandon to slam the passenger door shut before adding, "Or grab some pizza and beer. Your call." Even as Nick rattled off the options, none sounded remotely appealing. "Things'll be a little crowded on New Year's Eve, but it's not even four yet."

Brandon buckled the lap belt then stared at his hands. They rested—limp—in his lap. "I wanna fuck."

It took a moment for those three words to sink in. Stunned, Nick twisted in the seat to face Brandon. "What?" Of all the things he could have said that was the one Nick had expected the least.

"I want to go somewhere and fuck my brains out until I'm so worn out I can't think anymore." Hard, exhausted eyes swung up to lock on Nick's face. "I want to touch you, and feel you and forget, for just a little bit, that my life ended a few days ago."

Nick figured Brandon was depressed, terrified, but the utter hopelessness of that statement chilled him. "It's not over." He tried to put as much confidence into those three words as he could muster. "I know you're down. But, shit man, you can't think like that." He couldn't think like that. The police would find Shayna.

"Yeah, whatever, Nicky," Brandon huffed. "I'm not up for an argument right now. Let's just go find someplace and fuck around."

"Okay," Nick stammered. "Ah, we could do that." Shit, the question was where. He didn't want to take Brandon to some seedy little by-the-hour joint with vibrating beds. "Just give me a moment to think." There might be a reporter or two tracking them and he certainly didn't want to be followed to a place like that. They'd have to be fucking blind to miss the hearse.

Since the options were to have Brandon ride bitch on the bike, without winter gear, or take the van and leave Edith stranded without wheels—no way she could drive the fussy old Cadillac— they'd opted for the hearse. The big navy vintage Endloader was about as low key as an elephant walking down the street, but it would have to do.

Orozco had warned them, all of them, that there was just enough media appeal in this story for the possibility. A cop's kid had been taken. That in and of itself was pretty good for a sound bite. Top it with she'd been taken by someone now believed to be gunning for his "best friend" —a Nevada Gaming Control Agent—and the scenario was ripe for a mid-afternoon drama. Watching everything they said and did was tempered by not having to push media outlets to keep Shayna's face in the public eye. It was one of the best shots they had to someone coming forward with a tip.

They could easily lose themselves in any one of the big casinos. Goddamn, some of the Vegas giants had a bigger footprint than McCarran International Airport. The strip was too dangerous, or at least Nick thought of it that way now. That's where he'd been followed. That's where he'd been photographed. How something so simple could feel so invasive still stunned him. Anonymity had been ripped away. He'd been hunted like an animal. That this someone would take whatever deranged ill will against Nick out on a nine-year-old girl made him sick. It was terrifying.

He also didn't want people snarking about Brandon's daughter being gone and he hits the strip. Plus, New Year's Eve, they'd have better odds at winning the Megabucks Jackpot than landing a room in town, or even Henderson or Green Valley. Somewhere reasonably quiet, outside the city would be good. Nick threw Querida in reverse, backing out of the drive. Brandon'd moved the van out to the street earlier.

He headed toward State Line and a set of resorts there that catered to the camper crowd and truckers. If anyone ever questioned it, well that's where they could get away from the well meaning people who kept asking what was going on. Folks there were less likely to have caught the media blitz. It was a passing-through along the highway kind of place. Still, when compared to Atlantic City, where Nick'd been to gaming conferences, these locals' *dives* were huge. Where Nick headed boasted three resorts, close to seven-hundred rooms, a massive pool and a roller coaster people traveled across the country just to ride. If the GCB put every Electronic Services Agent on 24/7 detail they might be able to test each slot on the floor by the inside of two years. So, while casino employees might have seen the local publicity, probably the average Joe yanking the slots would be clueless and he and Brandon could disappear into the crowd.

A little less than an hour and fifty some odd miles later, Nick pulled into an asphalt lot surrounded by a small collection of resort casinos. Above their heads in the outdoor parking, late afternoon winter wind carried the rattle of the roller coaster some two hundred feet above their heads. When they hit the casino doors the hard sound of metal rain hitting a hundred trays assaulted them. Casinos everywhere had one thing in common, chaos. Nick could stomach chaos for Brandon. They threaded their way to one of the video poker bars. A table off to the side, sans inset screens and slot play, hopefully would keep Nick's bosses from roasting his butt since his employment contract nixed gambling. Nick stuck to Diet Coke and rum, pacing himself. Brandon went for harder flavors—premium cost extra but Nick just threw it on a card. After a cocktail waitress recognized Brandon from the news, even the good stuff came for free.

Alternatively drifting in silence and rehashing the week minute by minute, Brandon was getting sloshed. Nick could only repeat, "I know. I know.", and hope it was enough for the moment. They only had a few hours to be together—home by midnight or so to keep Brandon from freaking out. Brandon needed to unwind, relax some and then everything he'd held inside was going to pour out. When that happened, Nick wanted to be off the floor.

Late afternoon, heck anytime, drinking wasn't uncommon in any casino. Drunks lost. The casinos wanted you to lose. Of course, that usually meant they expected people to play. Still when Nick wobbled from the barstool and announced they needed a room to avoid a DUI he got a Casino Host. It wasn't like they had gambled for that courtesy. But notoriety had its rare benefits. Nothing special, just a typical room offered at the advance reservation price. Considering that, even this far off the strip, the resort was fairly packed, it equaled a distinct advantage.

Nick stashed Brandon at a fast food franchise with a couple of burgers then took care of the details. When he returned, maybe fifteen minutes later, a soccer mom chatted with Brandon while her kids ran wild. Her hand was on his arm and she offered up a thin smile every so often. Trying not to come off as possessive, Nick dropped his hand on Brandon's shoulder, "You okay?" He almost missed, considering how much he'd had to drink and how little he'd eaten that day.

"Well I keep getting hugs from little old ladies I've never met," Brandon barely slurred the tail end of his vowels. The only reason Nick noticed was he tried to keep at least a moderate tab on how bombed they both were. A jerk of Brandon's chin indicated the woman across the table. "This is Margo, we've been talking." He shoved the last bite in, chewing it like he didn't taste it. "Food was a good idea though."

"Hi Margo," Nick mumbled as a little blonde boy crawled into the woman's lap, demanding attention. Brandon's face went hard with a combination of what looked like jealousy and sadness. "The next good idea is let's go grab some sheets." For Margo's benefit he added, "I don't know about Brandon, but on top of everything else, kicking it on my couch for the last few days hasn't helped." Nick flashed a tight smile at the woman, "You know with strangers all over and the phone ringing almost 24/7."

Patting Brandon's hand as she shifted the boy to her hip, "People are praying for your angel."

"Thanks," Brandon mumbled as he stood. He grabbed his jacket and stuffed it under his arm. Pensive, quiet, they threaded through the casino. A few times, Nick thought he should say something and then just didn't. Once on the elevator, Brandon sighed. "Do you believe in God, Nicky?"

Nick chewed on his bottom lip. That wasn't a subject he ever thought too much about. Yeah, he'd done the whole first communion, altar boy to confirmation shtick when he was young. But, truthfully, other than funerals or weddings for people he knew, Nick hadn't stepped into a church in ages. "I don't know, babe." The bell chimed and they stepped into the hall. Rubbing Brandon's arm, thinking as they walked toward their room, Nick huffed, "I guess not so much at times like this."

The door opened onto a cramped little box with two queen-sized beds. Nick shucked his leather duster as he walked inside. Too many patterns, too little space, the ceiling felt low and the one window barely took up a third of the wall. The floor was covered in gold and brown zebra stripes. Add the pale wood laminate of the furniture and you had a fairly nauseating package. Well it wasn't designed to be where you spent your time. That was supposed to be the casino floor. And for their purpose, décor didn't much matter, either.

Sage, tan and chocolate flowers exploded under Brandon as he flopped across the first bed. His jacket slid off the end and onto the floor. God he looked so drained. Every time he moved it was like all his energy had seeped out through his boots. Nick couldn't stand seeing Brandon this torn up. And it hurt like hell that he was the reason why.

As he walked past the bed, Nick grabbed Brandon's jacket off the floor. He tossed both onto the other mattress and continued to the tiny window. "Maybe you should just sleep." Nick pushed aside the ivory chintz drapes, staring eight stories down toward the four-lane strip of the 15. Another perfect Nevada winter sunset bathed the sky in gold and blood.

Could Shayna see it where she was? Did she see anything anymore? As soon as the thoughts popped into his head, Nick booted them out. He had to focus on more mundane things…think about what he could deal with. "You can't have been sleeping well on that tiny little cot." He pushed past the fake plant and perched on the arm of the lone guest chair. Picking at the hound's-tooth upholstery, "Edith's right. You need to just relax some."

Brandon held out his hand. "Shut up and come here Nicky." His fingers beckoned Nick to the bed.

"You know." Nicky stood and shoved his hands in his jeans pockets. "I didn't think to grab anything." They'd left in a bit of a rush. And since he'd been thinking food and booze, not sex, he hadn't raided the nightstand. "I guess I could run down to the gift shop." Shit, he should have done that while he was arranging the room, at that point, though, he'd been more focused on getting back to Brandon. That's what he got for drinking.

"Don't worry." As Brandon sat up, he yanked his T-shirt over his head. "I've been thinking since, you know, the talk with Edith." Tossing the shirt on the floor, Brandon jerked his chin toward the pile of leather coats. Then he went to work on pulling off his boots. "I kinda started planning things. I grabbed stuff out of your drawer before we left. It's in my jacket pocket."

"Okay." Unbuttoning his shirt, Nick walked to the bed. He shouldered out of the shirt and laid it to one side. After sitting down on the end, he messed with getting his combat boots off. By the time he was done, Brandon'd shucked the rest of his clothes and lay waiting for him. With him face down, the labyrinth of ink on Brandon's back undulated every time he flexed. His tight ass begged to be fucked. If everything wasn't so desperate at that point, Nick would have savored the sight. Quickly, Nick reached over and dug through the various pockets in Brandon's biker jacket. The only thing he found was a small, flip-top vial. "Hey, I found the little thing of lube." He looked over at Brandon. "I don't see any condoms."

"Didn't bring those." Brandon rolled his head to stare back. "Like I said, I've made some decisions today. One, I want to feel you, Nicky."

Nick just sat there, staring at the bottle with its obnoxious label. What all of it meant was a little more than he could process right then. "Of course you'll feel me."

"No." Brandon propped himself up on his elbows. "I wanna

feel you, nothing between us."

Fuck, this was not the time to be making those types of decisions. "I don't know if that's such a good idea, Brandon." If it wasn't for all the other emotional crap coming Brandon's way at that point...well Nick would have been *right now* instead of second guessing.

Nick hated to be neurotic, but, shit, the last time he threw caution to the wind, he'd caught his boyfriend cheating on him. Quick jack offs at clubs: not cheating. Screwing an underage waiter from a pasta joint, raw, using Nick's own bondage gear: cheating.

The qualitative difference was hard to articulate and whether it was just the whole unprotected sex issue, Nick's own trust issues, or all the problems with Brandon and commitment, but Nick held to it. Shit, he'd even gone the route of private, expensive RNA tests just to be certain.

Brandon huffed. "It's been two years since I've been with anyone else—you know full on. My physicals all come up negative, and they test us for that shit."

Nick stood and unbuttoned his jeans. Wasn't easy with the little bottle in one hand, but he managed. "My tests came out negative," he shrugged, "but that doesn't mean anything. I mean for HIV it does, I guess. But there's other crap I've been exposed to."

"Look," Brandon huffed, "every time I stick my hands in a perp's pockets for a pat down search, I'm playing Russian Roulette. I trust you a shit load more than that."

"It's not the same..."

"Nicky." Brandon rocked up so that he knelt on the bed. "I don't ever intend to be with anyone else again. You're it."

"You've decided?" Nick kicked the jeans away as he stepped out of them. "I mean, what we talked about, before, you know?"

"Yeah, I've decided a lot of things." Brandon managed

something of a smile. "It all came to me in a flash, you know. These past few days I couldn't even think straight and then bam, it hit me. Now I'm kinda clear on what needs to happen." He scooted across the bed to the edge. With a heavy shudder, Brandon bent down. "This is part of that. Okay?"

Dick rising to half-mast, Nick moved to stand behind Brandon. He slid his hands across the toned ass and firm thighs of his lover. "Yeah. Okay." They both trembled a little...probably because of the emotional hell they'd been through the last several days.

Brandon, knees on the edge of the bed, head pillowed on his arms and ass in the air, waited for his cock. A totally submissive position. Feral and primal, it hit Nick right in the gut. Half-hard went to full and aching in a matter of seconds. After snapping the cap and drizzling a little gel over his cock, Nick ran his hand over the shaft a couple of times to slick up. Then he held the bottle a few inches over Brandon's butt and squeezed. The thick line of clear, viscous liquid drizzled into the V between Brandon's cheeks and down through the crack of his ass. Shit, in a moment Nick would feel that ass. Feel it all without the dampening effect of latex.

Tossing the bottle to the side, Nick moved between Brandon's legs. Brandon shifted, backed up a bit and spread his knees. "I want you to pound me," he mumbled. "Fucking hard."

Nick set his shins against the lip of the mattress, trying for a little purchase, and then eased forward until his rock hard prick rested between Brandon's hot cheeks. After a moment's hesitation, Nick pushed against that puckered bit of skin. Brandon was right, both of them played it safe and Nick was sick of the worry and the hassle.

Both he and Brandon sucked in desperate hisses as Nick penetrated Brandon's hole. Savoring the sensations, Nick slowly pushed past the initial resistance. Inch by inch, the length of his prick slid inside. Slow, steady, burning: God he felt everything and more. Once their hips met Nick didn't move for a while. He didn't want to. This was enough for the moment. Adjusting to the intensity of the contact, Nick concentrated on trying to breathe.

He savored the tight, hot softness of Brandon's ass caressing his prick. Not that it wasn't always good, but the feeling of skin to skin rushed from his balls to his brain and overwhelmed him.

It was too much and not enough. Slowly, as Nick pulled out, he whispered, "I love you." Even if Brandon couldn't say it, didn't mean he didn't need to hear it. Especially right now.

Instead of responding in kind, which Nick didn't really expect, Brandon growled, "Just fucking drill me!"

If Brandon needed rough, he'd give him rough. Nick held onto Brandon's hips and drove deep. "Fuck, Brandon." A couple of quick, sharp thrusts got him seated. Then Nick picked up the tempo, slamming hard. He could hear his balls slapping against Brandon's own. Just as Brandon would catch his breath, Nick would drive deeper and faster into his ass. Groans got louder and breathing more rapid.

Brandon rocked back against Nick. He pushed the pace to insane. "Shit, yeah." Grunting it out, Brandon slammed his ass onto Nick's cock. "Slam me."

The fuck ratcheted to beyond frantic and desperate. Yeah it was both, but more. His gut burned to cinders. Every nerve sparked into ashes. Somehow, Nick tried to channel everything he felt for Brandon through his dick. It was the best he could offer at that point. Reassurance, connection through sex. He lacked the words for more...not that Brandon accepted words well. A few more thrusts and Nick's senses boiled over.

Nick was going to cum in Brandon's ass, and he loved it.

White, hot spunk funneled through his dick and filled Brandon. Nick felt it bathe his cock in heat. Brandon moaned. "Goddamn, yeah!" Nick kept driving his dick in. Nothing felt quite like the friction of cum as lubrication in a guy's hole...in Brandon's hole. The overwhelming blanket of sensation robbed Nick's lungs of air and his brain of blood.

Brandon groaned then collapsed onto the bed. His ass still raised some and his legs spread wide, Nick enjoyed the view of Brandon's heavy sac smashed into the comforter. The head of his prick, obviously bent backward, poked out from the curtain of his balls. A tiny trickle of spunk leaked out of Brandon's ass. Nick hissed at the sight.

Brandon groaned and rolled onto his back. His semi-limp dick rested on his thigh. Other than the drops of Nick's cum that leaked from Brandon's ass, Nick couldn't see any evidence of spunk on the bed. He crawled up next to Brandon and ran his hand up a taught stomach. "What's the matter?" He'd clean off his dick in a bit. This was more important.

Brandon covered his eyes with one arm. After a few deep breaths he muttered, "Nothing."

Nick's hand wandered down Brandon's belly. "Want me to suck you?" That might help.

"I'm just too wound up, Nicky." Brandon ran one hand through his sweat damp hair. The other tugged his limp prick. "It's like I'm strung out, I guess. Jacking on stress."

Trying to drive away the worry, Nick kissed Brandon. Long, hard and deep. When he had to breathe, Nick pulled back. "Don't worry about it," he mumbled against Brandon's jaw. "Happens to a lot of guys who don't have half as much shit going on."

"Not worried." Caressing Nick's neck, Brandon huffed back, "I got what I needed." After another deep pant, Brandon added, "We can try a bit later. But I'm exhausted, and, you know, stressed. I ain't freaking about it right now."

Brandon must have been completely drained for that not to freak him. "Okay, baby, I'm here for whatever you want." He pulled Brandon tight against his chest. Exhaustion, or something more, stole the resistance from his lover's body. Brandon lay limp in his arms. Nick squeezed again and whispered, "Forever." Brandon shuddered in his embrace.

"Just rest some." With a sigh, Brandon heaved himself to sitting. "I'll be back in five, got to hit the can." Then he ran his knuckles down Nick's sternum. "I'll get you a towel first." As he stood, Brandon waved toward the little digital clock on the nightstand. "Why don't you set the alarm for a few hours from now? We should probably be back to the house before midnight... gives us about seven hours." Padding toward the small bathroom, Brandon muttered, "Might as well try and sleep."

Nick doubted either of them would, but Brandon was right... they might as well try.

clickjacked.blogroads.net—*Private Post, Jan 1, 12:35pm*

A new year. Now everything would change. Had to change. Everything set in motion and rolling. One change made already, so much easier not hearing it yap, yap, yapping. Already there was less noise about it from everywhere too, fading. Once it faded a little more then it would be time. Time to do what needed to be done. Like everything else things couldn't be rushed, just have to wait for the right time and then make a move. See the opportunity and go for it. Once that happens, everything changes.

CHAPTER 19

Brandon hunched his shoulders deep into his leather jacket and walked against the freezing wind toward Nicky's place. Another jogger, this one seedy, but buffed and dressed in thick sweats, passed him as he walked. That made the third in the last fifteen minutes. Never in his life had Brandon gotten up to jog on the morning after a New Year's Eve blow out. Hell, most of the last nine years he'd worked extra detail on checkpoints and drunk driver patrols—ticking off the minutes until the year rolled on the dashboard clock—and then slept through the day. Being single with not much of a social life might as well get put to good use earning double time and shift differential for holiday work. Closest he'd ever got to a party was signing up for Pasadena PD's outsource crowd-control detail for the overnight campers on the Rose Parade route.

For the second time that morning, Brandon traded a round of glares with a couple of tatted up bangers in flashy parkas and jeans slung low enough to show off their boxers. Why the fuck they were up so early Brandon didn't try to really fathom. Maybe they hadn't gone to sleep after rounds of cheap champagne and gunshots fired into the air.

Or maybe, they were like Brandon and just couldn't sleep. He'd been around the block at least five times since before sun-up and gone through half a pack of smokes already. Walking always helped him sort things out, plan. A lot of crap had to be taken care of pretty quick. Nothing monumental, just loads of little loose ends so that he could take the next step knowing things would be settled.

The cold fingers of winter dawn tinged the sky gray-blue: a dismal day to start a dismal new year. Maybe he'd try and sleep again. He and dreamland barely managed a nodding acquaintance these days. Fits and snatches were all he could manage and those were tinged with dreams he dreaded. Even the prescription he relied on in regular times to knock him out seemed to do no more than give him a woozy, crapped out headache.

Last night had been better. Close to four hours in one go. Probably because one side of his brain didn't have to recycle the what-nexts that kept him up. The nightmares about Shayna hadn't dissipated, but other stuff eased up. Just the vague outline of his future gave Brandon something to focus on and that calmed him down.

As he got closer, Brandon noticed someone lurking in Nicky's front yard. He slowed, surveying the scene: small woman, large coat and cradling something in her arms. She bounced from one foot to the other as if unsure whether she should head up and ring the bell. Since most perps fell into the stay-up-late and sleep-in category, Brandon figured she wasn't much more than a nuisance. Plus, she seemed hesitant, almost timid. Attitude, time of day and the fact that anyone passing on the street could see her hanging around, got the woman shuffled through his cop filter into the not terribly threatening category.

Brandon tossed the butt of his cigarette on the sidewalk and ground it out under his boot as he walked. When he got close enough, he growled out, "Can I help you?"

She jerked and spun. "Who are you?" She sputtered it out seeming far more frightened by his appearance than most people. Brandon, teetering on the edge of sleepless haze and sporting the unshaved, unwashed look figured he probably looked more disturbed than she did. Then, initial shock apparently passing, she blinked. "Oh, sorry. You're Agent O'Malley's, Nick's friend. With the kid."

Why the fuck was she lurking around Nicky's house before seven in the a.m.? Especially on New Year's Day. Of course, it'd be pretty reasonable to assume they wouldn't have been out partying 'til the wee hours. Basic social parameters still kinda drew the line at not calling or dropping by before nine. "Yeah, I'm the guy with the kid," Brandon growled. "Who the fuck are you?" He stamped down the urge to add *besides a moron* that threatened to slip out.

"Sorry. I work with him." She thrust a pink cardboard box with a chain grocery store sticker slapped on one side. "I brought some doughnuts."

Another person with food. Why did everyone think people whose lives had gone to hell needed food? "Great." Brandon didn't even bother to feign enthusiasm.

"Is Nick around?"

"No, he's asleep." At least one of them was able to sleep halfway decently. Could be because Nicky finally had his own bed back. They'd gotten back from the casino a little before midnight. Nick's bedroom door stood wide open, the bed made and cover turned down. Edith hadn't been in sight and the door to the office was shut tight. Besides the little creeping nausea caused by his stepmom *knowing*, possessiveness crawled in and gnawed at his heart. Shayna's stuff was in there. Her bed, her pillow... the little bits of things that kept Brandon centered. He wanted to keep those to himself as long as humanly possible.

"Asleep?" The whined out question yanked Brandon's attention back to the woman.

"Yeah." Brandon reached out and took hold of the box. "What's your name?" He almost had to tear it from her hand. "I'll tell him you came by."

"I want to see him." She shoved her hands in her coat pockets and shuffled her feet against the concrete walk. "Tell him myself."

"Look, I'm not going to wake him up." Brandon couldn't decide whether she was pushy or just stupid. Finally he decided he didn't care all that much anyway. "If you give me your name, I'll tell him you came by."

"Jen." She almost swallowed her own name. "I work with him."

"You said that." Brandon juggled the box with one hand and fished in his pocket for the keys with the other. "I'll let him know you were here."

As Brandon started to walk away she grabbed at his arm. "Is he okay?"

If his tone hadn't said *go away now* the turning and walking away should have clued her in. He paused and glared. "What?" Felony stupid; that had to be her problem.

"I'm sorry." Jen retreated with an embarrassed attempt at an apology. "I mean…I don't really know you, and—"

Once again Brandon reminded himself that civilians focused on small pictures—like who they knew. "We're all getting by," he huffed. "I guess he's as shook up as any of us." Deciding that he needed to be more forceful, Brandon added, "Good-bye, now. I'm going inside. You should go home." Hopefully, spelling it out for her would make her leave. "I'll tell him you came by." Not bothering to check on whether she followed or not, Brandon let himself in Nicky's house, shut the door and locked it. If the dismissal hadn't told her to *fuck off* that should have.

He wandered through the dim house. Neither Nicky nor Edith seemed to be up yet. Once in the kitchen he juggled the box while shucking his jacket and draping it over a chair. Then Brandon deposited the container on the counter next to the coffeemaker. The dregs he'd left from earlier got a quick warm up in the microwave. As he waited for the beep, Brandon inspected the offering sent by Nick's coworker. The standard bakers' dozen of glazed bars and rings…none of which looked all that appetizing.

After the ding told him the coffee was warm, Brandon fished a doughnut from the box and retreated to the kitchen table and tried not to think too much. He wished he had a white noise machine to blur all the things running through his mind. When the world was quiet, when he was quiet, was the worst. Then he could almost hear Shayna crying out for him or her mom. All the unimaginable shit human beings did to little children exploded like rancid blisters in his brain. Brandon took a deep breath and reminded himself that it would get better. He had a purpose and ruminating over what he couldn't change wouldn't help him get there.

"What are those?" Nicky's voice in the kitchen startled Brandon so hard he jerked. He'd been so caught up in his own thoughts he'd lost track of time and where he was.

Brighter sunlight filtered through the dust hanging in the air. The world seemed to move so slow these past few days... an unending purgatory of time. At least, knowing what would come next Brandon could appreciate little things. Like how the morning light warmed Nicky's skin. How even unshaven and bleary eyed with sleep, Nicky was a handsome son-of-a-bitch. And, God, Brandon loved him, more than he could ever begin to say. Nicky deserved so much better than dealing with a paranoid, closet-case cop who couldn't keep tabs on his own kid. Soon, Brandon would give him the better that he deserved.

Instead of saying any of that, Brandon growled out, "Donuts." Rather stale, fat soaked and over iced donuts at that. Brandon realized he'd eaten two between the time the woman had come by and Nicky crawled out of bed. He had no memory of actually getting up to get the second one. "Some chick you know from work brought them by."

"Who?"

"Fuck, I don't remember." Brandon took a swig of his coffee and grimaced as the cold, bitter brew slid across his tongue. "Said she worked with you...sorry, that's about all I recall." Looking down at his hands, Brandon spun the mug between his fingers. "I'm dead tired, Nicky. Shit. I normally don't forget crap like that."

"Well, what'd she look like?"

"Maybe blond? Came up to about here." Brandon used the side of his hand to indicate a spot just under his nose. Trying to dredge up more of a memory, Brandon added, "She was wearing a big winter coat." Shit, he was slipping. The life-blood of a cop, an ability to focus in on the minutia of height, weight, hair and eyes so he could recognize a perp from a bulletin a hundred yards away. Now he couldn't even recall the face of a woman he'd spoken to not an hour earlier. If she hadn't brought doughnuts Brandon wasn't certain he'd even remember her at all.

"S'okay." Nicky shrugged, oblivious to the uncertainty ripping apart Brandon's sanity. "I'll just figure it out tomorrow at work. I wish I didn't have to go in." The clunk of the carafe getting pulled out of the coffee maker dragged Brandon's attention out of the spiral of self-doubt. Nicky stared at the pot before setting it back on the counter. He popped the lid of the container that usually held the coffee. After a glare, Nicky left the lid propped open and moved to rifle the cabinet. He must not have been successful. Nicky turned and rested his butt against the counter. "What happened to the coffee?"

"I don't know." Brandon shrugged. "I made a pot around four this morning." Maybe he'd made two? Brandon couldn't zero in on that memory, either.

"How many cups have you had?"

Brandon offered up another shrug. "Beats me."

"Crap," Nicky huffed and shook his head. "Well we're out now." After rolling his neck, Nicky stretched his arms behind his back and grumbled. "Let me grab my shoes." Then he ran his hand through his hair. "Lend me the keys to the van and I'll run out to *Terrible's.*"

Okay, without sleep, the idea of Nicky running over to a local's slot joint for coffee just didn't make sense. Perplexed, Brandon sputtered, "The casino?"

"No," Nicky stared at him like Brandon had grown two heads, "the convenience store chain."

"Oh." That solved one piece of the puzzle but left a second one hanging. "Why do you need my keys?"

Nicky drawled out, "The van." Somehow he managed to put three syllables into that tiny word. Then, as Brandon just stared, the obvious seemed to hit him. "Fuck, you're right; I parked the hearse behind the van last night." Nicky snorted and palmed his face. "I'll take Querida then. Be back quick."

Brandon went back to spinning his mug between his hands. A little bit of action to distract his brain from the thoughts lurking in the shadows. "If I'm not here, I'm taking a walk." How could he be losing his grip like this?

Nicky paused at the door. "You okay?"

"No." Brandon glanced up. "But thanks for asking." He didn't even try for a smile. "I'm as good as I've been in days."

"I'll just be a minute."

Brandon nodded. "Yeah. Okay." He muttered to shoo Nicky on his way. The sad look Nicky gave him just before heading out of the kitchen kinda told him that Nicky didn't want to leave him by himself. It didn't matter much. Brandon'd been alone with his own thoughts for so long now—the difference between five minutes and five days was negligible. He just had to hold on a little longer and everything would work out. It wouldn't be *good*, 'cause nothing ever would again, but it'd be an acceptable status quo.

A little bit longer, Brandon promised himself and he could take a deep breath and move on.

"Brandon!" Nicky's muffled yell came from outside. Enough terror carried through to flick up the hairs on Brandon's arms.

He bolted out of his chair and out the back door. As he careened around the corner of the house he caught sight of Nicky standing near the driver's door of the hearse. Brandon slowed to a jog and panted out. "What happened?"

Shaken, pale, Nicky turned to stare at Brandon. "This!" He held out a crumpled manila envelope. Nicky ran his free hand down his face. "It was on the windshield." The top had been ripped open. The ragged flap gaped and Brandon caught a glimpse of glossy cardstock inside.

"Hold on." If Nicky found something on the windshield and he freaked...that meant it might be tied to Shayna's disappearance. Brandon sucked in a deep breath. Slowly, he asked, "You opened it?"

"No." Nicky denied it with a shake of his head. "I just grabbed it and it opened up."

Almost afraid to speak the words, Brandon managed to stutter out the question, "What's in it?"

Nicky scuffed his Vans against the concrete. He bit his bottom lip and then hissed out, "Pictures," like the word might bite him.

What pictures? Brandon needed to know. He stepped up and caught himself short before grabbing the envelope. Nine years of police training stopped him from adding another layer of fingerprints. He pulled back and waved toward the hood of the hearse. "Well, dump them across the —"

"No." That one syllable cracked out of Nicky's mouth and stopped Brandon cold.

"Why not?" Suddenly, the horror of what might be in that envelope hit Brandon. He swallowed and licked his lips. "Are they, you know?"

Nicky blinked. Something in Brandon's tone must have conveyed the direction of his thoughts. "No! Thank God, no." He massaged the envelope in his grip. "Dude, they're me."

When Nicky didn't seem ready to add more, Brandon prompted, "And?"

"And," Nicky shrugged, "I mean I just saw the closest one and, you know, it's off one of the sites." Nicky rolled his eyes. He looked like he wanted to run and hide. "Whips chains, the whole nine yards. I think it's one Jake took like almost two years ago. Long before you and I."

"Is it bad?" Well, in the scheme of things, any picture without blood and guts wasn't horrid. Still, Nicky's hesitation wouldn't have been evident if the photos were of the garden-variety family snapshots. Brandon figured something was up.

Gritting his teeth, Nicky muttered, "I'm not wearing a whole hell of a lot except a collar and some boots." He sucked in a lungful of air. "Puppy-tails and ballgags…I don't know where the fuck this shit got dug up."

Brandon reminded himself to breathe. Nicky's prior sexcapades on display vs. the other images Brandon's mind had dredged up…they'd deal. Embarrassing, but not fatal. Like the envelope sent to his office, this equaled an attempt to intimidate Nicky and, by extension, Brandon. Of course none of the messages was a lock of hair or voice recording or bit of clothing from Shayna. Nothing said 'look she's still in play.' Every message so far was just a sledgehammer blow.

Stilling his hands—they'd started to shake—Brandon reached for his phone. By the second swipe at his hip, he realized he'd left the cell inside. Brandon looked at Nicky. It felt like his face was ripping apart from the strain of not screaming. "Call Metro, see if Orozco's on shift," he managed to spit out the directive. "They need to process the scene."

A sign.

He needed a sign to remember what this all was about. It'd been hard to find the pictures…hidden things, so cleverly hidden. A test. But they were out there. Only those smart enough, cagy enough could find them. A trail of breadcrumbs dropped through the forest of the net. Of course that's what he intended by hiding them, things not meant for public consumption. If you looked hard enough, deep enough, you could discover the tiny clues that lead you to what you needed.

CHAPTER 20

How could he cope? The best Brandon could do was sit in Nicky's kitchen licking designer ice cream, in a flavor he hardly tasted, off the back of a spoon as he dug it out of the tiny carton. He didn't even have the energy to put the shit in a bowl.

Hollow.

He was hollow. No other word could describe it. There was this big empty mess inside and every so often it heaved and threatened to swallow his sanity.

All the times he'd delivered horrid news and told people it was all right. They'd get through it. The police were on the job. One hundred and fifty percent committed. Every resource available brought to bear. Everything will be okay.

But it wasn't okay.

Brandon knew. He knew better than all those civilians watching on TV, wondering where Shayna was. He'd seen it in the detective's eyes, when they'd offered the *'we're doing everything we can'* line. There wasn't anything they could do. Nothing. Because they knew, too. Kids didn't come home from things like this. Not after this long. You pulled them out of drainpipes or chiseled their bones from concrete blocks, or they just vanished and you never knew.

Brandon sank back down into the hell of being a cop. The hell of knowing the real odds. What a stranger kidnapping really meant. The past few days he'd manage to function, push the thoughts down and then night would fall, the world would go quiet and they'd overwhelm him again.

Did Shayna beg? Did she cry? Had she called out for Mommy? For Frank? For him? There was no use fighting the thoughts. If he tried to shove them to a small corner of his brain, they just coiled and sprang back up with more venom. Cycling into horror show scenarios. All of it more real because he'd seen things as bad or worse than most people could ever imagine.

What was the point, really? Of fighting? Why go on? How could he ever again deliver that rote patter: *I'm so sorry for your family. We're doing everything we can. You need to trust us.* He'd know, know exactly the chances, remember what he felt right now, and they'd see it in his eyes, his face. No one would ever trust in him again.

Worse yet, he'd never trust himself, believe in himself. Shell shocked and going through the motions…eventually, a cop without focus, who second guessed everything, would go down.

Everyone joked about suicide-by-cop. What no one ever laughed at were the officers slowly killing themselves through booze or drugs. Worse yet, the crazy fucks. The ones no one in their right mind wanted to partner with. Guys who went looking for the hairy situations and then ramped them up to insane because they wanted to go out with their boots on. Nobody on the force would acknowledge those nut jobs existed…not outside of innuendo and hushed conversations about cowboys and head-cases. And when a guy like that imploded, the collateral damage of civilians and other officers spread like a nuclear wind.

Brandon knew he couldn't go down into burning his brain cells out with a chemical blowtorch. 'Cause Nicky, his dad, hell even Edith, they'd stick by him trying to pull him out. If he fell apart they'd be scrambling for the pieces. Jeff, his partner, man he'd be torn up watching, messing and trying to pull Brandon out of the pit.

And the other way, shit. Even bangers who rolled hard, they had somebody who loved them. Take a guy like that out, while he took you out and the chain of misery just kept rolling on. Brandon didn't want to do that to someone else's family. Might as well just finish it now. Everything was done and over already.

Of course Edith and Nicky wouldn't really understand that. They didn't know…not like Brandon did. Not like any cop did. The scenarios, more graphic, more sick each time, played like an endless porn loop in his head.

There was really only one way to turn it off.

For the first time in days he was alone. No time like the present. Edith was off to wrangle Dian. When she'd come out to see what all the commotion was about, they'd dodged the issue. He'd mumbled something vaguely coherent about new evidence the cops needed Nicky to look at. No sense in getting her freaked out about Nicky's gay bondage cyber life. Brandon convinced the detective who'd showed up to keep the newest development close to the vest, interview Nicky downtown and take the hearse to the police lot for processing. After Brandon dredged up the few details of who he'd seen in the neighborhood that morning that group headed off. Nicky would be tied up at the station for a while, tracking down the pictures on the net.

Then Edith started in on half-a-dozen things, like more flyers, meeting Dian and talking with the rabbi again. The moment his stepmom started in with her plans, he seized the opportunity. Brandon begged off of accompanying her with the excuse of not having slept much. Not that it was a lie, but when she took off with the van Brandon didn't go back to bed.

Brandon hadn't expected to have this much free time this soon, but he could manage. He'd started planning anyway, since the day Nicky got the first set of photos. He knew then there wasn't anything to be done. This whole thing screamed of revenge—cold, bloody business and nothing Brandon could do would change the outcome. A few things were left undone, but they'd sort themselves out. Might as well deal with it sooner than later.

But not here.

Brandon didn't want to do that to Nicky. Doing it in someone's house was anger and hate for that person: screaming *you'll be so sorry* in a big messy statement. The childish, last ditch effort to say *I told you so*. This wasn't that. He didn't hate anyone. Well, yeah, one amorphous phantasm who stalked his daughter in Brandon's dreams…did horrible things. Even if they caught him there wasn't enough hell in the system to make it right. And all the statistics said they'd never find the guy who did it or Shayna in any recognizable form. Even with the cold, well, Vegas sat in the desert with half starved coyotes and other scavengers. It was hopeless. Brandon just didn't want to keep putting one boot in front of the other.

No, he needed to go somewhere. Somewhere away. There was a ton of away in Vegas. Dingy dives, low rent hotels, but those meant some schmuck he didn't even know would be left with the aftermath. What seemed acceptable: several hundred miles of desert—he could be *with* Shayna then. Leave a note at Nicky's, leave a vehicle on the side of the road, eventually someone would find him.

If he got going now, Brandon figured he had a good couple of hours. 'Course, he was kinda stuck. Edith copped the minivan for her run to Green Valley—he hadn't really even paid attention to what his stepmother had outlined for her day. Nicky drove the hearse to the station so the technicians could process the hood for fingerprints and had mumbled something about a car wash when he was done.

The whole not having wheels threw a monkey wrench into the *do it now* part of things.

It took another few mouthfuls before the solution hit. His bike…Nicky's bike. Nicky kept it in the garage. So where the fuck did he leave the spare keys? Everyone had spare keys. Kitchen drawers, desk drawers…they'd be somewhere accessible. If Brandon's police training made him an expert at anything, it was figuring out where people stashed shit.

That would work. Course it would leave Nicky sans bike; crime scene impound and all. Brandon could fix that, too. It'd take awhile for probate, but a note and the keys to Brandon's Harley, that'd be fair. His will on file with the department left everything to Shayna in care of his dad. And since Shayna was gone—he knew she was gone—then what little he left would be turned over to his dad. If he left a note, Edith would see that Nicky got it.

Brandon headed through the house to the computer room. Nicky had all sorts of office supplies there. When he stepped into the room, it hit hard again. Shayna had slept here. Her clothes still packed in the suitcase pushed into the corner, Brandon could smell them...bubble gum lip-gloss. His breath caught up in his chest, pushed against his ribs like a fist. Brandon rubbed his eye with his wrist as he dug out a sheet of printer paper and snagged a pen.

Goddamn, how to say it? Simple. It wasn't like there was a ton of reasons, he didn't need to say sorry or explain. Notes rarely did more than give the family more questions that couldn't be answered. Brandon tried about three different starts, crumpling each failure and tossing it. Finally, he settled on the bare minimum. *Edith, make sure Nicky gets my Harley.*

He folded the paper and jammed it in an envelope before scrawling Edith's name on the front. Then Brandon pushed back from the desk, dropping the envelope on Nicky's keyboard as he stood. Quickly he shook down the room...no keys for the bike there. Out the door, down the short hall and into Nicky's bedroom, Brandon knelt down next to his own duffle.

At the bottom he found what he needed. Not the keys, but the other component: his Sig Sauer. Too bad his piece'd wind up slated for disposal after this. Most weapons used in a crime were destroyed and technically what Brandon contemplated equaled a form of homicide. Since Nicky didn't like guns much, there wasn't anyone who'd want it after him. Brandon checked the clip, round and safety. Then he tucked it in the front waistband of his jeans. Not the most comfortable way to ride a crotch rocket. It would royally fuck up his plans, though, to be pulled over if some guy on patrol noticed the butt end of the Sig sticking out of the back of his shorts.

Now he needed the keys. All the reasonable, and unreasonable, places for Nicky's keys to hide got a thorough searching: bedroom, living room and kitchen. Shit, Brandon even tossed the bath. No keys. Brandon dropped down on the coffee table, using it as a chair. He ran one hand through his hair as he adjusted the weapon in his waistband and tucked his T-shirt behind the metal; right against his belly, not the most comfortable place to pack heat.

Dropping his hands between his knees, Brandon blew out an exasperated breath. Where the fuck did Nicky keep his goddamn spare keys? The last time he remembered seeing Nicky with them was in the kitchen. Shit, he must have missed them. It was the logical place. Back door, garage was back there. He headed back into the kitchen and slowly, methodically began re-searching the drawers.

About the fifth one in, the rattle of a key in the back door froze Brandon in place. Nicky sauntered through the door. "Hey, Brandon, how you holding up?"

There wasn't half enough time for the cops to have processed the hearse and put Nicky through a detailed Internet search. "You're done quick." Brandon hissed it through a plastered-on grin as he stood. The drawer stuck out of the cabinet and he tried to bump it back in with his hip. Since crap still stuck out everywhere from his rifling, the draw lodged about a third of the way closed.

"Yeah, it's New Year's Day." Seeming not to notice, Nicky shucked his duster and tossed it across the back of a chair. "Not a lot of technicians on staff. I gave a statement. They attempted to get fingerprints off Querida. Pointed them at a few websites I recognized stuff from. Orozco came by while I was there… somebody called him, I guess." Nicky hooked one foot through a chair leg, dragged it out and sat down. "I'm supposed to go back tomorrow with a printed out list of the sites I used to post that kind of crap on."

Brandon had wanted to get out before Nicky came back. "Where are the keys to the Kawasaki?" Since he'd committed to the course of action, however, Brandon figured he had to follow through.

Nicky rubbed his eyes with the butt of his palms and muttered out, "Why?"

"I kinda felt like taking a ride." Brandon lied, tried to feed Nicky a line he'd buy. "Get out on the road for a bit. You know it's how I usually unwind…but the 74' is back in Riverside. Cost me close to a hundred if I rented a Harley on the strip."

"I have them." Snorting, Nicky reached over to his duster and pulled out the big fob he usually toted about and another ring with about three keys on it. "I took both sets since I wasn't sure if I'd be allowed to drive my ass home." He bounced the smaller set in his palm. "Hate to get stuck without my spare house key, you know."

Brandon held out his hand for the keys. "Cool." He took a step forward. "Can I borrow the bike?"

"Brandon," Nicky licked his lips, "why do you have your gun?"

Shit, the butt end of his piece, Nicky had to have seen it sticking out of his pants. "Don't worry about it. I'm usually carrying it somewhere. You just don't notice it." Brandon shrugged, trying for nonchalant. "Give me the keys to the bike, I need to borrow it."

Wrapping his hand around both sets of keys, Nicky shook his head. "Ahh, no." He set his balled fist against his thigh.

"Nicky, I need the keys to the bike." Brandon tried for reasonable, reassuring. "Don't be an ass. I just want to go for a ride." With another fake grin for effect, Brandon held out his hand again. "Give 'em to me."

Nicky stared at the butt of the gun then flicked his gaze up to Brandon's eyes. He licked his lips again. He took a deep breath. After what seemed like forever to Brandon, he asked, "Why don't you put the gun on the counter and we'll talk?"

"No. I don't give up my service piece." He swallowed. A little more insistently he added, "Let me have the keys."

"They're right here." Tense—Brandon could almost taste how tense he was—Nicky held his hand with the keys over the scarred tabletop. "Look, I'll put the keys on the table if you'll put the gun on the counter."

No way was he giving up his weapon. It was part of the plan.

He had to stick to the plan. "Look, don't worry, if something happens to your bike, I'll give you mine."

"Why do you think something would happen to my bike?"

"I don't." He tried to brush it off. "Just you know, in case."

"Why would you think something would happen?" Nicky repeated.

"Look no, just in case," Brandon wheedled, "I'll give you the keys to the Harley. Collateral, you know?" Breathing hurt. "You give me the keys to your bike." Brandon forced himself into a mask of calm. "Hell, you'd look really hot on the 74'. Guys'd be all over you."

Nicky sat straight up and shuddered. "I don't need the keys to the Harley." After another deep breath he added, "Or any other guys, okay." A pitch of panic crept into the last word. "I got you."

"S'okay, you take my keys." Brandon swallowed hard. "You have to."

"I don't want them."

"I gave you everything you needed." Nobody'd ever gotten that from Brandon. Now he just needed Nicky to let him go. "You have to take the keys and give me yours."

Shaking, Nicky stood. "What I want is for you to put the gun on the counter." He kept the keys balled in his hand. "Christ, please, just do that for me."

"We're back boys." Edith's voice sounded from the front rooms. Two sets of heels clicked across Nicky's hardwood floors. "Came by to see if you need lunch." Edith swept through the swinging bar-style doors into Nicky's kitchen. "We have a five o'clock inter…" She glanced at Brandon; no way she could miss the butt end of the Sig sticking out of his pants. When Dian edged in behind her, Edith swept her arm out like she'd jammed the brakes on the car and wanted to keep someone from falling into the dash. Then she swept a panicked gaze to Nicky. "What's going on?"

Without diverting his attention from Brandon, Nicky hissed, "Edith. Get the fuck out of here." His voice cracked through three octaves just saying her name. "Go call Orozco!" He didn't elaborate; instead he kept his focus on Brandon. "Please, God, put the gun next to you on the counter." Brandon could see Nicky's chest almost spasming trying not to hyperventilate. "Okay, we'll just talk for a little bit."

"Oh my God."

Brandon couldn't tell whether it was Dian or Edith who spoke. And he really didn't give a shit. Everything, this whole plan was falling apart. "Nicky," Brandon pleaded. He wanted to go. Be done. "Just let me do this."

"No." Nicky shoved the hand with his keys into his pocket. "If you want the keys, you'll have to take them from me." Neither of the women moved. Edith stood there, wide eyed and sucking in her breath. Dian whimpered and bit her lip. Nicky flicked his eyes toward Edith and hissed, "Get out!" Neither moved.

Ignoring everyone else, Brandon tried to reason with Nicky. "I don't want to hurt you, Nicky." He didn't. Brandon only wanted to stop thinking, seeing, spinning out the scenarios.

Like he held terror at bay with just a thread, Nicky panted out, "I'm kinda counting on that."

In contrast, Brandon had never felt quite so centered. "It's gone too far." He was scared out of his wits, but calm all the same. Knowing that the endless slide show of hell would stop made it all seem worth it right then.

"No!" Nicky's face fell. "No. Never." Almost as if he tried to equate a physical presence to a mental one, Nicky balled his shirt into his free fist. "Look, I'm here. It's okay." Nicky huffed. "And Dian and Edith are here, even though I need them to *get out*." Then, gripping his skull, Nicky stammered, "I understand. Trust me."

"No you don't." There was no way he could.

"Okay," Nicky's voice hitched with the agreement. "Right now I don't. But you go do what I think you're planning, and I'm going to know real well, aren't I?"

Brandon palmed his face. He tried to explain enough so Nicky would let him go. "She's my own kid, Nicky. How am I going to tell other people to trust me? I can't even protect my own."

"We'll figure it out." Nicky stepped in toward him. "Everything's fine." Pulling his hand from his pocket, Nicky held it out to Brandon. He didn't have the keys. "Just put the gun on the counter and let's talk."

"Please, Brandon, listen to him." That was Edith. Brandon glanced at the two women hugging in the doorway. How the fuck did it get here? This was not how things were supposed to go.

None of it mattered anyway. Brandon turned back to Nicky. "Look, the last time we were together, I gave you it all." He had, every last emotional drop. Brandon said goodbye in that last, desperate fuck. Why couldn't Nicky let him go? "So you got that. Gimme the keys and let me go."

"Sex is not a consolation prize, Brandon," Nicky screamed without raising his voice. "It's not like…here's your parting gift: you get to fuck me without a rubber!" Brandon heard the terror in Nicky's voice. "No! I don't accept that!"

"What?" Dian did scream—nails along the chalkboard scream. "You did what with him?"

"Shut up!" Nicky spat. "Get out! You're not helping!"

"You're having sex?" Dian looked like she was close to puking. "With him?"

Edith stepped in front of her and grabbed her hands. "Dian, now's not the time!"

Now, more than ever, he just had to follow through. Everything was over. "Nicky," Brandon growled. "Give me the keys. Now."

Nicky took a step back. "No." He shook his head and swallowed. "You'll have to take them."

Nicky wasn't going to give him the keys. Things had gone too far. He couldn't stop now. "Okay." Brandon stepped in, going for Nicky's wrist.

Nicky threw his arm up and across. "What the fuck are you doing?" Their forearms collided. Brandon's blow went wild.

Get in. Get the keys out of his pocket. Get gone. "Taking the keys."

"Fuck you!" Nicky grabbed for Brandon's shirt. Or maybe he was stupid enough to go for the gun.

Brandon blocked the blow. Then he used the back of his half-closed fist to smack Nicky upside the head. Wasn't a hard hit, but it was enough to rock Nicky back. Somebody screamed and it wasn't him or Nicky. When Nicky grabbed at him again, Brandon's focus narrowed to just them and his objective: the keys. Again Brandon brushed the blow aside. Nicky tried a few hesitant jabs, trying for a hold, and Brandon avoided them without much effort. When Nicky overextended on one grab, Brandon caught his hand and spun him.

Far more used to fighting, Brandon used the energy to swing around and catch Nicky under the arm. His boot slammed against the inside of Nicky's ankle. Brandon twisted. Momentum carried Nicky to the floor.

Nicky lunged as he dropped and grabbed Brandon's knees. Brandon tried to kick him away and skidded instead. He fell back, banging his shoulder against the cabinets as he went down. Nicky scrambled on top of him, trying to use his weight to pin Brandon. Nicky might have been lighter, but he wasn't a slouch in the muscle department; lean, quick and stronger than he looked. Brandon slammed the butt of his palm into Nicky's chest. Nicky coughed and reared back. Not even thinking, Brandon reached between them and yanked his gun out of his pants.

He came up with the business end of his Sig pointed at Nicky's face and bellowed, "Give me the fucking keys!"

Nicky stilled. His chest heaved. A little bead of sweat ran down the line of his sharp cheek as he stared into Brandon's eyes. "What are you going to do, Brandon?" He hissed out the question. "Take me out with you?"

Brandon's hand shook. Reality hit him. He'd drawn down

on Nicky. It felt like Brandon breathed water. Once before, it'd happened, but that was an accident. This...this was Brandon pulling his piece on Nicky. His Nicky.

Everything fucking derailed. Edith knew. Dian now fucking knew. Shayna was dead, she had to be. And now, now Nicky would hate him because he was a coward. A freaking coward who would hurt Nicky to get what he wanted.

Brandon sucked in air in rapid gulps. He rolled out from under Nicky, scuttled a few feet away and wedged himself into the corner of cabinets. The only thing propping him up was the wood at his back.

"I just can't—" It hurt to talk. His face felt hot and tight. "I can't sleep." Brandon stared at his weapon, his hands. They seemed like they belonged to someone else. "Every time the world goes quiet I get all these thoughts. Every time I close my eyes I see it...over and over and over what that bastard must have done to her. I can't live with that shit in my head, Nicky." Brandon looked up...Nicky's features blurred as heat prickled Brandon's face. He hiccupped and managed to stutter out, "I just can't take it anymore."

"It's okay." Nicky scrambled to his knees and eased up next to Brandon. He slid one strong arm around Brandon's shoulders. "I'm here," he whispered. Brandon felt it as Nicky eased his piece out of his hand. Brandon didn't have the strength left to resist. Pulling Brandon against his chest, Nicky held out the weapon... thumb and fore finger holding it away from his body in a pinched, disdainful grip.

"Edith!" He called Brandon's stepmom. Nicky didn't take his gaze away from Brandon's eyes. He hissed, "Do something with this," out of the corner of his mouth. "Get it out of here." Cell phone pressed to her ear, Edith stepped up behind Nicky. Gingerly she took the gun. Then Nicky wrapped Brandon in a fierce, protective hug. "I'm here." Mouthing the words against Brandon's temple, he added, "I'll always be here for you."

Vaguely, Brandon registered the sound of something opening and closing. Edith was talking to someone on the phone...and fuck knew where Dian got off to. He could hear her crying somewhere in the house. Brandon shuddered. He couldn't control the tremors running through his frame. It was as if some force grabbed him by the collar of his shirt and shook him. "I'm sorry, Nicky," he mumbled it, not even sure Nicky could hear him. "I'm sorry."

"No." Nicky kissed his forehead, the bridge of his nose. "It's okay."

"I can't stand it." Brandon licked his upper lip and tasted salt. He sucked in a ragged breath. "I can't keep going like this." The sound of Edith's heels on wood told him she backed out of the kitchen. Maybe to give them space. Maybe to check on Dian. Really, what did he care? Nothing mattered.

Nicky just kept holding him, kissing his face and whispering, "It's okay," over and over. Brandon felt himself sliding into the hypnotic chant. He didn't know if Nicky was reassuring himself or Brandon, but it probably didn't matter. Then Nicky's lips found his. A deep, soul searing kiss. It burned away the threads stitching the bits of Brandon's sanity together.

Brandon balled his fists into Nicky's shirt. He pulled back. He sucked down a breath. He tilted his head back and roared out his hate and fear and how much he despised himself and his failure. It wound out of his system in almost tears and left him hollow again. Empty. Except Nicky was there.

Brandon had no clue how long they just sat there, Nicky holding him, telling him it was okay. It wasn't okay. It never would be okay. Maybe, with Nicky there, Brandon might learn to function at a not okay level. "I can't keep thinking about it, Nicky. And I can't stop thinking about it."

"It'll fade." Nicky held him tighter. "It'll get bearable with time." His strong gentle touch. Nicky's kisses that hadn't stopped. His presence gave Brandon the tiniest little strand of reason to cling to. He didn't want to hurt Nicky. That wasn't his intention. And he'd have hurt him. Brandon rubbed his eyes against Nicky's shoulder. How could he ever really tell Nicky just how sorry he was?

A cough at the door startled them both enough that Brandon banged his head against the cabinet and Nicky jerked toward the sound. Emanuel Orozco stood framed in the door. "Sorry to interrupt, gentlemen." He looked sad, drained. Somehow those emotions on Orozco didn't seem shallow or forced. "I got a frantic call and rushed over. I thought I was going to have to pull someone's gun—not someone's tongue—out of their mouth."

Nicky squeezed Brandon's shoulder. "Two minutes earlier and you would have been right."

"Agent O'Malley." Orozco grimaced then cast a quick glance behind him. "There's two very distraught women in your living room. Why don't you see if you can calm them down while I have a chat with Detective Carr?"

"I, ah…" Nicky hesitated.

"Look." Orozco's already strained expression went just a hair tighter. "I need to assess the situation a bit. To do that, I need you, Nicholas, to keep Brandon's stepmom and ex out of the way. Can you do that for me?"

One of Nicky's hands rested on Brandon's leg, the other gripped his arm. "I really think I should be here."

"Nicholas," Orozco's voice was low and commanding. He didn't *order* compliance, but he sure as hell suggested it with his tone. "Go. I'll be here. I need your help."

Brandon pushed Nicky's hand off his leg. "Go on." He tried for humor. "You took my gun. What am I going to do, stab myself with a fork?" Nicky didn't look at all amused, but he did stand. Brandon reached up and grabbed the lip of the tile counter. Then he pulled himself up. "Go and make sure the gals are all right, okay? I think we need to do some cop talk. Okay?" Shit, Orozco was going to bust his ass and he sure didn't want Nicky to see that. He'd earned a 5150: restraint for self-protection. Maybe Orozco would let him walk out on his own at least, not call the white jackets to haul him off. "Go on. What am I going to do with another cop here?"

"You sure?" Nicky's touch trailed down the front of Brandon's shirt.

"Yeah." Brandon managed a load of confidence he didn't feel. "You'll be right in the other room."

Nicky stepped in. A brief kiss stole Brandon's breath. Then Nicky backed away. "Just yell if you need me."

Brandon jammed his hands in his pockets. As Nicky eased around Orozco, Brandon promised, "I will." He didn't even try to force a smile. It would have been so wrong.

Orozco did offer a smile to Nicky and a pat on his shoulder as he passed. They both waited until a mumble of voices in the front room told them Nicky was occupied. Orozco turned to Brandon. He glared and shook his head. "Sit down, Brandon. We need to talk."

CHAPTER 21

Nick stumbled out the front door, fishing a cigarette out of the pack with his teeth. Nausea roiled in the pit of his stomach. Every few seconds his gut threatened to erupt up and out. Hopefully a little air outside and the smoke would calm that.

God, he was surprised that he hadn't shit himself when Brandon pulled the gun on him. How the hell could Brandon do that? To Nick? Those few moments had scared him worse than anything he'd ever encountered. Even when the Mexican Mafia had gotten to Nick…well they weren't anybody he trusted. His whole body still jangled.

Nick tucked the pack back in his pocket and exchanged it for his lighter. Why hadn't he seen it coming? Nick knew Brandon was barely hanging on, but, you know, to do that? Not like Brandon communicated well about anything. Still, Nick figured he should have seen how far Brandon sunk with this. He couldn't believe Brandon wouldn't say something, trust Nick to help. Nick felt so useless, clueless and alone.

And what felt worse…the little seething pit of anger in his chest. Nicky wanted to just strangle that self-centered bastard. How could Brandon do this to him?

"Where's Edith?" Dian's voice grated over his nerves and caught Nick up short. Shit, he could have done without *her* right now.

He cupped his hand over the end, flicked the lighter and inhaled in a long, deep drag. After a few seconds, while he debated whether to tell Dian to just get lost, Nick decided on a more forgiving course of action. "She said something," Nick mumbled around his smoke, "about calling Brandon's dad." Not like Brandon's father could do much. Last Nick heard he was stranded at JFK.

Dian paced the length of the walk between porch and driveway. As Nick settled to sit on the top step, Dian stopped, turned and glared at him. "What are you doing out here?"

"Passing out poppers," Nick snapped with more venom than even he expected. Tucking the lighter next to the cigarette pack, Nick dropped the bundle twice before managing to slip it back in his jacket...his hands shook like an old man's with palsy. He could barely handle the morning—between the photos left on his car and Brandon's meltdown—Nick was pretty certain he really couldn't handle Brandon's ex-wife. "What the fuck do you think I'm doing here?" He took another drag. It marginally helped to calm him down. Marginally. "Orozco told me to get lost and, unlike some people, I follow directions in a crisis."

"Things are falling all apart, I'm falling apart, Brandon's falling apart," the shake in her voice mirrored the tremble in her hands and lips, "and I should just do what you say?"

Nick tried to dredge up a forgiving attitude and couldn't find it. He'd hit rock bottom about ten minutes earlier. "You trying to make things worse for Brandon?" he spat with a lot more anger than he'd intended. "Is that it?" It was as if every time he opened his mouth someone else spoke.

"Worse for him?" She hugged herself. "Who do you think you are?" Her mouth drew up tight and nasty. "My daughter is gone and you're talking about what's worse for him?"

"I'm sorry, maybe you think I give a damn about you?" Nick didn't try to even mask his irritation. "No offense." All of his twisted up, overtaxed emotions came spewing out at the only available target. "I mean, I feel sorry for you, but I don't *care* about you." Pointing back toward the house, Nick hissed. "I care about the idiot in there who is so screwed up he was going to— fuck I don't even want to think about what he was going to do."

"This is my baby we're talking about!" She yelled.

Nick yelled back. "And that's the fucking moron I love!" He had to will himself to stay put. "She's his kid, too." Puffing on his smoke helped some, gave him a physical outlet, however minor, for his agitation.

"Why did he bring my little girl into this?" A deep ragged

breath punctuated her thoughts. "Why did he bring her here?"

"Because maybe, just maybe, he and I were getting beyond just dating." She didn't deserve an explanation, but Nick gave one anyway. "Figured maybe it was about time she met me." Nick stared across the yard out at the street. Smoking and talking at the same time, he added, "I mean, Brandon's told me you and your new husband got together when Shayna was like two," Nick huffed. "I'm sure you eased her into meeting him and that's what we were doing, you know?"

"No, I don't know." The line of her mouth went tighter still and her shoulders tensed. "How can he be with you? I can't even picture it."

"Well," he mumbled, "that's the way it is so I think you need to chill."

"You're having sex with my ex-husband!" Dian stepped in and sneered down at him. "I should care what you think?"

Staying where he was got harder and harder. "Yeah, I am." Nick threw her sneer right back. "Get used to it."

"Get used to it?" It came as almost a laugh. "What, it's okay to be that way?"

"Actually, it is." Nick pinched off the end of his cigarette and tossed it in the flowerbed. Half of it'd burned to ash before he'd even got a chance to really smoke it.

"That is not Brandon." Disbelief and disdain warred across her face. "Brandon wouldn't do that!"

"Do what?" Nick's voice echoed cold.

"He wouldn't, he wouldn't be with you." She swallowed, hard. Looking back to the house, Dian insisted, "That's the father of my little girl. He wouldn't ever be with a man." She returned her glare to Nick. "It's not how he is!"

Nick laughed. "Like you would know."

"Of course I would know!" This time she didn't sound as confident. "I was married to him."

"Yeah." Nick wrapped one hand around the wrought iron porch rail and stroked it a few times. "Nobody changes after all, figures out who they are in eight, nine years?" Although he wanted to, Nick didn't hit her with the obvious about why their marriage had probably gone to hell. And by the deep insecurity of the accusations and emotions that seemed to be riding her, Dian probably figured it out and just didn't want to admit it.

One arm clutched about her middle, Dian kneaded her shirt in her hand. The other hand went up to cover her mouth. Her whole body shook. After a few hiccups, which Nick guessed might be an attempt to stifled sobs, Dian stuttered out from behind her fingers, "Did you expose my daughter to this lifestyle?"

Nick shot to his feet and took a step down. "*Expose her!*" All the anger that dissipated over the past few moments swarmed back. Dian took a pace back and Nick willed himself to be calm. "Brandon and I are together." He shoved his hands in his pockets and glared. "We didn't hide it, but no we didn't take her down to the Rainbow Bookstore for the kids reading hour, either."

"You were together?" Now she sobbed. "With each other?"

"No we were together with five random guys I invited for a circle jerk." Nick regretted the nastiness of the sentence the moment it passed his lips. No way to pull it back. Instead, Nick softened his tone, a little. "Of course we've been together all fucking week."

"So he lied to me." More sobs. Fuck, Nick hated it when people cried. "He brought my little baby out here so he could be with his…oh my God." It made him feel all icky and useless inside, like he should do something. "I mean, oh God, did you like have sex in front of her?"

Blindsided by the utter idiocy of the question, Nick sputtered. "Gay does not mean pervert." His jaw didn't seem to function right, 'cause Nick couldn't keep it closed. "Do you and your husband have sex in front of your kids?" On top of every other insane thing that happened, Nick couldn't handle her. What, on any other day might rate as clueless and annoying, pushed all of his buttons wrong. "I don't think so." His patience ripped to shreds by more guilt, anger and fear than anyone could be expected to bear, Nick snapped, "Don't go there, bitch!"

"How dare you!" she spat.

"No." Nick threw her attitude right back. "How fucking dare you." When she started to open her mouth to say something, Nick cut her off. "Why don't you go, fucking find Edith and whine on her shoulder." He pushed past her and headed toward the drive. "I need to get out of here before I say something I'm *really* going to regret." Nick just didn't want to be around anyone else at that moment.

He stalked around the corner and down the concrete. Querida still had fingerprint dust all over the windshield. Maybe a little mindless busy work on the hearse might get Nick to a place where he could figure things out. Things like whether he was more furious at Dian for acting like an ass, Brandon for trying to—he couldn't even name that thought—or himself for not seeing how low Brandon had sunk.

CHAPTER 22

Detective Orozco stared from across the room. Long and hard enough for Brandon to start to fidget. Finally, Orozco eased over to the table and pulled out a chair before indicating the one Nicky had sat in earlier. "Sit down, Brandon." Even if it was a command, the man's voice broke the tension a little. Still, it was all Brandon could do to comply. Orozco eased into the chair. As Brandon twisted his chair to face Orozco, the older detective huffed, "What the fuck were you thinking?"

Brandon dropped into the seat. "Don't know." The hoarse whisper that came out hardly sounded like himself. Brandon stared at his hands and tried to will them to stop shaking. Placing both palms flat on his thighs seemed to help a bit. "I just can't think straight." Of course, since his hands were stilled, the rest of Brandon's body started to jangle.

Orozco crossed his arms over his chest and leaned back in his chair. "That is obvious."

Shit, everything had gone straight to hell. A simple little plan to just go away and stop thinking…royally fucked up. "Can we, at least, let me walk out of here on my own?" Brandon swallowed and stared at the floor. "No handcuffs or shit?" That's what happened when anybody, much less a cop, went off the deep end. Brandon'd drawn down on Nicky. That equaled off the deep end: hazard to himself and others.

"Think I'm going to have you tossed under 433A?"

Brandon shrugged. "That's your code section?" Most cops referred to that particular *public safety* issue by code number. "Involuntary restraint, mental health eval?" It was either that or veiling it in euphemisms like *squirrels* or *loosing marbles* and most modern departments frowned on that type of language.

"I'm thinking about it." At least Orozco didn't sugar coat shit.

Brandon snorted. "I'd 5150 my ass." He deserved it: the humiliation, departmental reviews. And it would put him somewhere where he couldn't hurt Nicky.

"You're not a squirrel." Orozco tapped the table with two meaty fingers drawing Brandon's attention from the morass of his own mind to Orozco's face. "You're fucked up, but I'm not sure locking you up would help things." He shook his head and growled. "Still, you think you're gonna get out of this hell by checking out like that, you deserve to be knocked upside your thick head. Everybody's life is in the shit-can and you're gonna go make it worse."

Brandon never had a great deal of training in crises debriefing…what he did, didn't equate to anything Orozco said. "Great way to talk someone down, Orozco."

"Manny." He rocked forward a bit. "I'm Manny to you now." Orozco's stare fixated Brandon. "No more of this arms length bullshit we all play. Maybe I'm saying it because that's what you need to hear, you stupid dumb shit." One arm unwound from around his chest and Orozco pointed back toward the living room. "You mean something to those people. What makes you think you got the right to do that to everyone else?"

Brandon managed to convert enough shame into anger to spit back. "What gives you the fucking right to get in my face?"

Orozco fell silent for long enough that Brandon figured he'd nailed it. Then the older detective rocked his hip up and fished in his back pocket. He pulled out a billfold, spent a second flipping through the credit card insert until he found whatever he sought then tossed it on the table. "That." He used his chin to indicate the wallet.

Brandon didn't look. "What, your wallet?"

"Look at it." Orozco snapped and reluctantly Brandon complied. A young man, not quite grown into himself yet, but with nice features and a tiny feathering of a mustache stared out from a school photo. The gold robe on his shoulders, plus collared shirt and tie, pegged him as a senior. "That's my son."

Brandon could see the hints of that relationship in the boy's eyes and the structures of his nose. "He would have been twenty-five two months ago."

"What?"

"You think, because you're a cop, you'll see it. I know what's out there. Kept an eye on his friends, thought I knew pretty much where he was most times. Figured if his grades were decent then things must be okay. I never had to worry. He'd come home after soccer practice, do his homework and take out the trash." Orozco sucked in a huge breath like he was steeling himself for the memory. "And then one day, I came home early and my gut screamed at me that something's wrong. Found him in the basement, foam all dried in his mouth and his head arched back off the couch we kept down there. Probably been dead a couple hours by then."

"Fuck."

"He wasn't doing small time shit, either. To this day, I still don't know where he kept his stash and I tore that house apart from top to bottom trying to figure out what I'd missed." Another huff sounded as Orozco rubbed his eyes with his left hand then pulled it down across his face. "I lost it, big time." He reached out and fingered the photo. "There's a good two years I don't remember much of…spent so much of it drunk. I wasn't one to take the direct route."

It couldn't have been too bad, Orozco still had his badge. "You're still working."

"I got help." Picking up the wallet, Orozco stared at the picture for a bit. "Just earned my five year chip." Then he snapped the billfold shut and tucked it away. "You been drinking a lot?"

Brandon hedged. "Define a lot." He was definitely putting back more than normal for him, but Brandon didn't think he gone over the edge with it.

Nodding, Orozco clarified. "Anything this morning?"

"No." Derisively, Brandon snorted. "Fuck, it's not even noon…much less like five o'clock."

"Hey, my motto was, 'it's five-o'clock somewhere.'" Orozco's snort echoed with self-depreciating amusement. Then his tone went a little more concerned. "When did you go to bed?"

Brandon dropped his face into his hands. "You mean go to bed," he mumbled out through his fingers, "or actually sleep?"

"Sleeping at all?"

Shaking his head, Brandon confirmed what Orozco probably already knew. "Not much."

"Look, Brandon, we're all taught to not show it. Weakness on the streets gets you killed. So we put on blinders to get us through the job, but sometimes they block out too much; don't see it in ourselves or the people we love." He paused for a moment then shrugged. "I guess it's because we think it means we're weak." Playing with his mustache, Orozco paused again. It was like he searched for a way to put his thoughts into words. Finally, he spread his hands on the table and spoke. "So we pack all this crap away in the mental trash can. The shit we see, the things we have to do. And then something happens and there isn't any more room." Orozco sighed deep and hard. "All that garbage spills back out over our brains. Because we don't talk to each other, the only other people who might know what we're going through, about shit like this, we think we're the only ones messed up. And we think we can't talk about it. We're the ones in control. We're supposed to help people deal with their shit. But we can't admit we need help."

Brandon picked at his cuticles. He couldn't look at the other detective. "You think I need help, but you're not sure I need a rubber room?"

"No," Orozco chided, "'cause you don't trust those head-doctors any more than any other cop. You'd tell them exactly what you thought they wanted to hear and nothing would get done." Reaching across the corner of the table, Orozco popped Brandon's shoulder with his fist. "Talk to me."

What the hell could he say? "I don't know if I can be a cop anymore, Oro—Manny." *I can't stand it? I can't live with the hell in my head? I'd rip out my brain just to stop the dreams, the nightmares?* Instead, Brandon choked out, "If this one thing can take me so far down…"

"First, Brandon, you're going through the worst hell a parent can imagine." Orozco shifted his chair so that the table wasn't between them anymore. "I mean, I went through hell." He leaned forward, resting his elbows on his knees and kneaded the knuckles of one hand with the other. "Honestly, though, at least I know where Beanie is; over at Palm Cemetery in Green Valley." Then he reached over and gripped Brandon's knee. "And second, it isn't just this one thing. You're vice, which is amped up shit all the time. About the only thing more crazy making is patrol… which we've all had to go through. Add onto that, you do guys and you lie about it to everyone you work with."

Brandon rolled his eyes and slumped back against the hard spine of the chair. "It actually kinda came out this summer."

"Intentionally?" Orozco prodded.

"Ah, no."

Nodding like he expected the answer, Orozco threw out another question. "How long have you been on the force?"

Brandon laced his fingers across the back of his head. "Going on ten years." Shit, the most committed he'd ever been to anything. With Shayna gone, ten years mattered about as much as ten seconds.

"How many suicides, murders, family things you think you've worked in those ten years?"

"Fuck if I can remember," Brandon rolled his eyes, "hundreds."

"Yeah." Orozco shared the sentiment. Too many tragedies for any one cop to witness…it came with the uniform. One of those things that any cop—any cop with any time under their belt—understood. "Shot anyone?"

"Discharged, hit a couple. Never fatal." Thank God for that. "I can't remember how many times I've drawn down without firing."

Again Orozco seemed to expect the answer. Maybe not the specifics, but a cop who, in a decade, never had to shoot at someone was either a coward who wouldn't draw or fucking lucky. "You ever talk to Nicholas about it?"

Brandon actually laughed. "Are you fucking crazy?" Cops didn't discuss that shit with anyone except other cops…and most times not even then.

"No. I'm not." Orozco assumed the fatherly, but stern, hands crossed over his chest position. He stared down Brandon until the younger cop broke eye contact. "Look," the gentle tone in Orozco's voice drew Brandon's attention back. "I was a drinker. I drank so I didn't have to talk. Goddamn, I've only known you about a year. And while I don't know you well, I know your type well. You're a bottler." Orozco rapped his knuckles on the tabletop. "Saw it when Nicholas almost bought his ticket up on the Grapevine. You squash it all down," he ground his fist against the wood as though mimicking Brandon squashing his feelings into tight space, "and the pressure keeps building and every little sliver of stress shakes that bottle just a bit. And then something horrible happens, like this, and the cap pops off and all that shit comes spewing out."

"Pop psychology 101?" Brandon growled out to keep from admitting how close Orozco hit it.

"Peer counseling training." Orozco shrugged. "Two Metro cops started it back in the 80's. One of them eventually got elected Sheriff. It's a mix of cops and civilians. We're on call 24/7—just like Vegas. They pulled me up. I'm going to help you pull yourself up outta this. So I'm going to give you my home phone, my cell and we're going to make a contract."

"I don't want you to have to do that."

"Look, *Detective,*" Orozco leaned into Brandon's personal space, "which do you think I'd rather…get woken up at three in the morning because you're having a hard night? Or get woken up at three a.m. to come out here so I can try and find all the pieces of your brain, or Nicholas', for the coroner?" He paused to let the importance sink in. "Your stepmom said you drew down on him before you snapped out of it."

Brandon couldn't believe Edith had told him that. Then he realized, of course she would have. It was probably the reason Orozco got there so fast. "Fuck, I didn't mean to." Brandon didn't want to remember that moment. "I don't want to hurt him."

Orozco rocked back in his chair as he fished in his pocket for his note pad. "Yeah. So that's why we need a contract."

What the hell did he mean by that? "Contract?"

"Yeah, you are going to write down a promise to me." Having secured the small notebook, Orozco searched his pockets and came up with a pen. "You're going to promise me that you're not going to off yourself. I'm going to tell you what you're going to write down."

Brandon actually laughed. "Why would I do that?"

"Because if you don't," Orozco tossed the pad and pen on the table in front of Brandon, "I am going to 433 you. And I will make it big and messy and involve as many people in my department and in your department as is humanly possible. Take you out fucking kicking and screaming." He held the pen out to Brandon. "You gonna write?"

Brandon grumbled, "Like I have a choice?" He took the pen.

"Yeah, you do."

"And you think just 'cause I write something down I'm not gonna swallow my piece?" How a little slip of paper could stop someone didn't compute in Brandon's mind.

"Well, I'm taking your weapon with me." Orozco at least was cautious; Brandon would take the weapon of anyone who was a threat to themselves as well. It was standard operating procedure. "And I saw you when I came in. You and Nicholas. You don't want to do that to him. Look, today's crisis has passed, but you'll probably go low again." Orozco tapped one meaty finger at the top of the pad. "This contract is how I know I can leave you here. So write this down. 'I, Brandon Carr, promise Manny Orozco that I will not harm myself or try to kill myself.'" When Brandon hesitated, Orozco barked, "Write it."

"I feel stupid." Brandon started to write.

"I know." Again, Orozco's voice dropped to gentle and fatherly. "Just do it."

It still didn't make sense how a piece of paper could change things. "Why?"

"Because when you write it down it gives you something concrete to look at and remember that it's not okay to off yourself. Got it?"

Brandon nodded. "I guess." It made a bit of twisted sense.

"Trust me." Orozco pointed at the pen, indicating Brandon needed to write again. "Okay, 'I understand it's not acceptable, under any circumstances, to kill myself. If I feel like killing myself I will: Call Manny no matter what time of the day or night it is.'"

Not breaking off from jotting down what Orozco said, Brandon asked, "Are you sure about that?"

"Positive." Orozco definitely sounded positive. "Keep writing. 'If I can't get a hold of Manny, or Nicholas…'"

Brandon never, ever called Nicky anything, but Nicky. "I don't call Nicky, Nicholas." At first it was because, well, he had to admit it made it a kids' name, something not serious. But then, you know, it became *Nicky*. The little private name that Nicky didn't allow anyone else to use, just Brandon.

"Whatever, Nicky then." Orozco waved it off. "'Or Nicky, or my stepmom,' put her name in." He paused and sized up Brandon. "You trust your partner?"

Trust Jeff? Hell yeah, more than he'd ever trusted any partner. "Jeff, yeah."

"Would you call him?"

"No." Well there was trust and then there was having to explain a ton of things Brandon didn't want to get into. "I don't want him to know I fell apart."

"Who else?" Orozco seemed to understand. "Got a priest?"

Brandon thought for a moment. "The rabbi Edith's been working with gave me his card." It was the best he could come up with.

"Would you call him?"

The guy had said to. That's what religious types, at least those who lead other people, said they did. Still, Brandon had never had much truck with religious leaders. "I don't know."

"Put him down, 'If I can't reach any of these people I will either call the suicide prevention hotline or 911.' Okay, now sign it."

Brandon scribbled the last of it out. It took up three of the small pages of paper. As he signed off on the last line, he asked, "So you're going to take this to wave it in my face any time I start losing it?"

"No." Orozco took the notebook, tore the pages off and folded them in half. "You're going to keep it." He leaned over and tucked the paper into Brandon's T-shirt pocket. "And if you start getting those thoughts again, you're going to take it out and you're going to read it. Once you've read it, you're going to do what it says." He spread his hands. "That's the contract."

"That's it?" Brandon couldn't believe that's all Orozco planned.

"For now." Orozco stood and stepped close. He griped Brandon's shoulder and squeezed. "Look, you're beat." Jerking his head toward the front of the house, Orozco instructed. "Why don't you go lay down and I'll send your stepmom in."

"I'm a big boy." Brandon didn't need Edith to watch him while he slept—or tried to. "I can take care of myself."

"No, actually, you can't." Orozco thumped Brandon's ear with the back of his hand. "For the next however long it takes, I'm telling them not to leave you alone." He moved back so Brandon could stand and explained, "You go to take a dump, you don't even get to lock the goddamn door. That's part of this contract." Then he pointed toward the front of the house. "So you go take a rest. I'm going to have a chat with Nicholas."

As Brandon moved past Orozco out of the kitchen, he mumbled, "I don't think…"

"No see," Orozco cut him off, "you don't get to think." He slapped Brandon on the back. "You lost that option for a while. You don't get it back until I or Nicholas say you do." When Brandon turned to glare, Orozco shoved his hands in his pockets and gave the attitude right back. "Look, if you don't do it this way, then I'm taking you in. And like I said, I'll make it messy, nasty and embarrassing." The words weren't half as threatening as Orozco's tone.

Part of Brandon wanted Orozco to take him in. He deserved it. The shame. The humiliation. All of it. What little was left of his rational self understood and appreciated the favor. It still didn't make the up-close and personal family hell he would have to suffer go down easier. Brandon swallowed back his comments as Orozco called for Edith. He only half listened to Orozco's instructions for his stepmom as he headed into Nicky's bedroom. Brandon didn't even bother to kick off his boots. Flopping face first onto the bed, he pulled a pillow over his head. Then he waited for his guard-slash-stepmom and her inevitable interrogation.

CHAPTER 23

Nick gripped the lip of the old wooden workbench at the back of his garage. Everything he knew about the world spun out beyond his grasp. It felt like he stood on a piece of cork floating in the ocean. Nick only moved in reaction to waves created by events he couldn't control. A sea of dark thoughts threatened to drown him, kill him, swamp his emotions under a deep, black abyss.

Bending over, Nick rested his forehead against his toolbox. Cold and tangible, the metal gave him an exterior focus. The past half-hour, the past few days, seeped into his pores like acid. As if someone pulled his nerves like wires, his face, neck and shoulders tightened up until it felt like the tendons might snap. "Stupid, fucking son-of-a-bitch," Nick hissed through clenched teeth. He slammed the butt of his palm against the bench. Almost a release, pain shot up his arm. "Goddamn selfish bastard!"

All the tension and fear he'd suppressed erupted at once, shredding his control. Bellowing an incomprehensible mishmash of expletives, Nick jerked upright. He spun and lashed out with his boot. The blow struck an old bucket full of stripped bolts and cast off car parts. The container slammed against Querida's fender, spewing metal bits as it spun off into a corner. Nick's blood sputtered with the rattles.

"Fucking bastard!" He roared and kicked again. This time his target was the front tire of the hearse. Slamming his fists against the hood, kicking the tires and fender, Nick yelled, "Asshole, fucking asshole," over and over. With each repeat the blows got wilder and his voice broke just a little more.

Fear mixed with anger and poisoned Nick's thoughts. "Why? Why didn't you say something?" Right then and there he hated Brandon. Hated him more than he ever thought possible. And he wasn't certain he could ever go back from that point. "You stupid son-of-a-bitch!" Nick pounded the car, taking his rage out on unyielding metal when he really wanted to slam his fists into Brandon's face. "What's your fucking problem?"

A huge shudder ran up his spine. Nick braced his palms on the hearse and shook. His chest was so tight he could barely suck in air. For a bit Nick stood frozen. Nothing made sense, least of all Brandon and him. Asshole fucking pulled a gun on him. The thought crested on a wave of nausea. Nick gagged. He retched. Stumbling from the garage, Nick managed not to puke until he hit the lip of the drive. Then he bent over and spewed that morning's doughnuts and coffee across the scraggly grass that pretended to be his back lawn. He braced one hand on the wall of the garage, the other on his knee gulping down a few breaths. Then he puked again and kept going until nothing but foam would come up.

He heard the back door open then slam shut. Someone, someone big, dropped down the steps. Nick turned his head and looked between where his arm and leg formed a frame. Orozco strode toward him. Shaky, Nick stood and propped himself against the side of the garage. He waited, not trusting himself to speak, until the detective stopped in front of him. Nick managed to gulp out a, "Hey."

Instead of a greeting, or commenting on Nick's physical state, Orozco asked, "Where's his piece?"

Nick had no clue what Orozco meant. "His what?" Maybe if he wasn't still so freaked out he might have been able to process the question more coherently.

With a frown, Orozco clarified, "Brandon's weapon." Conceding to the chill of the New Year's Day, Orozco flipped up the collar of his heavy jacket. "I'll take it."

Nick tried to remember the chaos of those few minutes. He didn't want to revisit that awful scene. Just thinking about it bubbled the need to puke again up into his throat. Nick fought the urge to gag and mumbled, "I think Edith put it in the freezer." She'd taken the gun from him and then the thunk sounded. Yeah, probably the freezer. Why she'd stick it in there, Nick didn't even try to fathom. None of them were acting rational.

"Okay. I'll get it before I leave." Orozco jerked his chin at Nick. "Nice shiner you have there Nicholas. Did Brandon lay into you?"

"Yeah." Nick fished another cigarette out of his jacket pocket, lit it and inhaled. The flavor masked the bile in his mouth and quelled his gut a little. "Brandon got me once when I tried to take his gun away." Shit, he sounded like some freaked out meth-head at the clubs. He was freaked out...for better reason than drugs.

Orozco nodded. "How are you hanging on?"

"I'm scared shitless." Banging his heel on the wall, Nick tried to get a grip on the situation. "Goddamn, somebody went after me, detective." He rolled his head back against the wall, shoved his free hand in his pocket and stared at the cold gray sky. "They reached out and tried to hurt me through him." He took another deep drag. "I feel so fucking responsible." Somehow he managed to fake a semblance of calm. "And Brandon, he's falling apart. Holy crap." Nick still couldn't really process the past half-hour or so. "I mean, he was going to do it."

"Looks like, yeah." Orozco shrugged. "I'm getting the sense that's what he planned."

Not trusting himself to speak, Nick smoked. Orozco waited, like he knew that Nick barely hung on to his composure. When he'd gone about halfway through the cigarette, Nick thought he could talk without losing his sanity. "What do you normally do in situations like this?"

"Normally?" Orozco sucked on his mustache like he was thinking on how to say it without freaking Nick out more. "Normally we'd throw the suicidal dip-shit on seventy-two hour hold at some mental health ward. I don't want to do that here."

"Why?" Nick didn't want that either, but if that's what people did in situations like this then that's what they should do. "Isn't that what's best?" A little, nasty voice in his own head pointed out that if they took Brandon away then Nick wouldn't have to deal with him...not for a while. Not until maybe he could make sense of the world again.

Orozco frowned again. "It'll trash his career. He comes out of there depressed, but not wanting to off himself and then they'll throw him through a 'fit for duty' investigation. Double kick in the teeth. It'll ruin him."

How could Brandon's department do something like that? "Somebody fucking took his kid." How could anybody not understand the situation? "She's not mine and I'm fucked up. Don't you think they'd cut him slack?"

"No." Orozco's bitter laugh sealed the denial. "Suicidal is suicidal. If you crack for this, you'll crack somewhere else."

Frustrated, Nick banged his heel against the wall again. "Holy, crap, how do they expect you guys to get help?"

"They don't." This time Orozco sighed. It sounded tired, resigned and just as bitter. "Look, I sent Edith in to watch Brandon for a moment." He jerked his head at the house. "I'm going to take his ex back around to where she's staying…give you some space. Before I leave though," Orozco reached out and squeezed Nick's shoulder. "I got to get your promise that you're not going to leave him alone. Not for a moment, not to take a beer out of the fridge, grab a smoke or even take a freaking piss. Somebody's always got to be with him all the time. And it's a lot to put on his stepmom, 'cause she's dealing with her own shit right now. So, that means, it's pretty much you."

Nick couldn't process the necessity of that level of attention. "Why do I have to babysit him like that?" God, that would mean he'd have to be near Brandon. Talk to him, interact with him and try not to slam the asshole's head into the wall. Nick didn't think he could manage that. He needed time to get his own thoughts in order, figure out what he might do next.

"Because, Nicholas," Orozco squeezed harder, "there's a chance he could try it again."

CHAPTER 24

Brandon walked out into the hall, zipping up his fly as he moved, to where his shadow, Nicky, waited. He didn't have to unlock the door because Nicky'd pitched a fit when he tried to lock it in the first place. This routine grew old quick. Bandon almost regretted his contract with Manny…almost, by a very slim margin.

"I can't even take a piss without you there, huh?" Brandon grumbled.

"Nope." Nicky glared. "That's the deal. Live with it."

The constant presence of either Nicky or Edith already grated on Brandon's nerves. Since Nicky'd dogged him from about the time Orozco took off, Brandon figured he could use a change of guard. He leaned against the archway between the hall and living room. "Hey, Edith." She looked up at the sound of her name and Brandon forced a smile. "You going to be up for a bit?"

"No." Edith stood and smoothed her skirt. "I was thinking of lying down and watching a movie." Smiling as she walked over, Edith held up her hand and, almost hesitantly, reached out to touch Brandon's face. "Nick pulled out a portable DVD player he had and found me some old classics." She patted his shoulder then and Brandon stepped aside so she could pass. After a couple of steps Edith turned. "I thought I'd use the headphones," after a heavy pause, "so I don't disturb you." As she moved through the door, she added, "Just forget I'm even here." Then she shut the door.

Fuck, stuck the rest of the night with Nicky. Brandon covered his eyes with both hands and rubbed the heels of his palms across his cheeks. He shouldn't think like that, Nicky was just doing what Orozco told him. "Look, I'm beat." Brandon huffed and turned to face Nicky. "I think I'll crash. Why don't you watch the big TV out here? I'm okay, Nicky." He shrugged. "You don't have to babysit me 24/7."

"No." Nicky crossed his arms over his chest and cocked his hip against the bathroom doorjamb. "Wherever you go, I go."

"You can trust me." Brandon shouldered past him and into the bedroom, flipping on the light. "I just want to try and sleep." Brandon made it to the bed, twisted and flopped onto his back.

Nicky followed him into the room. He rested his butt against the old wood dresser then reached over and swung the door shut with the tips of his fingers. The little snick of the latch sliding home sounded as final as a prison door slamming shut. "No, actually, I can't." Running his hands over his scalp, Nicky added, "I mean, honestly, Brandon...holy crap." Like he was getting ready for bed, Nicky undid the D-ring buckle on his black army style canvas belt.

Brandon unbuckled his own double tongue belt, lifted his butt off the bed and pulled the leather through the loops.

"Why don't you just put that on the bed next to you?" Confused by the request, Brandon looked up at Nicky. He stood there, end of the canvas belt clutched in one hand, bouncing the rings against the palm of the other.

"Why?"

"One, I said so." Nicky glared. "Two, because I think, I need to touch you Brandon." He stood and dropped his hand to his side. Flicking the rings against his thigh now, Nicky smirked. "I need to, we both need to remember that I'm here for you, you're mine."

Letting the belt just fall onto the bed, Brandon sat up. "I don't know, Nicky." He was tired, deep down soul tired if not physically exhausted. And the last time...shit he hadn't even been able to keep it up enough to cum. He yanked his T-shirt over his head and tossed it on the floor before kicking off his boots. Then he struggled with shucking his pants and shorts.

"Look." Nicky reached into his pocket and yanked out his phone. Fingers dancing over the display, obviously searching for something, he mumbled, "We both need this." Apparently he found what he wanted. Nicky tapped the screen then twisted and

nested the phone into the dock. "I need to connect with you…
otherwise, I may just kill you myself." Music, *Enigma* if Brandon
wasn't mistaken, swelled out of the speakers staged around
Nicky's bedroom. After fiddling with the volume on the small
AV control panel, Nicky turned his attention back to Brandon.
"We haven't touched each other since this shit happened."

Wearing just his socks, Brandon swung his legs off the bed
and dropped the whole pile of clothes on the floor, except for
the belt. He left that where Nicky told him to. "We've fucked,"
he corrected. It almost seemed like too much effort to either go
grab a shower or find his pajama pants.

"Yeah," Nicky stared at the ceiling for a moment, "and that's
what it was…a fuck." Then he swung his dark stare back to
Brandon. "I need to remind you what this is about." Nicky stood
up and slapped the belt hard against his thigh. "I need to remind
myself."

"All the crap is out in the garage." Brandon huffed and he let
his hands dangle between his knees. "You going to drag all that
back in here?"

"No." Nicky took two steps closer to the bed. "Stand up."

"Nicky." Although he protested, a little flicker of heat swelled
in his belly and moved lower.

"Look, Brandon, guys have been into this far longer than
the *Stockroom*'s been selling gear." Nicky slapped the canvas belt
against his palm. "So shut up and stand up."

"Nicky, Edith's in the other room." Even as he protested
Brandon stood up.

"And this door is closed." Nicky moved closer while using
the buckle of the belt in his hand to indicate the rest of the
house. "The TV's on in there and music's spinning here." When
he reached the pile of Brandon's clothes, Nicky toed around in
them for a bit, kicking Brandon's boots out of the mess. "Now,
put on your boots."

"Nicky…"

"Shut the fuck up and do what I tell you."

Bending down, Brandon reached for one of his motorcycle boots. "Are you going to beat me with my belt?" He looked up at Nicky as he tried to stand and pull on the boot. "You know, like all those old leather stories." He stomped into that one and then grabbed the other to put it on.

"You sound like you want it."

Brandon hedged. "Maybe." He wanted it, but he wasn't certain if it was to get off or to feel punished.

"I don't know." Nicky ran his free hand threw his hair before shaking his head. "Slap and tickle is probably not a great idea right now."

"Why not?"

After running the length of the belt through his fingers a few times, Nicky finally answered, "Because I'm not sure I can trust myself not to beat the hell out of you."

"Fuck." Brandon shuddered with a mixture of fear and anticipation.

"Turn around." Nicky grabbed his wrists and pulled Brandon's arms behind his back. Brandon could hear the canvas, feel the stretch in his muscles as Nicky crossed Brandon's wrists, wrapped the canvas belt over them and tightened it down.

"Look." As much as he wanted it, like Nicky said, Brandon really didn't know if he could trust himself either. They both walked on eggshells. "Get the fucking belt off my hands." He rolled his shoulders trying to wiggle his arms enough to create some slack in the belt. "It's probably not a good idea right now," Brandon hissed. "Edith'll hear something."

Nicky grabbed Brandon's shorts off the bed. "Then I guess we got to make sure she doesn't," Nicky hissed back and shoved Brandon's briefs in his mouth. Brandon tried to spit the fabric out. He kept working at the belt binding his wrists by twisting his arms against each other. The D ring buckle wasn't the most secure. He had no clue what the fuck Nicky was up to, but he wasn't stopping Brandon from trying to get loose.

A few seconds later, Nicky snagged Brandon's hair in his fist and yanked Brandon's head back. He stared down into Brandon's eyes, his expression tight and almost angry. Brandon shuddered. Nicky licked his lips before dangling a Christmas themed tie over Brandon's face. "Got this in the secret Santa thing, might as well get some use out of it." Then Nicky slipped the tie across the makeshift gag and tied it behind Brandon's head. About half the fabric of his briefs stuck out from his mouth like fake foam, but it effectively stifled Brandon.

Nicky wandered back to his closet. Unable to do much other than worry the binding on his wrists, Brandon turned to watch. Nicky snagged several other ties and a few canvas belts off the hooks on his door. One of those Goth things, BDUs required canvas belts in coordinating colors and Nicky kept a ton of them. He wouldn't be caught dead wearing a black web belt with camouflage. A couple of Nicky's own leather belts came out as well: one in black with double tongued eyelets running from buckle to base.

Before coming back to the bed, Nicky wandered over to the window and pulled the old broom handle out of the sash window track—the one he used to prop the window open when it got hot. For a brief moment Brandon wondered if Nicky would use it to beat his head in. He deserved it after the morning, after drawing down on Nicky. Then that thought passed and Brandon was just confused as to what Nicky needed a three-foot long, inch thick dowel for.

Brandon had no clue what thoughts were spinning in Nicky's head. "I hated you this morning." Nicky's voice drifted down, answering Brandon's unspoken question. "You son of a bitch." Nicky walked up twirling the wood in his hand. He dropped the belts and ties on the edge of the bed. "You pulled a gun on me." He walked around Brandon, like sizing up a piece of meat. With every step he bounced the broom handle against his own calf. "And I wanted to hurt you back," Once circuit, two circuits, "But I won't...ever."

Fuck it was hot. Stern, angry Nicky, dressed in combat boots and black BDUs prowling about him. The tap of the rod against Nicky's leg in time with his booted steps, Brandon found his breathing coming in pace to the rhythm. Finally, Nicky stopped at his side. Brandon looked back and down. Nicky held the bar behind Brandon, parallel to the floor. Then Nicky dropped just a bit. He popped the rod across the back of both Brandon's knees. It stung. More shock than pain caused Brandon to bite against the shorts stuffing his mouth.

"Kneel, bitch." Nicky hadn't hit him hard enough to take him down, just make him feel the blow.

Brandon knelt. He figured Nicky would remove the dowel when he was down, that it was some kinda control play. So far they had a prisoner-officer vibe going on. Brandon's dick responded by going half-hard. Especially with Nicky's attitude. Nicky pushed the rod against the joint as Brandon went down. Until the last few inches, Brandon managed pretty well, even with his hands tied behind his back. When he did lose balance, thumping his knees on the floor, it barely stung.

"And then," Nicky's voice drifted from above and behind, "I got mad." Body upright, hands behind his back, Brandon waited. "Not at you, but at me." Nicky stepped behind him. "Asshole, how dare you make me think that way?" With the toe of his boot, Nicky messed with the bar and Brandon raised up a little thinking Nicky could pull it out from between his thighs and calves where it'd slipped to.

Instead Nicky used his boot to shove the rod back into place. He gave another order, "Spread your legs more, knees wide," and punctuated it with the heel of his boot tapping Brandon's inner thigh. Brandon shuffled around on his knees. "Don't drop the pole." The rod behind his joints made it more difficult than it otherwise should have been, but he managed. "Here I am thinking, 'It's my fault,' and it's fucking not."

Nicky, shirtless now, moved around him again. He must have shucked it while Brandon adjusted his position. Still, he was hot. BDUs hung on a solid runner's frame, one strung with a decent amount of muscle. The whole punitive-captive vibe—as Nicky walked around his body, correcting Brandon's posture with the insistent touch of two fingers between Brandon's shoulders or the back of his hand lifting Brandon's chin—lit Brandon's nerves. "I resented you for making me think I was fucked up for not seeing it coming." With a huff of breath through his nose, Brandon shut his eyes. The fall of Nicky's footsteps, the corrective contact, the binding of his wrists even the gag, soothed him.

On his knees, back erect and focused on the sense of Nicky, Brandon allowed himself not to think, just react. He trembled a little from the anticipation of Nicky's skin against his, no matter how minimal the contact. Every time he slumped or shifted, Nicky brought him back into line with an insistent tap.

When he realized the tread of Nicky's boots on the wooden floor had stopped, Brandon opened his eyes. Nicky squatted down in front of him. "Then, then I figured it out." Anticipation shot up his spine as Brandon waited for what would come next. "We're both massively fucked up right now. You. Me. This situation. We need to get back to our heads being halfway on straight." A leather belt—double-tongued and with a double row of holes spanning the full length—and one of Nicky's crappy work ties dangled from Nicky's hand.

"Okay, bitch, look up." Brandon rolled his eyes toward the ceiling. Nicky snorted then knocked the underside of Brandon's chin with the buckle of the leather belt. The blow, hitting where skin barely covered bone, stung. Brandon shuddered, savoring the pain. "I meant, tilt your head up."

Brandon did. He felt as Nicky slid the leather behind his neck. Keeping his fingers between the belt and Brandon's skin, Nicky cinched it down and bucked it. It was tight, not so much as to restrict breathing, but it definitely felt confining. Then Nicky slid the tie between Brandon's neck and the belt. Nicky grabbed the end and tied it around the belt leaving the long end brushing against Brandon's chest. A collar and a leash, Brandon shuddered.

Nicky reached around Brandon and snagged more ties and

canvas belts off the bed. With one belt in his hand, the rest dumped on the floor next to Brandon's leg, Nicky knelt at Brandon's left. Nicky hooked one finger through the back of the collar and tugged back and down slightly. Assuming it was what Nicky wanted, Brandon sat back, butt resting on his heels. He twisted his head to watch as Nicky slipped the belt under Brandon's ankle. He cross the ends and threaded them between Brandon's leg and thigh. Then he buckled it over the top of Brandon's thigh in a half-assed tower tie. Nicky shuffled over to Brandon's right and repeated the bind on that side.

"Now." Nicky stroked Brandon's cheek with the back of his hand, before moving his grip around to the back of Brandon's skull. Steering Brandon's actions as he spoke, Nicky muttered, "Look at the floor." Encouraged by Nicky's guidance, Brandon bent forward, his back arched, his head down. Nicky took the loose end of the tie and, reaching under Brandon's body strung it through Brandon's legs. Like he was unaware of Brandon's dick in the way, Nicky bumped it with his arm as he moved. Nicky shuffled back and leaned over Brandon's body. The skin of Nicky's belly pressed against Brandon's bare lower back and butt. Brandon shuddered.

Then Nicky reached from behind Brandon's ass, between his legs, and grabbed the end of the tie off the floor. He pulled it taut. The fabric rubbed against Brandon's half erect prick. Although he couldn't quite see from his position, Brandon sensed more than saw, Nicky tie the leash to the bar strung behind Brandon's knees. When Nicky rocked back on his heels, apparently finished, Brandon jerked his head up. He hissed as the movement pulled the rod tight against the back of his knees.

A little stiffly, Nicky stood up. He caught the last of the ties with the toe of his boot and lifted it off the floor. Brandon assumed Nicky grabbed it since he could barely move more than twisting his head a bit. He could feel Nicky walking around him again. The vibrations from each step vibrated through Brandon's knees and toes. Canvas from Nicky's BDUs brushed Brandon's side. Brandon hissed and shuddered. All of his senses ramped up when Nicky bound him down. Too little and too much all at once.

"You will be mine again." Nicky grabbed Brandon's wrists. "I will be part of you again." He lifted. "Remember." The strain pulled against Brandon's shoulders. A sweet burning tightness in his biceps and elbows flowed through him and set Brandon trembling. Brandon felt as Nicky secured the last tie around the belt binding his wrists. Oh, God, he deserved anything Nicky dished out. Keeping the tension on the binding, Nicky moved toward Brandon's head. "It's always just us." The tie pulled Brandon's arms until his wrists were almost halfway up the plane of his back and Brandon's elbows stuck out at right angles from his body. Nicky slipped his fingers under the back of the collar and then slid the end of the tie under that. After securing the last tie, which Brandon only sensed by touch on the back of his neck, Nicky stepped away.

Kneeling on the floor, legs spread open, hands tied behind his back and gagged with his own shorts, Brandon closed his eyes. His toes flexed in his boots, the break in the leather pushed against the top of his foot. The warm puffs of air from the floor vent wafted across his otherwise naked body. Balled in and over himself, bound to his own body, Brandon's senses began to collapse inward.

Yet the complete awareness of Nicky's presence suffused him. He circled Brandon again. The tread of his combat boots a hollow thump on the old wooden floor that reverberated up through Brandon's knees and toes. Each step mirrored the inhale or exhale of air through Brandon's nose. The sharp jar of sensation flared when Nicky paused and knocked Brandon's inner ankle with the toe of his boot. Subtle shattering of his nerves swept through him when Nicky brushed his fingers across Brandon's shoulder or butt. Layers of sensation folded in over Brandon's brain forcing him down into himself.

Brandon shifted. The muscles of his wrists and biceps pulled against their bindings. His back strained with the position of being bent over with arms behind him. His thighs ached. The leather chafed his neck. Brandon shuddered. Then he shifted again so he could feel the restraints tugging at his muscles. Bound into a position of submission, Brandon listened to Nicky walking around him.

The strain of head down, back arched and arms pulled up and back toward his neck drifted into the ache of muscles held too long in one place. Slowly the ache melted into a burn in his shoulders and thighs. The rhythm of Nicky's steps lulled his consciousness. Little numbing needle stabs danced over his calves. A pleasant, low-intensity fire smoldered throughout Brandon's frame. Brandon sank deeper and deeper into the cradling arms of tender pain.

Centered into himself. Losing his physical self. Dropping away from the hurt in his body, but still intensely focused there, Brandon slid into the spinning of his own thoughts. Locked into his mind. The sucking black cesspool of his nightmares swirled through his consciousness. Dark, angry things that threatened to shred his mind into bits. He tried to rear back, stand, run away and came up against the reality of the restraints. Brandon whined and shook. He wanted out. He wanted free. He needed to fight back, tear things apart. Beat his fist against the walls. Kick the doors.

Screaming into the gag of his own shorts, Brandon fought his bindings. The toes of his boots scrabbled against the floor. Brandon jerked his hands. The belts and ties cut into his skin and pain shot through his arms. His eyes flew open, but he really couldn't see—terror, adrenaline and sweat blurred his vision. Twisting, struggling...maybe a half an inch of give gained. Sweat poured down his face, his back, his legs. He fought to not drown in his mind. It felt like his heart would burst into bloody foam... his lungs might explode from all the screams held back for so long.

All those evil, thick thoughts chewed at his sanity. Things he didn't want to imagine and couldn't help but. Terrified screams and hopeless pleadings echoed in his brain, conjured by too much knowledge pounded his psyche. He couldn't escape them.

Then the touches started. Nicky's thumb drifted down his spine. His knee brushed Brandon's shoulder. Fingers across the back of his neck. Strokes over his side. Brandon shivered. His skin recoiled from the contact. Brandon didn't want to feel anything. He wanted to die. Silence it all. Why had he let them stop him? Brandon thrashed against the bindings. He jerked so hard that he butted Nicky's legs and he heard Nicky land heavily on the floor.

The sense of Nicky's presence disappeared for a moment. Brandon heard a metallic grinding and then the pressure on his arms vanished. His bound hands dropped against his back. Brandon still thrashed and jerked. He fell on his side. Nicky's hands roamed his body. Soothing, but not. Brandon gasped for air, his chest heaving in short, sharp spasms. Something cold and thin and dull slipped between his cheek and the tie gagging him. Another grind and the tie holding his shorts in his mouth slipped loose. Brandon spit the briefs out. His mouth was so dry. He shuddered again, a hard convulsion that ripped through every nerve.

He wanted to scream. All that came out was a strangled, bubbling groan. He couldn't get his head up. Then another grind and the pressure gave. Silk still rested between the belt and his neck. In the back part of his brain, Brandon realized Nicky was cutting him free so Brandon wouldn't hurt himself. Fuck that. Brandon slammed his head against the floor and rolled onto his back. It pinned his arms under his body and his legs were still tied…still Brandon's lungs stopped clawing for air.

Nicky touched him again. His hands wandered over Brandon's chest and belly. "Stop struggling, bitch." Hard words and gentle touches set Brandon shaking. "I'm here. Lean on me." Sweat slicked Brandon's skin so that the wood rolled and Nicky pulled it free and tossed it to the side. Nicky shuffled up between Brandon's legs and leaned over him, bracing himself with his arms on either side of Brandon's chest.

Still shaking, sweating Brandon stared up at Nicky. Those deep, dark eyes didn't seem to judge and Brandon couldn't understand why. "Now you're here." Nicky dipped down to run his tongue over Brandon's sternum. Brandon arched into the touch. It licked heat down into his belly. "I'm here and that's all that matters." Nicky's kisses worked lower. When he wrapped his lips over Brandon's dick, Brandon's hips bucked off the floor. His shoulders jerked and his hands, still bound under his back, twisted against his spine. Strong, unexpected, the rush hit Brandon so fast it robbed him of reason for a moment. He went from kinda with it to rock hard in seconds.

Nicky slid his tongue around the head of Brandon's cock, just where it flared. Then he mouthed the glans, not really closing over Brandon's prick, just skimming the sensitive surface with his lips. Brandon shuddered. Nicky ran his tongue up and down Brandon's shaft several times before licking Brandon's balls. As Nicky sucked one nut and then the other into his mouth, Brandon moaned again.

Brandon heard the grind of the zipper on Nicky's BDUs. After a bit of shuffling and adjusting, Brandon assumed Nicky pushed down his pants, Nicky finally sucked him down deep into his mouth. He sucked up and down Brandon's prick. Occasionally, Nicky stopped to give the tip some attention, licking around the flare or tonguing the slit. He toyed with Brandon's balls, rolled them in his hands.

Hands bound and pinned under the small of his back, legs still bent and harnessed by the belts, Brandon couldn't do much more than writhe under Nicky's attentions. Insistent heat built in his gut. Brandon didn't want to cum yet. But it wasn't his choice. That belonged to Nicky. Brandon belonged to Nicky. He couldn't fight it. He didn't want to fight it. Everything wasn't okay, but it was bearable with Nicky.

Nicky sucked him down again, hard, so hard Brandon hissed and his hips jerked, the heels of his boots pushing Brandon's ass an inch or so off the floor. Nicky came up, running his teeth along Brandon's skin. Brandon shuddered. Pain and pleasure screamed through his nerves. At the last moment, when Brandon didn't think he could stand more, Nicky jerked away and Brandon's dick slapped against his belly.

While he caught his breath, Brandon stared across his chest and belly to watch Nicky. He couldn't get his head up enough to really see, but he could feel Nicky stroking Brandon's inner thighs and along his cock with his porn-star dick. Nothing between them...never again...just gel and skin and lust. Nicky grinned at him, those feral canines and worship filled eyes sent Brandon reeling. He knew he wanted Nicky, always like that.

Moving lower, Nicky gripped his own dick and rubbed the tip up and down between Brandon's ass cheeks. Giving Nicky as much access a possible, Brandon let his bound knees fall to the side and rocked them back toward his chest as much as he could. It was hard as hell when he lay flat on his back with his arms bound under him.

With a chuckle, Nicky used his dick to circle Brandon's hole. The slick gel and a little pre-cum made Brandon shiver. Nicky gripped Brandon's leg with his free hand as he guided his slick, bare dick to Brandon's ass.

Nicky pushed, barely inserting the tip of his cock. Brandon hissed at that little sharp bite of pain. Waiting for God only knew what, Nicky just knelt there between Brandon's legs. His hand came up and Nicky rubbed the lube over Brandon's dick with his palm. Brandon arched up into the heat of the touch. After the blowjob, the almost too intense touch frayed Brandon's nerves. Then Nicky moved again, driving a little further in.

Brandon's ass opened up for Nicky as he pushed inside. The initial sting blurred into pressure and heat, it had never been as intense with anyone else. Especially now, so full, almost too much to take. Brandon's own hard cock throbbed against his belly, burning under Nicky's strokes. Brandon loved the feeling of Nicky fucking and jacking him, especially when he couldn't resist. He rolled a little, just to feel the sting from his bound hands and lower back. Flexing his legs reminded Brandon of the belts around his thighs and calves. With sweat they loosened and shifted down. As long as he knew they were there, that was all that mattered.

A low ragged breath came out as a moan when Nicky sank in to the hilt. Brandon felt Nicky's hips settle against his ass. So good, that thick hard cock deep inside, overfilled. Brandon savored the awareness of Nicky as he withdrew, his cock slowly pulling out until just the tip remained. Then Nicky filled him again. Nicky started slow, pushing it in and pulling back methodically. The powerful feel of Nicky's prick sliding in and out of Brandon made him shudder.

The shakes hit. After the blowjob and with Nicky's hand stroking him off, Brandon couldn't hold back. The rolling heat in his gut blew through Brandon's frame. An explosion of sparks hit behind his eyes as Brandon came. Nicky hissed and pumped Brandon's dick, milking hot spunk. Exhausted, sated, Brandon lay panting.

"Okay," Nicky licked his lips, "My turn now." He grinned as he let go of Brandon's dick. Then Nicky hooked his arm, the one with the good shoulder, behind one of Brandon's knees and leaned in. The position rolled Brandon slightly, brought his ass farther up off the floor and pushed his shoulders harder into the wood. Nicky picked up the pace. He varied his thrusts, giving Brandon long slow strokes as well as fast and hard. He pounded Brandon's ass, ramming over and over.

Nicky grimaced, his face going tight. Brandon knew Nicky was going over even before hot cum filled him. After a few shudders, Nicky let Brandon's leg slide to the floor. He dropped his head onto Brandon's sternum. "Damn," Nicky hissed. "Fucking needed that." Then he looked up. His hair was plastered to his scalp and down along his neck with sweat. Brandon never knew anyone could look so hot after sex.

As Nicky sat up he tugged the belts off Brandon's legs… it wasn't like the binding was terribly secure anyway. He rocked back and his dick slid from Brandon's hole. "Okay, come on and roll over." Nicky slapped Brandon's inner thigh with the back of his hand. "I don't want to have to cut the damn belts off." When Brandon didn't budge, Nicky whacked him again. This time with more force. "Move, bitch."

Brandon couldn't believe how relaxed he was. Sane, well, he might not go that far, but his emotions weren't quite as twisted up as an hour earlier. He rolled his head and snorted, "Make me."

"Oh no." Nicky glared. "You are not allowed to get all pushy on me. Roll over now…or wait 'till your hands go numb. Your choice."

Unfortunately, that choice was already being made. Brandon could feel the first little nettle barbs of his hands falling asleep. "Bastard." He grumbled and rolled onto his side. Nicky worked the belt loose. When he was free, Brandon sat up and rubbed his wrists. "So whenever it gets bad, you'll just tie me up?" He shifted and felt a little wetness between the floor and his butt. "Make me all better?"

"Fuck no." Nicky used a hand on the bed to help himself off the floor. "You need therapy. I don't give a shit what Orozco says or you say." Tossing the belt onto the bed, he stretched and glared down at Brandon. "You need a professional to work through some of this shit. All this does," he held a hand out for Brandon, "it get us through today and tomorrow." Brandon took Nicky's offered grip and struggled up off the floor as Nicky continued. "I'll talk to the guys at the teen center, they'll probably know someone out in So. Cal. you can talk to, keep it down-low." When Brandon started to protest, Nicky shut him down with a two-fingered thump against Brandon's chest. "You have to get help Brandon. You can't keep your life bottled inside like that. I can't trust my life to that…get it? 'Cause what happens the next time? I don't want it to end with a bullet in my head."

CHAPTER 25

Brandon shoveled cereal into his mouth and watched the changing of the guard with bemused resignation. The whole situation still sucked donkey balls, but seeing Nicky fuss about leaving him with Edith was kinda funny. "Nicky, go to work." Brandon growled between mouthfuls. "I'll be fine."

Half in and half out of the back door, Nicky hesitated. "You sure?" He bumped his helmet against his thigh and kept his other hand in his jacket pocket where the jangle said he messed with his keys. All of it, when filtered through Brandon's nine years of being a cop, spoke of nervous agitation.

"Yes, mommy." Brandon stood, grabbed his bowl and walked to the sink. "Edith managed to get three boys through high school." After dumping the dishes in the sink, Brandon turned. "I think she can handle this." Nicky still stood by the door. If he left it open much longer Brandon was going to need to grab his own jacket off the chair. "Look, I'm coping today. Sleeping some helped, you know."

"Okay." Nicky's voice may have agreed but his body language still read hesitant. "I'll see if I can't cut out early, maybe bring some work home."

"Go." Brandon glared. "I'm going to go watch TV with Edith. I promise I will be here in one piece and still breathing when you get back."

Nicky chewed his lip for a moment longer before he nodded and headed out the back door. When the door banged shut Brandon blew out a heavy breath. He rubbed his eyes with the palms of his hands. Sleeping through the night, well through a good chunk of the night, had actually helped…some. Brandon still jangled like a tweaker hard up for a meth hit, but he didn't feel quite like road-kill anymore.

The subtle purr of Nicky's Kawasaki started in the garage and then the almost electric whine amped up and dissipated as the bike accelerated past the kitchen windows and off down the drive. Brandon figured that gave all of two minutes of alone time before Edith came looking for him. "Edith," Brandon pushed open the bar style door into the living area and yelled, "I'm stepping out back for a smoke." Then he headed over to the table to snag his jacket. He figured that bought him another minute or so.

"Wait," Edith answered from somewhere near the front of the house. "I'll be right there."

Brandon pretended he didn't hear. Shrugging into his jacket, he hustled out the back door, letting it bang shut behind him. He stopped at the bottom step and fished his cigarettes and lighter out of the jacket pocket. It took a couple of tries to fire up the Zippo and light his smoke. A cold, leaden morning burned in his lungs when Brandon sucked in the first nicotine for the day. Snow had fallen during the night. The light dusting of white was enough to dampen the world down another notch. He managed to get a second puff in before he heard Edith come through the door.

As he turned and settled his butt against the stair rail, Brandon looked up. He didn't say anything. Edith smiled, tight and strained, and pulled her coat close around her. "You should have waited for me."

Brandon shrugged. "Why? You already took my shoelaces."

"What? We didn't—" The reference seemed to sink in, "Oh. You got your father's horrible sense of humor, you know that?" When Brandon didn't respond she continued, "Speaking of which, I just talked to your father." Of course she had. Nicky's phone bill was going to be through the roof this month. "He's worried about you. I'm worried about you."

Turning away, Brandon stared off across the small yard. The twisted branches of the winter bare tree in the center of Nicky's patio scratched the sky as desolate as Brandon's thoughts. "I don't want to talk about it, Edith." Fuck, she'd told his dad, probably everything. "You didn't, like, tell him everything, did you?" Thirty years old and that thought frightened Brandon like he was thirteen again getting caught lying about something…like about who he was since puberty.

"About how you're holding up? Yes. He's your father he should know about that. Everything else, that's for you to tell him, not me." She paused and sighed. "He should be in this afternoon. With all the messed up flights in New York, they stuck him on a plane to Miami. He'll have a layover there and get out, hopefully, late this morning. We won't see him until sometime in the afternoon."

"Why does he have to come?" Brandon grumbled to no one in particular. "There's nothing for him to do here."

"Shayna is his granddaughter and he's your father and he loves you."

After another puff of the cigarette Brandon snorted, "Yeah, right." Brandon didn't doubt his dad loved him. Liked him? Respected him? Those were completely different matters all together.

Edith came down to stand on the step above Brandon's. "Why do you say that?" It put her voice almost right behind his ear.

"Dad hates everything I've done in my life." Brandon took another drag. "He hates who I am—the fuck up cop." They'd had knock-down drag-out fights over every choice Brandon had made since high school. One more deep drag and then Brandon finished his thought. "If he finds out I'm gay, he'll just have one more thing confirming that I'm a total fuck up."

"Like I said," Edith tugged at the collar of Brandon's jacket. He swatted her hand away, but it made him look at her. "He hates the biker look. He doesn't hate the man wearing it." Edith wrapped her arms over her chest and stared Brandon in the eyes. "He worries about you." A sad smile didn't back up her words very well.

"He'll be so embarrassed by me…his gay kid." Not that that was anything new. Holidays at his dad's house, some gathering, and his dad always introduced Jacob the doctor and Benjamin the CPA first. Then, like an afterthought it'd be, '*and you know my son*

Brandon, the cop.'

"No he won't," Edith chided. "Like I said before, you have no idea how proud he is of you."

"You're so funny," Brandon choked on a bitter laugh, "we could get you a gig on the strip."

Edith rolled her eyes. Then she smiled and leaned in a bit. "All the time he talks about you. His son Brandon making a difference." Rubbing her hands over her upper arms like she was cold, Edith added, "You know that you're the one who inspired him to volunteer. His practice was wonderful, but knowing how you gave yourself to the people, protecting them...well he thought he could take a couple of years to help people who needed him."

Brandon took one last puff before tossing the butt on the concrete. He crushed the cigarette out with the toe of his boot. "This would ruin that."

"Why do you think that? You're a wonderful person, Nick is a wonderful person." Reaching out, she brushed her thumb across his cheek. "Give your father some credit. He's human, but all he ever wanted was for you to be happy." Edith added a small, embarrassed laugh. "This may take a little bit of getting used to for him. I know your mother would have just been tickled by Nick. Might have given you a little grief about him not being Jewish, but she would have adored him."

Whether his mom would have liked Nicky didn't matter. She'd been dead twenty years. "Dad, just—I don't think he'll ever accept who I am."

"Don't close yourself off from the possibility before he's even had a chance to see you and Nick together."

"He'll freak," Brandon huffed. "I've blown every expectation he ever had of me." Brandon could barely say it. His face got all hot and the edges of his world started crumbling again. "This will just confirm for him what a loser he has for a son." He managed to mumble his thoughts through tight lips.

"Oh, Brandon, no." Edith reached out and hugged him.

Brandon stiffened, but didn't push her away. "Don't ever believe that about yourself. Do not for a moment think that your father believes that." Rocking them slightly, Edith whispered, "You are a wonderful man." Edith pulled back and wiped the corners of her eyes with her fingers. "You were becoming a great man."

"I have no clue what you're talking about, Edith."

"A truly great man is not measured by his accomplishments, but by the love and respect others give him. A great man sees when he makes a mistake and tries to set it right."

"What the fuck do you mean?" Brandon kicked the rail behind him. "'Cause I don't get it."

"You reached out to love someone, even if it scared you about what others would think. You connected with him. You realized you made a mistake with Shayna and began the steps to bring her back into your life. You have to keep working on this great man inside you."

He shoved his hands in his back pocket and glared. "How the hell do I do that?"

"Are you asking for my advice?"

"Depends on what it is."

"Stay with Nick. I didn't know, but somehow the first time I saw you together, I just felt the emotional connection between you, how special it was. So don't let your fear of what your father, or anyone else, thinks rob you of that." Like she'd done when Brandon was an errant teen, Edith slapped his shoulder. "On a practical level, from someone who used to be a nurse, both of you quit smoking. Now come on. You're finished and I'm cold. Let's go back inside and I'll make some more coffee."

CHAPTER 26

"Have you seen Jen today?" Nick called to Ada as she exited the break room. He'd been searching the office since a little after his arrival. First he'd met with the lab manager, brought him up to speed on everything personal and professional. Then it'd been the hunt for the data monkey named Jen and the reports he needed.

"No." Ada waited while he jogged up. "I think she called in sick."

Nick hissed, "Shit." Almost immediately he wished he hadn't. He never cussed in front of Ada.

Like she hadn't heard, Ada smiled and asked, "Why are you here…after everything on Monday?"

"Because I have work to do and no PTO left." Running one hand through his hair in frustration, Nick huffed. "Although, since I've got to get the project finished, the Chief said I can grab the preliminary reports and work the data from home today. Thank God."

"I thank God every day," Ada smiled, "but what's going on?"

"It's nothing." Nick shrugged.

"Nick." Gently she reached out and took his hand in hers. "Nothing in your life is nothing right now."

Ada, they'd never been close. Somehow though, she had the right sensibility and even keel that made Nick trust her. He stuttered a little, "I just need to be home to keep an eye on Brandon."

"What do you mean?"

"Like I said, it's nothing." Nick shrugged again. That, in itself must have tipped her off because Ada frowned. "Don't stare at me like that," he grumbled. "Okay, he's not dealing well.

Not thinking rationally." A bare bones explanation at best, but hopefully that would get Ada off her inquisitive track. "I had to take his gun away from him yesterday. It was pretty intense."

A little hesitantly, Ada pointed at Nick's face. "Is that how you got…?"

"The bruises?" He confirmed it with a nod. "Yeah. So, his stepmom is with him right now. I want to go back and keep an eye on him. We're just not letting him be alone right now."

In a gesture of faith mixed with sympathy, Ada crossed her hands on her chest and looked up. "He's got to be devastated."

"Yeah." Nick reminded himself that Ada had kids. She, of anyone he knew, could empathize with Brandon's mindset right then. "Pretty much torn up and screwed up right now. He had a talk yesterday with Detective Orozco. Seemed to help him some. You know, cop to cop. And Edith has asked a rabbi she knows out here to come talk with him this evening." Nick never connected to his own religious upbringing and, from what he knew of Brandon, neither had he. Still, if someone said that painting their faces blue and running around naked in the desert would solve it, Nick would have been the first one undressed. "Don't know if Brandon will actually talk to the guy, but he might."

Again, Ada touched his arm. "Do you have someone to talk to?"

"What?" They were talking about Brandon, not him.

She added a squeeze. "I may be assuming wrong here, but when you say 'I had to take his gun away,' and 'it got intense,' and now you are all watching him…" Sucking in a deep breath, Ada forced the rest out in a rush. "He was going to hurt himself, wasn't he?"

Damn, she was too perceptive or, more likely, he was way less subtle than he intended. "Yeah."

"You love him, Nick." Ada stepped close. With one hand still on his arm, she moved the other to his shoulder. "In all the years we've worked together I've never seen you so involved with someone. You've dated several people. But you've never seemed to connect with them the way you have with Brandon."

Nick managed a self-depreciating laugh. "Figured that out from the couple times you've met him?"

"No." She smiled and shook her head with the denial. "From the way you talk about him. That you talk about him at the office other than just a passing mention." A long heavy pause followed before Ada continued, "You were living, I think, with that other guy and I don't believe you ever mentioned his name or anything more than he had money because he was in banking or something." Given what Nick knew of Ada, struggling for words didn't usually happen. She was the person who always had something earnest, but kinda scripted, to say for any occasion. "I'm rusty at this. Ah, I worked a suicide line in college, feels like forever ago. There's got to be so much hurt on your end because of this."

"It's not important." Not terribly comfortable with Ada being so understanding, Nick brushed it off and stepped physically back. "Getting Brandon through this is important."

She didn't push, at least with contact. "You can't get him through it, if you can't get yourself through it. If you're both going to survive, with each other, through this ordeal, you have to deal with how it makes you feel."

Confiding in Ada wasn't what he planned, but when Nicky opened his mouth that's what came out. "It makes me feel like absolute crap, okay." Maybe it was because she was not involved in the whole fucked up mess. "I want to hurt his selfish ass. And then I'm mad at myself for thinking like that." Still, his feelings embarrassed him. He felt like he should be all understanding and a rock for Brandon. That's what people expected. Adding some snark to cover his admissions, Nick flashed a fake smile. "There, I've talked about it, make you feel better?"

"That wasn't my point," Ada challenged his bravado with a gentle voice. "Do you have a pastor you confide in?" When Nick went wide-eyed at the question, she fluttered her hands in front of her chest like she could dispel Nick's negative thoughts with gestures. "Don't look at me like that...I know there are gay congregations out there. A counselor. You do some volunteer work with some mental health type places. Maybe someone there would be willing to listen. Professionally, so they could actually help." She spread her hands in what looked like resigned frustration. "I can listen and I will, but I can't teach you how to cope."

Fuck, Ada was being all earnest and Nick pissed on her. "Look, I'm sorry." He really meant it. "I didn't mean to shut you down. I'm just frazzled."

"I know. It's okay." Ada gently pushed him toward the pit of Electronic Services. "So get your reports and go home, Dracula. Tell Brandon I'm praying for him, okay?"

Nick stopped them by sidestepping. "I would, but Jen has the reports I needed."

"Oh. Well they should be at her work station." Screwing up her face like she was thinking, Ada pointed back to the area occupied by Investigations. "Let me grab the master keys from my boss in case her bins are locked."

That caught Nick short. He hesitated and asked. "Just go through her stuff?"

"We're government drones," Ada chided as she headed toward her boss's office. "Needs of the job come before privacy."

Following, Nick voiced his concern, "I still feel weird about it."

Ada stopped and glared over her shoulder. "We can look for it or you can reprint all that data and start from square one."

There was privacy and then there was too much fucking effort. Nick shrugged. "Let's get the keys."

It took a bit to find the keys...well actually the keys to get the keys. Why Ada could access them, but not have direct access to them, Nick's mind wasn't in a place where the wonders of government could be processed. After wrangling the correct set they hustled to Jen's workstation. Standard modular cubical set up. Laminate desktop, keyboard tray...the only components that locked were the flipper-door unit and the bottom file drawer. They searched through the various piles of easily accessible paper. When that proved futile, Ada used the keys.

Nick, being taller, got the upper bin. He popped it open, dropped the keys into Ada's hand and slid the panel up and back. Chaos confronted him. "What's this shit?" Piles of paper mixed with trash stuffed the space. Nick could barely bring himself to touch it. "This is nasty. Garbage pail goes *under* the desk." He stepped back and grimaced down at Ada. "How does she find anything she needs?"

Ada shrugged. "It's only slightly better in the file drawer." Gingerly she pulled items from between the file hangers. "Magazines, open candy, stress ball shaped like a skull."

Nick did a double take. "That's mine." Picking it up, studying the soft toy, he flipped it upside down. The club logo stamped on the base confirmed his statement. "I lost it like three months ago."

Ada screwed her face up tight. "Well obviously you didn't lose it."

First Nick snagged a pen off Jen's desk then he used it to probe around the cabinet. "What is all this junk she keeps in here?" He really didn't want to touch it.

"More candy wrappers," Ada kept the running commentary as she tossed stuff from the file drawer onto the desk, "cigarette packs with butts tucked in. Djarum Lights? Jen doesn't smoke, does she?"

"I smoke Djarum." Nick glanced down at the crumpled pack. It had landed in front of the computer monitor…right on top of the open pages of a half-sized spiral notebook. Probably more trash from her file drawer, Nick dismissed it. Then the writing on the pages clicked and he looked back. "She's got my name written on that notebook with little hearts around it." As Nick flipped through a few pages, the various notes and scribbles were augmented, over and over again, with a pattern of misshaped symbols and the scrawl of his name. "That's like freaky."

Ada rocked back on her heels. She glanced from the drawer to Nick to the desktop. "This is not normal."

"She's so immature." Nick rolled so that his side was braced against the edge of the partition wall. Almost relieved he huffed out, "Total high school crush behavior."

"It is?" Wide-eyed, Ada stared up at him.

"Yeah," Nick shrugged, "you know, you can't tell a guy you like him. So you borrow his jacket for a month, sleep with it until the scent of his cologne is completely gone and it's lost the fueling the fantasy edge—" If anything Ada's eyes got bigger. "Okay," Nick flashed an embarrassed smile, "I'll stop there. You never did anything like that huh?"

"No." Ada smiled and then went back to flipping through the files. Absently, almost, she added, "Well, I did take Ramon Mendoza's student ID so I could have his picture. I was young." Stopping with her hands on several tabs, she stared at him again. "But, this is like creepier than that."

"I guess." It was and it wasn't. "Most of us grow out of that crap by eighteen, some maybe by twenty." A tiny weight dropped from his mind. "But, you know, this is actually a load off my shoulders."

"What do you mean?" She returned to sorting through labels.

All the issues with disappearing pens and appearing *tokens* suddenly sorted themselves out into a perverse logic. "I thought someone was taking my stuff because they hated me." Relieved, Nick palmed his face. "*If I make him miserable enough the gay guy will leave,*" Nick growled the inflection in someone else's tone. "We all know Jen's socially, ah, retarded. So now I can say, 'thanks, I'm flattered and I'm gay.' It's awkward, but it is so much more just the stupid-and-mundane-weird category than thinking someone is out to get you."

"That may be it," Ada mumbled but didn't look up. Then she added, "It's still creepy."

"Oh, yeah," Nick agreed. It was a little weird. "Not restraining order creepy, but I'll probably ask the Chief if he can pull her into another project so it's not coming from me, you know." At that Nick went back to his prodding of the upper cabinet. "Have him do that first and then I'll tell her."

"Considering everything that's going on," Ada's voice came from below, accompanied by the shuffle of papers, "I'm surprised you can plan that through."

"Honestly," he grimaced, "it's one less thing in my life I have to worry about now. I can focus on that someone is threatening me, Brandon's daughter is missing and my guy has completely gone off the deep end because he's convinced she's dead. Small crisis done and over. Three major ones pending."

Ada touched the back of his leg and Nick looked down. "He thinks Shayna isn't coming home?" The expression on her face echoed a loss that Nick couldn't even begin to fathom. He assumed it came from Ada's viewpoint as a mother.

"No." Nick swallowed. "He doesn't. She's gone in his mind. And he thinks the odds of catching the bastard that did this are pretty slim."

"Oh, Nick," covering her mouth with her hand, Ada shook her head, "I'm so sorry for him...to think it's hopeless." This time she reached out and ran her fingers down his arm. "Are you sure you want to take work home."

"Actually, I'm sure I don't, but I have to." Nick grimaced. "Little things like job, paycheck, bills." With a huff, he regained composure. "So, you said you saw the files?"

"Yeah, here." Ada fished out a file. *N O'Malley* was scrawled on the tab. Bundles of printouts filled the folder. "These look like the reports you gave her." Ada yanked the file free and held it out. "Hopefully, it's what you need."

"Well, if Jen didn't do it right, it'll give me something kind of mindless to work through." Nick took the offered file and tucked it under his arm without inspecting it.

Ada stood. She grabbed one of Jen's pens and a sticky-note. "Look, Nick, here's my cell number." Peeling off the top paper, she scribbled a number on the sheet before handing it over. "Call if you need someone's ear. You probably have friends who will listen, but not everyone is available all the time. So, if you need to call me you can."

At first Nick didn't take it. "I don't want to bother you more than I have."

"Don't ever think it's a bother." Ada smiled. This time, even as pained as it was, the smile echoed sincere. "I mean it. You need someone to listen you call me. Promise?"

"Yeah." He plucked the paper from her fingers and tucked it in his shirt pocket. "Thanks."

"Okay, Dracula, go home." Ada began to busy herself with putting things away. Not like Nick or Ada could figure out Jen's craptastic file system. A few items: Nick's stress ball and the cigarette packs Ada left out. "Take care of yourself."

"Thanks." Fingering the pages without looking at them, Nick added, "For everything."

"No problem," Ada looked up from the sorting, "anytime."

For a moment Nick toyed with asking Ada what she planned to do with the copped goods. It was too much. Where Nick belonged was with Brandon. Everything else, including the juvenile Jen shit, took a back seat to that. He silently thanked whatever powers might be and ducked through the deserted office. Mentally, Nick filed the need to complain in the back of his brain. All of it went to the mental memo sheet for the following workday. Now important stuff loomed. Like keeping Brandon from falling off the suicidal deep end.

Nick took the moment and bolted from work.

CHAPTER 27

Brandon lay on the little cot in Nicky's office and stared at the ceiling. The day hadn't been on the total suckage train he had predicted, but it skated damn close to the edge of suck. Of course, by the clock on Nicky's desk, since it was only about eleven-thirty, suckage could still materialize. All morning Edith kept trying to distract him, keep him involved. All it did was reinforce that he was a total idiot. Then when Nicky got home, well, Brandon felt like a guilty idiot.

Nicky twisted in his chair and held out his hand. "Give me your cell phone." From what he'd said, Nicky's boss let him bring some work home. "I want to load the video onto my drive. You know, what we took on the strip." That work all rested in the file at the foot of the cot. Instead of employment related tasks, Nicky tinkered with the website he'd built for collecting information about Shayna.

Brandon rolled a bit so he could dig his cell of his hip. "Here." He handed it over.

"Thanks," Nicky acknowledged as he took it. Fumbling with the cover on the micro-SD card slot, he mumbled, "So when was Edith planning on getting back?"

"Sick of me already?" Brandon sniped and Nicky looked up and glared. He probably deserved the glare for that. "I don't know." Brandon managed to shrug while lying down. "She was going to run over to one of the outlet places and get some clothes, basics. None of us planned on being here this long. And, from what she said, Dad has the clothes on his back and a change of underwear and socks. After that she's heading to the airport to pick him up."

Once he'd fished the tiny chip from the slot, Nicky tossed the phone onto Brandon's chest. "She told me you kept ditching her."

Brandon huffed, "I didn't ditch her." Even Brandon didn't

believe himself with that tone in his voice.

"Yeah, right." Nicky turned to hunt across his desk for the adapter card. "You'd, like, go for a smoke and not tell her." He tossed the comments over his shoulder. "Or lock the bathroom." When he found the card, Nicky twisted to glare again. "That, to me, equals ditching."

"Well, Warden," Brandon grumbled, "having my stepmom in the can with me... not happening."

Nicky pulled a small clear plastic case out of one of the drawers. Palming his face before extracting the adapter from the case, Nicky fiddled with fitting the tiny chip into the slot. "You know the fucking rules."

"Look, Nicky, I'm dealing today." Brandon sat up. He laced his fingers over the top of his head and tried to think. "Come on, ditching her means like taking a hike to the gas station...not two seconds of breathing time." Nicky just stared at him with that mix of massively pissed off and totally disappointed only he could manage. "Okay," Brandon swallowed, and tried to explain, "having her hovering is hard." He snorted and swung his feet off the cot. "Having you hovering is hard, but not quite as bad."

Nicky spun the little blue adapter in his fingers. "You keep breaking the rules and I'll call Orozco."

"You don't need to call Manny. Seriously. I mean, you're here and around, but you don't pester." Exasperated, worn out, Brandon dropped his hands in his lap. "Dude, you're my best friend. I can deal with you being right there. Her, not so much."

"Best friend?" Nicky made a sour face, like the words didn't taste quite right.

"Like my dad says, if the person you want to spend your whole life with isn't your best friend, don't bother." Brandon licked his lips and tried to rush past what he'd just admitted. "Look, with Edith, I sit down on the couch for two seconds and she starts asking if I'm hungry, or tired, or thirsty or if I like the program we're watching." Agitated, Brandon rubbed his thighs. "I'd say it was fine, but Edith wouldn't believe me. She'd start channel surfing with running commentary about, 'we could watch this, but it's depressing…or this, no it's violent…no this, oh it's a woman's drama.' I don't think we watched fifteen minutes solid of any show." Brandon snorted a laugh. "I drank enough coffee to float a battleship today just because when she'd ask if I wanted it, I'd say 'no' and Edith would do the round of twenty questions about why. When I said 'yes,' she shut up."

A soft, slightly twisted smile tugged at the corners of Nicky's mouth. "You want any coffee?"

"Fuck you." Brandon would have thrown something at him if there was anything lethal within reach.

"Not right now." Nicky turned back to the computer. "I'm tech geeking."

When Nicky started messing with programs for uploading and converting the video for the website, Brandon lost interest. Not that he wasn't interested in the outcome of Nicky's efforts, but the actual tech part of it was about as entertaining as watching paint dry. Of course, it wasn't as if he deserved to be entertained. Hell, everyone acted five times nicer to Brandon, than Brandon would have to them if their places were reversed.

"Why do I feel like such a shit?" Bored, Brandon flipped open the folder on the cot. He probably shouldn't pry, but, fuck, he probably wouldn't understand the data and shit Nicky dealt with.

"Ah," Nicky hesitated, "you don't want the answer to that, do you?"

God, who the fuck did these reports? Brandon teased a couple of sheets across the blanket. Absently, he grumbled, "That's the way to talk to someone on the edge." Weaver, on a bad day, had more organizational skills than this. Notes ran across the margins and tables of data seemed randomly ordered at best.

Brandon barely heard Nicky's retort, "I am not a shrink and I don't even play one on TV."

Pushing through a half dozen papers, nothing made sense to Brandon. Not in the way he thought it would make sense. The information wasn't data related to anything. Complete random nonsense, most of it scribbled in by hand. He looked up at Nicky, still messing around at the computer. "I thought you brought work home?"

"Yeah." Nicky didn't look back. "Boring, tedious work. And it's shit I can do in an hour. I figured I'd convert and upload the video. The stuff Dian gave to the news people is okay, but this shit's recent."

That wasn't what Brandon meant. "Nicky?"

"Yeah?" Nicky sounded slightly annoyed.

"I thought you like," flipping through more and more pages, Brandon realized it all made less and less sense, "worked with numbers and shit...like ones and zeros."

Now, Nicky turned. He looked slightly annoyed. "Thanks for putting my job in perspective there."

"No." Brandon looked up and held out a handful of pages. "I mean, uh, there's a log file in here."

Nicky shrugged. "Well that's part of the project which divisions are using what resources when and where." Obviously he didn't get it.

Time to make him get it. Brandon glanced at a random page. "Dude, does that include like when you hit the can?"

"Fuck no!"

"Okay." Brandon pointed to the place on the page he read from. "There's a log in here of...you." That's all it could be. Dates, times and what Nicky ate or drank or who he talked to. "Smoke breaks. What soda you got out of the vending machine."

"What?" Nick grabbed the page out of Brandon's hand. "And what do you mean me?"

"Well," tapping the top of the sheet, Brandon added, "Nick O'Malley is written at the top with like hearts around it." Brandon brushed the papers still on the cot. "It looks like it's all full of the same crap."

"No." The tone in Nicky's voice said he didn't believe it, or didn't want to believe it.

"Yeah," Brandon insisted. "Look." He snagged the papers and shoved them back into the file, then he handed the mess over to Nicky.

Almost reluctantly, Nicky reached out and took the file. He propped the open folder on his knees and leafed through the pages. After about the fifth one, he glanced up at Brandon. "Holy Fuck! Ada grabbed the file because of the label at the top. We were looking for the reports Jen was supposed to work up for me. Man I knew she was weird, but not that weird." Nicky shut the file and shuddered. Then he slid the folder onto his desk. He blew out an exasperated breath and rubbed his temples. "Look, apparently, Jen has a crush on me."

"Dude," Brandon pointed toward the records, "that is more than a crush."

"No." Nicky denied what Brandon implied. "You don't know Jen." He held up his hand and almost pushed the thoughts back at Brandon. Then Nicky turned back to the computer. He messed with some program and mumbled, "Social reject, pretty introverted." The video of them on the strip came up full screen. Nicky fiddled some more before adding, "This high school shit pretty much fits."

Brandon stood. He got right behind Nicky and leaned over, one hand on the desk the other on Nicky's shoulder. "This isn't jonesing on your favorite rock star, Nicky." Somewhere, after all the hell of the past few days, Brandon found his cop voice and cop attitude. He hit Nicky full with it. "This is stalking."

"Yeah right." Disbelief still threaded through his tone. "Not even."

Brandon watched the film of Shayna on the strip and tried to think of how to convince Nicky to take it seriously. Images of his daughter distracted him, captivated him. There they were, Shayna pausing by Nicky to watch the fountains. Dork that he was, Brandon had panned across the crowd to get a better shot.

As the camera moved, Brandon saw it. "Wait!" He yelled in Nicky's ear. "Stop the video."

Jerking back, Nicky fumbled the mouse and then managed to click the pause. "What?"

"Go back like five seconds or less," Brandon hissed.

"Okay." Nicky glared at him for a second and then did what he asked. "What did you see?" He clicked play.

As the feed came up near that spot, Brandon felt the excitement threading through his nerves. "Right there." For the first time in days he felt like a cop: proactive instead of reactive. "There," he pointed at a figure frozen at the far left of the frame. "That chick, she came by the house yesterday morning."

"That's Jen," Nicky hissed. He turned to Brandon. "How could you pick her out like that?"

"Cops, you got to be good with faces." What the hell was that chick doing there? "Remembering people." Nicky shifted and Brandon realized why. Brandon's brain may have made the connection, but Nicky just seemed confused. Brandon tried to prod him along. "Why would she be there? Think about it Nicky."

"It's the strip." Nicky's tone and attitude brushed him off. "Tons of people go to the strip."

"Yeah, but why is she holding a camera?" He'd seen the pictures Nicky received at his office. The detectives brought over copies and had everybody review them to see if anyone looked familiar. "It looks like she's taking pictures." If she was there, taking pictures, they could have been from her. If she took the pictures, she might be involved.

Nicky repeated, "Lots of people take pictures of the strip."

"She lives here," Brandon reminded Nicky of what seemed obvious to him. "Why would she take pictures?"

"It's the holidays." Nicky shot back and glared. "Lots of people take pictures of the big casinos all decked out."

Nicky obviously wasn't making the mental connection. "What

about the other pictures?"

"What about what?"

"All the pictures that someone sent you. Remember?" He tried to jog the mental connection. "Some in front of the penguin display thing." Nicky just stared at him like he'd grown an extra ear. "Remember we had that old lady take a picture of us? There were pictures in that bunch like someone stood over off to the side. Same pictures, weird angle…we talked about it. There were ones of us at the mall. Us at the mall." Brandon made the mental leap. "I bet she was there. One time that might be a coincidence. Nicky, the bitch is stalking you."

Shaking his head, Nicky still minimized. "She's just a little obsessive."

"Obsession is the cornerstone of stalking."

Nicky snapped, "'Cause you're an expert on that, right?" If he was agitated that meant the scenario hit a little too close to home for him.

"Ah, hello, I'm a cop." Brandon rapped the side of Nicky's head with his knuckles. "Yeah. And Nicky, has she been acting real strange?"

"She's Jen," Nicky shrugged, "strange is a relative term."

Brandon figured he needed to spell it out for Nicky. "Okay look, people involved in things like kidnapping and murder show up at like events around it." The Vegas cops had gone over it at the first briefing, but stuff like that might not have stuck in Nicky's head.

"What do you mean?"

"Press conferences. Media events. Shit like that. Have you noticed her at any of them?"

"She was at the initial press conference, but so were a lot of people." Nicky shut down the video. The WYSIWYG editor for the website popped into the front window on the screen. "And she's like crushing on me and I was there. So it means nothing." Nicky sucked in a deep breath. "And I see where you're going with that. Jen wouldn't do anything like that." Still in denial mode, Nicky shook his head again. "She's a mouse. She doesn't have the balls to complain when the other staff screws her over on shifts and shit. No way she'd be involved in something like this," he insisted.

"Nicky, people who are obsessed do unpredictable and crazy shit."

"Why would she hurt Shayna? I don't see it."

"Because you were treating her like your own." Brandon pointed to one of the pictures on the screen. Nicky, his hands under Shayna's arms, spun her; both captured forever in mid turn. "If she's this nutso stalker, she'd remove anything that got between you and her."

Staring at the screen, Nicky chewed on his bottom lip. "If that were true she'd come after you." He crossed his arms—classic defensive posture—over his chest.

Trying to give the words more impact, Brandon touched Nicky's shoulder. "And you don't think taking my kid is coming after me?" Then he let his hand drift down Nicky's arm.

"You know what I mean." Nicky didn't shake him off, but he definitely didn't relax either.

"Look, maybe you're right and she's not capable of that big step." Brandon figured he had to concede a little. Probably Nicky needed to take baby steps to move past his mental block. "But, if she's a little nutso, and if someone who wanted to hurt me or you, found Jen…" Brandon let the thought hang heavy in the air. "An obsessive chick, like Jen, if that person fed into her fantasy, it would be a great place to get information." Brandon didn't point out that the last set of pictures Nicky got were sexually explicit. That equated to the classic escalating stalker pattern. "She'd spout everything to some asshole just to be able to discuss her favorite subject: You. If she was talking about you, then she'd be talking about me, too." And if Jen was escalating, who knew what she'd be capable of all on her own.

"I don't see it."

Brandon crouched down enough that he and Nicky were eye to eye. "My gut tells me she's involved."

"Your gut told you to blow your brains out yesterday, too," Nicky huffed. "How reliable is that?"

Brandon stood and cupped his hands behind his head. He bit back the expletive and tried to be calm. "Nicky, this is serious."

"Okay." Nicky hadn't uncrossed his arms. That indicated he still wasn't sold on the idea. He kicked his legs out from his seat and crossed them at the ankles. "Then we should call the police."

"They'll tell you to get a restraining order." Brandon dropped his hands and shoved them in his back pockets. "That's about it."

"Wait—" Nicky sat up straight. "You're the cop and you're telling me it has to be this way," he spread his hands like he couldn't comprehend the situation, "that she's blown a gasket and capable of taking Shayna." His expression echoed the confusion in his body language. "But, now you're saying the cops are only going to tell me to get a restraining order."

"Look," Brandon tried to give Nicky a sense of the procedural problems, "They'll file it with the investigation notes and maybe follow up down the line. It's a lead, but not a critical one."

"Okay, you're nuts." Nicky returned to the crossed arms, crossed legs stare down position. "Cops won't do anything even if you, the cop, think it's something. That's about as random as you've ever been."

"First off, fuck off," Brandon snapped. "I'm thinking clearer than I have in days." Then he took a minute to try and order the explanation in his own mind. "Second, there's this whole set of hurdles we have to overcome to convince the cops that I'm right. Things like, you're a guy and she's a chick. Most stalkers are men stalking women." Brandon ticked the points off on his fingers. "You have no history with her. She's a co-worker, not someone you ever dated or slept with."

Nicky's expression went sour. "Like I would ever sleep with a woman, much less Jen."

"There you go," Brandon shrugged. "And you don't have a log of contacts. We've got her notes," Brandon pointed to the file on Nicky's desk, "but unless you remember her being at any of the places she recorded, it could be all fantasy. I don't think it is, but we can't *prove it*. She's shown up a couple of places, but we can't *prove* she's been dogging you. I mean this," Brandon swept his hand across the room indicating the whole set of circumstances, "kinda shows it, but she hasn't threatened you. The big thing, most cops don't believe gals get violent." This time Brandon's shrug conveyed his frustration with his brothers-in-blue. "They know they do, but they don't believe it."

"But we've got that file and the videos and photos." Emphasizing his words, Nicky tapped the manila folder on his desk. "That's what made you think of it."

"All we have right now is possible, and I mean, possible evidence of a misdemeanor." Agitated, Brandon tugged at the rings in his ear. "The bitch is stalking you, but you didn't really know it until now. You've gotten the weird emails and phone calls to your cell. But unless they connect them to her, it's not proof."

"Then they can use this information to subpoena her records." Nicky's tone indicated that the solution was obvious.

And it was obvious, just not feasible. "Do you know how much those subpoenas cost?" Brandon rolled his eyes as he said it. "Cell and internet providers don't give that information to the cops for free." His department rarely ponied up the funds for those shot in the dark searches. Even an agency as well funded as Vegas Metro would hesitate before shelling out the money. "You deleted the emails, so they can't be sure what her IP address is." Unable to stay still, Brandon rubbed the back of his neck and paced the short width of Nicky's office. "You ask your cell company to produce the records of calls into your phone, for even just say the past few weeks, it'll be hundreds of dollars and they'll take their goddamn sweet time doing it. It's not quite as simple as TV makes you think."

"But if she was involved in Shayna's disappearance…"

"For the cops to do something there has to be independent evidence that a crime has occurred." Brandon walked back to the cot and sat down heavily on the edge. "They'd probably believe us." He reached out and ran his hand over Nicky's knee. "But the Grand Canyon stands between believing us and being able to prove it." Brandon walked Nicky through the process as best he could. "Even if, say, Manny believes us and I think he would, he's got to take what we have and convince a District Attorney that it's worth the time and money. Then that DA has to go before a judge and convince him to issue a warrant for a search."

"What would push it over the edge?" Like he was trying to think, ward off a headache or both, Nicky rubbed his temples with his fingers. "Make them believe?"

Brandon tossed out the most obvious and, given everything, least likely solution, "Has she ever threatened you?"

"No," Nicky looked like he thought Brandon was sliding back into crazy territory, "she rarely even talks to me."

Brandon tried not to let Nicky see how that look kicked him in the gut. Finally, after all these days, Brandon was thinking rationally, but he could barely get Nicky to believe him. Convincing Manny would be three times as difficult. "Then it's going to be doubly hard making the connection with her to Shayna's disappearance."

"But Orzoco already says the main theory right now is that someone is after me."

"Look Manny's theory and my gut ain't going to convince a DA that this bitch is involved." Brandon palmed his face. "We need some hard evidence to convince them."

Nicky sniffed and shook his head. "I'm not sure you've convinced me."

CHAPTER 28

Nick walked up what was the path to Jen's porch and tried to drum up the balls to press the bell when he reached the door. Icy wind slipped down his collar and made Nick shiver; that or the sense that he was about to stick his hand into the proverbial hornets' nest. Glances to either side confirmed that nothing but lonely, cold stretches of desert faded off in all directions. The morning's snow had melted off before lunch. Still the barren area almost seemed like it held its breath waiting for something to happen.

Jen lived pretty damn near out in the middle of nowhere. Brandon skulked God only knew where around the property. What the fuck was Brandon doing? What the fuck was Nick doing there? Short answer, Brandon talked him into it. Of course that begged the bigger issue of why he let Brandon talk him into this insanity. Chalk it up to Brandon being the most persuasive bastard ever and one with the most supremely stupid ideas in the universe.

A little bit ago, they'd rolled up to a stop sign that Nick almost didn't stop for. There wasn't any other traffic within miles. One house was visible just beyond the rise. Jen lived in a suburb of a suburb, which equated to developers' wishful thinking. The few paved roads off of the highway were mazes of vacant cul-de-sacs cutting through the sand. The only way Nick even calculated that he was on the correct unpaved road was it fit the mileage count on the Internet directions he'd printed out. If those were correct, then the house ahead of them would be Jen's…at least if he'd wheedled the correct address out of Ada when he called her.

At that point, Brandon had popped the passenger door and slid out.

Nick managed to hiss, "What the fuck are you doing?"

Brandon paused, one hand on the top of the door and one hand on the top of the hearse. He leaned in, "Just keep her occupied."

"What?" Nick sputtered, "Why?"

"'Cause I'm going to go look around." Brandon glared at Nick like he was too stupid to even be driving.

It hit Nick what Brandon must be planning. "You're going to break into her house?"

"No." He denied it, but then Brandon's next words hedged his bet, "Probably not." He likely meant his smile to reassure Nick. "I'll just look in the windows see what's there."

Instead of encouraging, Brandon's expression reminded Nicky how low Brandon had dropped in the last twenty-four hours. "That's nuts." He'd let a suicidal cop talk him into a suicide mission. Jerking the column shift into the neutral position, Nick pushed in the parking brake, unbuckled and fought with the driver's side door.

Apparently oblivious to Nick, Brandon pulled back and muttered, "I won't do anything criminal." Then he slammed his own door shut.

Nick clambered out of the hearse and almost yelled, "I think going on her property uninvited equals trespassing."

Brandon stopped by the front fender. He turned and frowned. "Just keep her distracted."

"How?"

"Don't ask me," Brandon brushed him off with a wave as he started out across the desert headed vaguely in the direction of Jen's house. "The chick's obsessed with you...should be easy enough. She'll never see me." If Brandon dressed for covert, he missed it by a mile: black biker jacket, jeans and boots stood out in a landscape composed of ninety shades of brown.

"What if I need help?" Nick had yelled at his heels. "What if you need help?"

Without turning around, Brandon yelled back, "That's why God invented cell phones, Nicky."

Rather than standing there looking like an idiot, Nick had gotten back in the car. For about a minute he'd debated just driving off. But then thoughts like Jen calling the cops on Brandon or Brandon getting hurt or worse made him move. Nick had put the car into gear and driven the rest of the way to the house. He had just enough time during that drive to wonder if Jen might have heard them yelling at each other…sound carried a long way in the desert.

Now he approached ground zero. As his boots crunched over the gravel path a furious barking started in the house ahead of him. Shit. In all the insanity Nick forgot that Jen said she raised large dogs. By the racket they were definitely large. He didn't even make the concrete porch before the front door opened.

Two snarling dogs bounced against the mesh backed wrought iron security door. Without even thinking, Nick stopped and took a step back. The damn things looked like Dobermans on steroids: right height and coloring, but twice as heavy. One put his face to the screen and growled. Nick thought he might piss himself. If the damn door wasn't there he would have.

Jen stepped up to the door and snapped, "Netta, Leo, down!" As a switch, Nick would have subbed to Jen's command. The tone in her voice startled him more than her dogs had.

It took a second for Nick to regain composure. He swallowed and stuttered out, "Leo?" instead of a greeting.

When Nick spoke, Jen almost visibly faded back into the mousy shell he was familiar with. "Nick. Hi." She sniffed and then used the back of her hand to rub her nose. "Viscount Leopold de Rochelle meet Nick from the office." She spoke to the dog as if she introduced Nick to family. "Nick, this is Antoinette Le Désir de Chacun. Netta for short." Both dogs whined and scrabbled at the door as they milled around Jen's legs.

Nick blinked. "Your dogs have last names?" That equaled crazy dog lady weird. Of course that wasn't surprising given Jen.

"Tradition." Jen sniffled again. "All papered Beaucerons are given French names."

"Oh." Brandon told him to keep Jen distracted. "Cool." Having a conversation separated by a security door and a good five feet would have to work. "That's right somewhere someone told me you raised dogs." Hopefully she didn't invite him inside. He had zero desire to be in that house with those dogs. He had zero desire to be in that house with Jen.

"Yeah?" She nodded. And then Jen just stood there looking at him. The conversation dropped like a lead weight between them. Nick imagined he could hear it thud on the ground.

Finally, Nicky couldn't take either Jen's or the dogs' stares anymore. "Yeah." He parroted Jen's last word then fumbled for an excuse for being there. The one he planned out took off for the hills when the dogs started barking. "Ah, look, I know you called in sick, but I need those reports I gave you to work on," he lied. "I was on my way back to the office from a site inspection so I swung by here rather than go all the way back into Vegas, find your phone number, call and drive back out this way." Fuck, even coming out of Nick's own mouth it sounded like the horrible fib it was. Not the least of which was how Nick had Jen's address without having her phone number.

"Oh, they're back at the Board." The absurdity of the tale seemed to go right over Jen's head. "I hadn't finished them."

The dogs seemed to decide that Nick wasn't an immediate threat. They folded themselves down at Jen's feet. Both massive heads rested on forepaws and faced the door. Nick didn't figure either of them stopped believing he was a menace any more than he stopped believing them willing and capable of ripping his throat out. The door just created an uneasy truce at that point.

Nick swallowed and tore his gaze up from the dogs. "You hadn't?"

"No," Jen knelt and ran the back of her hand over Leo's head. "It's been kinda hard to concentrate lately." Nick assumed the dog on the left was Leo, but it could have been Netta.

Nick pushed the thoughts of big, irritated dogs to the back of his brain and tried to keep the stumbling conversation going.

"Coming down with the cold, I bet." Fuck, he hoped these were the only dogs Jen had. If Brandon jumped into a backyard of those beasts he'd be ripped to shreds.

"Cold?" Jen's question brought his attention back to her.

"Yeah," he shrugged and stuck his hands in his jacket pockets, "you called in sick today."

"Oh." It sounded like Jen didn't even remember doing that. "Yeah, I guess I did."

Steeling himself, Nick plunged into as much of a flirt as he could manage. He grinned and threw a tease into his voice. "You're not really sick are you?"

Jen chewed her lip. "No." The whine in her tone made both dogs look at her. After a few sharp breaths, Jen stuttered out, "I just, just had to take care of things." She stood and put her hand on the door. Nick prayed she didn't open it. "Don't tell."

"I won't." He smiled again and stepped forward a little. With a roll of his shoulders Nick stroked her interest with another question, "So what's worth taking a sick day?"

"Lots of things." Jen ran her hand up and down the back of her neck several times. "You know tons of stuff." She moved the hand around to scratch at her collar. "My other bitch, Chloe, just had a litter."

It took Nick a second to realize she was talking about another dog. "Oh, so you wanted to be home for that?"

"No. Just lots of things." When Jen snapped her fingers, both dogs rose up onto their haunches. One scooted back. "Do you want to see them?" She grabbed the doorknob with one hand and the key to the deadbolt with the other.

As Jen unlocked the deadbolt, Nick stammered, "Them?" Crap, just how many dogs did Jen own? He figured he should ask. "How many dogs do you have?" If the answer was more than say, three, he'd have to come up with a quick excuse and call Brandon.

Both dogs started a low throated growl as Jen eased the

security door open just enough to edge through. She seemed like she had control, but maybe appearances were deceiving. "Just three adults." Or, if Brandon was right and she was fixated on him...that might screw with the dogs' sense of who should be on top. Nick always figured dogs were the ultimate lifestyle submissives. Both of the dogs began to bark again. Jen ignored them as she shut the door behind her. "Do you want to see the puppies?" Like she might have been too forward by stepping outside, Jen fidgeted with the keys. Any subservient personality, human or canine, would freak out if their dominant acted unsure around someone else. "They're in the garage." She wheeled and Nick cringed. He didn't really want to go anywhere with Jen and other dogs.

Three adult dogs: two in the house and one in the garage. Brandon should be safe enough, unless he got stupid and crawled through a window or something. Nick shrugged. "I won't bother the mom?"

"Oh, no," Jen reassured. "They're kenneled and she's used to me bringing buyers to inspect the puppies they've reserved." She started walking off toward the detached garage. "I have older puppies, too, out in the rear kennel." Jen stopped, turned and hit Nick with an expression he could only define as rapture... like the Catholic saints he'd been brought up with. "Maybe you want one."

"They're beautiful dogs." He needed to keep the conversation going and keep Jen distracted. "I've been thinking of getting a dog. Not sure what breed."

Jen must have interpreted that as a willingness to view the dogs since she headed off again. "Beaucerons are wonderful companions." Looking back at Nick, she smiled. "Protective without being too aggressive." Jen seemed to develop a personality as she rattled on about the dogs. "They're big babies, really, just want to be with you." She flipped through the ring of keys she pulled out of the security door. "These litters are spoken for, but, but I could reserve one for you. You'd have to fence your yard though."

Although Nick had fallen into step behind her, he paused when she said that. "How do you know my yard's not fenced?" The only way she'd know that is if she'd been back around in the driveway. The thought scared the shit out of Nick.

It took Jen a few moments to respond. "I don't." Even with his reservations about Brandon's theory that sounded way too hesitant to be true. She knew and that meant she'd been around Querida the morning he found the pictures. Why had he let Brandon talk him into this insanity instead of calling the cops?

Jen rushed on both physically and with words, "Lot's of people's aren't." When Nick didn't contradict her, Jen kept walking. "Come on," she bubbled like Nick hadn't quite caught her in a hedge, "I'll show you the puppies."

Fuck, Nick hoped Brandon had a clue what he was doing. Jen, acting like this, tickled the hairs on the back of Nick's neck…and not in a good way. He sucked in a lungful of air, and then another. Okay, he had a good head on Jen, at least twenty pounds and a whole lot of desire to get the fuck out of there. That stacked up well for survival if she went psycho on him. Unless she had a stun gun or tranquilizer shots in the garage; Nick swallowed down the thought. Either just might be a possibility for someone who raised large dogs.

CHAPTER 29

Brandon shivered and tucked his hands into his pockets as he trotted across the desert. Scrub creosote, small washes and trash piles created an obstacle course. Even running, Nicky would get to Jen's way ahead of him. The timing bugged Brandon a little, but hopefully Nicky'd get some kind of rapport going that would keep her busy. Brandon pushed the fact that he'd sent Nicky into the jaws of a nut-job stalker out of his head. Nicky could take care of himself.

As he neared the back of what he hoped was Jen's property, Brandon heard the bark of dogs. Shit. He'd completely forgotten that when he'd mistaken Jen's van for his, Nicky had mentioned she raised big dogs. Brandon did a hasty backtrack to one of the dumpsites. Toeing around in the pile he found almost a dozen half-frozen lizards, a few used hypodermics and a hunk of lead pipe about the length of his forearm. He hefted the pipe and tested the swing against his boot heel. The blow knocked out a bit of rust although the pipe still felt solid. Wasn't half as good as his Sig, but it'd have to do for protection.

Jen's property seemed to be fenced by a combination of cinderblock wall and chain link. As he neared the fence, he could see several outbuildings and the main house. All of it looked pretty ratty...a lot like the run down areas of Riverside where he patrolled. One of the outbuildings didn't seem more than a cheap, rusted shed and another, located close to the big house, probably functioned as a detached garage. The last, set back a bit from the rear cinderblock wall, might have been a smaller home on the property—guesthouse possibly. It was long and kinda low, like seventies-era trailer home installed on a slab. The one window Brandon could see was covered with chicken wire and a big slide bolt and padlock secured the front door.

Taking cover behind a stand of brush at the top of a small rise, Brandon tucked the pipe into his belt. If he kept low, the combination might actually give him some cover. A little digging and he found a rock about the size of his fist. Brandon bounced it in his palm a couple of times before winding up, taking aim and pitching it at one of the poles. His high school fast-ball was still there. The rock zinged across and clanged against the metal.

Muffled barking responded to the noise. Brandon waited, but no dogs came rushing into the yard. Neither did their owner. That seemed reasonable. If Jen raised dogs for money, she probably wouldn't let them run loose. And, out here, there had to be lots of little noises that set the dogs off. No neighbors, but Brandon would bet money that coyotes and dirt bikers made the place home. He'd crossed numerous tire tracks of off-road vehicles on his way over. The wildlife…well that was an educated guess.

Brandon let a little more time tick off. Enough to be reasonably sure Jen wasn't going to rush out of the house. Then he crept up to the rear wall, the cinderblock wall. Chain-link would rattle if he climbed it. Plus the solid wall not only came barely up to his eye level while the other fences equaled around six feet or so, but was behind the smaller house. It would give him at least a bit of cover. Brandon found a good place, where a few toeholds had been knocked into the blocks, and hefted himself up.

Four fenced pens ran from the wall to the back of the guesthouse. Where the runs met the house, large doggie doors had been cut into the frame. All of them were shut against the cold—which explained why the barking probably hadn't been louder. A few abandoned, and well chewed, toys littered the pens. Brandon scuttled along the top of the wall to the far back corner where an L shaped gap between the fencing and the outbuilding would allow him access but afford some minimal cover. He dropped down into the space and scooted over to the wall of the outbuilding.

Every move he made garnered more barking. Not loud, in fact this close to the dog runs it seemed kinda muffled. He crouched down at the corner of the building and tried to think. What the hell was he looking for? Brandon could barely articulate it for himself, much less Nicky. The only reason he figured Nicky went along with him was that Nicky's gut must have been telling him the same thing.

All of it—the pictures, the timing, the notes—was too much to be coincidence. Brandon still didn't have a clue why the chick might have taken Shayna or even if she did it herself, but he damn well figured she played a part. If she was involved then most likely the evidence of that would be in the main house. He didn't have a lot of time, minutes maybe. The dogs still voiced their agitation in the building behind his back. He needed them to settle down a bit before he moved again. Brandon hunkered down to count off a few seconds. That was all he could spare. If they hadn't quieted, he'd have to risk it.

Planning his getaway in his head, Brandon studied the cinderblock corner he just came from. If he used the chain link on the pen as a step up he could vault the back wall easily and be off into the desert. Good enough. As he started to look away something caught his eye inside the dog run. He almost dismissed it, but then his gut told him not to. A well-chewed stuffed animal lay abandoned in the pen...a purple and gold stuffed dragon. Brandon focused on the paw with the virtual pet logo almost gnawed through. It wasn't really anything, but it was everything. What moron would let a dog tear up a thirty-dollar stuffed toy? Really? It could just be coincidence, but in Brandon's business, coincidence meant evidence out of context. A guy holding the right caliber gun a block from a murder went down for a DA as rough as a chick whose dog chewed on the exact same overpriced, stuffed piece-of-crap that Nicky bought Shayna a few days ago.

Busting into the main house was problematic. However, if something that probably belonged to Shayna sat abandoned in that pen, more concrete evidence that she, or her stuff, had been on the property might be in the outbuilding. The bitch might have held her there or dumped her things there before getting rid of it all. She'd have to be nuts not to have attempted to get rid of stuff once she got rid of Shayna. Of course, Jen pretty much equaled looney-toons in Brandon's book.

Brandon eased away from the wall he hid next to and studied

the building. A window, one not covered with wire, was at about chest height. Brandon stood and sidled up so he could look inside but pull back if anyone was in there. From his vantage, he looked down the one room building. There was an exterior door about a third of the way down the front wall. Beyond that a large front window faced the main house. Both he'd seen from off the property. On the interior the widow had been hung with heavy blankets, probably to act as noise dampeners. All he could see of the back wall was a set of interior dog runs. Directly across from him were two small interior doors that might lead to closets.

Brandon ran his hands up the glass until his fingers met the lip of the old sash window. He pushed and the window slid up. Once he got enough space at the bottom, Brandon slid his hand under the window and pushed it up and open. The dogs in the kennel went nuts. Brandon prayed that the dampers at the front of the building would keep the noise from reaching the house. With the window open he had the problem of keeping it up long enough to crawl through. He reached back to pull the pipe from his belt. Then he shoved it into the frame. With a deep breath, he hefted himself into the window frame and fought to crawl through.

CHAPTER 30

Four awkward puppies tumbled about Jen. Their dam had her head on Jen's lap, but kept her eyes on Nick. Nick kept his eyes on Jen. In the main house, the two other grown dogs hadn't stopped barking. It wasn't as rabid as when Nick showed up at the door, but they hadn't let up. Jen looked up from the pen of puppies and their mom. "Why are they still barking?" She mumbled the question more to herself. While all the puppies were the cute falling over themselves with big ears and big paws stage, mom dog looked willing and able to rip Nick's head off.

"Who knows?" Nick shrugged and tried to buy time. "Coyote or something maybe? I'm still here and the other dogs didn't seem happy about that."

"Maybe," Jen conceded. After a moment of indecision she smiled up at him. "So you like the puppies?" She held one up for his inspection. "Any one you see you really like?" Frankly all of the puppies looked alike to him. Black faces and gold throats. And way too big.

Suspicious and wary, given all of Brandon's theories mixed with his own gut feeling, he hedged. "I thought you said they were all spoken for."

"Well," Jen shrugged, "buyers sometimes fall through."

Nick scrambled for an excuse. "I really couldn't afford a dog right now." Last thing he wanted was a dog…especially one as big and nasty looking as the ones Jen raised.

Jen wrestled with one of the puppies. Almost absently she mumbled, "You wouldn't have to pay me."

"Ah." Okay, that just, no. "Aren't these expensive dogs?"

"Well, yeah, but—" Another spate of barking sounded. This time it seemed more agitated and Nicky could hear the muffled barks of several more dogs. "What is wrong with the dogs?" The mother dog rolled to her feet and glared toward the yard out back. "What is it Cleo?" A discontented rumble sounded in her throat.

Oh crap, Brandon had set off the dogs, big time. Not really wanting to, but knowing he had to, Nick walked around to block Jen's view of the rear door of the garage. "Maybe there's a stray out back or something?" The moment he said it, Nick realize how lame his excuse was.

"No, something's wrong." Jen set the puppy down and stood. Anxiously she pulled at the hair drifting across the back of her neck. She turned to Nick. Stricken didn't even begin to capture her expression. "Why don't you…" Not bothering to finish the thought she hustled to the gate and let herself out of the knockdown pen. "You need to go." Jen pushed his arm. Then she took a few steps toward the back door of the garage before scuttling back. "I've gotta go." She bobbed, pushing at Nick's hand. "I'll see you at work. And get you the report then."

Nick pulled his phone out of the holster and waggled it in front of Jen. "Look if you think something's going down maybe we should leave and call the cops." If he could get her to the edge of the property that would give Brandon a fighting chance.

"I'm fine," Jen backed away. "I got the dogs."

"Are you sure?" Nick dogged her steps toward the door. "You don't want to come and be safe."

"I'm sure," she insisted. "I'm fine. Just go." For a few seconds she danced between Nick and the door. "I'm going to get Netta and Leo."

"If it's anything, you're probably better with them in the house." Nick tried to stall her. "You don't want them hurt. Especially if it's a stray or coyote that's gotten in the yard. A fight could hurt them."

"Yeah, I guess." She rubbed her knuckles against the palm of the other hand. "Look, I'll see you at work. Bye." Jen darted through the door, leaving it banging in her wake.

Nick, not quite believing she'd left him alone, flicked to the icon of the Harley logo on his phone then double tapped it activating the add-on speed dial function. The moment Brandon picked up, he hissed, "Wherever the fuck you are, get out!" Nick raced out after Jen.

CHAPTER 31

The phone at his hip started playing *Bela Lugosi is Dead* and Brandon grabbed it out of the holster. When he hit accept and brought it to his ear, Brandon didn't even have time to answer. Nicky's hissed, "Wherever the fuck you are, get out!" barely carried over the barking of the puppies in their pens.

"What?" Brandon stuttered.

"Jen's coming," Nicky sounded stressed. "Get out."

"Fuck," Brandon tried to think of his exit strategy, "buy me like three minutes."

"What?" Nick growled, "How?"

"Just do it." Brandon cut the connection at that point. Shit, he was fucked. Well, he could take on the chick fine, but the big ass dogs were another issue.

As Brandon sucked in a breath he barely heard a whispered, "Daddy!"

No. That couldn't be, his daughter was dead. He spun around, confused, "Shayna?" There was nowhere for her to be...except the two doors. Tiny, but they could be closets. He rushed toward them and breathed out, "Shayna!" almost too desperate to believe what his ears heard.

From behind the smaller door, a plaintive, "I'm sorry, Daddy," issued from the gap between floor and door base. "Don't leave me here." Brandon's heart shredded at the thought that Shayna would think he'd ever leave her. "I'll be good," her promise whispered. "Let me come home!"

"What?" Brandon plastered himself to the smaller door. Shayna. Living and breathing, Shayna. "Oh, Princess, it's Daddy!" What the fuck. Brandon studied the door. Old fashioned and five panel with an ancient double lock set up. The barrier equaled a bitch, but not an impossible one to breach. A pre-forties era door in a barely maintained outbuilding...Brandon had enough motivation to manage busting it down. "Shayna," he ordered as he stood, "get as far away from the door as you can."

"But, Daddy," she whined.

"Do it!" Brandon hoped she complied. He stepped back and lashed out with his boot. Shocks slid up his shin and thigh, the door bounced in its frame but didn't give. Again Brandon kicked, his heel landing right on the old lock...the weakest point. The crack of dry-rotted wood shot into his bones. One more kick, then another and the structure around the ancient box lock mechanism shattered. The door banged against the wall.

A tsunami of rank dog, unwashed people and old sewer lines collapsed over Brandon. He didn't care. He stumbled into a tiny bathroom to find Shayna huddled in a chipped bathtub. Her hair was matted with dirt and sleep. Grime, tears and food crusted her face. Fuck it all, she was alive. Brandon's legs gave out and he fell to his knees at the side of the old tub. "Shayna," he whispered hardly trusting himself to reach out and touch her hair.

Almost like she couldn't believe it was him, Shayna whispered, "Daddy?" She touched the back of his hand and Brandon's heart collapsed into his chest. "Daddy!" The scream hit him as hard as her body launching out of the tub. "Daddy!" Brandon fell back against the bathroom wall cradling Shayna. Somehow he managed to stagger to his knees and lurch out the door carrying her. The cacophony of puppies barely registered over the wails of his daughter as she clung to him.

That's when Brandon registered the mousey little thing pulling open the front door. As many times as he'd drawn down on suspects...he'd never really wanted to kill them. He wanted to kill this bitch. A blood filmed skin slid over Brandon's vision.

"You're not supposed to be here!" The mousey monster screamed as she rushed him. Brandon twisted, using his body as a shield between Shayna and Jen. "Get away from her! You're supposed to be gone!"

Jen wrapped her arm around Brandon's neck. She scratched at his face with her other hand. Somewhere, he registered Nicky trying to pull her off. Screw that. Brandon lurched back against a wall. Nicky's startled face flashed for a second. Brandon thrust Shayna at him and yelled, "Get her out!"

Without warning a set of teeth, very human teeth, sank into Brandon's flesh. The bite landed solid; right where the muscle connected shoulder to neck. Brandon roared. "Fucking, bitch!" He reached back with the other hand. His grip found a fistful of hair. Brandon yanked. Jen screamed. She rolled off him. Brandon jumped. His not quite closed fist slammed into the side of her head.

Another scream sounded. Jen scrambled away. No. Brandon wouldn't let her go. Bitch needed to pay. He scrabbled across the floor and grabbed at her ankles. Jen kicked him, one blow landing on his abused shoulder the other on his chin. He lunged. She screamed and rolled. Wire banged between them. It took a moment for Brandon to realize she'd backed into a pen. He yanked on the door. She held the gate with her whole body.

"Bitch!" He bellowed and yanked on the gate. "I'll fucking kill you!" Five days worth of rage poured out through his voice. Brandon pawed the latch. His rage made his fingers thick. "Come here!"

"You were supposed to go away," Jen bellowed back. "Why didn't you go away?"

All of Jen's weight was on the gate. It was all she had to keep it closed. "I'm going to kill you," Brandon growled as he laced his fingers into the wire on the gate. "Tear you apart." He yanked on the gate and it swung forward a bit. Jen jerked it back. "Fucking kill you, bitch!"

"Daddy!" Shayna's scream cut through his rage. "Stop!" The puppies were going berserk in the pens and he could hear the other dogs somewhere on the property. Jen kept screaming for him to leave and Nicky was yelling something. With his heart pumping ten thousand miles a minute, Shayna's tugging at the back of his jacket and pleading wail of, "Daddy!" barely managed to reach in and mute the urge to rip Jen's throat out.

Brandon leaned against the gate, pinning it shut with his bulk. "Shhh, Princess. It's okay." He reached back with one hand and pushed her back a bit. "Don't worry." Right now, Jen was too scared to do more than try and keep it shut between them. In a moment that nutso persona might reassert itself. Looking back at Nicky, Brandon hissed out, "How do we keep her in there?" Shayna edged up to him again and Brandon shuffled to keep his body against the gate between his daughter and the nut-job.

"Nick, tell him to go away," Jen's voice jerked his attention to her. She crawled to the back of the pen, the farthest point from Brandon. "Take his thing and go away." Her voice barely carried over the puppies' frantic baying. "I didn't want it anyway. He needed to go so he wouldn't keep hurting you."

"Wow," Nicky huffed behind him. "I think you just need to stay in that cage." Somewhere, under all the sounds of hysterical dogs, Brandon heard shuffles and bangs indicating Nicky was searching for something to lock the cage with. "Bingo! Padlock and keys from the front door." Nicky hustled up and, while Brandon kept the gate closed, shot the latch, threaded the shackle through the padlock eye on the latch and snapped the lock shut.

Still jangling, Brandon turned and scooped up Shayna. "It's over, Princess." Almost more to reassure himself, he whispered again, "Over." Too much noise still reverberated through the building. "Come on, let's get out of here." Now that the adrenaline wound out of his system, Brandon registered the pain in his shoulder. He staggered out the door trying to manage Shayna's weight while favoring his left shoulder. Crap, it fucking hurt. Warm blood seeped across his chest and back…he needed to see what damage had been done. He turned to Nicky who dogged his heels. "Here, carry her for a sec."

"Come here, Princess." Nicky tried to take her off Brandon, but Shayna wasn't having any of it.

"Shayna, come on." Brandon pulled, as gently as he could on the arm with a death grip around his neck. "Go with Uncle Nicky for just a moment, I promise." Somehow he managed to pass a reluctant, and not quite willing, Shayna over to Nicky. "Crap."

Nicky took the lead and made for an open door in the garage near the house. Brandon hissed as he pulled his T-shirt away from the skin at the neck. He couldn't see the meaty part where shoulder met neck, but he could see the blood soaked into the material of his shirt.

As Nicky ducked into the garage, the barking from that area amped up. Brandon figured Nicky must know what he was doing. Brandon shot through the opening. A huge fucking dog lunged against the sides of a pen that didn't seem quite sturdy enough to hold her. Nicky darted around the cage and out a side door and Brandon followed. Just in case, he yanked the door closed behind him and raced across the front yard.

Nicky popped open the driver's door on Querida and sat Shayna down. Both of them knelt down in front of her. As Nicky pulled his phone off his hip, Brandon inspected his daughter. Dirty, disheveled and without shoes, but everything seemed to be intact; physically at least. Brandon barely listened to the conversation between Nicky and, hopefully, the police.

"Daddy, why did she say you were hurting Nicky?" What the fuck had that chick been putting into his daughter's head? And why, after all this shit, would that would come up? Unless Jen had been repeating it to Shayna for some reason.

"She's nuts, Princess." He took her little hands in his, "Nicky and I, we're fine together. Everything's good." Fuck, Shayna looked so scared, like maybe she didn't think this was real. Brandon could hardly believe it himself. "You can't believe anything she told you."

Shayna swallowed and looked back toward Jen's house. "She can't get out, can she?"

"No, Princess," Nicky reassured her, "I padlocked the latch." Brandon decided not to remind any of them that there were doggy doors out the back of each kennel. He couldn't remember whether the partitions he'd seen were pushed through the outside or the inside slides. "Orozco is on his way. Said something about the sheriffs."

"I'm sorry, Daddy." Shayna reached out to wrap her arms around his neck again. Since Brandon's weight was balanced on the balls of his feet, he fell back on his butt on the dirt. Shayna apparently didn't notice or care. She just huddled against him and mumbled, "I didn't mean to be bad."

"Did she tell you that you were bad?"

Shayna spoke through hiccups. "She said you were mean to Nicky and if I was good, you'd go away and then I could go home." With her face buried against his neck, Brandon couldn't tell if she was crying, but he'd lay odds she was. "But she wouldn't let me go home. I didn't mean to be bad."

"Oh, Princess. No." Nicky knelt next to Brandon and stroked her arm with his knuckles.

"It's not your fault." Brandon hugged her and rocked. "You didn't do anything." Off, somewhere down the maze of dirt roads, sirens wailed. "You weren't bad."

CHAPTER 32

Brandon stuffed his release papers and the copies of admittance paperwork for Shayna into his pocket. They'd been finished with him damn near an hour ago. Red tape always seemed to gum up getting home. Before bailing, he'd headed up for a quick goodnight for Shayna over in pediatrics. He'd almost had to crowbar her off his arm to get out. Not like he wanted to ditch her, but Dian was her mom and only one parent could stay in her room over night.

Gingerly he slid his biker jacket on. Even being careful, he caught the bite wrong and hissed through the flare of pain. A couple of people, those not asleep on the emergency room chairs, watched Brandon as he walked out the ER doors. The staff had informed him that most of the other doors were already locked for the night. He figured that meant, since Nicky wasn't in the waiting room, he'd be outside grabbing a smoke.

As he ambled out the automatic door, Brandon caught sight of Nicky's back and the large frame and abundant mustache of Manny Orozco framed in a pool of illumination. A haze drifted around Nicky's head. Brandon couldn't wait to light up himself. "Hey, Nicky." Brandon called out as he tugged the zipper up on his biker jacket. "Manny." He used the detective's name as a greeting.

Nicky turned at the sound of his name. "Hey, yourself." Brandon realized it wasn't a haze of smoke, but frost from Nicky's breath. "How's Princess?" He hunched his shoulders deeper into his trench coat and smiled.

"Doing okay." Fishing in his jacket pocket, Brandon managed to find his cigarettes, but not the lighter. "Her mom's with her right now." He dug through the inner pockets as well, without luck. "Said goodnight to her earlier. Saw Edith and told her I was coming out for a smoke."

Manny snorted. "Then you're shit out of luck."

"What?"

"The only place you can smoke," Nicky groused, "is all the way on the other side of the hospital."

Reluctantly, Brandon tucked the pack of smokes back into his pocket. "That's just fucking cruel." He really needed a fix of nicotine. "And why the fuck are you standing out in the cold then?"

"It's after visiting hours." It was Nicky's turn for a derisive snort. "Since I'm not related to you they wouldn't let me back to see you." He added a wry smile. "Then the waiting area of the emergency room was starting to creep me out. I went for air and Manny decided to keep me company."

With a bemused shake of his head, Manny asked, "So, how are you doing?"

Brandon shrugged and hissed as another flash of pain swept up his neck. "My shoulder hurts like hell. The numbing shit they put on it to look at it is wearing off. Got a tetanus booster and shot of antibiotics." The bite hadn't been bad enough to warrant real stitches, the doctors went with medical superglue to close the wounds and keep shit out of them. "Luckily, crazy bitch didn't rip anything out, just broke the skin and tore some muscle."

"You know," Manny crossed his arms over the front of his own winter coat and glared, "I knew Dracula here was a pain in my butt at times, but you, Brandon. This takes the cake." He drummed the fingers of one gloved hand on the bicep of his other arm. "Cop to whack job in less than a week."

"Look." Brandon didn't want Manny to think he went cowboy on Manny's case…even though Brandon pretty much had. "I just wanted to have a look around." He minimized, "You know?" The roll of Manny's eyes said he didn't buy Brandon's story. "I didn't think…well, that's probably the point. I didn't think. I just thought maybe Jen was involved after finding her weird ass notes and stuff. Give you something to point you in the right direction that was more than a hunch." It was the best apology he had. Manny was a good cop, a stand up guy. Brandon hoped his explanation let Manny know he didn't think Manny hadn't been on top of the case. "Honestly, I thought she was somebody's patsy. Never in a million years thought I'd find Shayna there. Especially not alive."

"Yeah." Manny blew out another snort of breath. In the cold air it looked like he breathed fire. "Next time, call me before you go off half cocked in my backyard." He kept the glower up for a bit. Brandon didn't see that there was really anything to say. Finally, Manny relented and smiled. "Lucky for you the sheriff's office is going to play ball about your little stunt." The tone in his voice told Brandon he'd probably used up a favor or two to get them to play ball. "They'll present it to the DA more as a trespassing matter than a full blown breaking and entering charge. I know of a few good attorneys, the guys I hate to see on the other side of my cases; they can probably make this go pretty much away." With a nod, Manny offered, "I'll shoot you their contact info."

"I told you to call him first," Nicky sniped. "Someday, you'll listen to me."

Brandon responded to Nicky by ignoring him. Instead he spoke to Manny, "Appreciate it. All of it."

"No problemo." Manny grinned. Brandon hoped that meant Manny didn't hold the shit against him. "That's what friends do for each other, right? On my way back to file my reports, but I thought I'd stop in and see how you all were doing."

"Thanks." Brandon jammed his hands into his jean's pockets. It was too fucking cold. "I already gave a statement to the Sheriff. Do you need one?" He'd have suggested they go indoors, but he'd seen enough of the inside of the hospital for the night.

"Later." Manny reached up to brush his mustache with his gloved hand. Brandon recognized it as his *thinking* gesture. "Both of you will need to do formal statements later. We spent some time interviewing that chick." He relaxed and shook his head like what they found out was beyond his comprehension. "Wow. Seems pretty normal on the outside, but it's all gooey mush up here." Manny tapped one finger against his temple. "She's spun herself some fantasies. Pretty much convinced herself that Nicholas was only playing gay to keep this whole office affair they had under wraps."

Nicky sputtered, "Excuse me?" He sounded completely blindsided by that information. Shocked the hell out of Brandon as well.

"Yeah," Manny confirmed the insanity. "From what she says, you leave her all sorts of notes and messages." Spreading his hands out, Manny seemed to weigh invisible absurdities in his hands. "In the world according to Jenifer you've been terribly agitated since Brandon hit town. So," he drew out the word, "in the way you arranged your desk and gave her projects and confided in your co-worker, the looker, so that little Miss Squirrel-Brains would overhear, you were *obviously* begging her to help you out. She seems to think you've got some job offer that would take you into California—read away from her—and that Brandon was forcing you to take."

"Actually," Nicky shuffled with what looked like embarrassment, "yeah, I did get an offer. I haven't decided."

Manny played with his mustache some more and his expression said Nicky's admission made a few things fit together better. "Well, and this is going to sound messy but it's about as coherent as I can make the jumble outta her mouth. She, while stalking Nicholas, overheard parts of a conversation between you two at a shopping center. How that Shayna was why things were serious. Ultimatums and crap."

"Nicky hit me with a throw down," Brandon confirmed that warped bit. "'I've got a job in your backyard. Say 'yes' to us and I take it. Say 'no' and it's *sayonara*, baby.'"

Like Nicky distanced himself from his ultimatum, he minimized, "I wouldn't call it a throw down." It was probably because Manny was there.

"What?" Brandon almost laughed. "You gave me four days to say yes or we were done. That's a throw down."

"Okay, well," Manny jumped in, "just enough reality to set

her off. So upshot is she's cruising the neighborhood hoping to catch sight of Nick. Apparently a pretty regular practice. Instead of you she sees Brandon's kid walking and recognizes her from that night." He shrugged. "Somehow she wraps around this plan that if she takes the little girl, Brandon will go home and Nick'll stay here in Nevada and be her one and only." Manny laughed at that thought. "I guess, 'cause your van kinda looked like hers she was able to get near Shayna, force her into one of the cages in the back. She's not terribly coherent about the whole scenario. At this point the only thing I'm surprised at is she hasn't claimed that the neighbor's dog told her to do this."

Brandon hissed, "Shit." Most people that unhinged...well you could tell. He'd figured Jen for a stalker and a loose cannon, but not a total whack job.

"So." Manny clapped his hands together. "I am going to leave you gentlemen and go close a case file. I know she's shaken right now, but we are going to have to talk to Shayna."

"Yeah." The police would need to know exactly what happened. "I know." Brandon wasn't certain he could stomach really knowing. "They're going to keep her overnight for observation." He could at least fill Manny in with the bare basics. "The building was heated, but for half-grown puppies not a kid. So, from what the nurse told me they're looking at exposure, she's a little dehydrated and hasn't eaten much in the last few days." All that equated to child endangerment on top of the kidnapping. "The water out of the pipes in that bath was pretty rank. Probably well water, so they want to make sure she hasn't picked up anything from it." Brandon tried to remember when the doctors said they might release her. "Maybe tomorrow sometime?"

"Works fine for me, Brandon." Manny jerked his chin back toward the doors of the emergency entrance. "Looks like someone looking for you?"

Brandon looked over. His gut sank just a little. A man in a black wool overcoat and dark slacks—older, refined and confidant—strode toward them. A little gray broke up his dark brown hair and blue eyes locked on to Brandon. "Oh great,"

Brandon swallowed. "My dad." All-in-all Robert Carr wore the mask of how Brandon might look in another twenty or so years.

"Brandon, there you are." The greeting rolled out of his mouth in a warm, polished baritone. "Edith said I'd find you outside since you still haven't given up that nasty habit of yours."

About par for the course, the first thing out of his dad's mouth was a dig. "Hey, Dad," Brandon dredged up a smile to mask the wound, "this is Manny Orozco." Brandon introduced Manny first since he said he had to get back to the station. "He's the lead detective on Shayna's case."

"Robert Carr." He held out a gloved hand. "Edith mentioned you and how you've been helping." When Manny took the shake, Robert gripped Manny's arm with his other hand. "Thank you. Edith's saying goodnight to Dian and Shayna right now. I know she'd want to thank you, too."

"Nice to meet you." As he pulled back his hand, Manny nodded to Brandon's dad, then to Brandon and Nicky. "I'm heading out." Walking off, he called over his shoulder, "We'll touch base, Brandon."

"Yeah, tomorrow," Brandon shot back. After a couple deep breathes, where Brandon really regretted not being able to light up, he turned his attention back to his dad. "So you came straight to the hospital?"

"We went to your friend's house first, before we got the news." He sounded as relieved as Brandon was. "At least I got a shower." Hunkering down into his coat, Brandon's dad gave him a rundown of the last few hours. "Checked on Shayna, talked with the doctors and made sure they're taking care of her right."

Basic catch up done, Brandon reached over and put his hand on Nicky's shoulder. "Great, ah, Dad—"

"Someone said," Robert broke into Brandon's train of thought, "you'd been bitten by that woman."

"I'm fine."

Again his dad took control of the conversation. "Break the

skin? Deep?" He went through his doctor routine, his way of avoiding crap. "You up on your tetanus shots? I would suppose as a police officer you would be. They probably didn't give you any antibiotics. I'll start you on a preventive course."

"Dad!" Brandon snapped. "The doctors here are top notch, I'll be fine," he huffed. "I want you to meet Nick O'Malley."

"Sorry." His dad blinked. Then he smiled in his version of Brandon's own thousand-watt grin. "I get on a track sometimes, too focused."

"No problem." Nicky quickly shook his hand and then shoved it back in his pocket. Brandon figured it was because Nicky didn't have gloves, not that he held anything against his dad. "He's your son and he got hurt." Smiling back, Nicky played down the slight. "Got to make sure he's okay, you know?"

"It's always a pleasure to meet any of Brandon's friends and especially one who's been so gracious under the circumstances."

"Robert, Brandon, Nick." Edith caught their attention as she walked out of the ER doors. "Shayna's asleep and Dian's staying with her." Pulling her gloves on, she kept walking and talking. "Frank is heading back to his cousin's house." When she came up next to his dad, Edith laced one arm through his. "I'd say we should all head out and try and get ten hours of sleep ourselves."

Brandon yawned. "Sounds like a plan to me." Although Brandon wasn't sure he'd sleep. There was this big awful ball of 'what if he'd actually offed himself and who would have saved Shayna then' just waiting to roll down on him. So far all the insanity of hospitals and statements and shit kept it at bay.

"Brandon." His dad touched his arm and started walking with Edith toward the parking lot. "I got us a suite at the Venetian."

As he and Nicky fell into step slightly behind them, Brandon muttered, "Great." Actually he meant it. A weight slid off his chest just knowing he wouldn't have to play host to his parents at Nicky's place. Plus, he could have Nicky all to himself for a while. When they reached the minivan, Brandon decided to say goodnight. "I'll catch up with you in the morning." Edith and his dad could keep the monstrosity for the night since Nicky's hearse sat a few rows down.

"No, I meant all of us." His dad sounded a little bemused and a little irritated, like he had to drill social skills into Brandon's head. "So you don't have to impose on your friend anymore."

"Ah, Dad." Oh fuck, why not? Brandon scanned through all the reasons he'd ever avoided telling his dad and decided none of them meant shit any longer. He swallowed hard then rushed out, "He's more than just a friend."

Close behind him, Nicky hissed, "Brandon, are you sure about this?" Edith echoed the sentiment with a little indrawn breath. Both those probably slid right under his dad's radar.

Keeping his voice low, Brandon answered Nicky, "Yeah, dude, I am." A little louder he reiterated, "Way more than a friend."

"I know," Robert's tone, sliding far more toward irritated, dismissed the connection. "Edith mentioned something about law enforcement." He talked to Brandon without looking at him. Instead he opened the passenger side door of the van. "I understand professional ties, trust me." Finally he turned back to Brandon. "I sometimes feel closer to some of the people I work with than Edith and you boys, spend more time with them."

"That's not what I'm talking about." Brandon stood his ground. God, he was so fucking glad that Nicky was right there with him, otherwise he'd probably chicken out.

"Why don't you tell your friend goodnight and let him have his house back?" It was delivered with the same attitude and voice his dad had used every time he thought Brandon behaved unreasonably. And like usual, the moment his dad turned it on, Brandon's back went up. "We'll all get together tomorrow." Robert focused his attention on Nicky. "I'm sure you're sick of the imposition."

"It's not been a problem." Nicky moved just a little closer to Brandon as he spoke, like he knew Brandon needed him right there. Nicky knew him better than he knew himself sometimes.

"You're too polite," Robert acknowledged Nicky's statement and then coolly dismissed it by turning on Brandon. "Don't impose on Nick any longer."

"Dad," Brandon had to bite his tongue not to get nasty too quick. "Nicky's been there through all of this."

"I know. He's a great friend." His dad stepped up close. "I wish I had a friend like him when your mom passed. Someone to support me." He reached out and patted Brandon's arm. "But your family is here now."

"No, Dad." Brandon drew back until he stood right next to Nicky. "I've been with my family." Over his Dad's shoulder he could see Edith with one hand over her mouth and her other pulling her coat tight. He really hoped that Edith's view of his dad was right. Otherwise, he was about to burn a bridge. "I've been with Nicky."

"Brandon, you need to be with the people you love and who love you."

Brandon huffed with frustration. "Dad, you don't get it..."

"Brandon." Nicky pushed his arm with a light touch. "It's okay." Brandon looked over to meet a dark eyed gaze that seemed to forgive him for shit he hadn't even done yet. "Just go with your dad. I understand."

"No, it's not okay." Brandon wouldn't let him down this time. He needed Nicky to know what really mattered.

"You don't have to do this right now, Brandon."

"Do what?" Robert's voice cracked across the cold air.

Brandon ignored him and whatever Edith said in response. His focus was on Nicky. "Yeah, I do. I'm not hiding us anymore, Nicky." He grabbed Nicky's coat collar and pulled him in so their foreheads touched. "Fuck the world, dude," he hissed. "I've been through the worst fucking week of my life, man! There's only two things that matter, really matter in my life. My little girl and you."

"What the hell is going on?" Brandon hadn't heard his dad

yell in ages.

Somehow Brandon managed not to raise his voice in response. Instead he stood straight, took a huge breath and managed to push the words out, "He's my boyfriend." The moment he said it, Brandon realized how inadequate that statement was. Almost to defuse the tension in his own body, he snorted, "God, that's a suckass word for it, huh?"

"Yeah," Nicky agreed, "it does sound a little wussy."

"What do you mean boyfriend?" His dad stared at him, then twisted back toward Edith. "What's he talking about?"

Settling onto the edge of the frame in the open van door, Edith offered a tight smile. "Something you need to listen to."

"Dad, I'm gay!" Shit, he never, not in a million years, thought he say that to his dad. "Nicky's my partner. That doesn't even convey it." Brandon laced his fingers behind the back of his neck. "I don't have the fucking words to tell you what Nicky is to me. How much he means to me."

"What?" Robert stuttered. "What are you telling me?"

"Just what I said—I'm gay." The second time the statement came out a little easier, but not by much. "How hard is that concept?" Brandon realized how ironic the question was given how long it'd taken him to admit it to himself.

His dad kind of drew into himself. He covered his face with his hand and for a few moments just seemed unable to do much more than breathe. When he looked back up, Robert's demeanor shifted back to cool, calm and removed. "It's unexpected."

"Unexpected?" Brandon spat. Just like his dad to retreat from real emotions. "Is that all you're going to say?" He was the dad that was never mad or angry, just disappointed.

"In a hospital parking lot…yes." He turned his back on Brandon and moved over as if to help Edith into the van. Then, only giving Brandon his profile, Robert added, "We'll discuss it later," and finished it with a final dig, "at the hotel."

"What do you want to discuss?" It was Brandon's turn to yell.

"It's my life. Nicky's part of it and I'm staying with him."

His dad spun and stepped right up into Brandon's face. "It's not acceptable," he hissed.

"Acceptable?" Brandon managed a sneer. Probably pissed his dad off even more. "I'm fucking sick of being acceptable to everyone else. I've been acceptable my whole life and hated myself every goddamn minute of it. I'm accepting me and that somehow—jackass that I am—Nicky accepts me. I don't give a shit if I'm acceptable to you. And, you know what, deal with it."

"What do you want from me, Brandon?" Somehow his dad managed to rein it all back in. "Do you want me to break down in tears?" He scoffed at the thought. "Or hug you and say it's all okay?" Probably the only one who didn't realize how impossible that would be was Nicky. "It isn't. This isn't one of those sappy movies Edith always drags me to. You're my son. This changes everything about you."

"No. I've always been this person." Somehow, Brandon managed to stand his ground as well. "Dian was a lie. I love Shayna, but I should never have done that to her mom. Fuck, dad," Brandon pointed at his boots for emphasis, "the guy I was half an hour ago, is the guy I still am right now. Except I'm not going to lie about who I am anymore."

"You can't do this to your family."

"Be honest? Can't be who I am?" Brandon threw the questions at him like knives. "Or can't do this to you?"

"This is not who I raised you to be!"

"Robert," Edith stepped in and grabbed his dad's arm, "don't say something you're going to regret."

Both of them vibrated. Brandon knew his dad would never back down once he dug into a position. And yeah, Edith was right. At that point Brandon wasn't sure he could keep from tossing a few accusation grenades into the fray. Still, he couldn't just walk away. "Look dad, I didn't choose to be made the butt of jokes, harassed or beat-up. That's pretty much what being gay still means...fuck, especially as a gay cop. I'm putting my fucking life on the line by being out. So it doesn't have shit to do with how you raised me. It has everything to do with admitting what the fuck I am inside. Accept it or don't, but you can't fucking change it. Fuck knows I tried hard enough to."

"I failed you when you needed me," he huffed out. "That it's right? After your mom died, I couldn't remember to take a shower much less make sure you got breakfast. You're punishing me for that."

It hit Brandon that his dad would rather take a fall in parenting department than accept that Brandon got hit with a genetic roll of the dice. "Yeah, mom dying fucked me up, fucked us both up." After all, people would forgive a grieving husband of a lot of sins. "But you're a fucking surgeon. You don't even believe the crap that's coming out of your mouth right now."

"It's not acceptable!" his dad reiterated.

Brandon twisted it and hit him back. "I'm not acceptable?"

"No," his dad spit back. "That's not what I'm saying!"

"Yeah it is." Brandon hit him with the reality. "The only other time you used that is when I signed up for the academy. That was a choice. This ain't." Robert Carr had always drilled into Brandon and his stepbrothers that you don't make judgments about people based on what they can't control—skin color, disability—didn't change that they were human. "So if it's not acceptable, then neither am I. Too bad." Brandon pulled up the only shot he had left. "So, Dad, you're still talking to me after I chose to be a cop. Defied you with something I could have walked away from. I didn't choose this. I wouldn't change me, but I didn't decide just to piss you off to be on everyone's shit list because I like guys."

"Brandon—"

"Stop." Brandon held up both hands and backed away. He was done. "Know what? I'm going to give you the advice you always gave me. Go sleep on it. See if you still feel the same way tomorrow." He turned on his heel and headed toward Nicky's ride.

His dad yelled at his back, "Brandon, get back here!"

Although Brandon wanted to flip his dad off, he resisted. Instead he shoved his hands into the pockets of his jeans, lowered his head and stalked off to Nicky's hearse. Yeah, not terribly mature, but better than a family fight in a hospital parking lot. When he got to Querida, Brandon just stood by the fender and stared at the hood of the classic meat wagon. He couldn't trust himself to move.

He heard Nicky come up behind him. "You okay?" Nicky's touch drifted down Brandon's back.

Brandon blew out a shit load of tension. Ten tons still remained. "You didn't say much." He wanted to pull that back in the moment it passed his lips.

"You know what?" Nicky swatted his ass before walking over to the driver side door. "Getting between you and your dad at that point—" He unlocked the door and slid onto the bench. After reaching over, popping the lock on the passenger side and waiting for Brandon to clamber in, he finished the thought, "You would have been pissed if I did." Nicky pulled his door shut.

Brandon slammed the door. "Maybe." Then he tried to find the lap belt in the darkness.

As Nicky slid the key into the ignition he finally commented on the row. "Wow, coming out with fireworks and all."

"Fuck, dude." The belt latch slid into place, punctuating his curses with a snap. "Shit. I can't believe I told him."

"You did," Nicky sounded proud. "And, I think he'll come around. Edith'll lean on him. He just wasn't prepared for it, you know."

Brandon looked across the lot as Nicky backed the hearse out. He saw the headlights of the van flutter on. Edith would work on his dad. And even if he never came around...it wasn't Brandon's problem. Two big hurdles in his life and one of them he'd managed to get over. Even if Brandon tripped and stumbled his way through it. "Well, at least that's one down." He stared at Nicky across the dark interior.

Nicky pulled out onto the street. Almost absently he asked,

"One down what?"

"Things I got to say." Brandon leaned against the door, his hand stretched across the bench seat. "Look, Nicky." He brushed Nicky's shoulder with his fingers. "I'm an idiot and a jerk and a fucking asshole at times, but, fuck, Nicky, I need you. I need to be with you."

Waiting until they hit a red light, Nicky finally asked, "Are you serious?"

"Hell, yes." This was far easier and far scarier than the confrontation with his dad. "I'll quit the fucking force." He would. Brandon realized he'd do damn near anything for Nicky. "I'll move here if you want. Find a job…maybe Metro." Even if it meant being a fucking rent-a-cop in a casino, Nicky was worth it. "All this, after all this shit, you matter. I don't want to lose you, Nicky."

"I'm the one with the job offer," Nicky reminded him. "You love the force."

"You love the GCB," Brandon countered.

Nicky smiled across the half lit interior. The light had turned green, but he hadn't put the hearse into gear. "I'm not hating the six figure offer they made me to move to So. Cal."

Brandon squeezed Nicky's shoulder. "Okay." Holy fuck, he was saying yes, committing to Nicky. And it felt absolutely right. "Okay. Let's go home."

CHAPTER 33

"Ah, Nick." Nick looked up from scanning the windows into a room full of people he didn't know to find Dian standing in front of where he'd parked himself on the lip of a planter. "Can I talk to you for a moment?" In a sea of relatives and volunteers thronging the cultural center, which once hosted the command post, Dian had found him. Considering Nick had bailed outside to avoid the crush inside that meant she'd sought him out. Intentionally.

They'd basically taken over both meeting rooms and a good deal of the enclosed garden areas. With the help of a couple of police organizations, the group that the rabbi was part of and the local alliance they'd scrabbled together a hasty thank you to the community and cops for their efforts. Pizza, egg rolls, cookies, coffee…wasn't a posh reception, but donated food and Dr. Carr's wallet did the trick. From what Brandon said, it was more thanks than most people ever gave the police or volunteers.

Why would Brandon's ex-wife want to talk with him? "Yeah, I guess," he stuttered.

She took a deep breath, "I wanted to give you something." Holding it with one hand on the spine, Dian offered out an oversized paperback. "I got it years ago, in case I ever needed to talk to Shayna about her father and what he does." She wiggled the book a little, like she tried to get him to take it. "I had my sister grab it when she took the boys by our house to get more clothes before they came down."

Suspicious, given their prior interactions, Nick took the book. A simple cover of a blue uniform shirt and black tie was over written by white lettering. Nick read the title out loud. "*I Love a Cop.*" Not quite sure why Dian would give him anything, much less that book, he probed. "What's this?"

"It's a book about living with someone in law enforcement, how to cope." Massaging one hand with the other, she tried for a smile. "Think of it as a peace offering." She took another deep breath. "Look, I want...no, I need to apologize for some of the things I said to you."

Nick slapped the book against his palm. With everything that had happened he wasn't really sure that he shouldn't just hand the book back. But, Brandon's ex-wife was about as close as he'd ever envisioned to having in-laws, so he took the high road. "Don't worry about it."

"Thank you for saying that," Dian settled onto the planter next to him, "but I am so sorry." After rubbing her hands a while longer, she dropped them both into her lap. "I didn't mean to attack you like that." She glanced off toward the park like she needed to collect her thoughts. Then she turned back to Nick. "I said very hateful and very personal things and I didn't even really know you."

"Well, we were all a bit stressed." Okay, it didn't seem just for show, Dian appeared to really want to apologize. "I had my moments, too."

She offered him a rueful smile. "That I pushed you into."

"Ahh," Nick shrugged, "you had a big ugly mess going on..." He let the thought trail off. What else could he say to her? What she'd hit him with really wasn't forgivable, if she believed it. Losing her cool in a completely fucked up situation, well, Nick could understand that.

"I'd like to start over if we could." Dian lightly touched his arm. From what Nick knew of her, that was majorly bold. "If you could see your way to forgive me."

"Like nothing ever happened?" He hoped he didn't sound as snide as he probably did.

She gave a small, embarrassed laugh. "I'm realistic, that's probably not possible. But we can try and look past that and say from right now we're going to move forward and try not to look back on the bad." Dian crossed her arms over her chest. It didn't seem defensive, more like she didn't know what to do with her hands. "It's probably a more honest form of forgiveness, don't you think?"

"Yeah." Nick shrugged. "I'm game." He'd play it by ear. If she really worked at smoothing shit over, well Nick might revise his rather critical opinion of her.

"Good." She smiled again. This time it was a little warmer. "So you're, ah, dating my ex-husband?"

"Yeah." He nodded. "I might be moving to Riverside to take a job down there. Probably makes it more than just dating."

"Really? Well, Nick, you seem nice enough." Nick gave an inch more. This conversation had to be so far outside her comfort zone as to be beyond comprehension, yet here she was trying. "And, very brave. I'm not sure I could have ever handled the situation in the kitchen like you did. Even if I wasn't already falling apart. You're very committed to Brandon. You stick by him." She shrugged. "I'll be honest, I'm not sure I'm all that comfortable with it. But I guess it's not my life is it? I'll have to talk with Brandon about visitation and such."

Since she seemed to be drifting back toward the attitude she'd handed him on his porch days ago, Nick reminded her, "Gay doesn't equal pervert you know."

"I know." Dian stared at the ground at her feet. "I'm sorry I, ah, was shocked and scared and angry at Brandon for lying to me." Then she seemed to pull herself together. She looked at him and chewed her bottom lip. "I'm not comfortable, but I'm not going to deprive my daughter of knowing her biological father." She unwound her arms from around her chest, but reverted to rubbing her hands together. "One of the things I'm concerned about is something I'd worry about whoever you were. Brandon's not the most stable person in a relationship. I don't want Shayna becoming attached to someone he's with and then they're gone from his life after a few months."

"I can get that." He really could. For most of the time he and Brandon had been together he'd wondered if he wasn't going to wake up one morning and just find Brandon gone.

"And, you're not Jewish."

"No." Of course he wasn't Jewish and why the hell did that matter anyway? "I was raised Catholic."

"My daughter's heritage is very important to me." She acted far more certain of that issue than the landmines she'd been treading earlier. "I expect her to be raised in our traditions." It clicked for Nick. Dian probably figured one day that she'd have this conversation with someone Brandon was dating. She'd just never anticipated it'd be a guy she was having it with.

"Trust me," Nick reassured her, "last time I was in a church was for somebody's funeral like more than six months ago. So, you're going to forgive him for all this—"

"No." She stopped fussing with her hands. Almost coolly she stated, "I'm not."

"What?"

"He's never asked me to." As though it were completely reasonable she explained, "If, when, he comes to me and says he's sorry…and means it, I might be ready to forgive him. Right now, I think he's on that road, understanding that he can't lie to people like this, but he's not ready to seek forgiveness and I'm not certain I'm ready to forgive him. Maybe, by the time he is, I'll be ready to release that debt. Let it go. And don't worry; I won't punish Shayna because her father's a jerk."

After all the bullshit about making peace she was going back to that. "You want him to ask you for forgiveness for being gay?"

"No," She turned to stare at him like Nick had lost his mind. "I want him to ask me for forgiveness for sleeping around with strippers while we were married and then abandoning his father role for a good portion of his daughter's life."

Boy, he'd kinda misread that. "Oh." Now he felt like a jerk himself. He sat there with the book wedged between his thigh and his palm, fanning the pages with the tip of his fingers and trying to figure out how the hell to move back into the conversation.

Dian saved him, both from embarrassment and figuring out what to say next. "Was he, well, like this when…?"

There was only one way to answer that question. "You know, you'll need to talk to him about that."

"And never get a straight answer. Even an answer." Smoothing her long, dark skirt before she stood, Dian nodded like things might be on the right track. "Okay, then we'll see how things go. I guess I should wish you luck with Brandon, you'll need it."

If he didn't know that himself, he'd have thought Dian was being snide. "Thanks." Nick stood as well.

"Thanks for what?" Brandon, carrying Shayna in something vaguely resembling a fireman's carry, sauntered up. Edith drifted along behind them and fussed with trying to adjust the hood of Shayna's parka while Brandon walked. She wasn't terribly successful.

Since they'd got her back, Shayna clung to whichever of her relatives seemed to be around. She extended that circle to include Nick at times. Victims Services said that was normal after trauma like she'd been through…that and how subservient and quiet she'd become. Might take months or years for her to get back to her normal self. If she ever truly did.

Nick shrugged. "We're drafting a truce."

Brandon shifted a suspicious glare between Nick and Dian. "Should I be worried?"

"Why would you be worried, Daddy?" Shayna wiggled until Brandon set her down. She immediately stuck her thumb in her mouth and drifted over to tangle her hands in her mother's skirts. The regression, apparently, was also normal under the circumstances. She popped her thumb out of her mouth long enough to add, "You and Uncle Nicky aren't fighting anymore? Like the mean lady said?"

"No, Shayna," kneeling down, Edith tucked her granddaughter's hair back under the hood and reassured, "they're not. They never were. Don't believe the things that woman said, she was sick."

Nick couldn't quite fathom how calm and sanguine Edith'd been. "I so don't know how you kept it all together." Nick tucked the book under his arm.

"Me?" Startled, Edith looked up at Nick. "Honestly, I did what most women of my background and age do." With a laugh, she shook her head. "You'd all be asleep. I'd go out on the back step, cram the hem of my coat into my mouth and scream it all out." As she spoke, Robert walked up behind her. Nick could see a ton of his dad in Brandon. Edith fussed a bit more with Shayna then stood. "Then I'd take a deep breath, go back inside and do what I had to do."

"You are a survivor," Robert mumbled and leaned in to kiss Edith on the cheek. For all his reserved air, Nick sensed someone who was deeply committed to his wife. Hopefully, that boded well for he and Brandon.

"Daddy," Shayna reached out and tugged the bottom buckle hanging loose from Brandon's biker jacket. "How come you didn't kiss Uncle Nicky when you saw him?"

The statement looked like it hit both Brandon and his dad like a two-by-four between the eyes. Brandon seemed to recover a step ahead of Robert, "I was carrying you; didn't have the timing right."

"It's okay to kiss Uncle Nicky, Daddy." She petted her dad's thigh like he was a scared animal.

Brandon huffed for a moment. "It must be if you say so, Princess."

"Come on, Shayna." Catching her daughter's hand, Dian steered her toward the building. "Your aunts and cousins want to see you." Shayna, after a small wave to Nick and Brandon let herself be pulled away.

The clearing of his throat brought everyone's attention back to Brandon's dad. Dr. Carr stared somewhere between Nick and Brandon. "We're heading home tomorrow." Nick resisted the urge to step into his line of sight to see if he flinched.

Edith had none of her husband's reservations. She moved in to hug Nick. "You'll have to come up sometime and visit." Then she moved to embrace Brandon. Maybe, hopefully, she'd wear Robert down.

Brandon hedged, even as he accepted her squeeze. "We'll see."

"Don't make me wait until Passover to see you again." Edith stepped back and glared. "Jacob's son John is having his Bah Mitzvah in February. You both will come up for that." It was less of a request than an order.

Brandon shrugged, "Just depends on work, Nicky's job, you know?" When Edith's glare turned to a glower, Brandon spread his hands in surrender. "We'll try. Really, I mean it."

"All right." She smiled. "I'm cold, Robert. And I need coffee." Edith steered Brandon's dad off toward the main meeting room. "You need some, too." It was as though she recognized the tension between father and son, but didn't want to acknowledge it. Edith paused and turned back to face them. "You will have breakfast tomorrow with us," again, she didn't ask…she stated a fact wrapped in a question, "before our flight?" When Brandon nodded, she smiled and pulled his father into the building.

Nick waited a bit before he commented, "So, your dad seems to have gotten over it." He really hadn't much, but Nick said it anyway.

Brandon almost choked, "Not by a million years."

"But—" Nick started to point out that nobody went off yelling this time.

Brandon broke in. "No, see, Dad's just going to be pissed off about it," he shoved his hands into his jeans and stared after his dad and stepmom, "but not say anything to me. Edith will pretend like everything's great. We've been playing that same game about me and the force as long as I've been a cop."

Nick had to take that dig. "So like father, like son."

"What?"

"Repressing shit until you go nuts." Nick grinned.

"Bite me, Nicky." Brandon rolled his eyes and then went back to watching the people inside. About the time Nick started to wonder if they should head in as well, Brandon spoke. "We're going to have to get you a new bike."

That comment came out of left field. "Why?" He had a decent crotch-rocket. "My Kawasaki is a great bike. Reliable."

"Yeah, no see," Brandon started walking and Nick followed, "if we're going to be riding together, a lot, a classic like the 74' can't be sharing the road with a rice rocket." A sound approaching a gag swelled in Brandon's throat and he shuddered. "I know a guy with a custom Duce he's gotta sell," Brandon ticked the features of the Harley Softail off on his fingers, "mini-apes, dropped low, wide rear tire and custom pipes. Sweet bike." It sounded almost like Brandon would want her himself. "She's got pretty low mileage and cheap enough." Then he grinned at Nicky. "Custom paint: high gloss black with a flaming red demon skull on the tank. It's so you." Brandon paused at the door to the center. "Been sitting a while, she'll need an overhaul and gaskets. But I wouldn't be embarrassed to park the Electra-Glide next to it at a rally."

Nick leaned on the door, preventing Brandon from opening it. "We're going to be riding a lot together?" he teased.

"Well, yeah," Brandon swallowed hard, but didn't stop smiling, "when you take that job in Cali."

"You saying you want me to?" Nick crossed his arms over his chest. "I mean I know you said it the other night, but I thought it might be a little more in reaction to your dad and maybe not what you were really wanting," He shrugged. "We haven't talked about it since."

"I guess," Brandon shrugged as well. "I mean, I want you. I want you to stick around."

Nick stepped back and yanked the door open. A rush of warm air hit them as they stepped inside. "In that case, I thought the new Harley Rockers were pretty cool."

"No, the Duce man." Slightly behind him, Brandon grabbed Nick's shoulder and gave him a couple of bumps with his fist on Nick's back. "Two of us working on it, we'd have it up and running in a month…two at most." Brandon stepped to the side, the opposite side of where he still held Nick's shoulder. He kept walking, his arm behind Nick's back. "Seriously," he tugged Nick in close, "don't embarrass me with a wanna-be chopper."

Nick slid his hand into Brandon's back pocket. "Wouldn't think of it, baby." Although he felt Brandon tense, he didn't flinch or draw away. Instead, Brandon took a deep breath and smiled as the rabbi who helped Edith so much headed over. Nick whispered, "Love you, man."

Brandon didn't even hesitate. "Love you too, dude."

ABOUT THE AUTHOR

JAMES BUCHANAN, author of over ten novels and single author anthologies, lives in a 100 year old Craftsman in Pasadena with her SexyGuy, two demon spawn and a herd of adopted pet dogs, cats, rats and fish. Between managing a law practice with SG, raising kids and writing books, James volunteers with the Erotic Author's Association and Liminal Ink as well as coordinates the newsletter for the ManLoveAuthor's co-op. James has spoken and read at conferences such as Saints & Sinners and the Popular Culture Association. In the midst of midlife crises, James bought and learned to ride a Harley – it went with the big, extended-cab pickup. James has been a member of CorpGoth since 1993 and been known to wear leather frock coats to court. If you don't find James at the computer working on her next book, you're liable to find her out on the bike.

Visit James on the web at:

http://www.james-buchanan.com/

http://eroticjames.livejournal.com/

http://groups.yahoo.com/group/eroticjames/

SERVICEMEMBERS LEGAL DEFENSE NETWORK

Servicemembers Legal Defense Network is a nonpartisan, nonprofit, legal services, watchdog and policy organization dedicated to ending discrimination against and harassment of military personnel affected by "Don't Ask, Don't Tell" (DADT). The SLDN provides free, confidential legal services to all those impacted by DADT and related discrimination. Since 1993, its inhouse legal team has responded to more than 9,000 requests for assistance. In Congress, it leads the fight to repeal DADT and replace it with a law that ensures equal treatment for every servicemember, regardless of sexual orientation. In the courts, it works to challenge the constitutionality of DADT.

SLDN
PO Box 65301
Washington DC 20035-5301
On the Web: http://sldn.org/

Call: (202) 328-3244
or (202) 328-FAIR
e-mail: sldn@sldn.org

THE GLBT NATIONAL HELP CENTER

The GLBT National Help Center is a nonprofit, tax-exempt organization that is dedicated to meeting the needs of the gay, lesbian, bisexual and transgender community and those questioning their sexual orientation and gender identity. It is an outgrowth of the Gay & Lesbian National Hotline, which began in 1996 and now is a primary program of The GLBT National Help Center. It offers several different programs including two national hotlines that help members of the GLBT community talk about the important issues that they are facing in their lives. It helps end the isolation that many people feel, by providing a safe environment on the phone or via the internet to discuss issues that people can't talk about anywhere else. The GLBT National Help Center also helps other organizations build the infrastructure they need to provide strong support to our community at the local level.

National Hotline: 1-888-THE-GLNH (1-888-843-4564)
National Youth Talkline 1-800-246-PRIDE (1-800-246-7743)
On the Web: http://www.glnh.org/
e-mail: info@glbtnationalhelpcenter.org

CPSIA information can be obtained at www.ICGtesting.com
Printed in the USA
LVOW110837131011

250307LV00001B/8/P